P9-EAJ-103

BOOK SIX

THE FIVE FAKIRS OF FAIZABAD

Children of the Lamp

BOOK SIX

THE FIVE FAKIRS OF FAIZABAD

P. B. KERR

ORCHARD BOOKS/NEW YORK
AN IMPRINT OF SCHOLASTIC INC.

Library of Congress Cataloging-in-Publication Data
Kerr, Philip.
The five fakirs of Faizabad / P. B. Kerr.
p. cm. — (Children of the lamp ; bk. 6)
Summary: Fourteen-year-old djinn twins John and Philippa travel from the Himalayas to Yellowstone National Park seeking to uncover and protect five holy men before the wicked djinn responsible for upsetting the balance of the world's luck finds them.
ISBN 978-0-545-12658-8
[1. Genies — Fiction. 2. Magic — Fiction. 3. Luck — Fiction. 4. Twins — Fiction. 5. Brothers and sisters — Fiction. 6. Himalaya Mountains — Fiction. 7. Yellowstone National Park — Fiction.] I. Title.
PZ7.K46843Fiv 2010
[Fic] — dc22
2009043656

10 9 8 7 6 5 4 3 2 1 10 11 12 13 14

Printed in the U.S.A. 23
First edition, November 2010
Book design by Elizabeth B. Parisi

For Linda Shaughnessy

BOOK SIX

THE FIVE FAKIRS OF FAIZABAD

CHAPTER 1

TARANUSHI

The twins John and Philippa left their house on East 77th Street in New York, and walked around the corner to the Carlyle hotel where their uncle Nimrod, who was staying there with his butler, Groanin, had invited them both to come and have lunch.

Following her complete and irrevocable renunciation of her djinn powers, Nimrod's sister, Layla, who was also the twins' mother, had made it adequately clear to her brother that she and her husband no longer cared to have any djinn matters even mentioned in their presence. Although Nimrod strongly disapproved of any djinn denying his or her true nature, his impeccable British manners required that he respect his sister's decision — enough to have written a short note to her informing her exactly why he had invited her two children to lunch.

Since no objection to their lunch had been forthcoming, Nimrod had gone ahead and booked a table in the hotel's swanky restaurant where he and Groanin now met the twins.

After a very large feast of Cornish lobster bisque, peekytoe Maine crab, pan-seared Hudson Valley foie gras (which Philippa did not eat), Atlantic black bass, roasted Amish chicken, and desserts from the trolley, Nimrod finally arrived at the subject he wished to discuss with his nephew and niece.

"Since you have both recently turned fourteen," he said, "the time has come when you must observe a tradition in the Marid tribe that we call *taranushi*."

"Why is it called *taranushi*?" asked John.

"Well," said Nimrod, "as you may know, Taranushi was the name of the first great djinn. Before the time of the six tribes, he was charged with controlling the rest, but he was opposed by another wicked djinn named Azazal, and defeated. This Marid tribal tradition is meant to commemorate his overthrow by wicked djinn."

"Why was he opposed?" asked Philippa.

"For the simple reason that he tried to improve the lot of mundanes —" Nimrod glanced at Groanin, who was loosening a button on the waist of his trousers to accommodate his enormously full stomach. "Sorry, Groanin, I was speaking about human beings. I meant no offense."

"None taken, sir."

"Yes," continued Nimrod. "Well, as I was saying, Taranushi tried to improve the lot of human beings by occasionally giving some of them three wishes. In fact, it was he who initiated the custom of giving three wishes."

"So what's the tradition?" asked John.

"The tradition is that each of you will go somewhere of your own choosing and find someone you consider to be deserving of three wishes. But it has to be someone truly deserving because upon your return, you have to justify it to a panel of adjudicators that includes me, Mr. Vodyannoy—"

"*After* I get back from my holiday," said Groanin. "I say, after I get back from my holiday. And not before. It's been ages since I had a proper holiday."

Nimrod continued with the names of the panel of *taranushi* adjudicators. "There's Jenny Sachertorte, and Uma Ayer the Eremite. Also, it ought to be a secret where you two go, just in case anyone tries to put themselves in the way of being granted three wishes. So, even I shouldn't know where that is. Although that's not so important, given it's me. But either way, you're very much on your own for this one."

"Anywhere we want?" said John.

"Anywhere you want," confirmed Nimrod.

"Maybe I should go on holiday with you, Groanin," said John. "There must be something I can do for that funny little town in Yorkshire where you take your vacation. Bumby, isn't it?"

"Oh, no," said Groanin. "You're not coming there and that's final. Bumby is just fine the way it is without you messing the place up with three wishes 'n' all."

"There must be something I could do for it," teased John.

"Nothing," said Groanin. "Nothing at all. Things are just dandy in Bumby the way they are."

"Please yourself." John shrugged. "Either way, it doesn't sound so difficult."

"Doesn't it?" Groanin laughed. "It's also traditional," he said, "in case you'd forgotten, for a young novice djinn like you to make a complete pig's ear out of granting three wishes. And to have little or no idea of how a wish will turn out. That's why I don't want you within a hundred miles of Bumby, young man. Especially not when I'm on me holiday."

"All right, all right." John laughed. "I was just kidding, all right?"

"Maybe," said Groanin. "But just remember what old Mr. Rakshasas used to say? 'A wish is a dish that's a lot like a fish: Once it's been eaten it's harder to throw back.'"

"I remember," said John. "I'm not about to forget anything he said, okay?" He frowned. "I just wish I knew what had happened to him for sure."

There was a moment's silence while everyone spared a thought for Mr. Rakshasas, who, it seemed, had been fatally absorbed by a Chinese terra-cotta warrior in the New York Metropolitan Museum of Art.

"Groanin makes a good point," said Nimrod, returning to the subject in hand. "Because it's not just that the recipient has to be judged deserving of three wishes. You also have to justify what they do with their three wishes. And, as I think you know, that can be a very different kettle of fish. People are unpredictable. And greedy."

Groanin managed to stifle a burp. "You can say that again," he said, and, waving the waiter over, he ordered himself a second dessert.

"Even the most honest, upstanding sort of person can turn rapacious when three wishes are involved," added Nimrod.

"Aye, it's not everyone that wishes for world peace," said Groanin. "I say, it's not everyone that wishes for world peace these days. Even if that was something within your power."

"Which, sadly, it isn't," said Nimrod.

"How are we going to discover if someone is really deserving of three wishes?" said John.

"Research," said Nimrod. "Read books. Read the newspapers. Find out what's happening in the world."

John groaned. "I might have known that there'd be some reading involved."

"It saves time finding out things for yourself," said Nimrod.

"It does that," agreed Groanin.

"Maybe I'll go to Canada," said John. "I bet there are lots of people in Canada who could do with three wishes." He grinned. "Stands to reason, doesn't it?"

"Don't tell me," insisted Nimrod. "Even your parents aren't supposed to know. It's a secret, remember?"

"He doesn't know how to keep a secret," said Philippa.

"I like that," said John. "You're the biggest gossip I know."

Noticing that Groanin had a newspaper in his pocket, John asked to borrow it and, absently, Groanin agreed. It was an English newspaper called the *Yorkshire Post* and, to John's surprise, there was a story on the front page that described Bumby as the unluckiest town in the world, and listed all the reasons why.

"You know, I could do a lot worse than go to Bumby," said John. "There's a story here in your newspaper, Groanin, that makes me think Bumby is the perfect place to go and offer someone three wishes."

"Oh?" said Nimrod. "May I see that please, John?"

Groanin pulled a face. "You keep away from Bumby, I tell you. I don't want you mucking up my holiday with your djinn power."

"I wouldn't 'muck things up,' as you put it," insisted John. "I'd only be going to help."

"Why don't you go to Miami and that Kidz with Gutz awards ceremony for young people who have demonstrated selflessness or presence of mind?" said Groanin. "You might have a lot in common with one of those interfering young so-and-sos. I'll bet you'd find one of them who would be deserving of three wishes. Or better still, why don't you go to Italy and try to help that bloke what's supposed to be the unluckiest man in the world? I say, why don't you go and help him?"

"Where in Italy?" asked Philippa.

"I think he works in Pompeii," said Groanin. "Fellow called Silvio Prezzolini."

"Tempting fate, isn't it?" snorted Philippa. "To be the unluckiest man in the world and working in Pompeii?"

"Why?" asked John.

"Duh! Because Pompeii was a Roman town destroyed by a volcano," said Philippa. "And the volcano, Vesuvius, is still very active." She shook her head as if in pity of her brother's ignorance.

"I know that," said John.

"You know something, John?" Philippa smiled. "It's true. You get everything I get, only it takes just a little longer."

Privately, Philippa was considering going to India. For one thing, in India they believed in the djinn, and experience had already taught her that it was a lot easier granting someone three wishes when they believed such a thing was even possible. Another thing was that there were lots of deserving people in India. Just about everywhere you went you could see them. But the more she thought about it, the more the Kidz with Gutz awards or even Pompeii also seemed like attractive options. She'd never been to Pompeii.

"Suppose you and these other adjudicators decide that the three wishes were not justified," said Philippa. "What happens then?"

"I'm glad you mentioned that," said Nimrod. "There's a penalty to be paid."

"You mean like a punishment?" said John.

"What could be a bigger punishment than being related to him?" asked Philippa.

"Not a punishment exactly," said Nimrod.

"Well, what is it?" said John. "Come on."

"You lose your power for a year," said Nimrod.

"What?" John was outraged. "Well, how does that work?"

"A simple djinn binding made by me and the others on the panel," explained Nimrod. "You have to be able to demonstrate that you can use your power responsibly."

"A year seems harsh," said Philippa.

Nimrod shrugged. "That's the tradition."

"Did you and Mom have a *taranushi*?" asked John. "When you were our age?"

"Yes," said Nimrod. "Your mother passed, of course. But I was failed. By Mr. Rakshasas, as it happens."

"And you lost your power for a year?" John's eyes widened.

"Best thing that ever happened to me," said Nimrod. "It taught me . . . humility, among many other things."

"This must have been a long time ago," said Groanin.

Nimrod handed John back Groanin's newspaper.

"Bumby at this time of year must be very beautiful," he said pointedly. "I should be interested to see what you might make of it. A silk purse out of a sow's ear, perhaps. We shall see."

CHAPTER 2

THE UNLUCKIEST TOWN IN THE WORLD

Every year, Mr. Groanin took two weeks' holiday and, not being fond of "abroad," as he was want to call anywhere outside of England, he almost always went to the seaside town of Bumby, near Scarborough in North Yorkshire.

For Nimrod's nephew, John Gaunt, who, in spite of the butler's loud objections, had chosen to accompany Groanin on his annual Easter vacation after all, it was hard to associate the little Yorkshire town with holiday making. Bumby was a grim, inhospitable place. The skyline was dominated by the black ruins of St. Archibald's Cathedral, high on Bumby's North Cliff. Below the ruins, on the other side of the River Rust, was a maze of dark alleyways and sinister, narrow streets that ran down to the once busy, but now almost derelict, quayside. The fishing industry that had once helped to sustain the town was no more. And Bumby was now only famous as being the place where Count Dracula had stopped, very briefly, before continuing his voyage to the nearby town of Whitby, in an earlier, unpublished version of Bram Stoker's famous book *Dracula*.

"So bad that even Count Dracula wouldn't stay here" was how the people who lived in Bumby were jokingly apt to describe the place. But like many jokes it also contained a grain of truth.

John could see Dracula's point. The town seemed utterly miserable. And the idea that the steady rain, gray skies, and biting north wind that seemed to persistently afflict the town had anything to do with spring or a vacation was, to the young djinn, incomprehensible, and prompted him to ask the bald butler a question.

"If this is what Bumby is like in spring, what's it like in winter?"

"Aye, well, there's no denying it's not been the best of weather this year," admitted Groanin. "I say, it's not been the best of weather. But when you do get a fine day, you can't beat Bumby."

"I find it kind of hard to believe the sun could ever shine in a place like this," said John. "Why do you come to such a crummy place for a vacation, Groanin?"

They were on the beach at the time, seated on deck chairs and swaddled with blankets against the stiff sea breeze. John was eating an ice cream that was more ice than cream.

"Habit," said Groanin. "I always come to Bumby at Easter. I used to go on holiday to Harrogate. But that got very expensive. Bumby's a lot cheaper."

"I can easily see why," said John.

"Nobody asked you to come, young man," said Groanin. "So I'll thank you to keep your views about Bumby to yourself."

"You know why I came," said John.

"That I do," said Groanin. "And let me just remind you that you've agreed to leave the place alone until my holiday is nearly over. I don't want you mucking things up for me here with your djinn power, just yet."

"I'm not here to 'muck things up,' as you put it," insisted John. "I'm here to help."

The boy djinn searched his pockets for the newspaper clipping from the *Yorkshire Post* that had prompted him to accompany Groanin on his holiday. And, finding the cutting, he unfolded it and spread it on his knee, which was not so easy in the cold sea breeze.

"Here," he said. "Read it yourself. 'The Unluckiest Town in the World.'"

"I know what it says," Groanin said stiffly. "It's me what reads the *Yorkshire Post*, not you, young man."

"I don't get it," said John. "Why you're so dead against this. You heard what Nimrod said. Now that I've turned fourteen I have to go somewhere and hand out three wishes, for my *taranushi*. It's traditional for a young djinn like me."

"I told you why," grumbled Groanin. "Because it's also traditional for a young whippersnapper novice djinn like you to make a complete pig's ear out of granting three wishes."

"C'mon," said John. "I'm much better at this than I used to be. I fixed your arm, didn't I?"

Formerly, Groanin had been a butler with one arm (the other having been eaten by a tiger) — until John and Philippa and their friend Dybbuk had used djinn power to give him a new one.

"Aye, but you had the help of others to do it," said Groanin. "Your sister for one. And that makes a big difference."

"Are you implying she's better at this than me?"

"I'm not implying it," said Groanin. "I'm stating it as a bald fact."

"We're twins, so that's impossible," insisted John. "Anything she's good at, I'm good at, too. Stands to reason."

Groanin made a noise that indicated polite disagreement. "Besides," he added, "as for your wanting to help Bumby, I reckon the only reason your uncle Nimrod agreed to that was because he figured it wouldn't matter much if things went wrong in a place like this."

"That's not true," said John. "He just thought that if I was going to go somewhere and grant three wishes, it ought to be somewhere that needed a bit of good luck."

"I can see you don't yet know your uncle," said Groanin.

"And there's nowhere," insisted John, "that needs a bit of good luck quite as bad as Bumby."

"Well, there's no denying that," admitted Groanin. "They've had it tough here, and no mistake. Tougher than tough. Hard. Harder than hard. Tragic, even."

John cast his eye down the length of the newspaper clipping to remind himself of the chapter of accidents that had befallen Bumby. *Tragic* didn't even begin to describe it.

First, the nearby chemical factory had accidentally discharged a large quantity of bright pink dye into the River Rust. And not long after this there had been an unusually high spring tide, which, following a whole month of rain, had caused the river to burst its banks and flood the town, turning everything — the church, the town hall, every shop, and every house — a hideous shade of pink. Bumby was so pink that on satellite pictures of England, the town looked like a sort of livid pimple on the country's shoulder.

Next, several residents of Bumby had been taken to the hospital after consuming a lethally hot curry at the local Indian restaurant. An investigation by the Food Standards Agency revealed that the restaurant's chicken Madras had contained a Yorkshire mamba — a chili pepper that is five times hotter than the Dorset naga, which had previously held the record as the world's fieriest chili. (The Yorkshire mamba is so hot that it is illegal to sell the seeds and grow one outside of laboratory conditions. Quite why England should have become the world center for developing hot chili peppers is anyone's guess.)

It is said that accidents come in threes. In Bumby they came in battalions.

Not long after the curry incident, a Ukrainian circus came to town. On the first disastrous night, the Magnificent Mikhail, a world-famous magician, managed to saw a lady in half for real, while Leonid the Lion Tamer got himself eaten by a hungry lioness.

Meanwhile, Bumby turned out to be the point of origin for a computer virus — the Bumby Bacteria — which infected half of the computers in Europe before it was contained and then destroyed. Then the *Bumby Foreign Language Press* published an English phrasebook in forty-two languages with many wrong translations so that, for example, foreigners who thought they were asking the way to the Tower of London were really asking to be sent to prison. Many of them were.

If all that wasn't bad enough, the Bumby gold mine had proved to be the biggest disaster of all. Following the discovery of several sizable nuggets of real twenty-four-karat gold in the famously deep Bumby caves, the town thought its luck had finally changed. Local people turned up in the hundreds to dig for the precious metal and make their fortunes. But no more gold was ever found. Not only that, but several gold miners were never seen again after one miner sank his pickax into some rock and somehow managed to restart an ancient volcano that had been long-thought extinct.

John had never encountered bad luck like Bumby's. Even while he and Groanin had been there, suffering the poor weather, the town had been further afflicted by a plague of extra-smelly stink bugs — *Nezara viridula* — which emit a foul odor when threatened. This meant that as well as being the unluckiest town in the world Bumby might also have been the smelliest.

Not surprisingly, the town was almost empty of the tourists who usually came to Bumby during the Easter holidays.

And John and Groanin were the only two guests staying at the inhospitable bright-pink-colored hotel that went by the unlikely name of the Oasis Guesthouse.

John flicked a stink bug off his knee and put away his newspaper clipping unaware of the fact that the insect had landed on Groanin's bald head and immediately made a smell.

"But are you sure that Bumby can wait for your holiday to finish?" John asked the butler. "I mean, before I try to fix the town's luck."

Groanin sniffed the air above his head suspiciously. "What's that you say?"

"Are you sure the town can afford to wait that long?" said John. "With luck like Bumby's, a meteorite could land here tomorrow. And your holiday would be over."

Groanin looked up at the sky wondering what the odds were of something like that happening. The movement of his head only served to make the stink bug feel even less secure and it made another smell, even fouler than the last.

"Aye, well, you make a good point," he said. "I suppose there's no point in delaying things any further. But mind you pay attention to what you're doing. What was the other thing old Rakshasas used to say? 'Having a wish is like lighting a fire: It's reasonable to assume that the smoke might make someone cough.'"

Groanin coughed. It wasn't smoke that made him do it but the smell of the stink bug.

"I really miss that guy," murmured John.

"Just make sure there's not much smoke generated when you start granting wishes is what I'm saying," said Groanin.

"Of course," said John. "Do you think I've learned nothing since I found out I was a djinn?"

Groanin sniffed the air again and looked around in search of the smell's origin. "How will you go about it? I say, how will you go about it, do you think? Granting the town three wishes and whatnot?"

"I was kind of hoping you might give me some advice there, Mr. Groanin," admitted John. "About the best way of handling things."

Groanin thought for a moment and put his bowler hat on, which, temporarily at least, contained the smell from the stink bug. "I've been thinking about that," he said. "And I reckon the best thing we could do would be to go and see the mayor of Bumby, Mr. Higginbottom, and just come right out with it. Tell him you're a djinn, like, and that you're prepared to grant the town three wishes."

"You don't think that he'll find me being a djinn a bit hard to believe?" asked John.

"Happen as he *will* think that," allowed Groanin. "Happen as anyone might look at a shaver like you and doubt you had the power to tie your own shoelaces, let alone grant someone three wishes. But then again, what's he got to lose?"

THE UNLUCKIEST MAN IN THE WORLD

Honoring the custom of *taranushi* is meant to remind a young djinn that granting a mundane three wishes isn't nearly as easy as it sounds. Very soon Philippa had bitter experience of this.

Her first search for someone worthy of three wishes had taken her to Miami and the Kidz with Gutz awards ceremony for young people who had demonstrated selflessness or presence of mind. In one way or another in their young lives, these were children who had shown themselves to be kids with *gutz*. Or so the organizers claimed. And maybe they had once been kids with guts, but Philippa herself had encountered a bunch of greedy, spoiled children who were ruthlessly determined to win the contest at all costs. She decided that none of them was in the least bit deserving of being given three wishes.

Truly, as Mr. Rakshasas had once told her, there was no point in giving an umbrella to a man who had holes in his shoes. Something like that, anyway.

So Philippa was now in Italy, in the ruined Roman city of Pompeii, to track down the unluckiest man in the world and grant him some better fortune.

Of course Pompeii itself had suffered more than its fair share of bad luck. In A.D. 79 the city had been completely destroyed and buried in several yards of ash, during a long and catastrophic eruption of the volcano Mount Vesuvius. Two thousand of the city's fifteen thousand residents were killed.

Today Pompeii is still big. At least the size of ten football pitches. It is one of Italy's most popular tourist destinations. And it looks exactly like what it is: a ruined Roman city. Everywhere there are paved roads rutted by the wheels of chariots, wide, paved squares called fora, and solitary standing Corinthian pillars. And above all of these is the huge volcano that dominates the Bay of Naples in a way that makes you think someone must have lifted the curtain of the sky to sweep something dark underneath.

Philippa thought Pompeii was one of the most fascinating places she had ever been.

Unlike John, she was traveling by herself. Being a more thoughtful and scholarly sort of person than her brother, she was combining her *taranushi* with a little sightseeing at the Uffizi Gallery in Florence, the Vatican Museums in Rome, and the National Archaeological Museum in Naples. She loved walking around art galleries and museums.

Besides, looking at pictures and ancient sculptures gave her a chance to think exactly how she was going to approach a complete stranger, persuade him that she was indeed a djinn, and grant the man his heart's desires without also ruining his life.

That was always a risk with giving anyone three wishes: that someone would speak without thinking, as King Midas had done when he wished that whatever he touched might be turned into gold. Unfortunately for him, this also included everything he tried to eat and drink, with the result that Midas was soon pretty hungry and thirsty. And things got even worse when he managed to turn his only daughter into a golden statue.

Philippa thought of all these things while she pondered contacting the man who, according to several Italian magazines and newspapers, was the unluckiest man in the world: Silvio Prezzolini.

Silvio was employed in the tourist shop at Pompeii, where he had worked for more than ten years, although he had only just returned to work after falling down a manhole — an accident that had left him with two broken legs. He was forty-nine years old and he had endured a whole lifetime of broken bones ever since the age of two, when he had fallen from a third-floor window and, uninjured, had then been run over by a Neapolitan pizza delivery van.

At the age of thirteen he had been sucked out of an Alitalia aircraft when the door fell off.

Silvio had celebrated his sixteenth birthday in the hospital after being struck by lightning on a soccer field. On the day of his discharge, there had been a violent thunderstorm and he had been struck by lightning a second time, on the roof of a multistory parking lot.

(The odds of being struck by lightning in any given year are about one in 500,000.)

Between the ages of twenty-one and thirty, Silvio had been involved in forty-two car accidents.

At the age of thirty-six, Silvio had gotten a job in the souvenir shop of the Rome zoo and, almost immediately, he had been severely assaulted by an escaped panda called Felix.

By this time Silvio was starting to get a national reputation as the unluckiest man in Italy. Which was why a Japanese television company agreed to pay Silvio fifty thousand dollars to follow him around for a year to see what happened to him; but when a whole year passed without anything at all unlucky happening to Silvio, the television company went bankrupt and Silvio got nothing. What was worse, the Japanese television producer himself suffered a terrible accident when he drove his car off a cliff and naturally, Silvio was in the car at the time.

Silvio survived, but only just. After a whole year in the hospital, Silvio changed his name and went to work as a tour guide on Mount Vesuvius. But his identity was leaked to the fascinated world by an Italian newspaper and this prompted several other guides to quit their jobs on the basis that, with Silvio's luck being what it was, their own was likely to take a turn for the worse. Since Vesuvius is long overdue for an eruption — the last one was in 1944, and that current lull in volcanic activity is the longest in five hundred years — this was perhaps understandable.

Silvio worked for several years at Vesuvius, falling into the dust bowl of the volcano's crater only once. During the same period he was severely scalded by a jet of hot steam, was concussed by a freak shower of hailstones, survived an earthquake, was run over by a German tourist bus, half drowned in a flood, and was hit by a piece of debris from a failing Russian satellite.

While working at the Pompeii souvenir shop, Silvio was currently being observed at a safe distance by a team of scientists from Princeton University who were studying global consciousness in an effort to determine if the effects of random or so-called unlucky events could be measured scientifically.

Of course the Princeton people were not the only ones watching Silvio Prezzolini: Philippa, too, was watching to see what kind of person he was. Just as she had done with the Kidz with Gutz awards ceremony. After all, just because a person has had a lot of bad luck in his life doesn't mean that by default he is a good person. Even bad people have bad luck.

Much to Philippa's relief, what she saw in Silvio Prezzolini was a small, balding man with a limp and a big smile, who was kind to animals and children. The more she observed him, the more Philippa was inclined to believe that if anyone looked like he deserved to be granted three wishes, it was surely Silvio Prezzolini.

Philippa knew he spoke good English, so the only problem that faced her — that faces any djinn granting a mundane three wishes — was how to make the poor man believe what she was saying without scaring him half to death and without him wasting one important wish.

Careful observation of Silvio revealed that he started each day in the souvenir shop by conscientiously dusting all of the merchandise. Mostly this was plastic junk, but there were some rather nice-looking reproductions of Roman cameo glass featuring scenes from Pompeii that Silvio treated with extra attention, polishing them all very carefully.

And this gave Philippa an idea as to how she might reveal herself to Silvio as a djinn ready to give him three wishes. She decided that perhaps the old-fashioned, traditional way of doing this was the best way, after all; and so, one morning, before he arrived in the shop, she transubstantiated herself into a cloud of smoke and hid herself in one of the Roman vases.

As soon as Silvio started to polish the vase containing Philippa, she turned herself back into human form, just like a djinn from the pages of the *Arabian Nights*. But by the time she had collected every smoky atom of herself so that she could talk to him, he had dropped the vase and was running away, and poor Philippa was obliged to run after him.

"It was never like this in the *Arabian Nights*," she puffed as she followed him across the Forum. "Who ever heard of a djinn chasing someone to give them three wishes?"

But Silvio wasn't very fit and Philippa soon caught up with him trying to hide in the Garden of the Fugitives — so named because here there were plaster casts of thirteen dead people who had made a futile attempt to seek refuge from the volcanic ash from the eruption of Vesuvius.

"Who are you?" squeaked Silvio, cowering in a corner. "What do you want with me?"

"Why are you running away?" Philippa asked Silvio breathlessly. "I'm here to help you."

Hearing her speak, he seemed to relax a little. "You're not from the volcano then," he observed. Silvio stood up and brushed some of the dust of Pompeii off his clothes.

"No," said Philippa. "Whatever gave you that idea?"

"Only the fact that you appeared out of a cloud of thick gray smoke," said Silvio. "You want to be careful about doing that kind of thing around here. People will get the wrong idea, that you're some kind of localized eruption. Or that you're something to do with Vulcan, the Roman god of fire and volcanoes."

"No, I'm nothing to do with him, or the volcano," said Philippa. "I'm a djinn. A genie, you might say. And I've come to grant you three wishes."

"You mean like in the fairy stories?"

"If you like," said Philippa.

Silvio regarded the girl standing in front of him skeptically. He supposed she was about fourteen years old. She wasn't very tall, with reddish hair, and glasses that made her look clever rather than magical. And undeniably she was an American, although not in a bad way.

"You don't look much like a djinn," said Silvio.

"What's a djinn supposed to look like?" Philippa asked.

"About thirty feet tall, with silk trousers, bare chest, little waistcoat, turban, and with a big curly mustache. Scary."

"Take my word for it. We're a little more modern these days."

"So, why me?" asked Silvio.

"Why not you?"

"What I mean is: I didn't do anything for you. Shouldn't I have released you from a lamp after a thousand years of you being in there, or something?" He shrugged. "Or maybe I did. In which case, you're very welcome."

"That does happen, sometimes," said Philippa. "But not very often. And to answer your first question, you don't always have to do something for a djinn to get three wishes. In this case I'm giving you three wishes because four Italian newspapers and two Japanese magazines voted you the unluckiest man in the world."

Silvio made a face. "I don't think of myself in that way at all."

"You don't?" Philippa sounded surprised. "Being struck twice by lightning in the space of one week sounds unusually unlucky to me. Especially on top of all the other stuff you've been through."

Silvio shook his head. "The way I see it is this: I'm still here. It's true, some dreadful things have happened to me, but I've survived them all. You'd have to be pretty lucky for that to happen. In fact, you'd have to be the luckiest man in the world. This is the way I look at myself, like the luckiest man in the world." He smiled kindly. "So, I think you ought to take those three wishes and give them to someone who really needs them. Not me."

Philippa was flabbergasted. "Look here, I really am a djinn, you know," she said. "I do have the power to make your dreams come true."

"Oh, I believe you," said Silvio. "I mean, it happened exactly the way I used to read about. Like in 'Aladdin' and those other stories. You may not be thirty feet tall with silk trousers, but you did appear from a vase, and in a cloud of smoke. It's not every little girl who can do that."

"Well, I never," said Philippa, who'd had no idea that granting a mundane three wishes would turn out to be quite so hard. "Are you sure?"

Silvio shrugged. "What would I do with three wishes, anyway? From what I've read, people either wish carelessly, which wrecks their life, or they end up being paralyzed with indecision about what to wish for. Besides, I'm at the kind of age when my life is pretty well set, you know. Having more or less anything I might want, just like that, would only complicate things now." He shook his head. "It would complicate life and, perhaps, make it less fun."

"Less fun?" Philippa sounded surprised. "A lot of people might disagree with that."

"Then they don't understand what life is all about," said Silvio. "To grant all a man's wishes is to take away his dreams and his ambitions. Life is only worth living if you have something to strive for. To aim at. You understand?"

"You're a very unusual man, do you know that?" Philippa couldn't help but be impressed. "Most people would give anything for a djinn to grant them three wishes."

"I stopped feeling like most people the day I got sucked out of an airplane at ten thousand feet," said Silvio.

"By the way," asked Philippa, "how did you ever survive getting sucked out of an airplane?"

"About two-thirds of the way down I hit a hot-air balloon," said Silvio. "It broke my fall quite a bit. Just as I slipped off the balloon, it was flying over a circus. I fell onto the big top and that helped to break my fall, too. Even so, I still went through the roof of the tent. And it just so happened that I arrived in the circus just as a high-wire act was in progress, and they had a safety net for the man walking the tightrope. Which I fell into."

"Gosh, that was lucky," said Philippa.

"Wasn't it?" Silvio grinned. "Didn't I tell you? I'm really a very lucky fellow. You want another example? The Japanese television producer who accidentally drove off a cliff with me in the car? The car burst into flames before it hit the ground but, fortunately for me, I had already jumped out. I missed some power lines on the way down. That was lucky, too. Then I hit some trees. Luckily for me, the man who was supposed to have pruned the trees that day was late; otherwise there would have been no branches to help break my fall. It's true, I broke a lot of bones that day. But I count myself lucky. Very lucky. You can't argue with that."

Philippa smiled. "I'm not even going to try," she said. "You know what? It's a real pleasure to meet someone who's not greedy for wealth or power or whatever. You've taught me something really important here: Not everyone wants something. Some people are just really happy the way they are."

CHAPTER 4

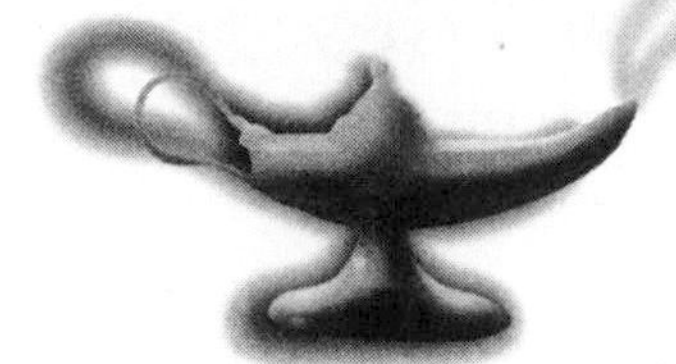

BUMBY'S JINX

John and Mr. Groanin went to Bumby Town Hall to see if they could make an appointment with someone important on the local town council.

In the entrance hall was a directory board that listed all the names of the people who worked for the town council. Through an open door was a room with uncomfortable-looking plastic chairs where several Bumby residents were awaiting their appointments. They looked like a typical cross section of the town's diverse population: There was a short, fat woman with a shopping bag and bad eczema; there was a tall, fat woman with a shopping bag and bad eczema and a small boy with eczema who was noisier than a campsite; there were two tall, handsome-looking men with very long beards and even longer hair; and a suspicious-looking character with red hair, narrow eyes, buckteeth, and — most suspicious of all to Groanin — a bow tie with polka dots.

Seeing him, Groanin nudged John and then nodded at the man in the bow tie. "Never ever trust a man that wears a bow tie in the daytime," he whispered. "Especially one with polka dots. Unless he's a clown in a circus. And even then you'd be wise to be on your guard."

"Winston Churchill wore a bow tie," said John. "What about him?"

"True, lad, but so did Karl Marx. And Sigmund Freud. And Frank Sinatra. You can bet that character is up to no good. You mark my words."

Groanin read out a few of the names of the people on the council from the directory board as he tried to decide whom they should see.

"Right then," he said. "There's Mr. Higginbottom, who's the mayor. There's Sheryl Shoebottom, the mayor's secretary; Henry Sidebottom, the town clerk; Arthur Shipperbottom, the press officer; and Colin Shufflebottom, the chief financial officer."

John sniggered. "Is everyone in this town called something-bottom?"

"It's not that kind of bottom, you daft little toe rag," said Groanin. "I say, it's not that kind of bottom. Trouble with you Yanks is that you think everything means what it says, when in fact it usually means something totally different. That's what comes of pinching our language — the *English* language — instead of inventing your own one. The word *bottom* was originally spelled 'botham,' and is an old English word meaning 'the broad bottom of a valley.' There's a lot of valleys in this part of the world. Hence the large number of 'bottoms' who live in them."

John sniggered again. "I can't help it," he insisted. "It

just seems kind of weird to have so many bottoms in one place."

"And this from a boy who lives in a state with towns called Cat Elbow Corner and Hicksville and Yaphank and Yonkers."

"There's a town called Cat Elbow Corner in New York State?" John sounded surprised.

"Seneca County," said Groanin. "It's near Glenora, if that helps."

"Nope," admitted John.

After thinking about it for a minute or two more, Groanin decided that they should first speak to the mayor's secretary, Sheryl Shoebottom. So they went up to her office and asked her if they could have an appointment with His Worship, the mayor.

"Can I tell him what it's about?" asked Miss Shoebottom.

She was a tall, thin woman with a long horseface, and a hairstyle and mouth that looked as if they had been set in plaster of Paris.

"The lad here is an eccentric millionaire," explained Groanin. "He's taken a shine to the town and wants to do it a good turn."

Groanin removed his bowler hat because he was speaking to a lady. This was unfortunate because the stink bug that had landed on his head while he'd been sitting on the beach had made several bad smells in its anxiety to escape from under Groanin's hat, and these had all accumulated to make one very large bad smell that was immediately noticeable once Groanin's bowler was removed from his bald head.

Fortunately for Groanin, and John, Miss Shoebottom did not hold him personally responsible for the bad smell. She was only too well aware of the plague of stink bugs affecting the town of Bumby and, as soon as her nostrils picked up the smell, she went into action with an aerosol can of something chemical that smelled only a bit like roses. She even sprayed a little inside Groanin's hat and on top of his head.

"There," she said. "That's much better."

"Thanks very much," said Groanin, uncertain if the smell of chemical roses was an improvement on the smell of stink bugs.

"You were saying," said Miss Shoebottom.

"Aye, well, merely that the lad here is an eccentric American millionaire, and that he's taken it into his head to do the town a good turn. Three good turns, as a matter of fact."

Miss Shoebottom looked at John critically, the way she might have stared at a scruffy dog that needed a bath. The boy was about fourteen years old. Quite tall for his age, probably, with darkish hair, and on the edge of turning quite handsome, she thought. His clothes were black and ordinary looking.

"Oh, yes?" She pulled a face. "Where's his gold watch?"

"You what?" said Groanin.

Miss Shoebottom sighed impatiently. "What I mean, luvvy — and no disrespect to you, sonny — is that he doesn't look much like a millionaire."

"Well, who does, these days?" said Groanin. "I say, who does look like a millionaire? And to be quite honest with you, I'm only using the word *millionaire* because it's a tad vulgar to go bandying around the b-word."

"The b-word?" Miss Shoebottom frowned.

"He means 'bottom,'" said John.

"I do not," said Groanin. "And I'll thank you, *sir,* to let me make the explanations." He looked at Miss Shoebottom. "The b-word. *Billionaire.*"

"If you ask me," she said, "he doesn't much look like one of them, either."

"Aye, well, I wouldn't disagree with you there, missus," said Groanin. "But the fact is, the lad's pockets are loaded with brass, and I have the honor to be his butler. It's my responsibility to help him dole out cash to them as needs it."

"We've never had a lad who had his own butler in Bumby," said Miss Shoebottom.

"It's only Yorkshire folk that think they've seen it all, right enough," observed Groanin. "And who think that what they haven't seen isn't worth seeing. Listen to me, missus. The lad's in a position to help this poor town get off its knees before it's too late."

"Tell you what, love," said Miss Shoebottom. "You leave your names and an address with me and I'll get His Worship, the mayor, to give you a call when he's got a minute. All right?"

Groanin nodded. "We're at the Oasis Guesthouse," he said.

"Mrs. Bottomley's place," she said. "I know it."

Only just managing to contain another snigger, John went outside the office.

"Just don't leave it too long or he's likely to take his charity up the road to Whitby," said Groanin.

Groanin thanked Miss Shoebottom and followed the boy out into the corridor, where he found him staring at the portraits of three previous mayors: Mr. Frederick Oakenbottom, Sir Geoffrey Longbottom, and Mrs. Hilda Longbottom.

"Don't say another word," said Groanin.

They went outside onto High Street.

"There are some weird-looking people in this town," observed John, catching sight of a man wearing a pink turban. "If you ask me, some of them look a bit sinister."

"It's true, that," agreed Groanin. "Yorkshire folk do look a bit sinister. Speaking as someone from Lancashire, I'd have to agree with you there."

"I don't get it," said John. "You're not from Yorkshire. So why not vacation in Lancashire?"

"Wouldn't be a holiday unless I could get away from everything," said Groanin. "Coming to Yorkshire is the next best thing to going on vacation in Lancashire, without actually going to Lancashire. See, if I went to Lancashire I might bump into someone I know and that would be a disaster."

"Why?"

"Because there's lots of folk in Lancashire I never want to see again as long as I live. Now put a sock in them questions and let's get back in time for our supper. It's sausages tonight."

They returned to their room at the Oasis Guesthouse.

It was not well named. John thought it couldn't have seemed less like an oasis if it had been an abandoned car factory. It wasn't even much like a guesthouse, since the place seemed to have more rules than a Carolina golf club.

"I was thinking," said John.

"That makes a change," said Groanin.

"I might go back to the mayor's office, invisibly, and see what kind of fellow he is. Get a feel for him, you know. I want to make sure he's not a crook or anything before I go handing over three wishes like a box of candy."

"Good idea," said Groanin. He sat down in a lumpy chair and shook open a copy of the *Daily Telegraph*. "I'll have a read of the paper while you're gone. But don't be late. It's sausages tonight."

John lay down on his hard bed, closed his eyes, and silently lifted his spirit from out of his body. It always felt a little strange leaving himself behind. He hovered near the ceiling for a moment, observing the dust and the trailing cobwebs that Mrs. Bottomley had ignored, and then swooped down beside Groanin to blow in his hairy ear.

Groanin shuddered visibly. "Give over doing that," he shouted, and swatted the air around his head with the newspaper for good measure.

Chuckling happily, John floated out of the guesthouse and into the street.

Mostly he behaved himself, but being of a mischievous disposition he could hardly resist stroking a policeman's fat neck and lifting up a whole tray of cakes in the Most Haunted Tearooms as he passed through the town. There were times when John thought that being invisible was the best fun anyone could have in this world and halfway toward the next.

But nearer the town hall John stopped floating for a moment as something unusual caught his eye: something that even he had never ever seen before — and John had already seen a lot in his fourteen years of life.

It appeared to be a species of small white ape.

Almost as interesting was the fact that the ape seemed to be invisible to everyone in Bumby except John. Not only that, but it was clear that the ape could see John *even though* he himself was invisible. And if all that wasn't remarkable enough, it quickly became apparent that the small, white, invisible ape could speak excellent English. Even better than Groanin, it seemed to John.

"Hello," said the ape.

"Hello," said John.

"My name is Cornelius," said the ape.

"Mine's John."

"You can't begin to know how pleased I am to see someone who can see me," said Cornelius. "It's been weeks since I spoke to anyone who spoke back."

"You can see me?"

"Just the faintest outline, it's true," said Cornelius. "Are you a ghost?"

"Er, no," said John. "A djinn."

"Ah. I've heard of those. But I've never met one."

"Are you an ape?"

"I'd agree with that description but for the fact that I can obviously speak. To my knowledge, apes are not capable of speech. But to be perfectly honest with you, I'm not exactly sure what I am. Cornelius is just a name I picked up in the local TV shop. There was a movie on called *Planet of the Apes* and one of the apes — one who looked like a darker version of me — was called Cornelius."

"How can you tell what you look like if you're invisible?" John asked reasonably enough.

"Oh, I'm not invisible to myself," said Cornelius. "Nor indeed to you."

"How did you get here, in Bumby?"

"I don't know that, either."

"So why don't you leave?"

"Where would I go? What's the point of leaving somewhere if you're lost? Besides, there was another TV program I was watching that said if you're lost, the best thing is always to wait where you are until someone finds you. And now someone has."

"Oh?" John glanced around. "Who's that?"

"You, of course." Cornelius frowned. "Apart from that, it's all a big mystery to me, I'm afraid."

John thought for a moment. "You know, I could maybe help you there."

"Could you? How?"

"Being a djinn, I might be able to give you three wishes," said John. "I say *might* because the plain fact of the matter is that I'm still learning how to be a djinn, so sometimes the wishes don't come out exactly right; and I also say *might* because I never gave three wishes to anyone but a mundane before now. That's what we djinn call a human being. I'm not sure how it works when I give wishes to . . . well, whatever you are. Let's call you an ape for now."

"All right. But what could I possibly wish for that might help my situation?"

"You might wish to remember something that you've forgotten, such as your real name, and what you are, and where you come from — where your home is. That kind of thing."

"Could I really wish for all that?"

John shrugged. "I don't see why not. The only trouble is I can't give you three wishes while I'm in my current transubstantiated state. I'll have to go and recover my body first and then sort you out. Of course, it's just possible that once I am in my body again, I won't be able to see you. After all, I'm sure I would have seen a white apelike creature wandering around the town before now. So we'd better think of something now in case that should happen." He shrugged. "Unless, of course, *you* know a way of making yourself noticeable."

Cornelius shook his head.

"All right, then," said John. "Follow me."

They returned to the Oasis, where supper was being served. As Groanin had promised, it was sausages. The house was full of their smell. John told Cornelius to wait in the garage, where Mr. Bottomley, the landlady's husband, kept his motorcycle.

"Listen carefully," John told his new friend. "In the event that I come back down here and can't see you, I want you to tap three times on the exhaust pipe of the bike to tell me you're here and that you're ready for three wishes. Let's try that, shall we?"

Cornelius tapped three times on the exhaust pipe as instructed. The sound seemed quite audible to John.

"Good," he said. "As soon as you've tapped that you're ready, make the three wishes we already discussed, and then I'll utter my focus word. My word of power. That should make your wishes come true. At which point tap three times again and I'll know that it worked. Then I'll lift out of my body and we'll talk. Got it?"

"It sounds complicated," said Cornelius. "But, yes, I think I can remember all that."

John floated back upstairs and collected his body. Groanin was already downstairs waiting for his supper. John got up from the bed and ran downstairs which, in the old guesthouse, sounded like a small earthquake.

Mrs. Bottomley came out of her kitchen with a frying pan in her hand and stared fiercely upstairs. "Do you have to make that racket?" she demanded.

"I'm sorry," said John.

"Boys," said Mrs. Bottomley. "You're all the same. Rude and noisy. A disaster area. If you're not clattering down them stairs, you're sprinting up them, or singing in the bath, or laughing like a drain, or slamming that front door, or shifting around in bed like a bear with insomnia."

John apologized again, only this time more profusely.

"It's all very well apologizing," moaned Mrs. Bottomley, who was ill suited to working in Yorkshire's tourist industry.

"But I'd rather not have the noise than have the apology. I wish I didn't have to listen to your racket, that's all."

For a moment John considered granting Mrs. Bottomley's wish and making her deaf for a day or two, or even transporting her to a desert island. But he was not a cruel boy and quickly thought better of it. Besides, a cloud of black smoke, like something from the crater of a volcano, was now billowing out of the kitchen door. Whatever was cooking on the stove was burning.

"The sausages!" screamed Mrs. Bottomley.

John ran outside before Mrs. Bottomley could blame him for that, too.

Straightaway he noticed that a mail truck had somehow managed to reverse across the flower beds in Mr. Bottomley's front garden and, even now, in his desperate effort to escape from the scene of the accident before someone saw him, the driver was revving the engine hard — so hard that the tires were gouging huge holes in the immaculate lawn.

But this was not the only disaster that had suddenly befallen the Oasis Guesthouse. A herd of goats from a farmer's field behind the house had managed to leap the fence and were now eating the bedsheets on Mrs. Bottomley's laundry line. Then the television — there was only one — exploded, which caused a large picture of Winston Churchill that was hanging on a wall above the staircase to fall on top of Mrs. Bottomley's cat and render it unconscious.

Meanwhile, the fire in the kitchen had spread to the so-called Sun Terrace, and as the mailman finally managed to speed away from the front garden, his van clipped a telegraph pole that fell over and flattened the greenhouse where Mr. Bottomley had been growing the largest marrow in Yorkshire.

John hardly hesitated. "ABECEDARIAN!" he said loudly, for this was his focus word. And almost immediately he managed to put a stop to any more disasters at the Oasis Guesthouse. Most important of all, the fire went out.

But the real damage was already done.

For a moment John worried that his earlier irritation with Mrs. Bottomley following her comments about him being a disaster area had somehow resulted in a case of him wishing a real disaster into existence so she might appreciate the difference. But since he had felt no power go out of him he was certain that he could not be held responsible for what had happened. Groanin would try to blame him, he was already certain of that much, but that couldn't be helped.

Worry that he had unleashed some kind of retribution on the Oasis quickly gave way to an instinctive realization that these disastrous events might just be connected with Cornelius.

John ran into the garage to find the beautifully polished motorcycle lying on the floor, with a large dent in the gas tank. He glanced around and, seeing no sign of the white ape, he shook his head and said, "Nope. Can't see you. But knock three times if you're ready for your three wishes."

Three taps on the tailpipe of the motorcycle confirmed the presence of Cornelius in the garage and that he was ready.

John felt something close to his ear, and then heard a small voice he recognized as that of Cornelius, speaking to him out of thin air.

"I wish I could remember my real name," said the voice. "I wish I knew exactly what I am; and I wish I knew where I come from and why I'm here."

"ABECEDARIAN," John said, again.

He felt the power go out of him a second time, and then slowly, like a light growing in brightness, Cornelius started to become visible until he seemed quite solid. But he was still totally white, so that, just as there are white leopards called snow leopards, he now looked like a species of white ape or chimpanzee that might have been called a snow chimpanzee.

"Did it work?" John asked anxiously, for he was keen to be out of the garage before someone could accuse him of knocking over the motorcycle. "Hey, Cornelius? Did it work?"

"First of all, my name is not Cornelius, it's Zagreus, and I'm from Greece. I'm here because some bad men captured me and then brought me here. I'm not exactly sure why, but I assume it's something to do with the fact that I'm a Jinx. Yes, it worked. Thank you."

"You're a what?"

"A Jinx."

"Er, what's a Jinx?"

"It's like this, John," said Zagreus. "I used to be something or someone else. I think it must have been a someone because I can still talk. Anyway, when I died I got myself reincarnated as an ape. Only the reincarnation didn't quite take. A Jinx is someone, like me, who doesn't make a proper reincarnation. I'm in a sort of halfway state between my old life and my new incarnation, which is supposed to be an ape. Which is why I'm white and sometimes invisible and why I can still talk. I'm neither one thing nor the other."

"Did you do something wrong in your previous life?" John asked Zagreus. "Is that why you've come back as an ape?"

"Actually I think an ape is considered pretty good," explained Zagreus. "It's something like a cockroach or a rat that you don't want to be. Reincarnation doesn't happen to everyone, of course. You have to believe in it, I think. And not everyone it happens to likes the idea of reincarnation. Some people try very hard to remember who or what they used to be and not everyone can remember. And that's one of the reasons the reincarnation doesn't take and how one becomes a Jinx. You see, Jinxes get very frustrated with things and cause all sorts of bad luck and accidents to happen as we try to remember who and what we used to be. My name, Zagreus, and the fact that I come from Greece is as much as I've been able to remember."

"So you're the one who's caused all this mayhem," said John. "Not just in this lousy guesthouse, but in this crummy town, too."

"Yes, but I didn't do it on purpose," explained Zagreus. "This kind of thing just sort of happens around me. I'd like to make it stop, but I don't know how."

"I think you'd better speak to my uncle Nimrod," said John. "He's a very powerful djinn. Very powerful and very wise."

"He sounds frightening," said Zagreus.

"Yes, he does, only he's not," said John. "He's English. But not English like they are here in Bumby. He's clever and kind and you can understand almost everything of what he's saying. I'm sure he'll be able to help you."

"That would be wonderful," said Zagreus.

"Now if we can just think of a way of getting you back to London and my uncle's house without causing a train crash or some other kind of disaster." John thought for a moment. "Hmm. Let's see now. Ah, yes, I have it. Do you know what a djinn binding is?"

"Something that holds someone under a djinn's power?"

"That's right. The binding I'm thinking of is called a diminuendo. It'll make you smaller and totally immobilize you until we're in a place of safety."

"It won't hurt or anything, will it?" asked Zagreus.

"No," said John. "You'll just feel and look like a sort of doll, or toy."

"All right. Let's do it. And then let's leave. I don't want to stay here a minute longer than I have to."

John had never carried out a diminuendo binding on anyone before, but he'd read about how to do it in the *Shorter Baghdad Rules*. This wasn't quite the same thing as actually doing it, but he couldn't think of any other way to transport the Jinx safely back to London.

"What's your favorite food?" he asked Zagreus. "Bananas, I suppose."

Zagreus shook his head. "I can't stand bananas," he said. "You forget, I only look like an ape. Inside, I'm Greek."

"What sort of food do Greeks like?"

"I don't know."

John thought of the sausages Mrs. Bottomley had been cooking. "How about sausages?" he suggested.

Zagreus nodded. "I think I like them."

"All right." John muttered his focus word again and produced a large plate of delicious-looking hot sausages.

Seeing it, Zagreus reached for one immediately.

"Wait," said John. "I haven't finished yet."

Frowning furiously, John concentrated all of his djinn thoughts on one particular sausage. He thought about small, shrinking things mostly, and focused all of his power on the idea that whoever ate the sausage would shrink and stiffen until they were the size of a doll.

Almost as soon as John had finished thinking very hard, the garage door opened. It was Groanin and he was looking rather grumpy.

"I've been looking for you everywhere," said the butler. "I said, I've been looking for you everywhere. Supper's finished. It was sausages. At least it would have been, only Mrs. Bottomley burnt them. Which is a great pity as sausages are my favorite. Anyway, I came to tell you that if we want anything to eat tonight we'll have to send out, or go somewhere else because the kitchen is out of action. And . . . wait a minute. *You've got sausages.*" Groanin licked his lips greedily. "Well done, lad. Well done. I don't mind if I do have one."

He reached for the plate with his fat fingers.

"No," said John. "You can't. Not that one, anyway."

"Why?" Groanin laughed. "Has it got your name on it?"

"No!" yelled John. "You mustn't."

But it was too late. Groanin had already taken and eaten the sausage containing the diminuendo binding.

"Delicious," he said. "I'll say one thing for you, lad, you know how to conjure up a good sausage."

"You're an idiot," said John.

Groanin laughed. "Another? I don't mind if I do."

A few seconds later the butler started to shrink.

CHAPTER 5

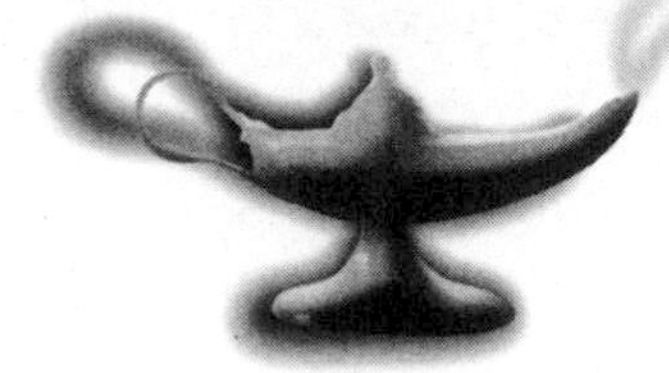

THE KGB AND THE LUCK OF THE BRITISH

In London, two hundred and forty miles south of Bumby, the weather was very different. It was a warm, sunny day and the curved black snakewood door of Nimrod's large white stucco house was creaking loudly in the heat. The hood of Nimrod's large black Rolls-Royce, parked immediately in front of the house in Kensington Gardens, was so hot you could have fried a whole carton of eggs on it. Sunny-side up, of course.

Not that anyone in possession of a carton of eggs would have dared to try and do such a thing. Nimrod's Rolls-Royce already enjoyed a reputation among London's criminal classes and general riffraff as something to be left alone, equipped, as it was, with some very surprising security precautions of the kind that only a powerful djinn could have taken. Because even in London a Rolls-Royce is not a very common car and can, upon occasion, excite a degree of envy and resentment among the more scrofulous members of the London nefarious. And while it is certain that one Rolls-Royce can make a street seem fortunate, two Rolls-Royces can make it seem downright prosperous. Which is how it might have appeared on that particular day as a second Rolls-Royce — equally large and almost identical but for the fact that this one was light blue — attempted to park next to Nimrod's.

This Rolls was driven — none too carefully, and almost invisibly, she was so small behind the wheel — by an old lady who was about seventy years old. She was wearing a large flowery hat with a net on it and a pair of glasses that were so large and horn-rimmed she could have gone head-to-head with a decent-sized moose and probably won. She was wearing elbow-length lilac gloves, an elegant lilac-colored dress, several strings of pearls, and, when she got out of the car, she was carrying a saddle-leather briefcase. Her face wore an expression of cold command, as if she was used to being obeyed, like Ozymandias.

She paid no apparent attention to the man wearing a striped pullover who dismounted a motorcycle a short distance away — or so it seemed to the man himself, who leaned on a wall and started to read a newspaper. But the old lady was watching him carefully and no sooner had she locked the door of the blue Rolls than she had marched over to him and confronted him crossly:

"Are you following me, you wretched little man?"

"Me, lady? Whatever gives you that idea?" He grinned unpleasantly. "You're a bit old for my taste, know what I mean?"

"And you are a bit too suspicious for mine," said the old lady. "I wouldn't be at all surprised if the police were interested in you, my man."

Panicking a little, the man hesitated and then tried to snatch the old lady's briefcase, only to find that it was securely handcuffed to her wrist.

The old lady did not scream, however, as might have been expected. Nor did she cry out for help or fall to the ground when her attacker tugged with all his might at the briefcase. The man now discovered to his cost that the immediate result of his offense was a surprisingly disproportionate degree of defense. For this was no ordinary old lady. She was no djinn, but she was someone who was an expert in the ancient art of *Kuttu Varisai*, which is a variety of Indian self-defense.

In a matter of seconds the old lady had tossed the man through the air as if he were a large pillow. The man hit a set of railings and lay stunned on the ground for several seconds; then he picked himself up, jumped back onto his motorcycle, and drove quickly away before the old lady could do him some more permanent damage.

There were no people around to witness the incident unless you counted Nimrod, who had watched the entire scene from his drawing room window. And he wasn't in the least surprised at the sight of this elderly lady throwing a mugger through the air. The old lady might have looked like someone's aged grandmother, but he knew that she was none other than μ — a Greek letter that means "mu," pronounced Moo — and that she was in charge of an important section in MI6, which is what Britain's secret intelligence service is called.

Or at least it used to be.

If you ever go onto the website for MI6 (http://www.mi6.gov.uk), you will learn that the name MI6 fell into official disuse many years ago and that the proper name for the agency that secretly goes about protecting the security and well-being of Great Britain is the Secret Intelligence Service, or SIS for short.

Taking the virtual tour on the SIS website, you will discover that there are a wide range of clubs and sporting associations that exist underneath the SIS umbrella. One of these SIS associations is the King's Gambling Board (KGB), which was set up in 1938 during the reign of King George VI, who was himself a keen gambler. The KGB trains SIS agents to become expert in all forms of gambling, especially hard-to-understand games played in French casinos where lots of money can be won or lost on the turn of a single card. This is considered essential for British spies, as making a bit of easy money on the side often prevents them from accepting outside employment with the Russian secret service.

The KGB was headed up by Moo, although for many years she had been rather better known as Lady Silvia Stone and as the headmistress of a girls' school in India, before a chance meeting with Mr. Rakshasas, then the representative in India of the British Security Service, had resulted in her joining MI5 and, later on, MI6.

Moo walked up the steps and, taking hold of the fist-shaped knocker, rapped loudly on the door.

After a longish interval the door was opened by Nimrod himself.

"Moo," he exclaimed. "What a lovely surprise." He glanced up the street. "Which is more than that poor fellow you just tossed through the air can say."

"Thank goodness I was wearing gloves," said Moo. "Filthy man. Let us hope the fall knocked some sense into his addled head."

"Yes, let's," said Nimrod.

"He was following me for several miles," said Moo. "Doubtless with the intention of mugging me. That's one of the hazards of being an old woman who drives a Rolls-Royce."

"Perhaps you should drive something else," said Nimrod.

"Oh, I couldn't do that. It's such a good car. Oh, no."

"What can I do for you?" asked Nimrod.

"I hope I'm not disturbing you, Nimrod. I dislike calling on people unannounced, especially when I find that they are answering their own doors. I deduce you are without your butler."

"Clever of you," said Nimrod.

"Elementary," said Moo. "I do hope Mr. Groanin is not unwell."

"Groanin is on holiday," explained Nimrod, and showed her inside without further delay. "And I'm having to look after myself."

"That ought not to be too difficult, given who and what you are," observed Moo.

Moo was an old friend of Nimrod's. She was one of the few mundanes in the world who knew that he was a djinn. He knew that Moo would have contacted him at his home only if the country — perhaps the world — had been facing some sort of crisis.

Nimrod led Moo into his drawing room and offered her a seat.

"Do you wish for tea?" he asked her.

"Yes, please," said Moo without a thought.

"QWERTYUIOP!" said Nimrod, and a tea table with a stiff white tablecloth and a silver teapot and beautiful china and cakes and scones and cucumber sandwiches appeared, all in the blink of an eye.

"Goodness gracious," said Moo. "How clever of you."

Nimrod poured Moo a cup of tea. "I hope this is all right. Tea is not the same when you have to make it yourself. I'll be glad when Groanin gets back. He is the most curmudgeonly fellow, but he can make a spectacularly good cup of tea."

Moo sipped her tea politely, with a pinkie extended, the way she had been taught as a little girl in India.

"Delicious," she said. "Only do warn me next time if you're going to do anything like that again. At my age, surprises can seem a little too surprising."

"Of course," said Nimrod. "It was rude of me not to mention it before. And may I say, you're looking very smart. The hat is most becoming."

Moo smiled. "It's my Ascot hat," she said. "I am on my way to the races, where I have a horse running in the three thirty. It's been my greatest wish, for over twenty years, to have a horse that wins the Ascot Gold Cup."

"Good luck," said Nimrod.

"That's what I came to see you about," said Moo. "Good luck seems to be in rather short supply at the moment."

"Are you speaking personally, Moo, or in general?"

"In general," said Moo. "Reports have reached my department that there seems to be rather more bad luck around than is normal."

"I haven't noticed anything unusual," said Nimrod.

"Are you sure?"

"I'm certain of it."

Moo sighed.

"Look, Nimrod, I'm sorry to press you on this, but it was my understanding that the djinn are the self-appointed guardians of luck in the universe. That there are three good tribes who try to influence luck for the good and that there are three bad ones who try to do the reverse. And that there exists a balance of power that you call the Homeostasis, wherein there is neither too much good luck nor too much bad. Also, that there is a machine, a kind of clock called the tuchemeter, that constantly indicates the state of the Homeostasis. Am I correct?"

Nimrod nodded. "You state the matter perfectly, dear lady."

"Then might I also inquire when you last looked at this tuchemeter?"

"In point of fact, there is not one, but several. I have one here in London, and I glanced at it this morning. I have another one at my other house in Cairo. If the one here in London were ever to stop working, then I could rely upon the one in Cairo to give a true indication of the current state of luck."

Moo took off her glasses and began to clean them with her handkerchief. "And if the one here wasn't working, then how would you know what the one in Cairo was saying?"

"Supposing that there appeared to be an excess of bad luck around," said Nimrod, "then my servant Creemy would raise the alarm. Also, there is a larger, more sensitive tuchemeter in Berlin, but I'm afraid security forbids me to tell you more about that."

"I quite understand," said Moo. "And yet, at the same time, I don't. Understand. You say you've noticed nothing unusual on the tuchemeter. Perhaps. But is it possible you cannot have noticed that the newspapers are full of so much doom and gloom?"

"That's true," said Nimrod. "However, just because something is in the newspapers doesn't make it true. I tend to believe what's on the tuchemeter rather more than what I see in the newspapers or on TV."

Moo nodded. "Very wise."

"Equally," added Nimrod, "just because there is an excess of doom and gloom here in Britain and America does not mean that there is doom and gloom in Patagonia or Timbuktu. The world is a large place, Moo. Luck has a way of evening itself out. One man's cloud is another's silver lining."

"Might it be possible to see this tuchemeter of yours?" asked Moo.

"Of course."

Nimrod led Moo through to the back of the house. For a moment he remembered his young nephew and why he had gone to Bumby. Was it possible that what was happening in Bumby was connected with Moo's visit?

He opened a door and showed her into a room where there were only two objects: a large, round clocklike instrument that was hanging on the wall, and facing it, an ornate-looking chair. The tuchemeter was made of gold and was about six feet in diameter. Three words were painted in large letters on the tuchemeter's silver face: GOOD, BAD, and HOMEOSTASIS. The single hand, shaped like a muscular human arm with a human index finger, was pointing slightly to the BAD side of the word HOMEOSTASIS.

"It's an exact replica of the larger one in Berlin," explained Nimrod. "That one records the official amount of luck around the globe and gives the so-called BML: Berlin Meridian Luck."

"Fascinating," said Moo. "How does it work?"

"It may not look like it," said Nimrod, "but it's actually very scientific. Every day people all over the world get up and go through their day in one of two ways: They either smile or they don't. If they're feeling lucky they smile, and if they're feeling unlucky they don't. Their smiles, or frowns create tiny changes in the earth's atmosphere that lead to larger-scale alterations of events, for good or bad. If someone smiles it affects the trajectory of the system one way, and if they frown it affects the system in another way. Luck isn't quite as random as most people think."

"How are those changes in atmosphere measured, and where?" asked Moo.

"There are several dozen locations all over the world where that happens," said Nimrod. "Even I don't know where they are. The measurements are taken by a special djinn binding called an animadverto, which brings the results to the tuchemeter every fifteen minutes. It's the animadverto that decides where to go for its observations. Like a sort of telepathic opinion poll."

"And how do you know if it's working all right?"

Nimrod tapped the face of the tuchemeter with his fingernail, as if he had been correcting a barometer.

"Well, if this one wasn't," said Nimrod, "if it was giving a false reading, one of the other ones would show up the difference and —"

"Yes, I understand that," said Moo. "I meant, suppose it was the measurements that were wrong, or the animadverto that was at fault. How would you know?"

"Quite simple," said Nimrod. "To give a reading on this tuchemeter any animadverto has to travel through the atmosphere of this room. I should ask a mundane to simply throw a die a hundred times and see how many sixes he or she obtained. So close to the tuchemeter itself, I might expect to see any manifestation of good or bad luck — no matter how small — have an effect on the tuchemeter."

"Do it," said Moo.

"Dear lady, I can assure you that —"

"Please," said Moo. "Indulge me, Nimrod."

"Very well," said Nimrod. He went to a special drawer under the seat of the chair and removed a cigar box containing just one die, and, handing Moo the die, he added, "I keep a die here for just this purpose, although I must confess it's some time since I thought to measure the tuchemeter's accuracy."

"Can you memorize the results of all my throws?" Moo asked Nimrod.

"Easily," said Nimrod.

"Now then," said Moo. "You would expect each number from one to six to come up one time in six, plus or minus $\sqrt{(2n/6)}$. If we throw a die one hundred times and get more than twenty-two sixes, or less than eleven sixes, then you can judge me either lucky or unlucky, yes?"

"That's about the size of it," agreed Nimrod. "And I must confess, I'm impressed with your knowledge of mathematics and probability."

"You forget. I'm head of the King's Gambling Board," said Moo. "Gambling, luck, odds, probability all fall within my department's scrutiny."

Nimrod held the cigar box open for Moo and watched carefully as she began to throw the die. After a hundred throws it was clear to them both that Moo wasn't enjoying much in the way of good luck.

"You threw only five sixes," said Nimrod. "Half as many as the least number that might have been expected. It's not your lucky day."

"Oh, dear," she said. "It's not looking good for my horse this afternoon if I can only manage five sixes. Why don't I keep going and see if my luck improves?"

Nimrod, who could remember a thousand different numbers just as easily as a hundred, agreed.

But more than an hour later, after Moo had thrown the die another nine hundred times, it was clear her luck could never have been described as good: In a thousand throws she might have expected between 148 and 185 sixes. Instead, she had managed less than a hundred.

"Such a run of singularly bad luck so close to the tuchemeter," said Nimrod, "ought to show up here, any moment now."

He looked closely at the tuchemeter expecting to see some movement of the finger at the end of the arm, but there was nothing, not even a tremor. He waited for several minutes during which time Moo said nothing. Finally, Nimrod said, "That's odd. There's nothing at all. Not so much as a flicker." And then he added, "Excuse me for a moment."

Nimrod left the room and was gone for several minutes; when he came back he was carrying a hand mirror that was the size of a table-tennis paddle.

"Many people believe that breaking a mirror means seven years' bad luck," said Nimrod. "With us djinn, it has to be the right kind of mirror. Each of us has a secret mirror, a synopados, that reflects a portion of our soul. With humans, the belief attaches to mirrors in general."

Moo nodded. "You're not asking me to break a mirror deliberately?" she said.

"I'm afraid I am," said Nimrod.

"You ask a great deal," said Moo, "of someone as superstitious as me."

"It's the only way to know for sure if something is wrong with the results we're getting on this tuchemeter. Perhaps on all of them."

"I suppose it was me who started this inquiry," said Moo. "I suppose it had better be me who answers it."

She took the mirror and looked at it for several seconds before she shrugged and then dropped the mirror onto the floor, where it shattered into a hundred small pieces. Even as Moo did it she let out a large sigh of self-reproach and told herself that in the light of what she had just done it now seemed so unlikely that her horse stood any chance of winning its race that she was thinking of telephoning her trainer and telling him to leave the animal in its stable.

Nimrod scrutinized the silver face of the tuchemeter for some sign that the almost-palpable bad luck that now seemed to affect the room would show up in some small movement of the finger at the end of the instrument's arm.

"Nothing," he said. "Nothing at all. Most peculiar. I really thought that you breaking a mirror would do it. But this seems to put it beyond argument. You were right. There is something wrong here."

"I do wish I wasn't," said Moo. "And I wish I hadn't had to break that mirror."

"Can't help you with the first wish," announced Nimrod. "But I can grant the second. And indeed a third. QWERTYUIOP!"

Immediately after he spoke his focus word, the tiny shards of glass lifted themselves up off the ground and began to reassemble themselves like some celestial jigsaw puzzle. For a moment a little galaxy of glass seemed to rotate in the air like a spiral nebula, and then became a mirror that was in Moo's hand once more.

Moo was so surprised that she almost dropped the mirror again.

"Oh, I say," she exclaimed. "How wonderful. Does this mean I won't have seven years' bad luck after all?"

"Yes, it does," said Nimrod. "You might also place an extra-large bet on that horse you've entered in the Gold Cup this afternoon. I've a very strong feeling it's going to win. In fact, I can guarantee it."

"Capital." Moo chuckled loudly. "Capital."

"Now then," said Nimrod. "Let's go and finish our tea and you can tell me exactly what made you think there was something wrong with the Homeostasis in the first place."

CHAPTER 6

THE MENDICANT FAKIRS OF BENGAL

No sooner had Nimrod and Moo returned to the drawing room than there was a loud knock at Nimrod's front door.

"Who can that be?" said Nimrod.

Opening the door, he was delighted to find his young niece, Philippa, standing on the doorstep and carrying a suitcase. She was looking sunburnt and was wearing a T-shirt that read WHEN IN ROME.

"Excellent," said Nimrod. "You've arrived back at a most opportune time. I suspect another adventure is afoot."

"Afoot," said Philippa. "Oh. And I was hoping to put my feet up for a little while. I'm kind of tired after my flight."

"No time for being tired at a time like this, child," said Nimrod, as he hurried her inside. "I fear that there's important work to be done."

"Don't you want to hear how it went?" she asked him. "My *taranushi*?"

"Plenty of time for that later," said Nimrod. "There's someone here I want you to come and meet. Someone who has just brought me important news."

He explained that something seemed to be wrong with the tuchemeter and then introduced Philippa to Moo.

"I think," said Nimrod, prompting the KGB section head, "that you were about to tell me what made you think that there's an abnormally large amount of bad luck around at the moment."

"I don't just mean the stock market," said Moo, "although things have been bad there. For business in general. I mean *everything*."

"Everything?" Nimrod sounded surprised.

"I don't know how much you pay attention to these things, Nimrod," explained Moo, "but recently it was Friday the thirteenth. It's not unusual for a few superstitious people to stay at home on a day like that, but this year employers reported a twenty percent increase in the numbers of employees reporting sick on Friday the thirteenth. Not just here in Great Britain, but in America and Canada as well. It wasn't just individual employees who were reacting to a perception that there is more bad luck around, either. NASA refused to launch a new satellite on Friday the thirteenth. And the president of the United States postponed a visit to Dallas, Texas, that was due to have taken place on Friday the thirteenth."

"Probably very wise," said Nimrod. "After all, you never know with Dallas. Fascinating. A certain amount of paraskavedekatriaphobia is not, as you say, unusual. But it seldom manifests itself at such a high level."

"Para, what?" exclaimed Philippa.

"Paraskavedekatriaphobia," said Nimrod without so much as a stammer. "An abnormal fear of Friday the thirteenth. A specialized form of triskaidekaphobia, which is a simple fear of the number thirteen. Also sometimes known as friggatriskaidekaphobia."

"Precisely," said Moo.

Philippa nodded and decided that if ever she decided to change her focus word, *paraskavedekatriaphobia* might just be the word she would choose.

"Meanwhile," continued Moo, "the cities of Las Vegas, Atlantic City, Reno, Macao, and Monte Carlo are reporting that the number of people entering casinos is down by almost thirty percent. And the sales of lottery tickets are in steep decline. In other words, people just don't feel lucky. Also, the sales of cars that are the color green — traditionally a color that some people find unlucky — have dropped through the floor. People are even missing doctor's appointments for fear of being told bad news, or canceling flights, worried that the plane might crash."

"It's true," confirmed Philippa. "The flight from Rome to London was half empty. And you're right. No one was wearing green."

"For this reason the British government has been monitoring the situation carefully." Moo opened her briefcase and took out a buff-colored file. "This is top secret."

"You can speak freely in front of Philippa," said Nimrod.

"Just last week," said Moo, "we arrested three men in London. One was in possession of a large quantity of fake railway timetable books. It's thought he intended to distribute them throughout the country with the intention of making everyone miss their trains and be late for work. The other two had recently opened a self-improvement center for company employees, to teach people personal growth through fire walking."

"You mean barefoot?" said Philippa.

"That's exactly what I mean," said Moo. "Many people manage it quite successfully, too. Only these two suspects were planning something rather more sinister. They planned on encouraging people to do it without first offering them any kind of psychological preparation on how to do it. We narrowly managed to save about a hundred people from badly burning their feet."

"Ouch," said Philippa.

"An idea mundanes got from us, Philippa," explained Nimrod. "In previous times, your *taranushi* would also have involved walking across live coals."

"These are the three men we arrested." Moo opened the file and showed Nimrod the pictures of three miserable-looking men holding numbers underneath their chins. "Mr. Puri, Mr. Parvata, and Mr. Sagara," she said. "Of course they deny being part of some larger conspiracy. In fact, they refuse to say anything at all. All we know for sure is that they seemed bent on creating mischief."

"Interesting," said Nimrod.

"I wondered if you might be able to get anything out of them," said Moo. "Like what they're up to. If, as seems quite possible, there exists some kind of plot to affect the country's luck for the worse. I was thinking of one of those djinn bindings you use to make people tell the truth."

"You mean a quaesitor?" Nimrod shook his head. "No, I don't think that would work at all. Not with these three. You see, those three names. They're significant. One name I might hardly have noticed. But those three together. Well, it rings a bell, so to speak."

"You mean you know them?"

"No, I don't know them. But I know those names."

"You're being cryptic, Nimrod," said Moo. "Like the *Times* crossword."

"I don't mean to be," said Nimrod. "Those names belonged to three of the ten great fakirs. Long dead, of course. Which makes it all the more probable that these men are mendicant fakirs."

He sprang up off his chair and went over to his bookshelves.

"What, pray, is a mendicant fakir?" asked Moo.

"I was wondering the same thing myself," admitted Philippa.

"Centuries ago in India," said Nimrod, "fakirs were religious mystics who sought to imitate the powers of djinn by gaining great control over their own bodies. Walking through fire, lying on a bed of nails, going without food or water for many months were common physical hardships endured by these fakirs in search of true enlightenment. Over the years, however, fakirs became more interested in making money than in a wish to be closer to God. As common street beggars, or mendicants, they were little more than a nuisance. We might call them frauds or con men today, or even fake fakirs. Anyway, as they grew in number they became more and more lawless. Indeed, they became virtual bandits until, in the latter part of the eighteenth century, they were suppressed by the British.

"Ah, here it is." Nimrod pulled a thin green volume out of his library. "*Sannyasi and Fakir Raiders in Bengal,* compiled by the Bengal Civil Service in 1930." He opened the book's cover and read the inscription written inside. "'The Kent Walton Prize for Wrestling with the School Puma awarded to Nimrod Plantagenet, Charterhouse, 1949.'" Nimrod smiled. "Happy days."

Moo smiled back at him. "Were they?"

"No," said Nimrod. "Hated the place. But I rather liked the puma."

"Oh."

"These mendicant fakirs often joined fraternities, or unions of fakirs, upon which they would be given a new name after the ten great fakirs of Tirthankar. These ten great fakirs were Puri, Parvata, Sagara, Vana, Aranya, Keviin, Tirtha, Asrama, Swaraswati, and Bharati. That is why I believe these three men you arrested, Moo, are mendicant or fake fakirs. And that is why I believe a quaesitor would have no effect on them. Because they will certainly have trained their bodies to withstand a certain amount of physical discomfort. Nevertheless, I should like to see them."

"They're being held on HMS *Archer,*" said Moo. "That's the Tollesbury Marsh Prison Ship. In Essex."

She opened her bag and took out her cell phone. "I'll arrange it now," she said, and went out into the hallway to make the call.

"And then I suppose we'll be going to India," said Philippa.

"What on earth makes you say that?" said Nimrod.

"The title of your book. Bengal. That's in India, isn't it?"

"Used to be," said Nimrod. "You're right. Only these days it's called Bangladesh." Nimrod shook his head. "But it doesn't follow that we'll be going there at all, Philippa. It all depends on where the animadverto conducting the world's luck has been trapped or waylaid."

"Waylaid?" said Philippa.

"Interfered with," said Nimrod. "It's the only possible explanation why the tuchemeters are giving false readings. For some reason the animadverto's gotten stuck somewhere."

"Is that possible?" asked Philippa. "That someone could interfere with an animadverto?"

"Interfering with this particular animadverto is not something I can see any djinn, good or bad, bothering to do," said Nimrod. "I can see no possible advantage to any djinn in doing it. And only a mundane who was a skilled djinnfinder would ever attempt such a dangerous thing. It's a well-rewarded but precarious profession. The last djinnfinder I met, a woman called Montana Retch, is now a cat. Your cat, I believe."

"Yes, I'd forgotten about her," said Philippa. "Although

to be quite correct that cat is a him. But how do you know the other tuchemeters are giving false readings, too?"

"Stands to reason," said Nimrod. "Otherwise I should have heard from Creemy, in Cairo, and Faustina, in Berlin. Blessed be her name. No, I shall only know precisely where we're going after we have first had a closer look at these three fakirs."

Moo came back into the drawing room. "It's all arranged. Only we shall have to leave now if there's any chance of me getting to Ascot in time to see my horse running."

"In which case I had better do the driving," said Nimrod. "The Tollesbury Marshes, you say?"

CHAPTER 7

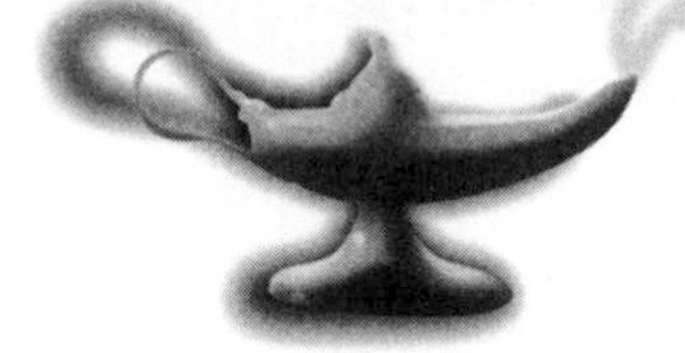

THE PRISON HULK

It used to be that any djinn in a hurry would travel by his or her own personal whirlwind, but global warming had affected the world's weather to such an extent that it was no longer safe for a djinn with a conscience to whip up a whirlwind for fear of creating a more violent and uncontrollable tornado or typhoon. As a result, good djinn were now obliged to travel like ordinary mundanes: by plane, train, or automobile. Naturally, these same, self-imposed restrictions did not apply to bad djinn, which partly accounts for the greater number of hurricanes that now affect the world, especially the southern United States and the Caribbean.

With Moo and Philippa in the back, Nimrod drove his own Rolls-Royce at great speed through London. Most traffic moves in central London at just ten miles per hour — which, as any fool knows, is the same speed as a running chicken. But Philippa's uncle seemed to know the least used, quickest roads, not to mention every shortcut and rat-run, and a car journey from Kensington to a place well beyond the east end of London, which any normal Londoner might have expected to take at least an hour, took Nimrod less than twenty minutes. In that twenty minutes it seemed to Philippa that they didn't just leave west London behind, but the good weather also, so that by the time they reached their destination, the sun had quite disappeared behind a grimy net curtain of gray clouds.

Tollesbury Marshes was a bleak, featureless place, a mixture of flat, waterlogged land, scattered lakes, and an empty sky that seemed to come out of a horizon of water. Philippa thought it was a grim, discouraging area, like something out of a bad dream. And then she saw it. Enveloped by a heavy mist, and marooned on a large spit of rat-infested mud like a beached whale, was the gray hull of an old warship — a destroyer from the Second World War. All of the guns and turrets from the deck had been removed, and there was just the rusting hull and nothing else. The name of the ship HMS *Archer* was just visible on the bow next to a sign that read HM PRISON ARCHER. Philippa felt sad just looking at the old hulk.

"Prisoners are held in cells belowdecks," explained Moo as they walked up a long gangway toward a reception area where the prison governor, Mr. Weston, was already waiting to greet them.

"What a horrible place to keep human beings," remarked Philippa.

"How else should a prison look?" inquired Moo. "People are put in these ships because they murder and because they rob and do all sorts of bad things, and because none of them ever gave a second thought to other human beings or their welfare as you do, child."

"It's still a horrible place," Philippa said defiantly.

"Rest assured, little lady," said Mr. Weston. "We've come a long way since Charles Dickens and Abel Magwitch. Our prisoners are well fed and allowed to bring one or two comforts from home. Although I don't think anyone has ever thought of comfort in quite the same way as these three fellows."

"How do you mean?" asked Philippa.

"You'll see." Mr. Weston chuckled and, lighting a candle — for the government was on one of its periodic energy-saving drives — he led the way down several flights of iron stairs into the gloomy, creaking bowels of the old ship where it seemed that several hundred men were imprisoned or awaiting trial.

Being in the ship was already making Philippa feel claustrophobic, which is a phobia that afflicts a great many djinn. She didn't like the smell, either. The ship smelled worse than the locker room in a boys' school — which was about the worst thing she could think of.

"Cabbage," she muttered. "Cigarettes, bleach, perspiration, French fries, and despair." Identifying each constituent part of the collective stink of the ship helped to keep her mind off her increasing claustrophobia. "Unwashed socks, cheap burgers, carbolic soap, and mildew."

Moo seemed to agree with Philippa's analysis because, along the way, she produced some perfume from her handbag and sprayed herself liberally.

On the bottommost level, Mr. Weston lit another candle, found a key on the wall opposite a gray steel door on which were chalked the words FAKIRS: THREE OF, and opened the door carefully.

Straightaway, Philippa was struck by a strong smell of castor oil and camphor that emanated from the cell. It was a curious smell but it made a pleasant change from the smell of the rest of the prison ship.

The three fakirs, Messrs. Puri, Parvata, and Sagara, were all housed in one large cell for four prisoners. They were tall, thin men, wearing loincloths — although one of the men seemed a head shorter than the others on account of the fact that he was standing on his head, which was completely buried in a fire bucket full of sand. The other two had long, straggling beards. One of these men was lying upon a bed of nails; the other was balanced cross-legged on top of a long bamboo pole that seemed to be without any sort of a platform or seat.

Philippa marveled that the three men seemed so comfortable, although it was a little hard to tell with the man whose head was buried in a bucket of sand.

"Doesn't it hurt?" she asked the man lying on the bed of nails. She pressed a finger on one of the nail points and found it was hard and sharp.

"Of course it hurts," he said.

"Then what's the trick?"

"The trick is really not minding that it hurts," he said.

"The answer of a true fakir," said Nimrod. "My compliments to you, sir."

The man lying on the bed of nails bowed his head, acknowledging Nimrod's courtesy.

"But I'm puzzled," continued the djinn. "Why would a true fakir try to sabotage Britain's rail network? Why would true fakirs allow innocent people to burn their feet, or perhaps worse, when walking through fire?"

"To bring about the answers," said the man.

"The answers to what?" asked Nimrod.

"What else but the questions?" said the man sitting on the end of the pole.

"What questions?" said Nimrod.

"If we knew the questions," said the man on the pole, "we should have little need of the answers."

"But without the questions," said the man on the bed of nails, "the answers would make no sense."

"Truly," said Nimrod.

"And when there are no questions left," said the man on the pole, "this itself is the answer. Is it not so, great djinn?"

"Do you know who I am?" asked Nimrod.

"Of course, great djinn," said the man on the bed of nails. "You give off a certain chi, or energy."

"Who are you working for?" asked Nimrod.

"Not who," said the man on the pole. "What."

"You won't get any sense out of this fellow," Moo told Nimrod.

"Very well," Nimrod said patiently. "What?"

"Did we not already tell you? To bring about the answers."

"If you know what I am, then you must know I could make you tell me," said Nimrod. "With a quaesitor. In case you don't know what that is, it's a djinn binding that's designed to find out the things you find most unpleasant and then make them appear in your mouth."

"As you can see," said the fakir on the bed of nails, "we do not fear that which others find uncomfortable and unpleasant. Least of all that which appears in our mouths."

"Indeed, we welcome it," said the man on the pole. "We live on an unusual diet."

At this point, the fakir standing on his head, which was buried in the bucket of sand, lowered his bare legs carefully until he was kneeling on the floor, at which point he lifted his head out of the sand and exhaled loudly as if he hadn't taken a breath in a long while. His hair and beard appeared to be even longer and filthier than those of his two companions.

"Which is now demonstrated, thus." And so saying, the fakir lifted his stomach into his rib cage and regurgitated a large cockroach, which appeared to be very much alive, and placed it, almost reverently, at Nimrod's feet. The cockroach hissed angrily — it was the hissing kind — and wriggled assertively.

Philippa was horror-struck. In her time she'd seen some very horrible things, but at that moment this seemed like the worst.

"Really," exclaimed Moo with distaste, and went out of the cell. "What a revolting person."

But there was more to come.

The fakir lying on the bed of nails opened his mouth very wide and put his filthy forefinger and thumb deep into his mouth, from which he then withdrew a living mouse by its tail. The smiling fakir held the wriggling mouse a few inches off the ground for a moment and then let it go.

The fakir on the bamboo pole wobbled his head and grinned. The grin turned into a wide-open mouth — rather wider than seemed possible, even in a dentist's chair — and, with an obscene flourish of fingers, he began to pull inch after inch of a snake from somewhere inside his throat. When there were as many as three or four feet of the reptile in his hands — it was a harmless grass snake — the fakir dropped it onto the floor, where it promptly swallowed the mouse (the grass snake is only harmless to humans and djinn).

"I've heard of the old woman who swallowed a fly," exclaimed Philippa. "But this is ridiculous."

"Gentlemen," said Nimrod. "Light my lamp, but it's been fascinating. And I begin to see why the British in India suppressed rascals, knaves, and vagabonds such as yourselves. For how else am I to describe men who make an intolerable nuisance of themselves such as you do? I tell you honestly that you will soon come before an English judge and you will do much better if you wear clothes. The English system of justice is more forgiving of a man who wears trousers than a half-naked man who feels he can do better with his head in a bucket full of sand. In spite of that I shall make it my business to see that you are given proper legal representation and that you are treated fairly. Good day."

They retreated into the corridor and Mr. Weston locked the door behind him. Then they went back upstairs and outside, where Philippa took a very welcome breath of fresh air. Right on cue, the sun appeared from behind the net curtain of clouds and warmed her face like a blazing fire. Djinn love heat, and Philippa was no exception.

"It's good to be out of there," she said, feeling suddenly euphoric.

"Isn't it?" agreed Nimrod.

"Well?" Moo asked him. "What did you make of them?"

"No doubt about it," said Nimrod. "They were mendicant fakirs, all right. Or at least as near as there exists to the mendicant fakirs in this degraded day and age. Did you notice that peculiar smell as Mr. Weston opened the cell door? Oils of cajeput, chaulmoogra, origanum, terebinth, and unguent of althea? Not to mention camphor. All of which mixed together is better known as the recipe for Indian balm, which for many years has been manufactured in England. It helps to keep them warm in the absence of very much clothing."

"But do you have any idea of what they're up to?" asked Moo.

"Only that you were right," said Nimrod. "That they are indeed religious scoundrels, part of a fraternity that is governed by laws of an uncommon or secret nature and that is bent on bringing about some change in the amount of luck that exists in the world. The question is, why? What do they hope to achieve? If only Mr. Rakshasas were alive. He might already have an answer. His knowledge of the sannyasi fakirs was second to none."

"I do miss that man," confessed Moo.

Nimrod nodded silently. "Rest assured, dear lady," he told her, "I shall find an answer to those questions. But first I must think awhile inside my lamp. Which I happen to have in the glove box of my car."

"In a glove box?" Moo's tone was one of disbelief. "Isn't that a little cramped?"

"The interior of a djinn's lamp exists outside time and space. I suggest you drive my car to Ascot, dear lady, and by the time the Gold Cup race is over I hope to have some sort of answer as to our next course of action."

CHAPTER 8

A SMALL PROBLEM

John sat in his uncle's house, awaiting his return from wherever it was he'd gone and rehearsing his story with Groanin and the Jinx. The grandfather clock in the hall ticked ominously, as if measuring out the seconds and the minutes before John was obliged to face the music about exactly what had happened in Bumby.

He could see that Philippa was back from Italy — her bag was by the stairs — and John was glad that at least he would have her there to support him. That was the good thing about having a cleverer twin sister. Sometimes she was able to come to his aid when he was having a little trouble explaining himself.

"This is a nice house," said Zagreus. "The person who lives here must be very rich."

"Did you ever hear of a poor djinn?" said John.

"No," said the Jinx. "I suppose not."

John glanced at Groanin uncomfortably. "What am I going to tell my uncle?" he asked.

"The truth is always best," said the Jinx.

"Is it?" John looked doubtful. "I don't know about that. Sometimes my mother asks me what I think of something she's wearing and I don't want to hurt her feelings by telling her I think she looks weird, and so I say, 'Mom, you look great.' And that's a lie. Plus, there are the times when you go to someone's house and they've cooked dinner and they say, 'I hope you like fish cakes,' and you have to pretend you love them, which is also a lie. Or if someone had a really horrible disfiguring injury and they said, 'You're looking at my scar,' or whatever and, of course, you say, 'I didn't even notice that you had a scar,' so as not to make them feel bad. Sometimes I think that lies oil the wheels of life's skateboard, you know? Because if you told the truth all the time, you'd have no friends."

John didn't usually talk so much, but he was feeling nervous.

"It's what you intend that makes the difference, I guess," said John. "If you tell a lie with a good intent, that makes it okay in my book."

"Clearly that won't apply here," said the Jinx. "I mean, there's no way of telling this other than the way it happened. And I still think it wasn't your fault."

"What wasn't your fault?" said an Englishman's voice.

John spun around.

Nimrod was standing in the doorway. John had been talking so much he hadn't heard his uncle come in through the front door. Immediately behind him were Philippa and an old lady wearing a silly hat and carrying a gold trophy in her hands. Nimrod pointed at the Jinx.

"Why is there a white monkey in my drawing room? And where is Groanin?"

John felt a sort of prickly sensation and a hideous feeling of guilt, together with a shortness of breath and sudden perspiration.

"Er, this is Zagreus," he said. "And he's not a monkey. Or at least, not completely. He's a Jinx. He used be something or someone else. And then he died, which happens, yeah? And when he died, he got himself reincarnated as an ape. Almost. Because the reincarnation didn't work, see? At least not completely. That's what a Jinx is, okay? Someone that doesn't make a proper reincarnation. He's a sort of missing link between his old life and his new incarnation, which is supposed to be an ape. Which is why he's white and sometimes invisible and why he can still talk. Which is not something that apes are supposed to be able to do. Obviously."

"I see," said Nimrod, and very quietly murmured his focus word.

"I wish I did," said Philippa.

Nimrod looked closely at Zagreus. "I've never actually seen a Jinx before," he admitted. Politely, he added, "How do you do?" so as not to make the Jinx feel like some sort of freak.

"Very well, thank you," said Zagreus. "Considering who and what I am."

"Unfortunately, he has this unlucky effect on things," said John. "He sort of makes things happen that you kind of wish hadn't happened."

"Like a jinx, you mean," said Nimrod. "All right."

"Exactly," said John. "That's what happened in Bumby. I mean, it could very well be that the Jinx is why all that stuff happened and why, for a while, I guess, it was the unluckiest town in the world."

"And you brought him here?" Philippa sounded exasperated. Then she looked at Moo. "Moo? This is my twin brother, John."

"I'm very glad I didn't meet your brother and his friend earlier on today," Moo told Philippa. She set her gold cup down on a table. "So far this has been the luckiest day of my life. So far."

"I say twin," said Philippa. "But you'll have noticed that he doesn't actually look like me. And hopefully, he doesn't think like me. Which is to say that he doesn't think at all. Sometimes, like right now, the twin thing is a bit of an embarrassment."

"I used to have a brother," said Moo. "He was killed in the war."

"Am I to assume that Groanin's holiday didn't go entirely to plan?" said Nimrod. "And talking of Groanin, where is he? I am quite desperate for a cup of tea."

"He's here," said John. "And then again, he's not. We had a bit of an accident. Or rather he did. Only it wasn't entirely my fault. If Groanin hadn't been so very greedy, things might be different."

"What kind of an accident?" asked Nimrod.

"A sort of djinn kind of accident," confessed John. "Involving sausages."

"Where is he?" asked Nimrod.

John pointed at the desk on the far side of the drawing room. "There," he said miserably.

Groanin was standing stiffly to attention on top of Nimrod's desk. He looked exactly as he had looked the last time Nimrod had seen him, except for the fact that he was only two feet tall and utterly rigid, like a doll.

"Fascinating," said Moo. "Most, most fascinating."

John explained what had happened. "The diminuendo was meant for Zagreus," he said. "So that I could transport him safely back here from Bumby. But it went wrong. As you can see."

"Doubtless our strange friend, Zagreus, had some effect on the outcome," said Nimrod. "He is a Jinx after all."

"Groanin ate the binding before I could stop him," added John. "It was inside a pork sausage."

"Yes," said Nimrod. "That sounds about right. Groanin is very fond of pork sausages." He produced a tiny flashlight on a key chain and shone a small beam of light into Groanin's eyes. "Since you would certainly have restored Groanin to his old self before returning here, had you been able, I must assume that you've forgotten how to lift the binding."

John said nothing.

"Or worse," added the djinn boy's uncle. "That you have forgotten the actual diminuendo you used to put him into this diminished state in the first place."

"I couldn't help it," said John. "I just did. I have. Forgotten the binding. I've tried to remember it. Honest. But so far, no luck." He shrugged. "After that, I didn't dare try another diminuendo on Zagreus here. For fear that I wouldn't be able to lift that one, either. You can't imagine all the problems we had leaving Bumby and traveling here."

"Oh, but I think I can." Nimrod shook his head. "It's not everyone who's brave enough to travel with a Jinx for company. No offense, Zagreus."

"None taken. I'm only sorry for the inconvenience I seem to have caused."

"What are we going to do about poor Groanin?" asked John. "We can't just leave him like that."

"I agree," said Nimrod. "So, let us hope you can remember the diminuendo, or I shall be looking for a new butler."

"You can't mean —"

"You remember Galibi," said Nimrod. "The boy we found in French Guiana."

"I've never forgotten it," said Philippa. "He consumed a diminuendo invoked by Iblis that turned him into a living doll."

"Just so," said Nimrod. "Your mother had hoped that her power, or that of Faustina, might be strong enough to overcome that of Iblis the Ifrit. But so far, the precise form of that binding has eluded them both. The poor boy remains exactly how we found him. And stuck inside a drawer in Baghdad until Faustina can figure out a way to return him from a state of suspended animation to real life."

"Do you hear that, John?" Philippa clouted her brother

on the shoulder. "You've got to remember, you great fathead. Or Groanin will be stuck like this forever."

"Don't you think I've tried?" John punched the side of his own head with exasperation. "But you can't remember what you have forgotten. Otherwise you wouldn't have forgotten it."

"That's very true," observed Nimrod. "In which case, you, Philippa, will have to remember for him."

"Me?" said Philippa.

"Yes," said Nimrod. "You'll have to go inside his head and have a good rummage around. And before you are too hard on your brother, you must bear in mind that it's not easy doing anything when there's a Jinx around."

"What?" John was outraged. "No way am I having her rake around inside my head."

"As I recall," said Nimrod, "you and Faustina shared Finlay's body with him once."

"That was different," said John. "That was Finlay's body. And that was bad enough. You've got no secrets when you share a body with someone. Dad says he isn't ever going to get over having Mom inside his head. And that was just for fifteen minutes. Who knows how long it'll take Philippa to find out what I've forgotten?"

"Do you really want Groanin to stay like this forever?" demanded Philippa. "Because unless you can remember —"

"No, of course not," said John.

"Well then," said Nimrod, "let's hear no more argument about it. The sooner Philippa slips inside your fat head and finds that binding, the sooner I can have my loyal butler back. He might moan and groan like a soldier with ill-fitting boots, but I can't tell you how much I've missed the blighter. Besides, I do so hate going to Morocco without my butler."

"Morocco?" said John. "Who said anything about going to Morocco?"

"I did," said Nimrod.

"You found something in Mr. Rakshasas's library?" said Philippa. "Something that means we have to go to Morocco?"

"Yes. To see someone I'd completely forgotten about."

CHAPTER 9

FEZ

Nimrod chartered a private plane to fly from London to Saiss Airport in Morocco. He was accompanied by John, Philippa, Moo, Zagreus, and Groanin, who was now fully restored to his old self after his ordeal at John's hands. This made him very happy. In fact, he was so happy he didn't even complain about the prospect of visiting a foreign country, which was something that he always hated. And he sat at the back of the plane singing, like a man in the bath.

"'We're off on the road to Morocco,'" he sang, even as the plane was taking off.

"What's that song you're singing?" Philippa asked the butler.

"'The Road to Morocco,'" said Groanin. "As sung by the great Bing Crosby in the film of the same name. Probably the greatest film ever made. Bing Crosby, Bob Hope, Dorothy Lamour." Groanin grinned as he recalled some scenes from the movie in his mind's eye. "Marvelous stuff."

Philippa, who had never heard of any of the names Groanin mentioned, smiled thinly and nodded. "If you say so."

"I do say so." He started to sing again.

Nimrod, who was so disturbed by Groanin's sunny disposition that he had already moved seats twice to be as far away from his butler as possible, winced. "Why is he so cheerful?" he asked his nephew.

"For one thing, he's no longer the size of a garden gnome," said John. "That might have something to do with it. And maybe he's looking forward to a few days of sunshine, after Bumby. The weather in Bumby was awful."

"But Morocco is a foreign country," said Nimrod. "They do things differently there. Very differently. Groanin hates everything foreign. Especially when it's as foreign as Fez. That's one of the reasons I like taking him with me when I travel abroad. Because he detests it so much. Having Groanin along always reminds me of everything I hate about England."

John smiled even more thinly than his twin sister. There were times when his uncle seemed really strange, even for a djinn.

"Besides," John said, "we'll probably be staying in a five-star luxury hotel, so when you think about it, maybe it won't seem all that foreign, so Groanin might actually enjoy it a bit. I'm kind of looking forward to it myself. Room service, enormous beds, huge bathrooms, plenty of first-class food, a swimming pool, a minibar."

"I can see I've been spoiling you all," said Nimrod thoughtfully. "And, as a result, neglecting your education." And very quietly he muttered his focus word.

"How do you mean?"

"Nothing." Nimrod shook his head and made a mental note to teach the twins something about economic and social reality as soon as they got to Fez. "Do me a favor, would you please, John? Tell Zagreus to come up here. I want to speak to him."

"Sure."

Nimrod had attached a binding to Zagreus to temporarily disable him from jinxing people and machines around him, but he had not yet decided if and how he could help the Jinx and, until he did so, he thought it best that Zagreus accompany them to Morocco. For his part, Zagreus was pleased to have been asked along and to have a chance to speak to Nimrod. He just wanted to help.

"My nephew, John, tells me that you were captured by some bad men and taken to Bumby."

"That's right," said Zagreus.

"Can you tell me anything about these men? Who they were? Not to mention how and why they did it? After all, when John first saw you, Zagreus, you were invisible. At least to human beings."

"I don't know for sure," said Zagreus. "But I believe it was them who interrupted my progress to my next incarnation. There was some kind of séance. One minute I was traveling through the spirit world, and the next there was someone calling me. At least I think it was me. Then I was in a room and there were these men standing inside a circle. In fact, there were two circles, one inside the other, with a lot of writing in between."

"A magic circle, perhaps," said Nimrod.

"Whatever that is. Either way, I seemed to have no will of my own. It felt like my spirit had been arrested. I can't explain it any better than that. The rest is all a bit of a blur. The next time I was aware of anything I was in that horrible little town."

"Bumby."

Zagreus shrugged. "I'm afraid there's not much more I can tell you, sir."

Nimrod nodded thoughtfully.

"Except the name of one of the men who arrested my spirit. It was Mr. Churches."

"Churches?"

"I think so. I can't be sure."

"What did he look like, this Mr. Churches?"

"A bit like you, sir. Very well dressed, very well-mannered. English, in an old-fashioned sort of way."

"Hmm." Nimrod glanced out the window of the plane. "We're coming in to land. Perhaps we can talk of this again. Right now you'd better make yourself invisible so that we can get through Moroccan customs without having to answer any awkward questions about importing live animals. No offense intended."

"None taken, sir."

A stretch Mercedes met them off the plane and drove them into Fez. The fourth largest city in Morocco, Fez was once the largest city in the world. Founded in A.D. 789, the city is situated just below the most prominently northwest point in Africa — a sort of continental thumb that pokes up at the soft underbelly of Spanish Europe. It was full of narrow, winding streets, minarets, and strange smells, not all of them good. Men in long striped-cloth hoodies stood around on street corners, shouting at one another and gesticulating wildly, while the women seemed all but invisible. Everywhere — spilling out of bars and shops, blasting out of open car windows — there was the infectious sound of Arabic music.

Nimrod told the driver, a handsome Moroccan named Saadi, to drive them into the new part of the city and, arriving at a graceful avenue of trees, he announced that they were looking at the Morisco Palace Hotel.

"This is the best hotel in Morocco," he explained. "It might even be the best hotel in the whole of North Africa. As you might expect, given the enormous price of a room."

"Excellent," said Groanin, who winked at John and reached for the door handle. "Room service, here I come."

"Which is why we're not staying here," added Nimrod.

"You what?" said Groanin.

Nimrod told Saadi to drive on.

"You mean we're not staying here?" said Philippa.

"I realized that I've been giving you and John an incorrect impression of what the world is really like," Nimrod told her. "Which is hardly fair of me. I've been thinking of my own comfort and convenience when I should have been thinking of your education."

"What does that mean?" asked Groanin.

"It means we're staying somewhere else," said Nimrod.

"So where *are* we staying?" asked Moo as the car neared the edge of the Sahara desert.

The car stopped outside what looked like a cross between a giant pyramid and a skyscraper.

"Here," said Nimrod. "One hundred and five stories high, three thousand rooms: Welcome to the internationally famous El Moania hotel."

"It looks like a rocket launchpad," observed Moo. "Simply awful."

"Why is it internationally famous?" asked an invisible voice that belonged to Zagreus.

"For the simple reason that this is without doubt the worst hotel in the world." Nimrod smiled at Moo. "Rest assured, dear lady; as I recall, you still have one wish left from yesterday."

"Do I?"

"Very much so," said Nimrod. "We always grant them in threes, for the sake of a harmony that includes and synthesizes two possible opposites."

"I always wondered why that was," said Moo happily.

"The worst hotel in the world?" John sounded outraged. "How is this going to help with our education?"

"It is my experience," said Nimrod, "that you can only really appreciate the finer things in life when you have had to endure some of life's hardships. And believe me, there's no greater hardship in the whole of North Africa than the El Moania hotel."

"I can see that," admitted Philippa. "But don't you think it might be better for us all if we just said 'thank you kindly' when we left?"

"No," said Nimrod.

"Well, I shan't put up with it," insisted Groanin. "I shall check in somewhere else. I said, I shall check in somewhere else. Like that hotel we were just at a few minutes ago."

"And pay with what?" asked Nimrod. "The Morisco Palace is a thousand dollars a night. Or whatever that is in the local currency, which is the dirham. I'm just guessing, but I'm assuming you don't have any of what passes for money in this neck of the woods."

"Then I shall make some, using djinn power," said John.

"You tell him, John," said Groanin. "That's the spirit."

Nimrod smiled. "You do that, nephew of mine," he said, opening the car door.

John winked at Groanin. "Don't worry," he told the butler. "You can rely on me. I'll sort things out. Just see if I don't. In just a few minutes we'll be checking into the Morisco Palace." But when John opened his mouth to utter his focus word, he found that he could not. "Ab-ab-ab-ab-"

It wasn't that he had forgotten it, merely that he couldn't pronounce the word.

"Your word is ABECEDARIAN," said Groanin. "I said, it's ABECEDARIAN."

"Ab-ab-ab-ab-" John shook his head. "What's happened? I can't pronounce my focus word." He looked helplessly at

Philippa, who discovered to her equal horror that no more could she utter hers.

"Fab-fab-fab-fab-"

Nimrod laughed. "Now you see the importance of keeping your focus words secret," he said. "I've attached a sesquipedalian binding to each of you for the duration of our stay here in Morocco. I'm afraid it specifically prevents each of you from pronouncing your own focus word."

The driver unloaded the luggage on the pavement outside the hotel entrance.

"I think this is so unfair," said John.

"So now you're stuck here whether you like it or not," said Nimrod. "You can either stay here, at the El Moania . . ." Nimrod pointed at the undulating sand dunes that marked the beginning of the Sahara desert. "Or you can stay there, I suppose." Shaking his head, he added, "But I really wouldn't recommend it."

Moo then made her final wish, which was to stay at the Morisco Palace, and Nimrod ordered the driver to take her back there.

"It's lucky I brought my usual supply of sterilized baby food from England," said Groanin. "At least we won't starve."

THE WORST HOTEL IN THE WORLD

For about five minutes the hotel didn't seem quite as bad as the twins and Groanin had feared it would be. The receptionist greeted them warmly and promised them each a room with an en suite bathroom and a panoramic view of the desert. Nimrod signed the register. Room keys were handed over. Groanin even admired the beauty of the entrance hall.

But things started to go a bit wrong when the hotel manager appeared and told Nimrod's party that the air-conditioning in the hotel was not working, nor were the elevators. And it was at this point they discovered that their rooms were all on the hundredth floor. What was more, the hotel porters were on strike, which meant that there was no one to carry the luggage.

"How do you expect us to get all the way up to the hundredth floor carrying our own luggage?" Groanin demanded.

"The stairs," said the manager. "You will find them very convenient as they go all the way up to the top of the hotel, where the view is the best in all of Fez."

"Couldn't we have rooms on a lower floor?" asked John.

The manager smiled sheepishly. "I regret that the rooms on the lower floors are not yet finished," he said.

This was something of an understatement as it swiftly transpired that most of the hotel between the second and the ninetieth floors was one large building site, and the noise of men drilling walls, hammering nails into wood, or operating cement mixers was deafening.

Arriving on the hundredth floor, hot and out of breath, Groanin kicked open the door of his room, flung his bags down on the floor, and collapsed onto the bed only to discover that his bed had no mattress.

"I suppose it could be worse," said Philippa, experimentally opening and closing her own door — which lacked not only a lock but a door handle, too.

Meanwhile, Groanin had discovered that his minibar was empty, which made him very cross indeed.

"Mine isn't empty," John reported. "There's a large cockroach living in it."

"Probably got the most comfortable room in the hotel, I shouldn't wonder," observed Groanin.

Philippa yelled for everyone to come to her room, and they all found her standing in the bathroom and looking down at the floor of the shower, which seemed to be made of bare earth. "There are no tiles on the floor of the shower," she said. "It'll just turn to mud when the shower is turned on."

"Actually, that's not true," said Nimrod, trying to turn the shower faucet. "For the simple reason that you can't actually turn the shower on. John, you'd better call downstairs and have someone see if they can come and fix it."

John picked up the telephone, which wasn't working. And then another, which wasn't connected to the wall. Finally, he found a phone that was working and managed to speak to someone.

"What you want?" said a hostile voice.

John explained that the shower in Philippa's room was not working.

"Why not just have a wash?" said the voice. "The hand basin works okay, I think."

John insisted that the shower be fixed and the voice said that he would send someone just as soon as possible.

Half an hour later a very tall man wearing a red tarboosh — this being a kind of hat that is also sometimes called a fez — and a white robe appeared and said he had come to fix the shower.

"You got any tools?" asked the very tall man. "To fix the shower."

John shook his head. "Er, no," he said.

The tall man glanced around the room, picked up one of Groanin's boots, and started to beat the faucet with it until, finally, the knob turned and water started to spray from the showerhead. Quickly, the floor of the shower turned to a small, square sea of mud. But he paid that no attention.

"Shower's working now," he said. Then he tossed the boot aside and walked out.

Philippa shrugged and went into the bathroom to turn off the shower and discovered that this was now impossible. "Hey," she shouted after the man, "now it won't turn off."

But it was too late. The man had gone.

Naturally a little shy, Zagreus had waited until now before rematerializing. He walked on his knuckles around the interconnecting rooms for a while and then sat down to watch Moroccan television. On one channel it was *Strictly Belly Dancing*, on another it was *So You Think You Can Belly Dance on Ice*, and on the third it was *Who Wants to be a Belly Dancer?* Zagreus decided that he liked Moroccan television a lot more than he liked English television.

Groanin glanced at the television and then at the Jinx uncomfortably. "Just tell me that you've got nothing to do with any of this," he said.

Zagreus gave a sheepish look. "Er, I really don't know," he said. "I mean, it's possible, I guess."

Nimrod grinned at his butler. "Really, Groanin, this isn't known as the worst hotel in the world for nothing," he said. "None of this has anything to do with Zagreus. Besides, I took the precaution of putting a binding on him while he's with us, so you can rest assured that his jinx won't affect us for now."

"Thanks," said Zagreus. "I was wondering about that myself."

Meanwhile, Groanin picked up his boot off the floor, where the man with the fez had tossed it. "What's this doing here?" And then, "Flipping heck, the heel's come off me boot. How did that happen?"

"The guy with the fez was using it as a hammer to fix Philippa's shower," explained John.

"My boot? A hammer?"

"Better put that boot on, Groanin," said Nimrod. "You're going to need a pair of sturdy boots where we're going."

"And where's that?" asked Philippa.

"A better hotel, I hope," said Groanin. "I said, a better hotel, I hope."

"The Atlas Mountains," said Nimrod. "Specifically Jebel Toubkal, the highest peak in Morocco."

"Anything's better than actually staying here, I suppose," said John.

"There's a man called James Burton who lives there," continued Nimrod. "He's one of the reasons we came to Morocco in the first place. Mr. Burton used to be a butler — a very good butler, actually. And now I urgently need his help."

The twins looked at each other with horror and then at Groanin, who was now looking thoroughly offended.

His lip quivering with self-pity, the butler turned his back on the three djinn and walked quietly across the room.

"I see," Groanin said stiffly. "So that's the way the wind blows. Maybe I should just stay here and start looking for another job?"

The butler leaned his forehead thoughtfully upon the windowpane; at least he did until the pane fell out of the window frame. He leaped back with fright, collided with a small table, knocked over a lamp, slipped, and sat down heavily on top of Zagreus. Nimrod helped Groanin to his feet.

"You mistake me," said Nimrod. "It's not Mr. Burton's skills as a butler I need to enlist. It's his experience as a holy man."

"You mean, I'm not being sacked, sir?" said Groanin.

"Of course not," said Nimrod. "Mr. Burton is a fakir. And a very good one, I believe. Which he should be, as he had an excellent teacher. Before he was a fakir, Mr. Burton was for many years a butler in the service of Mr. Rakshasas."

"He was a butler?" said John. "And now he's a fakir?"

"That's a career path I hadn't thought of," Groanin said wryly.

"Weird, isn't it?" said Nimrod. "Although there's not much an English butler can't do when he puts his mind to it. Isn't that right, Groanin?"

"Yes, sir." Groanin grinned back at his employer. "Might I inquire, sir, how we are to get to the Atlas Mountains?"

"I'm glad you asked me that," said Nimrod. "That's the other reason we came to Morocco. We need to go and get ourselves a decent carpet."

John inspected the floor of the hotel room.

"I guess this one is a little threadbare in parts," he said. "But it seems to me there are plenty of other things in this place that are a heck of a lot worse than the carpet." He shrugged. "Wouldn't it just be easier to go to another hotel?"

"I'm not talking about that kind of carpet, my boy," said Nimrod. "I am referring to the flying carpet of King Solomon."

"But I thought magic carpets didn't exist," objected Philippa. "That's what you said. Isn't it?"

Nimrod shook his head. "I said nothing of the sort. I said that nearly all modern djinn prefer to travel by whirlwind. Or airplane. And we did. But since it's no longer permitted for good djinn to travel by whirlwind, and since it is notoriously difficult to get to the summit of Jebel Toubkal, we must needs look to more old-fashioned methods of transport. Such as a flying carpet. Of the kind described — as I'm quite sure you will both remember — in night number five hundred and seventy of the *Arabian Nights*. And please don't let me hear you describing it as a 'magic carpet.' You know my views on the use of that word. A flying carpet is vulgar, clichéd, embarrassing — you, John, would probably say it was corny — but I can now see no alternative to owning one. A flying carpet must be procured. Which is why, before we do anything, we must visit the rug emporium of Mr. Barkhiya, in the medina, which is the old part of Fez."

CHAPTER 11

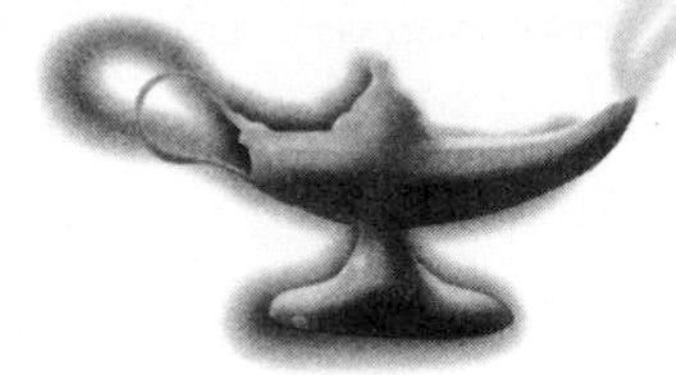

THE VERY SPECIAL RUG EMPORIUM OF ASAF IBN BARKHIYA

Entering the old medina of Fez through a dome-shaped gate in a high white wall, Nimrod led the twins and Groanin through a succession of narrow, winding streets and covered, shadowy alleys that were full of shopkeepers, tourists, chickens, dogs, and donkeys. Wonderful smells of spices and herbs assailed their nostrils, while their ears were filled with sounds of music and commerce that had changed little in centuries.

The twins considered themselves well-traveled, but the medina was like nothing they had encountered before. It was, thought Philippa, like stepping back into one of the seven journeys of Sinbad or, perhaps, the tales of Aladdin and Ali Baba. But Nimrod seemed to know the place like the back of his hand.

After ten or fifteen minutes, they arrived in a dusty, plain little square in the darkest and most ancient part of the medina, where Nimrod approached a small and very old-looking wooden door. And there he addressed his companions, who included Moo but not Zagreus, who had elected to remain in the hotel and watch *The Belly Factor* on television.

"This is it," he said. "This is the place."

"You mean this door?" asked Moo.

"It doesn't much look like a rug emporium," observed John. "It looks more like a prison."

"Certainly somewhere secret," said Moo.

"My dad used to work in carpets," said Groanin quietly. But no one was listening. "He was a carpet fitter all his life."

"This shop has been here for two thousand years," said Nimrod. "Mr. Barkhiya is the direct descendant of the vizier of King Solomon."

"You mean the chap in the Bible?" asked Moo.

Nimrod nodded.

"What's a vizier?" asked John.

"A high-ranking minister or advisor to the king," said Nimrod. "When Solomon died, Mr. Barkhiya and his family inherited the king's famous flying carpet. Originally, this was an enormous blue rug, sixty miles long and sixty miles wide, and when it flew, it was shaded from the sun by a canopy of birds. Thousands of djinn and people could ride upon it at any one time. On one occasion, so the story goes, the wind, which is not known for its patience, became jealous of Solomon and shook the carpet, and forty thousand people fell to their deaths."

"That's one way of trimming your frequent-flyer program," observed Groanin.

"Over the years, the carpet has been cut up many times," continued Nimrod. "Today all flying carpets are smaller pieces of the larger one once owned by Solomon. Of course in more recent times, flying on a carpet was deemed most unfashionable. And business was slow for Mr. Barkhiya. But all of that is different now. Which means that it may be hard to negotiate a fair price for exactly what we want. So it might be best if you say as little as possible while I'm bargaining with him. Because it's certain that Asaf will want something more than just money. Is that clear?"

The twins nodded. "Clear," they said in unison.

Inside, the rug emporium was more like a church — a huge, echoing, dark Byzantine church with a circular marble floor and many brass lamps hanging from a very high ceiling. The vast floor was surrounded with a series of enormous pillars that were unusual in that they appeared to be made out of giant rolls of carpet: a blue silk carpet with a gold weft.

Nimrod clapped his hands loudly, and lifted a hand in salute as a man wearing a plain white turban and silken white robes, who was seated cross-legged on a little square of blue carpet, floated across the floor toward them like a scoop of ice cream on a Frisbee.

"Peace be with you," said Nimrod.

"And with you," said the man.

Dismounting the carpet, which stayed floating several inches above the ground, the man bowed gravely and said:

"Let mountain and desert tremble. Let cities shudder and turn in fear of mighty Nimrod. Welcome, esteemed sir. Since I last saw you, great djinn, I have often thought of you and wondered how long it would be before you would come back to my humble establishment. And I bless this day, since we now meet again."

Philippa shuddered to look at the man. Mr. Barkhiya had the nose and eyes of a hawk, a large gap between his front teeth, and a long black beard that was divided into two points like a pitchfork. He was not very tall but he carried himself like a man of enormous height, and his voice was as deep and almost as dramatic as that of a great orator.

"Permit me to introduce my nephew, John, and my niece, Philippa," said Nimrod.

"I am your servant," said Mr. Barkhiya, and he bowed again. "May both of you continue to live happily until the very distant hour of your death."

"You too," said Philippa.

"May I also present Lady Silvia Stone and my servant, Groanin."

"The honor is all mine," said Mr. Barkhiya.

"We've come about a carpet," said Nimrod.

Mr. Barkhiya smiled as if such a thing was obvious. He bowed again and then lifted his arms.

"And when Solomon sat upon the carpet he was caught up by the wind and sailed through the air so quickly that he breakfasted at Damascus and dined in Medina," said Mr. Barkhiya. "And the wind followed Solomon's commands." The carpet seller grinned happily. "Of course you have come about carpets, my dear fellow. Why else would you be here? Just the one carpet, is it? I could perhaps let you have a discount for three. A very special price."

While he talked, Mr. Barkhiya stroked one of the great blue carpet pillars, which rippled and undulated under his touch like a hide of some great beast. He nodded at John and Philippa. "Come, children, touch it."

John and Philippa glanced at their uncle, who nodded his assent, and the twins stepped forward to rub their hands up and down the smooth surface of the blue carpet pillar. At the same time, Nimrod lifted the sesquipedalian binding that stopped the twins using their focus words. He wanted to make sure that they would feel the djinn power that was present in every fiber of the carpet.

"Is it not smooth?" Mr. Barkhiya asked John. "Is it not silky?" he asked Philippa. "Is it not marvelous? Is it not very special?"

The twins nodded.

"Very," said Philippa.

"It's like something alive," observed John.

"There's a vibration in every fiber," added Philippa.

"Truly," said Mr. Barkhiya. "But only a djinn such as yourself can feel this special vibration. I have never felt this sensation myself. I am merely the great carpet's custodian. Not its master."

"To weave such a carpet," said Moo, "that must have taken a very long thread."

"It is said that the thread used to make the first great flying carpet of Solomon was as long as eternity," said Mr. Barkhiya. "And the carpet was handwoven by a thousand djinn."

"And do you only sell to djinn?" said Moo. "Or to human beings, also?"

Mr. Barkhiya smiled his gap-toothed smile. "I regret, dear Lady Silvia, that only a djinn may control such a carpet as this, otherwise I should be delighted to sell you one, too. The tiny fragment of rug you saw me appear on earlier is as much as I am able to safely control myself. And even that is only thanks to my having been granted wishes by another grateful customer. Each knot of the carpet contains an uttered word of djinn power. What the djinn themselves call a focus word. Is it not so, Nimrod? And that this is where the power of the flying comes from. From the djinn power over mathematics and physics and the great Golden Ratio and the secret meaning of 1.61803."

Nimrod nodded. "That's quite right," he said. "Many human beings have been killed trying to ride a flying carpet."

"That's a comforting thought," remarked Groanin.

"I think an extra-large one for the great Nimrod, and two junior models, one each for your two young friends."

"Very generous of you, Asaf," said Nimrod.

Mr. Barkhiya said, "But you have not yet heard my price, O great one."

"I'm listening, old friend."

"Three wishes."

"That is fair."

"From each of you."

Nimrod shook his head. "No. That is too much." He nodded. "But the three wishes shall come from me."

"Very well, I agree."

"One more thing," said Nimrod. "I know you to be a religious man, Asaf. And a man of your word. So, you must state your three wishes in advance and confine yourself to wishing for them and only them, by all that's holy to you. Is that agreed, also?"

Asaf grinned. "Don't you trust me, O great one?"

Nimrod shook his head. "You're only human, my friend. It's been my experience that wishing for whatever your heart desires is more than any mundane can cope with. And it is always wise to remember to be careful what you wish for just in case you get it."

"True," said Mr. Barkhiya. "For power of such greatness as yours, it is good that you counsel caution. I am a poor man of the desert; however, I have wished before, and I have survived the extraordinary magic. I have eight sons and fifteen grandchildren and it will be my wish that my family shall remain in happiness and health. And so that all djinn who come here may know that I am not a selfish man, it will be my wish that the king, too, shall remain in happiness and health."

"And your third wish, Asaf?" asked Nimrod.

"Things have been difficult for my country of late," said Mr. Barkhiya. "People are fearful. They are superstitious.

And of late, luck has not smiled on us. The crops lack rain. There is much unemployment. Our country has many enemies and owes much money to the World Bank. Good fortune seems to have deserted us."

"That's interesting," said Moo. "This is what I suspected all along."

"But this is one of the reasons I came here in the first place," Nimrod told Asaf. "To consult with the English fakir who lives at the top of Jebel Toubkal. If Lady Silvia here is right, it's not just your country that feels its lack of luck. Many others do, too."

"I would change that."

"You ask the impossible, Asaf," said Nimrod. "Even I don't have the power to fix all your country's ills."

"I believe I have a way. So this will be my third wish, Nimrod."

"How?" asked Nimrod. "This interests me a great deal, Asaf. How would you change the luck of your country?"

"I will not say that it would change things in your country, Nimrod," said Asaf. "But it will certainly change things here. We are a simple people and some sort of a sign is needed that perhaps things are improving in my country. I think that the sign I would give with my third wish might change this perception. The ancient Romans had a saying: *cum mula peperit*. You will find this strange, Nimrod. But that will be my third wish. This is how it will be, O great djinn?"

Nimrod nodded. "This is how it will be, Asaf. As you wish. *Cum mula peperit*."

CHAPTER 12

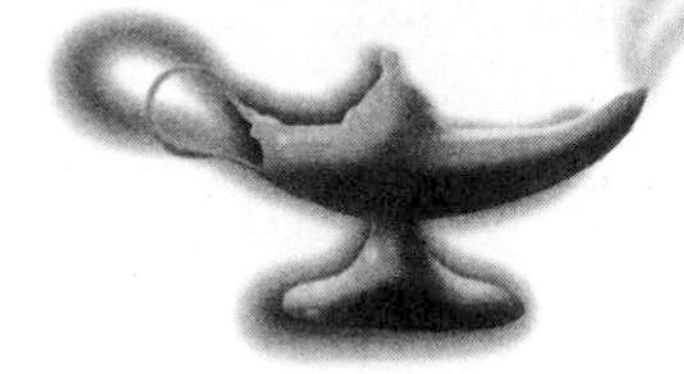

THE FLYING CARPET

Mr. Barkhiya took Nimrod and the others up to the rug emporium rooftop, where, in the late afternoon sunshine, his sons were spreading out the three carpets that had been bought. The biggest of the carpets — Nimrod's flying carpet — was about a thousand square feet and as blue as a sapphire. Under the hot Moroccan sun, the gold thread woven into the carpet seemed to glow like it was molten metal. Moo and Groanin sat close to the center of the carpet, which seemed like the safest place, and patiently awaited takeoff.

The emporium's rooftop was castellated like a fortress and was the highest in all of the old city so that local people might not be alarmed at the sight of a carpet ascending into the sky. The El Moania hotel was several miles away, although its distinctive pyramid shape was clearly visible on the horizon.

"If the carpet has not flown for a while," explained one of the sons, "then you should always leave it in the sun for a few minutes to warm the fibers up. Djinn power relies on heat, yes? Especially the heat of the sun?"

John nodded. "Yes," he said.

"You will wish to personalize your carpet," said the man. "Make it so that only you can fly it. In which case you must spill your blood upon it. For then your djinn blood will become part of the carpet. And the words of power will always be yours to command."

Mr. Barkhiya's son, who was called Mustafa, produced a large hat pin that he handed to John expectantly.

"What, now?" John stared at the hat pin.

"As good a time as any," said Nimrod. He took the hat pin from John, stabbed his thumb with it, and let a ruby of blood drop on the shining blue silk of the largest carpet. "And you certainly wouldn't want another djinn to steal it, would you?"

Philippa pricked her finger in turn and handed the hat pin back to her brother.

"I hate needles," mumbled John.

"Do hurry up, John," said Nimrod.

"Don't be such a wuss," said Philippa and, taking the hat pin back again, she grabbed her brother's finger and pricked it for him before he could protest.

"Ouch," said John. "That hurt."

Philippa squeezed his finger hard and dropped some of John's blood onto the third carpet.

"By the way," said Nimrod. "You'd better let me have some of that blood. Just in case."

"Just in case of what?" asked John.

"Just in case I need to fly your carpet myself," said Nimrod.

He ordered the two smaller flying rugs to be rolled up and placed on top of the larger one and, with he and Moo and Groanin and the twins now seated on the huge blue square of silk carpet, the English djinn muttered his focus word. A second or two later, the carpet started silently to rise into the air like a very well-behaved helicopter.

"Marvelous," said Moo, glancing over the carpet's edge at the retreating medina. "I never thought to fly on a real magic carpet."

"Don't say that word," muttered Groanin. "*Magic.* It irritates the boss. And I wouldn't want him irritated when he's flying. It's been a while since he flew anything other than a will-o'-the-wisp."

"Oh, right," said Moo. "Sorry. But I don't think I've had as much fun as this since I was a little girl, when I rode on an elephant at the London Zoo." She smoothed the carpet with the palm of her hand and thought it smoother than the fur of the cleverest cat that had ever lived.

Groanin closed his eyes. "You ask me," he said, "carpets is for covering floors with. Or vacuuming. Not gallivanting about the world upon. It isn't natural."

"Do shut up, Groanin," said Nimrod, and steered the flying carpet in the direction of the El Moania hotel.

"I didn't understand Asaf Barkhiya's third wish," said Philippa. "It was in Latin, wasn't it?"

"*Cum mula peperit?*" said Nimrod. "Yes. It's Latin. And if you had ever attended a decent school where they taught anything other than so-called 'computer skills,' you might also know that it means 'when a mule foals.'"

"That's a wish?" said John. "Sounds more like a riddle."

"In a way it is," said Nimrod. "A mule is —"

"The sterile hybrid of a horse and a donkey," said Philippa. "They do teach us biology."

"That's something, I suppose," said Nimrod. "Then you might also know that it's almost impossible, biologically speaking, for a mule to give birth. But it does happen. Once in a blue moon."

"So, when it does happen," said Moo, "word will quickly get around that something pretty special has happened. Which Asaf hopes will be seen as a cause for some optimism in the country at large." She nodded. "Yes, I can see how that might work. Very clever of him, really."

Nimrod stopped the flying carpet outside the hundredth floor of the El Moania and because there was no window — Groanin having leaned on it earlier and pushed it out of the frame — it was a simple matter for all except Moo to climb back into the room where Zagreus had remained behind watching television.

"Pack your bags," Nimrod told everyone. "We're leaving."

"First sensible thing you've said since we got here," said Groanin. "Thank goodness we won't have to carry the bags all the way down those stairs."

"Hey, what about the hotel bill?" said Zagreus.

"He's right, we should leave them something," said Philippa.

"The bill?" exclaimed Groanin. "For what? Ruining my boot? Making us climb a hundred flights of stairs? Confiscating my food supply? I've stayed in better prisons than this place."

"John?" asked Nimrod. "What do you think?"

"Well, it was certainly an experience," said John. "I don't think I'll ever complain in a hotel again. That is, as long as I don't ever have to come back to this particular hotel. I thought the Oasis Guesthouse in Bumby was bad. But this place is terrible."

"There's nothing wrong with the Oasis Guesthouse in Bumby," insisted Groanin. "Leastways not unless there's a Jinx staying there."

"Speaking for myself," said Philippa, "I think I've learned to appreciate how well-off I am and what a good hotel is. It's been an education, all right."

"Ah," said Nimrod. "Experience. Education. The all-important words. In which case we should certainly leave something to cover the bill. Experience and education are in short supply these days and are always worth paying for. After all, anyone can stay in a good hotel. But it takes a very special kind of person to stay in the worst hotel in the world."

"You don't half talk some nonsense," muttered Groanin, and pulled his bowler hat tight about his ears.

"Quiet, Groanin," said Nimrod. "Or I shall turn you back into a garden ornament." And, taking out his wallet, he thumbed several banknotes onto the table. "It's a pity more people don't get a chance to stay here. And then they might be a little happier with their lot in life." He shook his head. "But perhaps when we return to Fez, we'll stay in the Morisco Palace Hotel, after all."

Zagreus, who didn't have any bags, switched off the television and bounded out of the window, onto the carpet beside Moo.

"Is it safe?" he asked, stretching out and leaning his head on John's rolled-up carpet.

"Isn't that a question you should ask *before* you step out of a hundredth-floor window and onto a flying carpet?" Groanin threw Nimrod's bag out of the window, then his own, and climbed out beside the Jinx. He was followed by the twins and, last of all, Nimrod himself.

"Perhaps you're right," said Zagreus. "But then as someone who's neither properly dead nor properly alive, it's easy for me not to pay too much attention to these things. If I fall a hundred floors, I'm not sure I'll be any worse off than I am now. Can you say the same?"

Nimrod laughed at the sight of Groanin's obvious discomfort and set a course for the Atlas Mountains.

"Nimrod, you haven't yet explained why this man we're going to see is so important," said Moo as they climbed higher into the sky above the city. She tied a ribbon over her straw hat and under her chin so that the hat would not blow off her head.

"And how a butler comes to be a fakir," said John.

"Mr. Burton is the great-grandson of the famous English explorer and Orientalist Sir Richard Burton," said Nimrod.

"The man who was one of the first translators of the *Arabian Nights*. Inspired by his illustrious ancestor, Mr. Burton studied Arabic and Urdu at Harvard University and then went to live with holy men in India, where he met Mr. Rakshasas, who was persuaded to take the young man under his wing and teach him many ancient secrets and several esoteric mysteries.

"In return, Mr. Burton was, for twenty years, butler to Mr. Rakshasas. Then, according to what I was told by Mr. Rakshasas, Mr. Burton had some sort of vision and decided that he should go and become a holy man himself. Some people call these holy men sadhus or gurus, and some call them swamis or yogis. The most important thing is that Mr. Burton became an ascetic, which is to say that his life became one of abstinence and hardship, all with the aim of attaining wisdom and enlightenment. For many years now Mr. Burton has lived at the top of Jebel Toubkal, which is the highest peak in the Atlas Mountains, not seeing anyone, not saying anything, and not eating or drinking anything. In other words, he became a kind of fakir. And it is certain no one knows more about fakirs than he."

"He doesn't eat anything?" said Groanin. "Nothing at all? Not even a cup of tea?"

"So far as I know," said Nimrod.

"He sounds a bit mad to me," said Groanin. "I mean, what's the point of being alive if you can't eat? Or drink? You might as well be dead. Anyway, how are we going to get any information out of this character if he doesn't say anything? Have you thought of that, sir?"

"There are more ways of communicating with someone than just speech," said Nimrod.

"For you, maybe," grumbled Groanin. "Personally, I've always found speech is quite adequate for making myself understood."

After an hour's flying, they reached Jebel Toubkal, the highest peak in the Atlas Mountains. But at the summit of the mountain, which is 13,665 feet high and shrouded with clouds, there was no obvious sign of the English fakir. And, dismounting the flying carpet, they spread out to search the summit and its environs.

"Perhaps he went on holiday," suggested Groanin.

Moo shivered. "I wish I'd brought a coat," she said.

And because Philippa liked Moo and could already feel her own djinn powers starting to wane in the cold of the mountaintop — for djinn are made of fire — she quickly muttered her focus word and made warm fur coats, one for Moo and one for herself.

"Don't worry," she told Moo. "It's not real fur," and wondered why Moo looked a little disappointed.

"I like that," said Groanin. "She gets a warm coat but not me."

"Too late, I'm afraid," said Philippa. "My power's gone."

"Mine, too," admitted John.

Groanin glanced at Nimrod. "No chance you making me a fur coat, is there, sir?" he asked.

"Wouldn't it be simpler to look for something warm in your suitcase?" asked Nimrod.

Groanin shrugged and then opened his case. But there was nothing that looked like it might make the butler feel any more comfortable. "I packed for a hot climate," said Groanin. "Not a perishing cold one."

"We're supposed to be looking for some sign of Burton," said Nimrod. "Not a vest or a pullover."

"That's easy for you to say," said Groanin, rubbing his hands together.

Then John shouted from a place several yards away that was hidden in the mountaintop mist. "I think I've found something," he said.

"Where are you?" said Nimrod.

"Here," said John. "A few yards down the south-facing slope, there's a pile of stones."

When they found John, he was halfway up a little pyramid of rocks and taking hold of what looked like a tall, thin tree that was growing out the top of it. Except that it wasn't a tree at all but a rigid length of thick rope. John peered up the rope into the depths of the mist above his head and then tugged it experimentally.

"It seems to go up for quite a way," he said.

"Well done, John," said Nimrod. "I should say there's a very good chance that you've found Mr. Burton."

"What? You mean he's up there?" Groanin sounded outraged. "At the top of that rope?"

"Of course," said Nimrod. "Where else would he be?"

Groanin smiled a wry smile. "Where else indeed?" He shook his head. "You make it sound almost normal. Just don't expect me to climb up there, sir. I'm a butler, not a chimpanzee." He glanced sideways at Zagreus when he said this.

"What an unimaginative fellow you are sometimes, Groanin," said Nimrod. "Who on earth said anything about climbing up there? Why climb when we can fly?"

CHAPTER 13

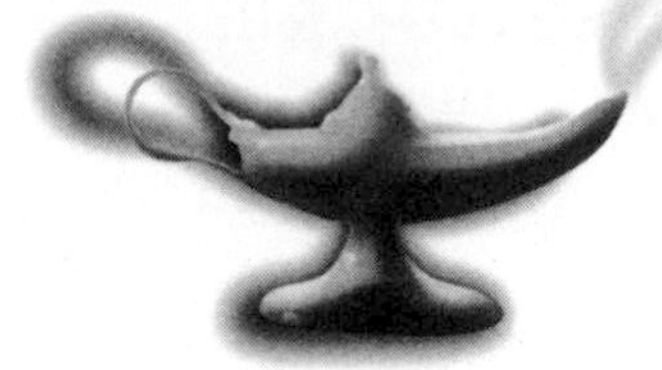

THE THREE RIDDLES OF THE FAKIR OF JEBEL TOUBKAL

Steadily, like an elevator in a very tall building, the flying carpet ascended in the air alongside the rope. Above their heads were thick white clouds and little sign that there was anything at the top of the rope except yet more clouds. As they continued their inexorable ascent, both air temperature and pressure dropped quickly and a thin layer of hoarfrost began to turn the golden edge of the blue carpet white. After a while, Nimrod took pity on Groanin, whose teeth were chattering like castanets, and made a warm silver fox fur coat for his butler, as well as one for his nephew. For himself, he made a red fox fur coat because Nimrod was always very fond of the color red.

Only Zagreus didn't seem to feel the cold, but then again, he didn't feel very much at all.

"Thank you, sir," said Groanin, shrinking into the warmth of the coat.

"Is that real fur?" asked Philippa.

"It is and it isn't," said Nimrod. "You see, it all depends what you mean by 'real fur.'"

"Don't you know that real fur is wrong?" said Philippa. "Synthetic fur is the ethical choice."

"Oh, I agree," said Nimrod. "But since I used djinn power to make these coats, then you can be assured that no animals were killed."

"Hmm." Philippa nodded. "I hadn't thought of that."

John was looking anxiously up the rope. "I think we're nearing the end of the rope," he said. "There are little bits of knotted string. And, in the knots, there are pieces of colored wool and paper, and cloth bags."

"Those are prayers, and offerings of food," said Nimrod. "From local people on the ground. The Berbers. Those probably get pulled up the rope by the fakir. An indication of the regard people hereabouts must have for him."

"I suppose this is a bit like the Indian rope trick," said Moo.

"I sincerely hope not," said Nimrod. "The point of the Indian rope trick is to disappear at the top."

"Oh, yes." Moo pulled an old lady sort of face. "I never thought of that."

At the top of the rope, the wind dropped and the clouds suddenly cleared to reveal a brilliantly blue sky bathed in bright, warm sunshine. The air seemed sweeter, too. As if someone had opened a box of strongly scented Turkish delight. Attached to the rope was a little triangular wooden platform, like a very small tree house, and sitting on the platform, surrounded by flowerpots, was a tall, thin man with white hair and the longest beard the twins had ever seen. Everyone fell silent as Nimrod brought the flying carpet directly alongside the fakir.

Mr. Burton wore a thin brown robe and a set of amber beads, and on his forehead were four streaks of yellow paint. In front of his bare feet was a garland of beautiful flowers. But most curious of all were his bright blue eyes, which stared into the most distant distance, as if he could see far into the next world. Groanin, who had seen holy men before, was more fascinated with the rope, which wasn't attached to anything at all. It just ended in a large knot, as if someone had tried to tie the rope to a very tall, faraway tree that had long-since vanished into thin air.

"What's keeping it all up?" whispered Groanin. "The rope? The platform? The bloke with the beard? Everything."

"Simply mind over matter," explained Nimrod.

"Is that all?" said Groanin.

"No man is just his thoughts," Nimrod told Groanin. "Sometimes it's important to take a step back from thinking. And to feel."

"Aye, perhaps you're right at that," admitted Groanin. "You could say that's why I support Manchester City Football Club."

"The rope stays up because the fakir *feels* that it stays up," added Nimrod.

"That never worked for Manchester City."

Nimrod got up, walked to the very edge of the carpet,

and bowed gravely to the fakir. Then he sat down again in front of the fakir and pressed his hands together in a gesture of respect and salutation.

"My name is Nimrod," he said. "Possibly, you remember I was a close friend of Mr. Rakshasas who you served for many years. And like him, I am a djinn of the Marid tribe. In respect of your vow of silence I should like to step inside your head and meet with you, Mr. Burton."

Nimrod waited for a moment before adding, "Alternatively, if your own level of enlightenment is sufficiently developed, you may communicate with me telepathically."

For several minutes the fakir stayed motionless and silent. But after a while his breathing grew a little more noticeable. His chest moved perceptibly and the sound of a loud intake of breath was heard by all who sat upon the flying carpet. Finally, the fakir brought the palms of his own thin, leathery hands together and he spoke:

"That will not be necessary," said Burton. His voice was surprisingly clear and strong for one who had not uttered a word in several years.

"Thank you." Nimrod was grateful that Mr. Burton had spoken to him so quickly; at the same time, however, he was surprised that a long-kept vow of silence had been abandoned with such alacrity.

"What brings you to this place that is no place?" asked the fakir.

"Mr. Burton, I'll be honest with you. I need your advice."

"Nimrod, is it?"

Nimrod nodded.

"I have heard of you," said Burton. "Mr. Rakshasas often used to speak of you when you were a boy. Tell me. How is my former master?"

"He died," said Nimrod. "An accident. Most unfortunate."

"I'm sad to hear it," said Burton. "He was the wisest person I ever met. And yet it seems to me that I should have felt something if he was indeed dead. Yes, I ought to have felt something, perhaps. No matter. Tell me, Nimrod. The children who accompany you. Are they djinn like yourself? And were they, too, friends of Mr. Rakshasas?"

"Yes," said Nimrod. "They are djinn. The boy is my nephew, John, and the girl is my niece, Philippa. And they were as fond of the old man as I was."

"If, as you say, they were fond of Mr. Rakshasas, then they will know his mind as well as their own. And they will be able to answer three simple riddles that were told to me by him more than two decades ago."

"We only have to join our minds for you to be sure about that," said Nimrod. "Perhaps I could join you in spirit and then we should know each other's thoughts."

But Mr. Burton shook his head. "But what if you are an evil djinn?" he asked. "If I let you into my mind, you might take control of it. And what then?"

Nimrod nodded. "You make a good point," he allowed.

"If the boy and the girl can answer three simple riddles," said Mr. Burton, "then I will agree to help you. For only then will I know that you and they are what you say you are. Friends of Mr. Rakshasas."

"Blimey," muttered Groanin. "It was hard enough to understand old Rakshasas even when he was trying to make sense, let alone when he was giving you a riddle."

"Wouldn't you prefer me to answer your riddles?" Nimrod asked Mr. Burton.

"Sure, the wolf never found a better messenger than himself," said Burton with a Rakshasas-like twinkle in his eye. "You might be what you say you are. But sometimes it's best to judge the wolf by its cubs."

"True," admitted Nimrod. "And sometimes the youngest thorns *are* the sharpest."

Nimrod waved the twins toward him.

The twins came over beside Nimrod and sat down in front of the fakir.

"Welcome," said Burton. "It's nice to meet children again. Especially nice when these are children of the lamp."

"Have you been here very long?" Philippa asked Burton.

"Yes," said Burton. "So long that I'd almost forgotten that such a thing as a child even existed."

"That is a long time," said Philippa.

"Don't you get lonely?" asked John.

"Long loneliness is better than bad company," said Burton. "And truth speaks even though the tongue were dead."

"Whatever that means," muttered Groanin.

"What's the first riddle?" asked Philippa.

"A woman gave birth to five children," said Burton. "And

exactly half of them were sons. And her husband said, 'How can this be?' And, indeed, please enlighten me: How can it be so?"

John frowned and scratched his head as he tried to imagine one of the children as a freakish half boy, half girl. But Philippa was already answering Burton's riddle.

"If exactly half of her children were sons, then all five of her children were sons," she said. "Because no one can be half of anything."

Burton nodded. "You answer well, child," he said.

John winced. Five children who were five sons. How else could there have been exactly half of them who were sons? It seemed obvious now that Philippa had given the answer. But all riddles were a bit like that.

Burton produced a large, silver inkwell and placed it in front of Nimrod and the twins, and then a fountain pen. He unscrewed the body of the pen and, squeezing the little reservoir, allowed one drop of black ink to drop into the inkwell.

"Now, please tell me this: Exactly how many such drops of ink can be dropped into this empty inkwell?"

John stared at the inkwell. He was certain that a bottle of ink held about twenty-five mills of ink, and that the well itself was large enough to have room for two such bottles, and that each drop of ink was perhaps a tenth of a milliliter, and that . . .

"The well is no longer empty after you put one drop of ink into it," said Philippa. "Therefore the answer is just one drop of ink."

"Once again, you answer well," Burton told Philippa.

"She's a clever girl that Philippa," Groanin told Moo. "I said . . ."

"Yes, I heard you the first time," said Moo.

John could have kicked himself. Once again, the answer seemed so obvious now that his sister had said it. What was more, he could see how he'd wasted time in a pointless math calculation of the inkwell's capacity when the question had really been about words and their proper meaning. And he told himself he simply had to answer the third riddle himself otherwise he'd never hear the end of it. As if to underline this fact, Philippa shot him a look that only a brother with a sister could ever have recognized. A smirking, triumphant look that said, "You're a dork."

"What's the third riddle?" John asked Burton, even more anxious to prove himself now.

"Please tell me this," said Burton. "Yes, tell me what is better than heaven, but worse than hell? Every poor man has this, yet the richest man in the world has need of it. And if you eat it, you will surely die. What is it that I speak of?"

John racked his brains and glanced sideways at his sister. Being a twin and given to an almost telepathic knowledge of what his sister was thinking — and vice versa — he even tried to sneak a look into Philippa's mind, but instead he found her thoughts blocked to him and her eyes staring back at his.

"Looking for something?" she asked.

"No, nothing," he said, and redoubled his effort to arrive at a solution before she did.

"Of course," she whispered. "That's it. That's the answer."

"What is?" said John, aware that he had said or thought something important that Philippa had picked up on. But what? What was it that he had said? He didn't know.

"Well, go on," she urged. "Tell him, John. Don't keep everyone in suspense."

John smiled thinly as a fourth riddle now confounded him: the riddle of how he had solved the riddle. He wrung his brain, like a wet sponge, with thinking for a moment and then shook his head. "Er no, I don't think I did solve it," he said. "At least, if I did, then I don't know how."

Philippa shrugged. "You said it."

John shook his head again, this time more irritated than before. "Nothing," he said. "I said nothing. I don't know the stupid answer, you idiot."

"That's the answer," said Philippa. "Idiot yourself."

"What is?" John sounded very exasperated.

"Nothing."

John shook his head again. There were times — and this was one of them — when he felt like the dumbest djinn ever to billow out of a bottle. "Tell me," he said. "Don't be such a dork, Phil."

"Nothing," repeated Philippa. "Nothing's the answer."

"There has to be an answer," said John. "It wouldn't be a proper riddle if there wasn't an answer."

Philippa gave up on him and turned to face Burton. "Nothing is the answer," she told the old fakir. "Nothing is better than heaven, and nothing is worse than hell. Every poor man has nothing, yet the richest man in the world has need of nothing. And if you eat nothing, then you will surely die." She nodded. "It's just what Mr. Rakshasas would have said."

"Once again, you answer well, girl," said Burton.

John cursed himself for his own stupidity. It was true. He remembered now. He'd said "nothing" after Philippa had asked him what he thought he was doing trying to sneak a look inside her thoughts. The answer had been right on his lips and even then he'd not understood.

"Never mind, John," said his uncle Nimrod. "We can't all be Stephen Hawking."

Burton smiled and placed a friendly hand on John's head. "Calm yourself, boy. And recognize that the true pleasure of a riddle is, as in life, finding your own pathway to the right answer. And though wisdom is good in the beginning, it is better at the end. 'Tis afterward that everything is understood."

"That's easy to say," said John, who was still beating himself up inside his own head.

"No matter how tall your grandfather was, boy, you always have to do your own growing."

"You will help me then?" asked Nimrod and, seeing Mr. Burton nod, he described the problem that had brought them all the way from London. "A group of religious scoundrels, mendicant fakirs most probably, but certainly part of a fraternity that is governed by laws of an uncommon or secret nature, seems to be bent on bringing about some change in the amount of luck that exists in the world. The question is, why? What do they hope to achieve?"

"Hmm. That is interesting. But you'll forgive me, Nimrod, if I say that I'm tired. This has been a busy day for me. You must come again tomorrow and we shall speak some more."

"We've only been here ten minutes," whispered Groanin.

"I think we have to respect the wishes of the fakir," Moo told him. "After all, it's we who are disturbing his peace and soliciting his help. It's what's called diplomacy."

Nimrod nodded. "Very well. We'll pitch camp down there, on the mountaintop. And speak again first thing in the morning."

CHAPTER 14

FALERNIAN WINE

In a matter of minutes after landing safely back on the mountaintop, Nimrod had used his djinn power to conjure several canvas pavilions from thin air, creating an elegant and comfortable encampment that would not have disgraced a desert-dwelling caliph. Meanwhile, Groanin gathered wood in the conventional way, made a large campfire, and before long had boiled some water for Nimrod and Moo and, of course, himself, for, being English, none of them were able to function without a cup of freshly brewed tea.

Tea was followed by dinner and, in honor of Moo, who said it had been years since she'd been on a picnic, Nimrod used his djinn powers to make her a whole roast wild boar stuffed with sausages and dates and all served with hundred-year-old Falernian (S.C.) wine. The twins, who didn't much care for wild boar or wine, were permitted to use their own djinn powers to make themselves cheeseburgers and sodas, and a plate of fruit for Zagreus. But Groanin, who was fond of sausages, enjoyed the wild boar and perhaps a little too much of the sweet Falernian wine.

"This Falernian wine is delicious," said Moo. "It has a most warming effect."

"Indeed." Groanin wiped the sweat from his forehead. "It's a cold night, but for some reason I don't feel cold at all."

"That's why we djinn drink it," said Nimrod. "So that we can nourish the inner fire that gives us all power."

"What exactly is Falernian wine, anyway?" Groanin asked Nimrod.

"Are you sure you really want to know?" Philippa asked him.

"Er, on second thought, perhaps not," said Groanin, who remembered how appalled he had been in South America upon discovering the horrible secret of the recipe for making a local beer called *chichai*.

"It was the most expensive wine in ancient Rome," explained Nimrod. "Falernian wine was served at a banquet to honor Julius Caesar following his conquests in Spain in 60 B.C. Both Pliny and Catullus describe the excellence of Falernian wine. It's made from black grapes from a variety of countries."

"That's a relief," said Groanin. "And the S.C.? Southern Campania in Italy, I presume." He chuckled politely. "Or perhaps these days it's Southern California. They make a nice drop of wine, them Californians."

"Falernian wine is perhaps the only wine that takes light when flame is applied to it," explained Nimrod. "But for some inexplicable reason, when we djinn make the stuff it seems to catch alight of its own accord. At least it does after you drink it. That's what the S.C. means. Spontaneously combusting."

"Spontaneously combusting?" Groanin smiled uncertainly. "You mean, it catches fire all by itself?"

"Exactly," said Nimrod.

"Am I to take it, sir, that the inside of my stomach is on fire?"

"Yes, just like the flame on a Christmas pudding." Nimrod grinned. "That's why you feel so warm on what is, after all, quite a cold desert night."

Groanin stood up abruptly. "I don't think I like the sound of that," he said, holding his ample stomach with both hands.

"Me, I'm glad I stuck to soda," observed John.

"Me, too," said Philippa.

"I'm glad I stuck to water," said Zagreus.

"Don't worry, Groanin," said Nimrod. "It's quite safe. Provided you don't drink too much of it. And even then —"

"Yes, but suppose the rest of me catches fire as well?" said Groanin. "Suppose me whole insides catch fire. What then?"

"They won't," said Nimrod. "I promise you that the worst that could happen is —"

"Water," said Groanin. "Quick, give me some water before I blow up or something!"

"I wouldn't do that if I were you," said Nimrod.

But it was too late. Groanin had already snatched the jug of water from Zagreus and was pouring the contents down his throat.

"Oh, dear," said Nimrod. "I wish you hadn't done that, Groanin."

"What?" Groanin frowned. "Why?"

"Falernian (S.C.) wine reacts badly with water." Nimrod winced.

"In what way badly?" asked Groanin.

"Nothing fatal, I can assure you," said Nimrod. "Not even painful. Just a bit inconvenient. Look here, Groanin, it might be a good idea if you slept outside the tent tonight. Just in case."

"Just in case of what?"

"And one more thing," said Nimrod. "If you happen to burp, don't, for Pete's sake, put your hand up to your mouth. And it might be best if you took several steps back from anyone whenever you felt a burp coming on."

"Why?"

Talk of burping caused Groanin to belch nervously. But this was no ordinary belch. It was loud. Only it was not the volume of Groanin's belch that made it unusual. What made Groanin's belch unusual was that it was the kind that might have been produced by a dragon, for most of the wind that was released from his body through his mouth now appeared in the darkness of the mountaintop as a tongue of flame, several inches long.

"That's why," said Nimrod. "Fire always tries its best to escape from water. They don't mix, you see."

John ducked as Groanin belched again, only this time with more spectacular effect. The flame flew out of his mouth, through the air, and caught hold of a dry olive bush, setting it on fire.

"Blimey," exclaimed the butler. "I'm a human flame-thrower."

"Wow," said John. "Good trick, Groanin." He grinned at Nimrod. "Hey, Uncle Nimrod, why don't you put a cigar in your mouth and see if Groanin can light it?"

"Sounds like a good way to lose some eyebrows," said Moo.

"John's right, you know, Groanin," said Nimrod. "I never thought of that. A butler who can light a cigar with one burp could be jolly useful."

"Very amusing, I'm sure," complained Groanin. "Isn't there anything you can do to help me, sir?"

"I'm afraid not, Groanin," admitted Nimrod. "Not now that you have drunk the water. You'll just have to wait for the effect of the wine to wear off."

Groanin muttered a swear word under his breath and, taking a sleeping bag, went away and found a quiet spot to sulk, which was, from time to time, illuminated by one of the butler's fiery explosions of wind.

CHAPTER 15

THE FAKIR'S ADVICE

After dinner, the remainder of the little party settled down in their sleeping bags and were soon fast asleep. That is, everyone except John, who had other ideas. Sneaking out of the tent, he found his new flying carpet and willed it to move. Instead, it wrapped him up like a parcel, which is not an unusual thing to happen to anyone who attempts to fly a carpet for the very first time. But after several further attempts, he succeeded in getting the carpet off the ground and was soon ascending the height of the fakir's rope.

Mr. Burton was exactly where they had left him except that the sun in the sky had been replaced by an equally bright moon — so bright that it was almost like the middle of the day. John steered the carpet closer to the fakir and, getting up, bowed gravely to the holy man.

"Mr. Burton," said John. "I apologize for disturbing you. This is going to sound weird, I know, only I have questions that need answers. I hate to sound like a hippie but you might even say that I seek enlightenment."

"Yes," said Mr. Burton. "Earlier on, I heard the voice in your heart that commands you to seek answers, which is why I said I would help you. And I shall, if I can."

"My sister is cleverer than me," said John.

"It could seem that way. But you are not your sister. You are yourself. So why does such a thing matter?"

"I just wish I was a bit cleverer, that's all," admitted John.

"Perhaps you have other strengths," observed Mr. Burton.

"Yes, but what?"

"That is for you to find out," said Mr. Burton. "The finding out is one of life's pleasures. And as my former master, Mr. Rakshasas, used to say, even castles are built one brick at a time."

"I miss him," said John. "I was kind of fond of that guy. I often wish I knew exactly what happened to him."

"If you look for him, then perhaps you will find him," said Mr. Burton.

"If he's dead, how can I look for him?"

"You only have to know the best place to look," said Mr. Burton. "Fortunately, I can help you there."

Mr. Burton took out his fountain pen — the one he had used earlier in the second riddle — and squeezed a little drop of black ink into a white saucer.

"Perhaps," he said mysteriously, "you will find an answer in this little drop of ink."

"How can anyone find something in a drop of ink?" objected John.

"Shakespeare did," said Mr. Burton. "And many others since. But have you ever actually looked inside a spot of ink?"

"No," admitted John. "I can't say that I have."

"Then it may be that you will find more in it than you might expect."

"Don't know unless you try it, huh?" John nodded, took the white saucer from the fakir's bony fingers, and stared at the little shiny concave black dot.

At first he could see nothing at all. But then as his eyes steadied on the ink spot, John saw the full moon reflected there and next his own face.

"I can see myself," he whispered.

"That's a start," said Mr. Burton. "Believe me, it's not everyone who can see himself. Already there is enlightenment where none existed before. What do you see?"

"I see someone strong," said John. "A seeker after truth. An explorer. Someone who is not afraid to act. Someone who would do things. But what? The answers are hidden. Perhaps lost forever."

"Then you must look deeper to find that which was lost," said Mr. Burton. "You must look beyond yourself to that which lies beneath. You have to search the very depths of the ink spot to find what you seek, my son. Oh, and try not to blink. You have a much better chance of seeing something if you don't close your eyes."

"All right."

John could not have said how long he sat there and stared into the ink spot. And for a long while it was like staring down the wrong end of a telescope. As if he was trying to look at something that was a very long way away from him. But then, after a while it seemed as though the length of the telescope shortened and what he was looking at grew nearer, and he had the idea that it was not the inside of a telescope he was looking at so much as the depths of an enormously deep well. No ordinary well, either, but a well that seemed to have been bored into time itself. And as he looked, he started to see places and people he recognized.

"Why, it's incredible," he whispered. "I can see everything."

John saw his house in Manhattan, and his mother and father, and Alan and Neil — the two dogs who were really his uncles. He saw his uncle Nimrod, and his sister, Philippa, Mrs. Trump, Dybbuk, Virgil McCreeby and his son Finlay, Iblis the Ifrit, and almost everyone he had ever met or known. None of them paid him any attention or perhaps even noticed him. It was like looking out of a window set into the sky and staring down at a selection of human miniatures. He could even hear voices he recognized and smell things.

And finally, he saw his old friend, Mr. Rakshasas.

"I see him," he said delightedly. "He's quite real. It seems to me I could almost reach out and touch him."

"You must not," said Mr. Burton.

"He's at the Metropolitan Museum in New York," said John. "And he's been absorbed by one of those horrible terracotta warriors. And . . . ah! So that's what happened to him. That's where he went. But no, that's impossible, isn't it?"

"What is?"

"That he should have . . . died," said John. "And started a new life without telling me about it."

"Did he?"

"Yes. And yet, he can't have, can he? Reincarnation? Surely not."

"Don't you believe in reincarnation?"

"I didn't," said John. "Until I met Zagreus."

"And now?"

"Well, yes. I do."

"Then perhaps that is why you and Zagreus were brought together in the first place."

"Perhaps," said John. "But surely someone as important as Mr. Rakshasas wouldn't come back as a dog, would he?"

"We don't choose who or what we come back as," said Mr. Burton. "If we come back at all. Not everyone does. And a dog is not so bad."

"Why do people come back at all?" asked John.

"Perhaps they have something left to do or say?" said Mr. Burton.

"Then it's not much use coming back as a dog," observed John. "They can't say anything."

"Tell that to another dog," said Mr. Burton. "It's my impression that dogs can say a lot. Even to us, upon occasion."

John shook his head. "No. It's not a dog. He's a wolf. Mr. Rakshasas has come back as a wolf. A young wolf. He's black and gray, with bright blue eyes. And I can actually hear him howling. He's living somewhere cold, too. It looks like Yellowstone National Park. Yes, it's Yellowstone National Park. Gee, I thought I'd seen everything. Well, a lot, anyway. But that's incredible."

John shook his head and found himself staring at a

simple ink spot. "What I was looking at," he said. "How long ago was that?"

"The past is the past," said Mr. Burton. "It could be anything from a few seconds to several years. The longer you look, the further into the past you can see."

"And the future?" said John. "Is it possible to see the future in the same way?"

"The ink spot you were looking at was concave," said Mr. Burton. "To see the future you must look into an ink spot that is convex."

"You mean like a lens?"

Mr. Burton nodded. "But to know the past is one thing. To know the future is quite another. It is not without danger."

"What kind of danger?"

"Knowledge of the future is the most dangerous thing in the universe," said Mr. Burton. "That is why I remain here. Because once, many years ago, I looked into the future and what I saw made me think that it would be safer for everyone if I came here where I could not put that knowledge into action."

"Can I look for something in particular?" asked John.

"Yes, but why would you wish to look into the future in the first place?"

"I want to make sure I'll amount to something, I guess."

"You can look but there is no guarantee that you will see anything," said Mr. Burton. "Visions of the future tend to be rare and rather unpredictable." He winced.

"What?" asked John.

"To be given a vision of the future is a rare thing. Upon seeing such a thing, however, it is difficult not to act on it. And yet you must also be aware that what you might see would only be a fragment and not the whole picture, therefore understanding might be similarly incomplete. Are you sure that you wish to do this, boy djinn?"

"Yes," said John.

Mr. Burton wiped the spot of ink off the saucer with the edge of his robe and, taking his fountain pen, dropped another spot of black ink into the saucer's center. "Then look again," he said.

John leaned forward and stared hard. First of all, he noticed that this time the spot of ink was convex and it impressed him that Mr. Burton could do this with ink spots.

"How do you make one spot concave and the other convex?" he asked.

"Practice," said Mr. Burton. "But it's best to look in silence. The future is like a great movie star. It does not like to have its picture taken, unawares."

John stared a while and saw nothing. Or so he thought. But just as he was about to blink and rub his eyes, he saw himself leaning over a body. A dead body. John was pretty sure it was a dead body because there was blood on John's hands. He couldn't see the dead man's face but there was no mistaking the red fox fur coat. It was his uncle Nimrod. And Nimrod was dead — by John's bloody hand, or so it seemed.

John blinked and, turning abruptly to one side, vomited over the edge of his flying carpet.

"No," he said. "It can't be. Say it isn't true."

CHAPTER 16

THE TEN FAKIRS OF FAIZABAD

Groanin spent a miserable night on the mountaintop.

First of all, he burped so much fire that his eyebrows and all of his clothes — including his coat and his favorite bowler hat — caught alight and were completely destroyed, and then his sleeping bag, too. That would have been bad enough. And Groanin was just thinking that there was nothing else the night could throw at him when someone vomited on his head from a great height.

"Well, that's just marvelous," said Groanin, and sat down to await the dawn.

The butler presented a sorry spectacle when Nimrod went to look for him in the morning to ask where his tea was.

"I'm sorry, sir," said the butler, standing uncomfortably behind a bush. "But due to my absence of clothes, not to mention this horrible mess on my head, you'll have to fetch your own tea this morning."

"Always got an excuse for not doing your job," said Nimrod. "Very well. I suppose you would like me to make you some new clothes."

"A hot shower wouldn't go amiss, either," said Groanin.

"Yes, you do seem to smell a bit strongly. Difficult night, eh?"

"You could say that, sir, yes."

"Still breathing fire?"

"No longer, sir. Them fiery eructations would seem to have stopped. I said, them fiery eructations would seem to have terminated. At least I can hiccup without setting fire to something, anyway."

"Well, let this be a lesson to you, Groanin," said Nimrod. "Don't ever mix water with Falernian wine again."

"No, sir, I shall endeavor not to." He shook his head and added, "I've never been lucky with food and drink. And people wonder why I stick to baby food when I'm abroad. Because you can't go wrong with baby food. That's why they give it to babies, see?"

Nimrod muttered his focus word — QWERTYUIOP — and soon Groanin was looking like a proper butler again, which is to say he was wearing a dark jacket, matching vest, pin-striped trousers, black shoes, black tie, white shirt, and a black bowler hat. And looking like a butler again meant that Groanin was soon acting like one, too — fetching tea for Nimrod and Moo and generally tidying up the camp. It wasn't long before he started to whistle, but only because he knew it annoyed Nimrod when he seemed cheerful.

"Anyone seen John?" asked Philippa.

"No," said Groanin. "Perhaps he's gone off exploring somewhere. His flying carpet is gone."

"So is Zagreus," observed Moo.

Philippa shook her head. Being John's twin, she sometimes sensed things about her brother that only a twin could feel — something that even human twins are capable of. "I dunno," she said. "It doesn't feel like he's anywhere close. Plus" — she kept on shaking her head — "he seems disturbed by something. But exactly what, I don't know."

"I expect he and Zagreus will turn up in due course," said Nimrod. "Boys will be boys. Even when they're djinn."

After breakfast, Nimrod steered the flying carpet back up the rope to see Mr. Burton. It was even colder ascending the rope than it had been the day before and Groanin's teeth were soon chattering noisily.

"What happened to your fur coat?" Nimrod asked him.

"Went up in smoke last night," said Groanin. "Like the rest of me clothes."

"Here," said Nimrod, taking off his fur coat. "Have mine. After all that Falernian wine last night I don't really need it now. I feel as warm as hot, buttered toast."

"Thank you, sir," said Groanin to whom hot, buttered toast seemed like the nicest thing in the world and certainly nicer than Falernian wine.

As soon as they saw Mr. Burton again, the fakir surprised them all by standing up. Then, leaving his precarious little platform, he stepped barefoot onto the flying carpet.

"I've been thinking about your problem," he said. "And I've come to the conclusion that you have urgent need of my help. Perhaps more urgently than you might have thought. But first I must tell you a story by way of an explanation."

Mr. Burton sat down in front of Nimrod, tugged his beard thoughtfully for a moment, and then started to speak:

"Ayodhya is an ancient city of India in the Faizabad district. Not a bad place. I spent six months there on a bed of nails after leaving the service of Mr. Rakshasas. It is one of the six holiest cities in India, and a city made by gods. Or so the people believe. Many centuries ago, there lived in the city a great Tirthankar, which is a kind of holy man. This holy man was so enlightened and full of wisdom that he had achieved perfect knowledge. Which is to say that he knew absolutely everything."

"How is that possible?" asked Philippa.

"It was easier then than perhaps it is today," admitted Mr. Burton. "After all, there used to be so much less to know than there is nowadays. But even so, it is certain that the Tirthankar had learned the five great secrets of the universe."

"Five?" Groanin looked doubtful. "Only five? Somehow I thought there'd be more."

"Oh, yes," said Mr. Burton. "Five. Five great secrets. About the meaning of everything. Anyway, sensing that he would soon die, for the Tirthankar was very old, which is how great wisdom is achieved, and in order that these great secrets should not be lost to mankind forever, he summoned ten very adept fakirs to his presence. Proper fakirs, not fakirs like me, nor these mendicant fakirs whom you spoke of earlier. These were proper Indian holy men, who were known for their extraordinary powers of self-denial and endurance. The Tirthankar entrusted each fakir with one of the five secrets of the universe. In other words, each secret was entrusted twice, for the sake of safety.

"All ten fakirs volunteered to go to the four corners of the earth and be buried alive, so that one day, when the world might have need of true enlightenment, the fakirs might come forth from the ground at an auspicious moment and provide the answer to one of these great mysteries."

"Buried alive?" exclaimed Moo. "But surely a man would die."

"And surely it would have been easier to write the secrets down on a piece of paper," objected Groanin.

"Paper can be stolen and read by anyone," said Mr. Burton. "Better to have men who could be trusted. Special men. This is precisely why the Tirthankar enlisted the help of the fakirs. For only fakirs have sufficient control over their bodies so as to be able to do without air, food, and water for many years. And, in this case, for many centuries."

"Well, I've heard of such men," admitted Moo. "But I always thought these stories were nothing more than fairy stories and exaggerations."

"They are, if you ask me," said Groanin. "No man can do without food and water, let alone air, for centuries. I certainly couldn't."

Ignoring the butler — which was easy for Mr. Burton, for he had once been a butler himself — Mr. Burton continued his tale: "Each fakir was accompanied by a *dasa* — a servant. The servant and his descendants were supposed to guard the secret of the fakir's burial place and be there to serve him whenever the fakir judged that the time was right for him to return. He would somehow respond to vibrations in the atmosphere, to a feeling of general bad luck or peril. Whereupon he would conclude that the earth had need of one of the answers to one of the great mysteries and then come up from his secret burial place, whereupon the *dasa* would help him apply the secret to the benefit of humankind."

"These mysteries of the universe," said Nimrod. "What sort of mysteries are we talking about? And how many remain to be revealed?"

"I'm very glad you asked me that," said Mr. Burton. "As far as I know four of the original ten fakirs have been resurrected over the centuries. But no one knows how many of the great mysteries have yet to be discovered. The mathematics of it would indicate at least one. But I am certain that the most recent revelation was at the beginning of the twentieth century, when one of these fakirs was accidentally uncovered by the Lahore earthquake. The next month Einstein came up with his theory of special relativity."

"Einstein?" said Philippa. "What's he got to do with this?"

"What happened was this," said Mr. Burton. "The *dasa* in Lahore and his descendants had long died out, which left the fakir of Lahore with something of a dilemma. He had a great secret to reveal but no one who could understand it. So he went to Europe. To Switzerland. And sensing he did not have long to live, because he was several hundred years old, he thought he might record his secret as a patent."

"What's a patent?" asked Philippa.

"It's a grant made by a government that confers upon the creator of an invention the right to make, use, and sell that invention for a set period of time," explained Moo. "But it's also a means of officially recording the existence of an invention or a theory."

"The fakir went into the Federal Office for Intellectual Property in Bern," continued Mr. Burton. "Fortunately for him, it was there he met someone who understood the meaning of his secret immediately. That man was Albert Einstein. It was the holy man's secret that helped Einstein develop his famous theory of relativity that changed the world."

"You mean *e* equals *mc* squared?" said Philippa. "That was one of the great mysteries entrusted to the ten fakirs by the Tirthankar of Faizabad?"

"Exactly so," said Mr. Burton.

"I'm beginning to see why someone might want to get his hands on one of these great mysteries," admitted Nimrod. "With a secret like that there's no telling what someone might do."

"Yes, you are right, Nimrod," said Mr. Burton. "It is generally supposed that each of the fakirs could reveal a secret that would bring about such an enormous change in the world, and which, if it fell into the wrong hands, might prove disastrous."

"That's putting it mildly," said Moo. "*e* equals *mc* squared was the theory that helped unlock the secrets of the atom."

"Not to mention the atomic bomb." Groanin shook his head. "Nasty things that make nasty-looking clouds shaped like mushrooms. I've never liked mushrooms. Not even with sausages."

"My suspicion," said Mr. Burton, "is that someone must know where one of these *dasas* — the fakir servants — is to be found, and is watching him closely. Probably they are hoping to create a feeling of bad luck around a particular location where it is commonly believed one of the remaining six must be buried alive."

"Bumby," muttered Groanin. "There must be one of them fakirs in Bumby. It's the only possible explanation for why the town's luck has turned so bad."

"The *dasa* has no control of the fakir's revival. It's even possible the fakir himself may already have arisen, but the *dasa* knows he's being watched and doesn't dare contact his risen fakir for fear of the secret falling into the wrong hands," said Mr. Burton.

"Light my lamp, Groanin," said Nimrod. "But you could be right. It could be Bumby."

"It would certainly explain why there were so many odd and sinister-looking characters wandering around the place," added the butler. "It must have been them fake mendicant fakirs you was talking about, sir."

"Yes," said Nimrod. "I think so, too. But who's behind them? The mendicant fakirs, they're just a bunch of troublemakers. They wouldn't know what to do with one of the universe's great mysteries if they found it inside a

Christmas cracker. No, this is something else. Something more sophisticated."

"I suppose it's back to Bumby, then," said Groanin.

"What, all of us?" exclaimed Nimrod. "I should say not. No, this calls for some subtlety. We must move carefully. Philippa, you must go."

"Me?" exclaimed Philippa. "On my own? Why me?"

"Because no one there will suspect you, my child. And besides, Groanin and John have been there before and it might draw attention if they went back there so soon. It's my impression that no one goes back to Bumby unless they are quite mad."

"I often go to Bumby," protested Groanin. "On my holidays."

"Then you make my point for me," said Nimrod. "You can go there on your flying carpet," he told Philippa.

"I shall accompany you, child," said Moo. "I may be of some use. In an official government capacity."

"Good idea," said Nimrod.

"What shall I do when I get there?" asked Philippa.

"Watch and observe," said Nimrod. "See if you can spot the mendicant fakirs and the *dasa*. And the genuine fakir, of course. The one with the secret. And if you can manage it without leading the fake fakirs to the real one, try to make contact."

"Where are you going to be?" asked Philippa.

"Er, I don't know," said Nimrod. "But I'm hoping Mr. Burton here is going to tell me."

Mr. Burton shrugged. "This is not so easy."

Nimrod thought for a moment. "I think that somehow we will need to alter the perception of luck in the world and to do it quickly before other fakirs start to come out of the ground and reveal their secrets," he said. "But for that to happen, something really lucky would have to take place. A quick-fix event of almost mythical good luck. But just how such a thing is brought about, I really have no idea." He sighed and, throwing up his hands, landed them loudly upon his head as if he hoped the impact might provoke a good idea. But it didn't.

"When Mr. Rakshasas needed inspiration and enlightenment," said Nimrod, "he would say that it was time to look for his navel."

"I can't see that helping somehow," observed Groanin. "For a start you'd have to find your navel. That's not so easy these days. You're not as thin as you used to be."

"I was speaking metaphorically," said Nimrod. "I don't mean *my* navel. I mean omphalos, which is Greek for 'navel.'"

"A navel is still a navel," said Groanin. "Whether it's a Greek navel or one from the Isle of Skye."

"That's where you're wrong, Groanin," said Nimrod. "An omphalos is also an ancient religious stone artifact. According to the ancient Greeks, Zeus sent two eagles to fly across the world and meet at its center, the navel of the world. And several omphalos stones were erected in several areas around the Mediterranean Sea, including one that was at the oracle at Delphi. Omphalos stones were said to allow direct communication with the gods."

"Yes, that's right," said Mr. Burton. "Mr. Rakshasas used to go and sit inside an omphalos stone when he wanted to do some serious thinking. The stone has a hollow center."

"Did he now?" said Nimrod.

"Oh, yes. He once said that he regarded the inside of an omphalos stone as a better place for thinking than the great British Library."

"That wouldn't be difficult," said Groanin. "Some of the stupidest people in the world work at the British Library. I should know. I used to work there myself."

"Do shut up, Groanin," said Nimrod. "So then, I suppose I'll have to go to Delphi."

Mr. Burton shook his head. "The one in the museum at Delphi is a fake," he said. "But there is a real one in Jerusalem. In the Church of the Holy Sepulchre. That's the one that Mr. Rakshasas always favored." He bowed to Nimrod. "It would be my honor to accompany you, Nimrod, as I did once accompany Rakshasas."

"Good idea," said Nimrod. "So, here's the plan: Philippa and Moo will fly to Bumby, while Mr. Burton, Groanin, John, Zagreus, and myself will fly to Jerusalem." Nimrod frowned. "Which reminds me. Where is that boy? And where is that Jinx?"

"You say that there is no sign of him down below?" asked Mr. Burton.

"No," said Philippa. "And frankly, I am a little worried."

Mr. Burton looked sheepish. "I think I might be able to provide an explanation," he said.

CHAPTER 17

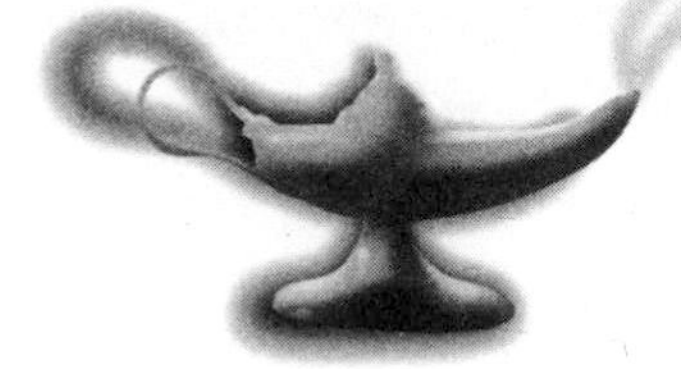

RESCUE MISSION

What is it, Mr. Burton?" asked Philippa. "Do you know where my brother, John, is?"

"No, I do not know that. But if your brother has left the mountain, then perhaps I can offer a reason why. He was most aggrieved at his lack of cleverness. Upset with himself that he did not guess any of the three riddles I set you yesterday. I think he wished to prove his worth in some way. That is why he came to seek my advice. Most particularly he wished to know what happened to our mutual friend, Mr. Rakshasas."

"And?" Philippa's tone was impatient.

"The boy asked to look into the past," explained Mr. Burton. "Into my ink spot."

"Ink spot divination?" Nimrod sounded surprised. "You can do that, too?"

"I learned it from a great Egyptian sorcerer," said Mr. Burton. "A Mr. Jonathan Burge, of Heliopolis, Cairo. A most capable fellow."

"Well, what did he see in your ink spot?" asked Groanin. He, too, was beginning to feel worried about John.

"In my ink spot he saw that Mr. Rakshasas has undergone samsara, the process of rebirth, and has been made flesh again. Or to be more exact, flesh and fur."

"What, you mean like reincarnated?" said Groanin.

"Yes," said Mr. Burton.

"Who is he now?" asked Groanin.

"Not who. What. According to what John saw in the ink spot, Mr. Rakshasas is now a wolf."

"A wolf?"

"A wolf living quite happily in Yellowstone National Park," said Mr. Burton. "That is a park in Wyoming, Montana, and Idaho, I believe."

"Thanks," said Philippa drily. "I know where it is." She looked at Nimrod. "Did you know about this, Uncle Nimrod?"

"No. But it's what Mr. Rakshasas believed would happen to him after he died. So I'm not particularly surprised. Mr. Burton? Do you think John might have gone to Yellowstone to see Mr. Rakshasas in his new incarnation?"

"Yes, it's possible," said Mr. Burton. "But I think there was also another reason that he has left the mountain. Something more serious, perhaps."

"What was that?"

"I cannot say for sure, but as well as looking into the past he looked into the future, and there he saw something that was most alarming to him. He didn't say what it was, however, and I didn't press him to tell me. My own experience of looking into the future has persuaded me that it's a very personal matter. I confess I warned him of the dangers of future gazing but still he wished to look."

"And you let him look?" said Nimrod.

"He wished it," said Mr. Burton.

"If you only knew the problems we have with wishes," observed Philippa.

"You got that right," observed Groanin. "I say, you have got that right, miss."

"But he's just a boy," Nimrod told Mr. Burton.

Mr. Burton shrugged. "I have no experience of boys except that I suppose I was once one myself, a very long, long time ago. Why should I say no to him? I liked him. I explained the hazards of looking at tomorrow and the year after, but he was adamant as Adam himself. Besides, this is no ordinary boy, Nimrod. He is a powerful djinn. Who better than he to look after himself, wherever he has gone?"

"You make a fair point," sighed Nimrod. "All the same it's very inconvenient that this should have happened now, in the midst of this crisis."

"Someone should go after him," said the butler. "And fetch him back home. A rescue mission, so to speak."

"I agree with you, Groanin. And it's brave of you to volunteer for the job. Stout fellow. Proud of you. I shall miss your tea, of course."

"Me?" said Groanin. "In Yellowstone?"

"I'd go myself but there are more pressing matters to attend to."

"Nimrod's right," said Philippa. "John will listen to you. He respects you."

Groanin looked pained for a moment. "But there are bears in Yellowstone. Large ones. With very sharp claws and even sharper teeth."

"Then I had better arm you with a discrimens," said Nimrod. "An emergency wish that you could use in the event of, er . . . well, an emergency, such as meeting up with a grizzly bear, perhaps. Or being hunted by a pack of wolves. Or a mountain lion. Or being charged by an elk. Or attacked by a rattlesnake. Yes, I think there are lots of rattlesnakes in Yellowstone National Park. To say nothing about the park being one very, very large active volcano that is several centuries overdue for an eruption."

Groanin smiled thinly. "Best say no more, eh, sir? Otherwise I shall feel quite unequal to the task of going at all."

"You'll enjoy it," said Nimrod. "At this time of year, Yellowstone is extremely beautiful."

"What time of year is it?" inquired Groanin. "In Yellowstone."

"Spring, of course," said Nimrod. "Although I believe there's still plenty of snow about, so you'd better take that coat with you. Plus one or two other things. In fact, I'd better set you up with some proper equipment. All that Jack London stuff."

"Yes, but how am I going to get there? The boy is using a flying carpet, which means he'll get there sooner than any plane I might catch."

"Hmm. Good point." Nimrod sighed. "I suppose there's only one thing for it. I'd better cut you off a chunk of my own carpet."

"I thought Mr. Barkhiya said that only a djinn could fly one of these carpets," objected Moo.

"That is true," said Nimrod. "But Groanin will merely have to sit on his piece of flying carpet. I shall be doing the flying. By means of my own willpower. Happily, this will be easy enough. You remember that Mr. Barkhiya told us that all flying carpets were made from the one larger carpet once owned by King Solomon? Well, when directed to do so, one rug will follow the other. I shall simply direct the smaller carpet I cut from my larger one to pursue John's carpet, with a special binding. Much as I would instruct a bloodhound to go after a scent. All Groanin will have to do is sit on the carpet until it gets to Yellowstone."

"And the rug," said Groanin. "This fragment of your own larger one. It won't give out in the cold, will it? I don't want to be stuck there in the middle of nowhere trying to fly a flipping yoga mat."

"I can't imagine why you think such a thing is even possible," said Nimrod.

"Because, sir, I've been on adventures before. Things go wrong. I suppose that's what makes them adventures, really. But I should much prefer it if they didn't go wrong, see? I'm not much of a traveler at the best of times. A day in which nothing at all happens — and certainly nothing at all remarkable — is my idea of heaven."

"Rest assured, Groanin," said Nimrod. "I shall endeavor to make sure you travel in style, comfort, and safety."

As soon as Philippa and Moo were airborne and bound for Bumby, Nimrod set about the preparations for Groanin's flight. He faced his own flying carpet and for several minutes contemplated the best way to cut the thirty-one-foot square of blue and gold.

"Do I cut a strip from the edge?" he mused. "Or do I cut it in half? And with what? I wonder what Mr. Barkhiya uses when he does this sort of thing? And if there are any ceremonies to be observed. Light my lamp, I do wonder about that. After all, this is no ordinary Axminster. This carpet was once owned by King Solomon himself. I'd fly back to Fez and ask Mr. Barkhiya if there was time, but there isn't. You really ought to get started after my nephew right away, Groanin."

"Can't you just use djinn power on it?" suggested Groanin. "Just zap it down the middle, laserlike?"

"I don't like to 'zap it' as you say," said Nimrod. "There's the small matter of respect involved here. Using my power on the carpet might offend the ancient power that dwells within its silky fibers." Nimrod shook his head. "No, using djinn power on this is quite out of the question. And quite possibly impossible."

Groanin thought for a moment. Then he said, "I do happen to have a carpet knife in my luggage, sir, if that might help."

"Perhaps the edge of the carpet is best. Ten feet wide still leaves me with twenty-one feet. What was that you said?"

"I have a carpet knife in my luggage, sir."

Groanin went and fetched his knife and handed it over to his master.

"A carpet knife, Groanin? How on earth is it that you have one?"

"That carpet knife were me dad's," said Groanin. "He were a carpet fitter all his life, in Burnley. I keep it with me for sentimental reasons. Sometimes I just get it out and hold it and imagine me dad slicing a Berber twist pile on the floor of some semidetached in greater Manchester. It's amazing, I can almost smell new carpets when I hold that knife."

"A bit like Marcel Proust, you mean," said Nimrod.

"I don't know about Proust, but I do think it's a bit ironic really, us planning to cut up this here carpet. If my dad was here now, he'd have it done in no time. No one could cut a carpet like my old dad."

Nimrod handed back the knife to his butler. "Then you shall cut the carpet, Groanin," he said. "We shall see if this is a talent you have inherited from him."

"Very well, sir." Groanin dropped down upon his knees and proceeded to cut the straightest line in a carpet that Nimrod had ever seen.

"Perfect," said Nimrod. "There seems to be no end to your talents, Groanin. Well then. On you get." Groanin fetched his luggage and sat cross-legged on the carpet and waited while Nimrod used his djinn power to add a large box of stores for the expedition. "Everything you might need is in those boxes, Groanin. Food, tents, a rifle, ammunition, materials for making a fire. And I've attached a discrimens to your person just in case the rifle should prove not to be enough."

"Thank you, sir. When I find John, what shall I do?"

"Go back to the house in Kensington and wait for me there. And don't let him go gallivanting anywhere else."

"Right you are, sir."

Under Nimrod's direction, the carpet carrying Groanin started to rise slowly in the air.

"Can't help feeling just a little bit nervous, sir," said Groanin. "After all, this is my first solo flight, so to speak."

"Relax. Sit back. Enjoy the experience. You'll be fine."

"And you, sir?"

"Off to Jerusalem. With Mr. Burton here. In search of inspiration. Hard to say what that might look like. But I have a feeling we'll know it when we see it."

CHAPTER 18

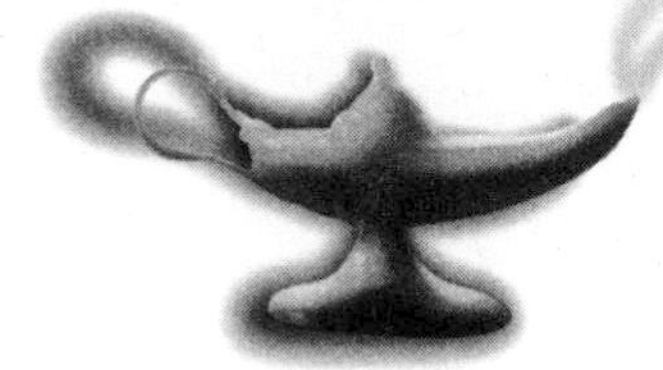

GROANIN GOES WEST

As anyone who has traveled on a flying carpet will tell you, the experience is a peculiar one. For one thing, the carpet itself feels quite solid, like a wooden floor; and for another, the air seems to slip to either side of the carpet so that the passenger does not have to endure the discomfort of having the wind in his face. All of this makes standing up on a flying carpet quite safe.

Groanin would have stood up but for his fear of heights. At only ten feet wide, the flying carpet seemed hardly wide enough and whenever the butler was obliged to fetch something from his box of stores, he had to crawl there on his hands and knees. It wasn't that Groanin was acrophobic, which is the proper word to describe someone who has a fear of heights, but unlike the djinn, who have no fear of heights, most mundanes feel a little uncomfortable when they are several thousand feet in the air with only ten feet of Moroccan silk carpet to support them. So, wrapping himself tightly in

Nimrod's fur coat, which was now Groanin's fur coat, the butler pressed his back against the box of stores, closed his eyes, and did his best to put out of his mind all thoughts of the cold Atlantic Ocean beneath him. And after a while he fell asleep.

When, several hours later, he awoke, Groanin's flying carpet was still over the Atlantic but it seemed to him that in some indefinable way his situation had somehow changed, and at least ten minutes had elapsed before he formed the idea that the carpet he was sitting upon was now narrower than it had been before.

Being a good butler, Groanin had a tape measure and, plucking up his courage, he hooked the end of the metallic measuring strip to one edge of the carpet and attempted to span its width.

"Flipping heck," exclaimed Groanin as he read off the number on the strip. For there was no doubt in his mind that the carpet that had been ten feet wide on takeoff was now only eight feet wide. He was so shocked by this discovery that his nervous fingers switched off the spring return mechanism and the metallic strip of the tape measure zipped back with such force that Groanin dropped it onto the carpet, where it bounced twice and disappeared over the side and into the ocean. It seemed a very graphic demonstration of what now threatened to happen to Groanin himself. "Flipping heck," repeated Groanin.

He crawled to one edge and found nothing amiss. And then crawled to the other — the edge he himself had cut earlier — where immediately he perceived the problem. A thread of the flying carpet had come unraveled from the back corner and was now trailing in the air for miles behind, like a fishing line.

"Flipping heck," said Groanin, and crawled back to his luggage to find a pair of scissors. Crawling back to the thread again, he snipped the thread off as neatly as he was able. And thinking he must have solved the problem, he went back to his former position leaning against the box of stores.

For a while he read a newspaper — Nimrod had thoughtfully added a copy of the *Daily Telegraph* to his box of stores — and this took his mind off things, which, of course, is why people read newspapers in the first place: to forget their own problems and enjoy reading about someone else's. Another twenty minutes passed before Groanin looked up and, once again, was possessed of the horrible sensation that the carpet was narrower than before. Crawling back to the corner where he had snipped the loose thread, he was appalled to find another loose thread trailing hundreds of feet behind him.

"Flipping heck," said Groanin, and he snipped the thread a second time. This time he stayed put to make sure that his scissor surgery had been effective and, after several vigilant minutes, he was just about to relax when several hundred feet of thread seemed to unravel at once.

Groanin yelped and snipped at the thread. But the same thing happened again, and again, and before long Groanin's scissors were snipping so much he felt like a demon barber in a gentleman's hairdressers.

It was now uncomfortably clear to Groanin that after cutting the carpet on the mountaintop in Morocco, he had neglected to finish the edge of the carpet.

It was true, Groanin ought to have knotted one of the threads although he could hardly have known which one: There seemed to be thousands of them, although, in fact, there was really only one thread.

By now the whole frayed edge of the flying carpet — previously eight feet wide, but now perhaps just seven and a half — was trailing threads. They were flying somewhere over the United States but Groanin was close to panic. A hard landing on the ground from several thousand feet promised to be just as uncomfortable as a hard landing in the ocean.

"Blast that man, Nimrod," Groanin shouted. "Blast him and his daft ideas. He'll be the death of me, so he will."

He shook his head in the hope that the motion might dislodge an idea that was sticking to the back of his mind like a boiled sweet.

"Flipping carpet," he muttered. "I wish I knew what my dad would have done about this. I really do."

For a moment, he pictured his dad, laying a carpet at Groanin's childhood home in Burnley, and a Proustian smell of burning carpets filled the nostrils of his own remembrance of things past.

"Of course!" he exclaimed as suddenly he remembered

his father melting the fibers along the edge of the carpet with something hot. And straightaway he went to his luggage, found a lighter, and applied a flame along the tattered edge of the flying carpet.

There were two reasons why this was a very bad idea. One was that most of the carpets Groanin's dad had fitted had been very cheap and made of nylon, which means it's possible to melt a neat edge on a carpet. However, the flying carpet was not made of nylon, but silk, which is extremely flammable. Which was the other reason it was a bad idea for Groanin to apply a naked flame to the edge of the flying carpet.

For a moment it seemed to work. And then things turned from bad to worse as the carpet caught fire.

"Flipping heck," yelled Groanin. "That's all I flipping need. A flying carpet that's on fire."

He stared anxiously over the edge at the ground, with no idea where he was in relation to Yellowstone.

"If this isn't an emergency, I don't know what is," said Groanin. Thinking to use the discrimens given to him by Nimrod, he added, "I wish this flying carpet would now land safely."

Nothing happened. The flying carpet did not slow or even dip toward the ground. If anything, the carpet seemed to climb a little higher to avoid a rain cloud that lay immediately ahead.

Groanin was baffled for as long as it took for him to remember that he had carelessly wished away his one discrimens when he had wished to know what his dad would have done to the edge of the flying carpet to stop it from unraveling any farther.

He wondered which of the two problems now affecting his mode of airborne transport would precipitate him to the ground first: the fact that the carpet was still unraveling at the rate of about six inches an hour, or the fact that it was also on fire.

CHAPTER 19

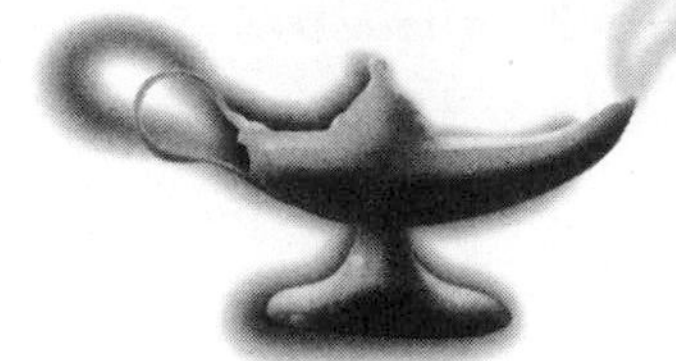

CHEESE AND BISCUITS

Bumby's luck had improved a little since John had persuaded Zagreus the Jinx to accompany him back to London. The local newspaper, the *Bumby Chronicle and Echo*, was even reporting that "green shoots of recovery" had been observed, which was a journalist's way of saying that people were feeling a little more optimistic about the town's fortunes. This newfound optimism was largely based on the recent success of the town's annual cheese-rolling festival, in which several hundred of the stupider inhabitants chased a ten-pound roll of Bumby Cheddar down the slope of a very steep hill. Normally, at least a dozen competitors were injured — mostly broken legs and concussions — and given the town's run of bad luck, the mayor, Mr. Higginbottom, had actually considered canceling this year's race out of fear that it might result in some more serious injuries or even a fatality.

Mr. Higginbottom's controversial decision to go ahead with the ancient race had been vindicated when, to everyone's amazement, the race had gone ahead without any injuries at all. Not even a sprained ankle.

"What a ghastly little town," observed Moo as she flicked through the newspaper with its stories of stolen tortoises, lost cats, dead badgers, and radioactive beaches. "And you say that Mr. Groanin comes here every year for a holiday?"

"Yes," said Philippa. "It's weird, isn't it?"

"Weird? I should say it is weird. The man needs his head examined."

"Groanin's always been a bit contrary," said Philippa. "But he has a good heart."

"Rag." Moo tossed the newspaper in a trash bin and followed Philippa into the small family beachfront hotel where they had decided to stay. Mrs. Lightbottom, the proprietor of the Stately Pleasure-dome Guesthouse, eyed Philippa's luggage, which included her rolled-up flying carpet, with unfriendly suspicion.

"What's with the blue carpet?" she said sharply. "Linoleum not good enough for you Americans, I suppose."

"It's my exercise mat," lied Philippa.

"Aye, well, I trust you'll keep the noise down," said Mrs. Lightbottom. "I wouldn't want your exercise disturbing the other guests."

"*Are* there any other guests?" inquired Moo.

"Of course there are other guests," said Mrs. Lightbottom, coloring a little.

"You do surprise me," said Moo, staring out the door so that she wouldn't have to look at Mrs. Lightbottom's unwelcoming fat face. Every time she saw its tight mouth and supercilious eyebrow she wanted to slap the woman, hard, and shout at her, "You're a disgrace to British hotel keeping!"

"For your information," Mrs. Lightbottom said crisply, "there's an Indian gentleman in Room 11. Mr. Swaraswati."

"Now there's a name you don't hear every day," murmured Moo.

"Yes, it's interesting," agreed Philippa. "Mrs. Lightbottom? What does he look like, this Mr. Swaraswati?"

"What's it to you?"

Moo sighed. She'd had enough of this woman's obstreperous ways. She opened her bag and took out the identity card that identified her as the head of the British KGB. "Police," she said sharply. "Just answer the question."

Philippa and Mrs. Lightbottom noticed the large gun in Moo's handbag, and the handcuffs, and the blackjack, which is a kind of police baton; there was also a police radio, a smaller gun, a pepper spray, a large roll of banknotes, and a makeup bag.

"Police?" Mrs. Lightbottom paled and then curtsied. "I'm sorry, Your Ladyship," she said. "I don't want no trouble or nothing."

"Just answer the question, you silly woman," Moo said brusquely.

Philippa was beginning to think Moo would be a useful person to have along on this adventure. She was a formidable old lady.

"Well, he's an odd-looking sort and no mistake," said Mrs. Lightbottom. "Very pale and thin — painfully thin — like he hasn't eaten in a long time. All he'll eat now are a few dried biscuits. I never seen anything like it. No appetite at all. A waste I calls it, me being such a good cook 'n' all. All he wants is dried water biscuits, almost like his stomach couldn't handle much else."

"What else?" said Philippa.

"Let's see now. Well, he's old. Very old. Hard to say how old exactly but I wouldn't be surprised if you said he was a hundred. He wears a long gray beard. And a robe, like one of them foreign monks. And, well, I hope he'll forgive me for saying so, but he's just a bit dirty, like he doesn't wash very much. And dusty, like he's been lying on the ground."

"Or in it, perhaps," said Philippa. "As if he'd been buried alive for a long time."

"You're right, Philippa," said Moo. "That could be our fakir. The one with the great secret that those fake fakirs are looking for."

"He goes out every day like he's looking for someone and just wanders around the town. A few years ago, he'd have stuck out like a sore thumb, but not these days. There are all sorts like him in Bumby these days. A regular Khyber Pass 'round here, so it is."

"That's probably why he hasn't been spotted yet," said Moo.

"Does he have any friends?" asked Philippa. She was thinking of the fakir's *dasa*, the servant who was supposed to guard the secret of the fakir's burial place and be there to serve him now that he had returned after many centuries of being buried alive.

"None that I've seen. He keeps himself to himself. He's always asking if anyone has left a message for him. But they never have. Not ever. Not so far."

"Who's paying his bill?" Moo asked suspiciously.

"He is."

"With what?"

Mrs. Lightbottom looked guilty.

"Come on, come on." Moo snapped her fingers. "We haven't got all day."

"Now look," said Mrs. Lightbottom. "I was going to give him any money that was left over, you understand."

"Left over from what?" asked Moo.

Mrs. Lightbottom opened a drawer in the reception desk and took out a cash box, which she unlocked with a little key that was hanging around her fat neck.

"This," she said, and handed Moo a gold medallion. "It was hanging around Mr. Swaraswati's neck when he came in and I said I'd hold on to it by way of a deposit against the final bill." Mrs. Lightbottom started to wring her hands. "You're not going to arrest me, are you?"

"Do shut up," said Moo. "No, I'm not going to arrest you. Not so long as you continue to help us with our inquiries."

Moo showed Philippa the gold medallion. On one side there was a swastika and on the other a goose.

"Nazi gold, is that?" Mrs. Lightbottom asked lightly.

Moo frowned at her. "What?"

"The swastika, I mean," said Mrs. Lightbottom.

Moo shook her head. "The swastika is an ancient Hindu good luck or religious symbol," she said. "Very ancient. The earliest recorded example is some three thousand years old."

"Is that so?" said Mrs. Lightbottom. "I didn't think he looked like a Nazi. Not with those sandals."

"It's him," Philippa told Moo. "It has to be him."

"I agree," said Moo. "Is he in his room now?"

Mrs. Lightbottom looked at the key rack behind her head. There were only three keys missing: the two she had given Philippa and Moo, and one other, which was the key to Room 11.

"Yes," she said.

Moo unfolded a sheet of printed paper and laid it on the reception desk. "Sign this," she said.

"What is it?"

"It's the Official Secrets Act. Basically, it means you'll be sent to prison if you tell anyone about the man in Room 11, or repeat the details of our conversation."

"And if I don't sign?"

"You'll be sent to prison immediately," said Moo.

Mrs. Lightbottom snatched up a pen, quickly signed the Official Secrets Act, and then curtsied again as Moo folded up the piece of paper and placed it carefully in her handbag.

"You mentioned a great secret," said Mrs. Lightbottom. "Is this Mr. Swaraswati dangerous?"

"I can't tell you how dangerous," said Moo. "What he knows could affect the safety not just of the country, but of the whole world."

Hearing this, Mrs. Lightbottom felt a little faint and sat down heavily.

Moo and Philippa went upstairs and along a cold corridor to Room 11.

"You know it's just possible he really is dangerous," Moo whispered.

"I was thinking the same thing," confessed Philippa. "At the very least he's likely to be a bit cranky. After all, you're buried alive for centuries you expect a bit of TLC when you surface again."

Moo took out her gun and checked that it was loaded.

But Philippa shook her head. "You won't need a gun," she said. "Really. I know what I'm doing. So, take it easy with that thing."

To her own surprise, Philippa realized that she really did know what she was doing. For the first time in her young djinn life she felt entirely equal to the situation that now presented itself. And she supposed that this was all down to what Nimrod would have called "experience." The kind of experience that told her it might just be a good idea to enter the room invisibly.

"Come on," she said, walking farther along the corridor and opening the door to her own room. "I think we'd best do this the subtle way."

Philippa lay down on her bed.

"This is no time to lie down on the job," said Moo.

"I'm going to slip out of my body for a few minutes," Philippa explained. "So that I can take a look in his room without any risk."

"The softly, softly approach," said Moo. "I understand. Good idea."

"You won't notice anything until I come back," Philippa added. "Except that I'll appear like I'm in a trance or something. So don't worry. I'm not dead. Okay?"

Moo nodded. "Understood." She sat down on a chair and slipped off her shoes to await Philippa's return.

Philippa floated invisibly out of her room and back along the corridor. Outside Room 11, she paused for a moment and looked more closely at the door. Over a period of time she'd noticed that some materials were harder to penetrate as spirit than others, with steel being the hardest. It was easier slipping through solids when you knew exactly what they were made of. This door was made of wood, which was relatively easy to walk through. That is, as long as you were spirit. A transubstantiated state was a different thing altogether. It always struck Philippa as a strange paradox that a djinn could be trapped inside a lamp or a bottle merely because a djinn's transubstantiated, smokelike form was very different from a djinn's disembodied, spiritual state. As different as it was from a djinn's physical body.

She braced herself and stepped through the door.

The room was plain and cold and, in this respect at least, it seemed to reflect Mrs. Lightbottom's forbidding personality. The floor was covered in brown linoleum. On the wall was a picture of a Chinese girl wearing a brown dress with a golden collar that was the same as the one in Philippa's own room and in the corridor outside. The Chinese girl had a sad, green face as if she'd eaten something that had disagreed with her badly, and for this reason it seemed like a strange picture to hang on a wall of a hotel where, if the smell from the kitchen was anything to go by, the food was likely to be quite horrible. It seemed more than likely that Mr. Swaraswati might have agreed with this: On the bed-side table was a large plate of water biscuits and a glass of water.

On the bed lay what looked to Philippa like the dead body of a very old man. He appeared to be a thinner, dirtier, more ancient version of Mr. Burton, although such a thing seemed hardly possible. A strong smell of earth hung about the man, the result, Philippa concluded, of having been buried alive for many centuries. His eyes stared straight up at the featureless ceiling. And there was no discernible sign of movement from his chest or stomach to persuade her that the man was alive. It appeared that she was too late.

"Oh, no," said Philippa. "Please don't say he's dead."

The man lying on the bed blinked slowly.

"Not dead," he said. "Just resting."

"Sorry to disturb you," said Philippa. "I just popped in to see that you were all right."

"I'm very much, as you can see," said Mr. Swaraswati. "Perhaps a more interesting question is why can't I see you?"

"Please don't be alarmed, Mr. Swaraswati," said Philippa. "I mean you no harm."

"I can tell that from your voice," said Mr. Swaraswati.

"You're looking for your *dasa*, am I right?"

"Yes. And the *dasa* should be looking for me. Has something happened? Are you the *dasa*?"

"No, I'm a djinn, called Philippa," said Philippa. "But I am here to help you if I can."

Mr. Swaraswati smiled faintly. "Now there's a coincidence," he said. "That's what I'm here for. To help. Or so I thought."

"You've been tricked," said Philippa. "By some wicked mendicant fakirs. Somehow, they were able to identify the *dasa* who lives here and have been watching him in the hope that he might lead them to you and your secret. We think they brought about a radical change in the luck that exists in this little town in the hope that it would provoke you to raise yourself up from your buried state. We think that the *dasa* knows this and is reluctant to come and look for you for fear of giving you away."

"Who is 'we'?" asked Mr. Swaraswati.

"My uncle Nimrod is a djinn, too," said Philippa. "He asked me to come and find you and offer you some assistance."

"How do I know that you're not in league with these wicked mendicant fakirs that you mentioned?"

"You don't," said Philippa. "Not for sure. But I think you can trust me just as long as I don't try to find out your secret. The one given to you by the Tirthankar of Faizabad."

"Good point," said Mr. Swaraswati. "But still, it's a little hard to trust anyone who remains invisible."

"That's for sure," said Philippa. "Perhaps if I was to go and fetch my physical body? It's in the next room with my friend Moo."

"Is she a djinn, too?"

"No. She's human. Would you like to come and meet us?"

"Yes. Perhaps that would be best."

"We're in Room 13."

Mr. Swaraswati sat up and swung his thin legs off the bed. Then he stood and arched his back with difficulty. "I'm rather stiff," he said. "It comes from being buried alive."

"If you don't mind me asking," said Philippa, "how did you get out of your grave?"

"You've seen a mole," said Mr. Swaraswati.

"Yes."

"Well, it's the same sort of thing. You just burrow up through the earth. The hardest part is the end, when you have to force your arms and head through the surface."

"Kind of like a zombie," said Philippa.

"I don't know what that is," admitted Mr. Swaraswati. He hobbled to the door and opened it.

Philippa drifted out into the corridor ahead of him and through the door of her own room, where she found her body on the bed, in the same place that she had left it, and Moo asleep in an armchair. Philippa lay down in her body, stretched herself out into the toes and fingers, like someone putting on a rubber glove, and then let out a breath.

Moo yawned and looked up as she heard a knock at the door that Philippa was already opening.

Seeing Philippa, Mr. Swaraswati pressed the palms of his hands together, bowed, and said, "You are Philippa, perhaps?"

"Yes. Come in, Mr. Swaraswati."

"This is my friend, Lady Silvia Stone," said Philippa. "But who prefers to be known as Moo."

"How do you do?" said the old lady, extending a gloved hand toward Mr. Swaraswati.

"Not so very well, thank you," said Mr. Swaraswati.

Moo thought the old fakir looked a bit like Mahatma Gandhi.

"Many centuries of burial have left me with a variety of ailments," he said. "The soil in this country is very damp. Things might have been different if I had been buried somewhere in India. The ground there is very dry and much kinder to the human body. Nevertheless, it seems pointless to complain about it now. I am here and surely must make the best of it."

"I suffer from quite a few aches and pains myself," admitted Moo. "Perhaps I could find you some ointments and medicines that might ease your discomfort."

"That would be very kind of you."

Mr. Swaraswati looked quizzically at Philippa.

"I must say you don't look very much like a djinn, my child."

"I know," said Philippa. "Everyone expects a very tall man with a bald head, wild eyes, and baggy trousers."

"And a mustache," said Moo.

Philippa shrugged. "Sorry to disappoint," she said.

"Actually," said Mr. Swaraswati, "it's really most reassuring that you are not at all like that. I should find it hard to trust someone as devilish as you have described."

"I was thinking," said Philippa, "that perhaps the best way of helping you would be to grant you three wishes. That way you might know that we really are your friends."

"You can perform such miracles?" said Mr. Swaraswati.

"Of course," said Philippa. "I wouldn't be much of a djinn if I couldn't grant some wishes."

"Well," sighed the old fakir. "That would be terrific. I should be eternally grateful to you, Philippa." He hesitated. "How does the magic work?"

Philippa smiled. "Just make a wish," she said.

"Very well. Oh, dear, this is most embarrassing. And you'll think me an idiot. However, it's been such a long time that I've been in the ground — longer than I would ever have thought possible — that I've forgotten that which I was supposed to remember."

"You mean, your great secret?" said Moo. "The one entrusted to you by the Tirthankar of Faizabad?"

"Exactly so. I wish I could remember the great secret of the universe entrusted to me. Yes, that is what I wish, most earnestly."

"Easy," said Philippa, and spoke her focus word:

"FABULONGOSHOOMARVELISHLYWONDERPIPICAL!"

As soon as the last consonant had been uttered, the old fakir breathed a sigh of relief, smiled, and sat down on the floor. "Ah, now I remember, yes," he said. "Oh, that's much better. I can't tell you how relieved I feel to have remembered that. Ever since I came up from the ground it's been a source of constant worry to me." He wiped a tear from his eye. "I'm so very very grateful to you, Philippa."

"No problem," said Philippa.

As soon as Mr. Swaraswati had gathered his fragmented emotions together, he stood up and pressed Philippa's hands in his own, and bowed his head to her.

"Three wishes, you say?"

Philippa nodded.

"You'll think me such an old fool," said Mr. Swaraswati. "What good is a man who forgets that which he is supposed to remember?"

"I'm always forgetting things," confessed Moo. "And I am not nearly as old as you."

"It's kind of you to say so, dear lady. Very well. My second wish is to remember the name of my *dasa*. For I confess that I have forgotten that, too. And I can hardly go and find a man whose name I can't remember."

Philippa spoke her focus word a second time — "FABULONGOSHOOMARVELISHLYWONDERPIPICAL!" — and, once again, Mr. Swaraswati smiled happily as, suddenly, he remembered what he had forgotten.

"Rejoice, rejoice," said Mr. Swaraswati. "Blessings be upon you, child. I have remembered it. Now, if I can just find out where he is. That is my third wish. I wish that I knew where to find my *dasa*."

"The wish is made," said Philippa, although in truth she had little idea how to make this so with djinn power. But it's not every wish that needs a djinn to come true, and Philippa sensed that Moo was probably best placed to do this for Mr. Swaraswati.

Moo was already opening a small computer and switching it on.

"Perhaps if you were to tell us his or her name," said Moo.

"Yes, it's Shoebottom," said Mr. Swaraswati.

Philippa smiled. "I don't know why it is that everyone in this town has a name that ends in 'bottom.'"

"Perhaps because a bottom lies at the end of everything," said Moo, and quickly typed SHOEBOTTOM onto her laptop keyboard.

Mr. Swaraswati frowned and then tapped his head with the flat of his hand. "The wish has not worked, I think. I still do not know where to find him."

"Patience," said Moo. "Some wishes take longer to come true than others."

"Truly?" Mr. Swaraswati looked at Philippa.

"Truly."

"Here we are," said Moo, pointing at the screen. "At the last census there was only one Shoebottom living in Bumby. Born here, too. As were all her ancestors. Interesting."

Philippa glanced over Moo's shoulder at the laptop screen.

"Sheryl Shoebottom, 74 Muckhole Terrace, Bumby, West Yorkshire."

"That is where the *dasa* lives?" Mr. Swaraswati looked amazed. "The shiny little tablet tells you this?"

"Yes," said Moo.

"Now that really is miraculous," said Mr. Swaraswati. "Where is this Muckhole Terrace?"

Moo was already accessing a website that showed a UK government satellite picture of the house where Sheryl Shoebottom lived, and directions on how to get there from the Stately Pleasure-dome Guesthouse.

"You're looking at it," said Moo.

Mr. Swaraswati continued to look and sounded amazed.

"That's interesting," said Moo. "Three weeks ago, Sheryl Shoebottom made a complaint to the local police that she was being watched by some strange-looking men. According to this the complaint was withdrawn before it could be investigated."

"Three weeks," said Mr. Swaraswati. "That's how long it's been since I came up from underground."

"You know, it might not be safe for you to make contact with her, Mr. Swaraswati," said Moo. "Not yet. It might be better if Philippa and I were to contact her first."

"Good idea," said Philippa. "You can stay in our room, too. Nobody will think of looking for you here. Not only that, but I can attach a special djinn binding to this room, to protect you from harm."

"Thank you," said Mr. Swaraswati. "You have both been most helpful."

"We'll tell Miss Shoebottom that you're safe," said Moo. "And take a message from her to you. And from you to her."

"Please tell her that I am the expected one," said Mr. Swaraswati. "It is a phrase she will be, er . . . expecting anyone who knows me to use. Tell her I am quite safe and that I hope to see her soon."

"And after that we should go and see my uncle Nimrod," said Philippa. "He'll know what to do next. He usually does."

CHAPTER 20

THE NAVEL OF THE WORLD

The capital of Israel, Jerusalem is an ancient city where religion seems not to unite men in the worship of God but to divide them in the service of several competing religions, each of which regards itself as the one true faith, and where tiny differences of what people honestly believe to be true apparently count for a lot more than their many common points of similarity. Historically speaking, it has always been a good place for an argument, and even today it is an excellent place to visit and then leave.

Nimrod always felt uncomfortable in Jerusalem. Even at the city's most famous hotel, the luxurious King David, he felt uncomfortable, if only for the reason that the hotel had once been blown up by terrorists. He felt no less uncomfortable walking into the honey-colored Old City with Mr. Burton, who hardly looked unusual in Jerusalem, where there are so many who dress in strange-looking clothes; ragged, half-naked pilgrims, not unlike Mr. Burton, have been turning up in Jerusalem since the fourth century A.D. It wasn't the oddly attired Mr. Burton who made Nimrod feel uncomfortable, however, so much as the fact that in the Old City everyone looks at you with suspicion, as if trying to decide whose side you are on in this seemingly eternal neighbors' dispute.

In some respects, the Old City of Jerusalem is not unlike Fez. There are many winding streets, and dark alleys that are full of Arab traders, although perhaps Jerusalem, being on a hilltop, is not as flat as Fez. And, of course, the city is full of tourists buying carpets, or water pipes, or drinking arak, or visiting the many holy places.

In the center of the Old City is the Church of the Holy Sepulchre, which is controlled by several different Christian churches in a complicated and sometimes fractious arrangement — the Greek monks have sometimes brawled with the Armenian monks — that has remained in place for centuries. The church is significant for its antiquity, and the visitors who flock there in the tens of thousands have always seemed to greatly appreciate its convenience as the place where Christ was imprisoned and crucified, and also the place where he was anointed and buried — four for the price of one, which counts as great value in an increasingly expensive world.

Entering the cool, dark, echoing interior of the church with its high ceilings and marble floors, Nimrod and Mr. Burton walked quickly away from the many tourists, some of whom were busy thrusting their arms into the brassbound holes of the crosses on Calvary, and found a quiet place to sit and give the appearance of being deep in prayer.

"Mr. Rakshasas used to kneel here," explained Mr. Burton, "and I knelt beside him. He would take his spirit off into the omphalos and I would remain here to keep an eye on his physical body. Once I caught a man trying to pick his pocket. Can you believe it? In a church, of all places." Mr. Burton looked around and nodded. "He loved coming here. There were many questions that were answered for him in this church. Once, when he returned from the omphalos, I was so impressed by the expression of peace and enlightenment on his face that I felt able to ask him a question that had been troubling me."

"Which was?" asked Nimrod.

"The meaning of life," said Mr. Burton. "I asked him what it was."

"And what did he say?"

"He said that there is no one meaning that suits everyone. He said that there are as many answers to that question as there are people in the world, because it's a different answer for everyone. But that once you recognize that fact, then all questions are answered. At the time I didn't really understand his answer. But I think I do now."

Nimrod nodded. "Exactly where is the omphalos?" Nimrod asked the fakir.

"On the east side, opposite the rotunda," said Mr. Burton. "On the floor across from the main altar of the church — what the Greek Orthodox folk call the catholicon, I think. You can't miss the thing. It looks like a large pie with a thick crust from a very good bakery. Or perhaps a garden urn. The Delphi omphalos looks very different. That one's rather more like a shell from the First World War. And completely useless for the purpose of communicating with — well, whatever it is you communicate with. The universe, I suppose."

Nimrod took a deep breath. "Wish me luck," he said, and bowed his head.

"Good luck," said Mr. Burton.

Nimrod had liftoff almost immediately. At his age he'd had so many out-of-body experiences that it was like second nature to the djinn. He floated across the red, white, and black marble floor to the high altar like a ghost. There, in front of a large, round brass table covered with a hundred lit candles, was the omphalos. Mr. Burton had been right. It was quite unmistakable to look at and did indeed look like a garden urn, albeit one with no room for earth or flowers for there was a convex surface in the urn, with a hole in it.

Nimrod slipped invisibly through the hole into the interior of the omphalos, which, like a djinn lamp, was much, much larger than could have been supposed from the exterior, and he floated around for a while, trying to get his bearings. Finally, he sat down, cross-legged — or as near to cross-legged as Nimród was able, given that he had no actual legs — and tried to give himself up to the ancient forces that once had dwelt there.

It was a solitary feeling being in the omphalos. Time and space had no meaning. After a while — he had no idea how long — Nimrod felt as if he was in the presence of great age and his own terrible insignificance.

"How small I am," he whispered. "And how little I know."

This feeling of great insignificance and ignorance was swiftly succeeded by the insight that he was in the actual omphalos from Delphi, and that the omphalos stone had been taken from Greece to Jerusalem by the Emperor Theodosius I in the fourth century A.D. How he knew this he had no idea, but he knew it to be true in the same way he knew his own address.

At the same time he seemed to hear some of the oracular statements that had once been forthcoming from the priestess at Delphi who, legend had it, would breathe the air of the omphalos — and very likely something stronger — before making her keenly attended statements:

Make your own nature, not the advice of others, your guide in life.

Love of money and nothing else will ruin Sparta.

Know thyself and to thine own self be true.

Nothing in excess and nothing excessively.

Sure, 'tis better to be a live dog than a dead lion.

Drink is the curse of the land. It makes you fight with your neighbor. It makes you shoot an arrow at your landlord and it makes you miss him, too.

Nimrod smiled to himself as he almost seemed to hear the Irish voice of Mr. Rakshasas in some of these words. Was it possible that some of his proverbial wisdom had been inspired by the time the old djinn had spent in the omphalos?

An intoxicating smell like incense filled the dank air of the omphalos and, not having any nostrils to smell it, Nimrod wondered how he did. And yet it was there and getting stronger until he perceived it wasn't a smell at all but some powerful force — older than antiquity itself — that seemed intent on becoming mixed in with Nimrod's own spirit. Instinctively, Nimrod felt himself pull away and, for a moment, the force fragmented like a broken window and a hundred ancient voices suddenly crowded in sharply upon his thoughts, as if in recrimination for his desire to be a thing apart.

"See not what *you* see and hear not what *you* hear," he seemed to tell himself, but when he tried to give himself up to the voices, he experienced a brief moment of panic as his mind struggled to accommodate all of these whispered sounds, and he cried out as the clamor of what he heard was too much for him.

And almost immediately, he realized that hearing wasn't required so much as feeling and, relaxing a little, he gave himself up to it and soon enough, their separate voices and his became one clear thought. It was as if his mind had suddenly expanded tenfold and he experienced insights into existence and the universe he had never even suspected were possible. Most of these insights could never have been put into words, for they were beyond articulation, which is sometimes the way with revelation. But gradually, one omniscient voice seemed to make itself plain. Nimrod could not have put a name to the voice that seemed like his own and yet was not; nor did the voice identify itself, but Nimrod was quite certain that the voice he heard inside his head was nothing less than Wisdom itself. And yet it was Wisdom with a definite love of the obscure:

"When a man shall become a mule, you will begin to have found what you are looking for," said the voice.

"I don't understand," said Nimrod. "Speak again."

"The way to the stars is not signposted, nevertheless it does exist. If you don't know the way, then walk slowly, in thin air, and you will find it between a rock and a hard place."

"You speak in riddles," said Nimrod.

"Of course. It's up to you to find the meaning."

"Really," said Nimrod, "this is most frustrating."

"A man may die of frustration, perhaps, but he'll never die of wisdom. The beginning of wisdom is the fear of God."

"Nevertheless, I would ask you to speak again," said Nimrod. "My mission is an important one. And not for myself, but for all mankind."

"I count the grains of sand on the beach and measure the sea; I understand the speech of the dumb and hear the voiceless. So, believe me, I know what your mission is."

"Well then," said Nimrod.

"Sharpen the claws on your feet and the one in your hand," said the voice. "Take hold of the field and don't let go. Stand on a shelf and reach for the sky. Hang yourself from a face and rejoice at every hammer blow for you will still be alive."

Nimrod sighed. "I was hoping for something a little more obvious."

"Look, you have to guess or I can't help."

"Very well," sighed Nimrod.

"You must climb over the bodies of those who went before," said the voice. "Those whom a winter blanket now covers and whose faces are hardened to you forever."

"Yes. Go on. I think I'm getting warmer now."

"There are several routes you can choose," said the voice. "They all reach the same place, but not all of them will get you to where you most want to go. When it becomes impossible to breathe then you will have succeeded where others failed."

Nimrod groaned. "Yes, all right, I get it now," he said. "You're talking about a mountaineering expedition, aren't you?"

The voice tutted loudly. "Yes, of course, I thought you'd never get it. Duh!"

"Sorry."

"All right. Let me unpack some of what I'm talking about here."

"I wish you would," said Nimrod.

"You wish to bring about the impossible: suddenly to make a great many people feel that the world is a better, happier place than it was before and that they themselves can actively share in the world's new good fortune."

"Yes. That's it exactly. Now we're getting somewhere."

"To do this is no small thing because you can't build a barrel around a bunghole," said the voice. "Nevertheless, you must do something very like it and make people believe that there is much more than there is. So look for that which is impossible or that which cannot be found."

"I thought this was you being a little less obscure," observed Nimrod. "We seem to be losing sight of clarity again."

"*Such as*," said the voice, raising its voice, "the cure for a disease, the white whale, the Holy Grail, El Dorado, the fountain of youth. Something like that. Or perhaps some utopia, a perfect paradise that exists hidden from man. My opinion is that this is the best thing to look for. Shangri-la. Hence all the mountaineering references."

"Shangri-la? That old fairy story about a secret earthly paradise in Tibet?"

"Is it? A fairy story?"

"I always thought so," admitted Nimrod. "Either that or something dreamed up by people suffering from oxygen deprivation."

"Maybe you're wrong. But you won't know unless you look, will you?"

Nimrod sighed. "Gosh, that's quite an undertaking. Finding Shangri-la. But you really think that might do the trick?"

"Yes. For while it's true that all men must die, be sure it takes much more than a lifetime to get used to the idea. Remember, the seeking of one thing will find another."

"The seeking of one thing will find another what?"

"That is my advice. I have spoken. Good-bye."

Nimrod shook his head, or at least he did something as close to shaking his head as he was able given that he had no head. "What a cryptic fellow," he muttered.

"I'm an oracle," said the voice. "Not a stupid fortune cookie. None of this is supposed to be obvious."

"It isn't," said Nimrod. "Really, it isn't obvious at all."

CHAPTER 21

A MEMORABLE BIRTHDAY

Sitting on top of the box of stores now occupying the last three or four square feet of the flying carpet that continued to smolder underneath him like a dying barbecue, Groanin prayed that he and it would stay aloft long enough to avoid a landing in the snow-covered tops of the trees that seemed uncomfortably close and pointed. Beyond the tall trees lay open fields of snow, which, he hoped, would be deep and soft enough to break his fall and not his neck. A thin plume of smoke drifted for miles behind him so that he felt he must have resembled a stricken airplane, or perhaps a meteor.

Groanin was reasonably sure he was over Yellowstone because a little earlier on, he'd seen an immense volume of water projected into the air to a height of more than a hundred feet for almost three minutes. He thought that this might be Old Faithful, which is the park's largest geyser. The water was hot, too — hot enough for the steam to warm his face — because, as Nimrod had said back in Morocco,

Yellowstone is an active volcanic area and the geyser effect is the result of surface water coming into contact with hot, melted rock called magma.

Suddenly, the flying carpet stuttered a little and dropped several feet, narrowly missing the top of an immense lodgepole pine.

"Flipping heck," yelled Groanin as the remnants of the flying carpet steered its way between the remaining treetops like a car on a fairground ride that had left the fairground far behind. After a couple of near misses with tree trunks and boughs, Groanin and the box of stores emerged safely beyond the tree line into the wide snowfield. The carpet, what was left of it, incapable of supporting its load anymore, dipped precipitously, and then died. Groanin and the stores flew on for several seconds before the realization that he was no longer flying but falling drew a loud yell from the frightened butler's lungs that lasted for as long as it took gravity to bring him back down to earth.

For a while, Groanin lay winded in a snowdrift that was several feet deep and that had certainly saved his life. And hardly moving, he contemplated a life that, as an English butler, ought to have been, he thought, a little less packed with incident. But at last he stirred, picked snow out of his ears, nostrils, and mouth, and forced his way to the surface.

The snowfield was covered with bright sunlight but the air was cold and still, and Groanin's angry, hot breath already erupted from his mouth like a mini-geyser. It was lucky he was wearing a thick fur coat because the temperature was well below freezing.

"I never signed on for any of this," he moaned. "I say, I never signed on for any of this malarkey. And when I get back to London — if ever I get back to London — I am going to give His Lordship a piece of my mind. No, I'll do more than that. I'll tell him I quit. That's what I'll do. I'll hand in me notice. He can stuff this job. Djinn or not."

He looked around for the box of stores and saw that it had broken on impact with something harder than his own place of landing; and most of the stores were spread out over a distance of several hundred yards. Slowly, for the snow was very deep, he walked and sometimes crawled after his supplies. Fortunately for him, almost the first thing he found was a pair of snowshoes and as soon as he had put them on, he found it a little easier to travel across the snow and retrieve the remainder of his stores: a backpack containing food and fire-making materials, a one-man tent, a good sleeping bag, a pair of thick fur mittens, a fur hat, a compass, a rifle with spare ammunition, a pair of snow goggles, and — what he thought was probably Nimrod's idea of a joke — a snorkel and a pair of flippers.

"Very amusing, I'm sure," said Groanin. "I'll show him where he can stick this snorkel when I see him again." He shook his head. "Idiot even left the price tag on." And he threw the snorkel and the flippers into the snow.

As soon as he was properly attired for cold weather — as Nimrod had said, he looked like something out of a novel by Jack London — Groanin searched his pocket for his cell phone. But switching it on, he found there was no signal and, cursing Nimrod for not adding a satellite phone to his stores,

Groanin thrust the cell phone back in his coat pocket and looked around, wondering which direction to go in. He decided his best hope was to find some sort of park guide who could direct him to a main road where he might hitch a lift to the nearest town.

Now that the flying carpet was no more, the idea of finding John in an area covering several thousand square miles seemed too remote a possibility. And it was only when he heard the howl of some wolves in the distance that he remembered exactly what Nimrod had told him: One rug could be directed to follow the other, much as a bloodhound could be encouraged to follow a scent.

John had come in pursuit of Mr. Rakshasas in his new incarnation as a Yellowstone timber wolf. Was it possible, Groanin asked himself, that the flying carpet had brought him nearer John than he might have supposed?

Encouraged by this idea, Groanin cupped his mouth with his hands and shouted John's name several times. And then comforted by the fact that he had a loaded rifle and could shoot anything that tried to eat him, he started to walk toward the sound of the howling wolves in the hope that one of them might be Mr. Rakshasas, and that John might be somewhere nearby.

Even in the snowshoes it was hard work walking across the snowfield, and after a couple of hours he had reached some trees where, with the sun already beginning to set, he decided to make camp for the night.

Groanin had little experience of camping beyond the kind of luxury, five-star camping practiced by his master, and he knew nothing about bear safety while camping. He had wolves on his mind and had quite forgotten that Yellowstone Park also has some of the largest grizzly bears in the world. If Groanin had remembered this, he might have taken a few elementary precautions such as cooking his food downwind of his tent, burning his garbage, and suspending his stores — even his toothpaste — from a tree. Bears have a very keen sense of smell, not to mention a keen and omnivorous appetite. Groanin took none of these precautions — but then he wasn't Jack London, but an English butler camping in the wilderness. And having made himself a pot of tea, he set about frying some pork sausages over the campfire in front of his tent, quite unaware that smelly, greasy food — which was, of course, the kind of food Groanin liked best of all — should always be avoided in bear country. If he had stuck to the jars of baby food Nimrod had also put in the butler's stores, it is certain he would not have encountered any problems. Worst of all, Groanin, whose eyes were always larger than his stomach, fried far too many sausages and was obliged to throw several away, thinking that some hungry birds would probably be grateful for them. In short, Groanin made every mistake that it was possible to make, including the mistake of not washing his frying pan after using it. Short of sending a bear a gold-edged and heavily embossed invitation to a picnic, there wasn't much else he could have done to ensure that he would have an unwelcome nocturnal visitor.

Not long after he had finished dinner, it started to snow heavily.

"That's all I flipping need," he muttered. "As if things weren't miserable enough out here. I hope that lad had the good sense to equip himself properly for this trip. Because there's fat chance of his djinn power working in these temperatures."

Groanin went inside his tent and, still wearing his coat for it was fearfully cold, he climbed inside his sleeping bag. Turning the lamp up, he tried to read a bit of *David Copperfield* before going to sleep. Or to be more exact, he tried to read a bit of *David Copperfield* so that it might send him to sleep. Some people take sleeping pills. Some people have hot cocoa. Some people count sheep. Groanin always read *David Copperfield*. He had been using this book as a sleep-inducing technique for many years and it had always worked, with the result that he had read no further than chapter nine, in which David has a memorable birthday. Reading this might have prompted Groanin to remember that it was in fact his own birthday and if, in the minutes after his crash, he had searched the bottom of the store box a little more thoroughly, he would have found the birthday cake and card that Nimrod had thoughtfully provided for his journey. The snorkel and the flippers he had tossed angrily away had been Nimrod's birthday present to his butler and the price tag had in fact been a birthday tag.

Despite the absence of cake and card and a present, however, Groanin was about to have a very memorable birthday of his own.

David Copperfield fell out of his fingers about halfway down the second page of chapter nine, and sleepily Groanin yawned and reached up to turn down the light. He was just drifting nicely off to sleep when he heard a short and muffled growl outside the tent.

The butler's eyes opened wide, and very slowly, he reached for the rifle, which was just visible in the dimly lit tent.

Slowly, he sat up and, cradling the rifle on his lap, listened carefully. Something was moving about in the snow outside his tent. Something large. Groanin swallowed loudly and tried to keep calm, even when something tore at the bottom of his tent.

"Flipping heck," he whispered. "Must be a bear."

Groanin worked the bolt-action rifle and prepared to fire even as a long, hairy, very muscular, *apelike* arm came under the bottom of the tent and an almost *human-looking* hand started to feel around the groundsheet that covered the floor. Groanin knew nothing about bears except that they were dangerous, but even he could see that this was no bear, but something rather more horribly mysterious and perhaps rare.

"Flipping heck," he remarked. "Must be a bigfoot."

But the rarity and mystery of bigfoot were lost on the terrified Groanin and, raising the rifle to his shoulder, he pointed the barrel at the wall of the tent and pulled the trigger.

Nothing happened. Nothing happened for the simple reason that Groanin had forgotten to release the safety catch on his rifle. This was just as well for the creature — whatever it was — that had thrust its importunate arm into Groanin's tent, but it left the butler in a state of near panic as he squeezed the trigger once again and, once again, the rifle refused to fire.

Bellowing loudly with fear, Groanin scrambled out of his tent and started to run away from the tent, which was enough to scare the shy humanoid creature away. In the full moonlight, the butler caught a glimpse of something tall and shaggy and vaguely apelike running into the darkness. Then, recognizing that he had scared the bigfoot away — by now he had little doubt that this was what he had seen — he walked back to camp, his heart still beating like the sound of feet on a fast treadmill.

"Flipping heck," he breathed. "That was frightening. I say, that was frightening." Full of bravado now that he had scared the bigfoot away, Groanin yelled after it:

"Now I know why it's called Yellowstone Park," he cried. "Because them as are daft enough to live in it are yellow themselves. I say, them as are daft enough to live in it are yellow themselves."

Chuckling nervously, Groanin was about to reenter his tent when he saw an enormous human footprint in the snow. A bare footprint about fifteen or sixteen inches long.

"Blimey," he said. "That's a big foot, all right."

Inside his tent, he climbed back into his sleeping bag and, wide awake with jangled nerves, he returned to chapter nine of *David Copperfield*. This time he managed to read as far as chapter twelve, in which David forms a great resolution, before he felt his eyelids droop.

"Can't beat a bit of *David Copperfield* at settling you down for the night," he said to himself and was reaching for the light when once more he heard a muffled growl. Thinking that the bigfoot had come back, Groanin cursed its nerve and crawled outside, intent on scaring the creature off again. As soon as he was outside he waved the lamp in the air and yelled loudly, expecting to see the apelike creature legging it into the trees. Instead, he found himself face-to-face with an enormous grizzly bear. Bears do not care to be yelled at, especially when they are licking a frying pan clean of sausage fat. Moreover, it's rare that a grizzly bear gives way to anything except perhaps an Abrams tank, or another grizzly. It's certain there's no record of one ever having given way to an English butler in a fur coat.

The bear reared up on its hind legs to a height of nine or ten feet and roared a terrible roar that lasted ten or fifteen seconds. Even before it ended, Groanin was already running for his life, which, as most bear experts will tell you, is as bad an idea as yelling at one, since bears are capable of running faster than most humans and certainly faster than a portly English butler.

The grizzly finished licking the frying pan and then gave enthusiastic chase.

CHAPTER 22

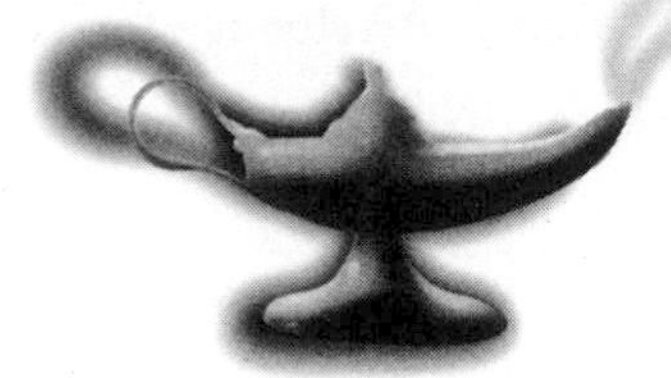

WHAT HAPPENED TO JOHN AND ZAGREUS

You could be forgiven for thinking that finding just one timber wolf among all the wolves that live in Yellowstone National Park would be impossible. In fact, there are just one hundred and twenty-four wolves living in Yellowstone, as John was to discover when he wished that he might have several books on the subject to read aboard the flying carpet en route from Morocco. Having also wished to have the power of speed-reading — something Philippa had told him about but that he had never before seen the point of, since he really didn't like to read at all — John quickly read all there was to know about wolves and their habits. And by the time John and Zagreus arrived in Yellowstone, the boy was already something of an expert on all things lupine, which is to say he knew a lot about wolves and their behavior. He had also applied a great deal of djinn power to put some of this new knowledge into practice.

First of all, John had wished with all his power to see and hear again the image of the howling wolf he had glimpsed in Mr. Burton's ink spot, only this time he wished that he might see a larger and more detailed version of the ink spot image that was lodged only very opaquely in his memory, so that he might study it minutely.

As a result, John was able to pinpoint some distinctive geographical features of that part of the park where Mr. Rakshasas and his wolf pack were living. He already knew where the twelve wolf packs in Yellowstone were located. After that, it was simply a matter of matching these twelve locations against the geographical features in the clearer image he now carried in his memory. In this way, he was able to steer his carpet to a spot within only a few hundred yards from where the pack to which Mr. Rakshasas belonged was now living.

As soon as John landed, he quickly set up camp with the stores he had made in the minutes before djinn power finally deserted him in the cold. For this same reason, John's camp included an Indian sweat lodge.

"We're on our own now," he announced as he made supper for himself and the Jinx.

"How do you mean?" asked Zagreus.

"I mean that djinn power doesn't work in the cold. Well, not for me, anyway. I'm a young djinn, see? And it takes a while for the power that's inside of me to mature and get really warmed up. Djinn are made of fire, so the colder I get the less power I have. That's why I built the sweat lodge. In case I need to get hot in a hurry."

"What about the flying carpet?"

"That's just a carpet, not something living," said John. "As far as I know, the carpet works no matter how cold things get."

Zagreus shrugged. "It's not that cold."

"Well, I think it is."

"But either way, we can leave whenever we want?" said Zagreus.

"Yes." John sneered at the Jinx. "Don't worry. We're only going to stay as long as it takes for me to find Mr. Rakshasas. It's getting dark now. So I guess we'll look for him first thing in the morning. He'll tell me the best way to deal with what Mr. Burton showed me in his ink spot. As soon as I've spoken to him we'll be out of here, I promise." John grinned humorlessly. "Man, you must hate this place."

"On the contrary," said Zagreus. "You know, it's weird, but I feel kind of at home here. This place is really, really beautiful."

"You surprise me."

"*You're* surprised. Think how I feel." Zagreus looked at himself. "And another thing. I don't know if you've noticed this. But my hair seems to be getting longer and darker."

"Hey, you're right," said John. "It is. Not only that. But you're getting bigger."

"Maybe," said Zagreus.

"There's no maybe about it. Look at the size of your feet."

Zagreus looked at his own feet and nodded. There was no getting away from the fact that John was right. His feet seemed huge. "Oh, wow, you're right," he said. "I didn't notice."

"Well, you don't, do you?" said John. "I dunno, but it seems to me that every time my mom takes me to buy a pair of shoes my feet are a size bigger. And I realize I've never noticed it before. Your feet seem to have doubled in size."

"You don't suppose that I'm no longer a Jinx," said Zagreus. "That I've started to make the complete transition from being a Greek man to being an ape?"

"That's not such a big transition," observed John. "I've been on a beach in Greece. Some guys there were so hairy they already looked like apes."

"Very funny."

"I don't know about a transition," sad John. "After all, you can still talk and I don't know how many apes can speak English. Or Greek."

"True," said Zagreus. "Nevertheless, it all seems to have happened since we arrived here in Yellowstone."

"True," said John. "Here, have some coffee."

When supper was over they went to bed.

Zagreus slept hardly at all. For one thing he felt stifled inside the tent, and for another he dreamed a very vivid dream. But when early the next morning they emptied out of the tent, it was plain that Zagreus had kept on growing throughout the night.

"Holy smoke, look at you," said John.

"What do you mean?" asked Zagreus.

"Well, look at you, dude."

"I'm darker, yes. And my feet are bigger. So what?"

"Not just your feet, dummy. Stand up."

Zagreus stood up and it was plain to see that he was now six or seven feet tall, with a shaggy brown coat of hair, like Highland cattle, and long, immensely strong arms.

"Also, the top of your head has gone all pointy and crested," said John. "Like the crest of a male gorilla."

"Wow, you're right. I'm huge. I was dreaming I was getting bigger all night and now I am." He frowned. "Hey, do you think I'm a gorilla?"

"Not a gorilla," John said. "You're too big." Then he smacked his fist into the palm of his hand. "Of course," he said. "It's the only possible explanation."

"What?" asked Zagreus.

"You're not an ape at all," said John. "At least, not an ape that zoology would recognize. Which is to say you're not an ape like a gorilla, or a chimpanzee, or an orangutan, or for that matter a man. You're an unknown species, most probably an ape-man."

"You mean like Tarzan."

"No. He lived in Africa. My best guess? You're new incarnation is to be a bigfoot. A Sasquatch. Like a yeti. Only a yeti is something different. I've met a yeti and that turned out to be a German pretending to be a yeti to scare off tourists in the Himalayas. So there's no such thing. Quite a few people were of the opinion that the Sasquatch was also a hoax. However, that would appear not to be the case, since, without question, you, my friend, are very definitely a Sasquatch.

Probably, it was coming here that triggered your full transition."

"You mean you think I'm home?"

"Yup. I'd say so. Congratulations, buddy."

"So, let me get this straight," said Zagreus. "I'm this legendary creature, a Sasquatch, that everyone thinks is just a hoax."

John nodded. "Does that bother you?" he asked.

"How do you mean?"

"Well, I dunno, someone like that might easily feel rejected," said John. "A person could get a complex about that."

Zagreus shook his head. "On the contrary," he said. "I kind of like the fact that people think I don't exist. Really I do. When I was human I always enjoyed my own company. Athens is a very busy city. Full of people. Especially in summer. And much, much too hot. I used to wish I lived somewhere cold where I could just be on my own."

John shrugged. "Looks like your wish came true." He looked around the snowy landscape. "Out here you couldn't be more on your own if you lived up on the moon."

After breakfast, John put on his snowshoes and picked up his backpack and told Zagreus that he was going to look for Mr. Rakshasas.

"Tell me, how are you going to recognize your friend Mr. Rakshasas?" asked Zagreus. "I'm no expert like you are, but it seems to me that all wolves are pretty much alike."

"I already thought of that," explained John. "When I still had my djinn power I wished that I might be able to recognize Mr. Rakshasas's wolf howl so that I might more easily distinguish him from the rest of his pack. Apparently, no two wolves howl in the same way."

"Want me to come with you?"

John shook his head. "No, I don't think that would be a good idea. No offense, but those wolves would take one look at you and skedaddle. I would skedaddle myself if I didn't already know you, Zagreus. You look pretty frightening. A grizzly bear with a machine gun would probably be frightened by you now."

"Suppose you meet a bear," said Zagreus. "What then?"

"I'll be fine," said John. "I know what to do to keep safe in bear country."

"Hmm. What shall I do while you're away?"

"I dunno. I guess you should do what the Sasquatch normally does in this part of the world at this time of year. Forage. Lurk around a bit. Skulk in some trees. Frighten a camper if you see one."

"Good idea," said Zagreus. "What will you do when you find your friend?"

"Depends on whether or not he recognizes me," said John. "If he doesn't, I'll probably come back here and sweat my spirit out in the lodge. Then go and find him again and climb inside his skin."

"You can do that, too?"

"Sure."

"Isn't it a bit crowded with two people inside the one skin?"

"It can be, yes. But it's only for a short while. Just long enough for me and Mr. Rakshasas to have a chat."

"But he's a wolf now. Won't that make communication a little difficult? Even at a spiritual level?"

"You might think so, yes. But once I'm inside the wolf's skin, I'll become a little bit of a wolf myself and that way we'll be able to talk about a great many things."

"Such as seeing your uncle dead in your vision of the future?"

"And me with his blood on my hands," said John. "That's the part that worries me. I'm sure Mr. Rakshasas will know what to do. He usually does."

"Impressive."

"I'm a djinn. That's what I do."

CHAPTER 23

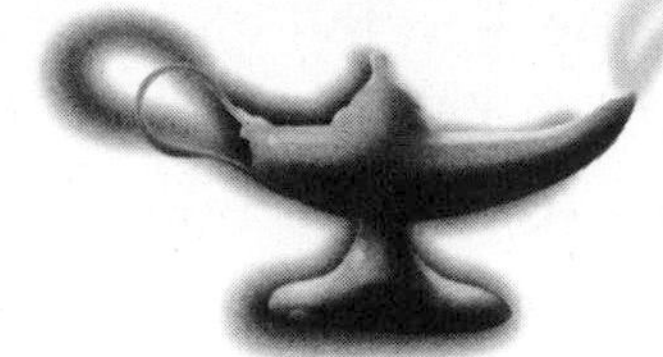

BIGFOOT PUTS HIS FOOT IN IT

As soon as John had gone, Zagreus went off on his own to forage, and lurk, and skulk about in the trees a bit, which was all rather enjoyable. The foraging part was the most consuming of all these activities because it meant digging up snow and eating the stuff that he found underneath, such as roots, grass, and insects; but best of all he found he liked the cones and the sweet pine needles and the tree bark of the park's plentiful supply of lodgepole pines — he even liked the honey fungus that grew parasitically on these tall conifer trees. When he was thirsty he picked up a handful of snow and sucked the water out of it — harmful to humans in the wilderness, but not to a Sasquatch. And it was quickly clear to Zagreus that with all the berries and nuts and seeds he would probably find in the summer, he would certainly never starve while living on his own in the enormous national park.

It was toward the end of the day when Zagreus became aware of the camper. He noticed his smell — or rather the smell of whatever it was he was cooking — at least an hour before he saw his tent. Not that Zagreus liked sausages very much anymore, but he found himself curious about the camper, which is a common trait in a Sasquatch. Also, he was keen to live up to his own reputation and frighten the man just a little bit, as John had suggested. He didn't mean him any harm. He just wanted to have some fun.

So, after dark, when the man had gone inside his tent to sleep, Zagreus wandered around his camp for a while leaving his impressively large footprints in the snow so that the man would find them in the morning and feel alarmed.

Hardly satisfied with this, however, Zagreus decided to push things just a little further, grunting loudly and then slipping his arm underneath the tent so that he might give the poor man a real fright. Only, Zagreus himself got a fright when the man came stumbling out of the tent with a rifle, and, thinking he might easily be shot on his first full day as a Sasquatch, Zagreus ran away.

As he ran away, he heard a familiar voice shouting after him:

"Now I know why it's called Yellowstone Park," he cried. "Because them as are daft enough to live in it are yellow themselves. I say, them as are daft enough to live in it are yellow themselves."

Zagreus stopped in his enormous tracks and looked back

at the man in the fur coat. It was Groanin, Nimrod's English butler. What on earth was he doing here? And Zagreus was just about to go back to Groanin's camp and say hello and apologize for his earlier behavior when he remembered what John had said: that he now looked pretty frightening and that John himself would have skedaddled at the sight of a Sasquatch if he hadn't already known that it was really Zagreus. Plus, there was also the danger that Groanin might shoot him with that rifle.

What on earth was he doing here?

And then it dawned on him.

"Of course," he said. "Groanin followed the boy djinn here to fetch him back home. The boy's uncle Nimrod must be worried about him, the way he just took off like that. I guess if he were my nephew, I'd be worried myself."

As he trudged back to John's camp to bring him this important news, Zagreus tried to remember if he had ever had a nephew himself, but almost all memories of who he was and what he'd been in his previous life were now gone; he couldn't even remember the fact that once he had been Greek. Which, it is sometimes said, is something a great many Turks can't remember, either.

It was almost dawn when Zagreus reached the camp again. He found the boy djinn sitting beside a blazing fire. As he approached the camp, something growled at him from the shadows.

"It's all right, Rakshasas," said John. "He's a friend of mine."

Zagreus sat down heavily in the snow. "You found him then," he said, smiling a big toothy smile as a young, blue-eyed wolf came slowly toward him out of the shadows and licked his outstretched hand.

"Yes," said John. "I found him." He reached out and stroked the wolf's thick gray coat. "Didn't I, old friend?"

Rakshasas the wolf made a whining noise that ended in a howl.

"Which reminds me," said Zagreus. "There's another old friend of yours in this park. Mr. Groanin."

"Groanin?" John sighed. "Here. In Yellowstone? On his own?"

"Yes."

"You're quite certain of that? Because I daren't go near their camp if Nimrod is there. For obvious reasons. I mean, I can hardly kill him if I keep away from him, can I?"

"Yes, I'm quite certain he's on his own," said Zagreus.

"I wonder how — no, wait, I can guess. Since they're all made from the one original carpet of King Solomon, I bet one flying carpet can follow another. Provided you know how to direct it. Nimrod must have sent Groanin here to look for me."

Rakshasas barked as if agreeing with this theory.

"That's what I thought, too," said Zagreus.

"Did you speak to him?" asked John.

"Er, no. I would have spoken to him but I was afraid I might scare him. Me being the size I am now. The last time he saw me I was about three feet tall and white-haired. Now

I'm seven or eight feet tall and covered in brown hair. He'd run a mile for sure."

"Thoughtful of you." John smiled. "Actually, I think you've grown some more since I last saw you."

"You think so?" Zagreus sounded pleased.

John nodded. "Look, is Groanin all right, do you think? Does he have food? Groanin's very particular about his food."

"Yes, he seems to be fairly well equipped. He had a big skillet on his campfire. I think he'd been cooking pork sausages. Really, I'm surprised you didn't know that. You can smell the meat for miles."

Rakshasas sniffed the air and barked as if to confirm what Zagreus had said.

"That's bad," said John. "That's very bad."

"What is?"

"This is bear country," explained John. "If you could smell those sausages, then so could a grizzly."

"I never thought of that." Zagreus stood up. "Then he's in danger. We should go and see that he's all right."

"Do you think you could find him again?"

"Easy. Like I said, you could smell those sausages for miles. I'm sure I could find my way back there with my eyes shut." Zagreus smiled. "And with the size of tracks I leave, I dare say you could find your way there, too."

John stood up and reached for his backpack. Rakshasas was already whining and looking back down the trail of giant Sasquatch footprints as if eager to follow them. And guessing that the wolf could probably cover the distance back to

Groanin's camp in no time at all, John clapped his hands and pointed.

"Go on then," he said, and Rakshasas took off down the trail like a greyhound.

"There's no time to lose," said John, starting to run. "I'll follow you."

CHAPTER 24

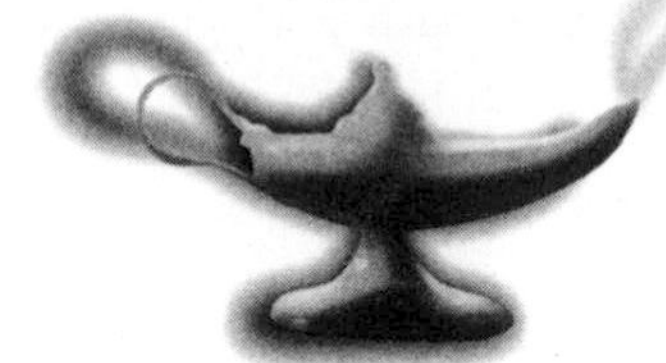

TERROR IN MUCKHOLE TERRACE

Muckhole Terrace was well named, part of a drab and derelict neighborhood of Bumby that was full of grimy, redbrick homes. Drying gray laundry fluttered over tiny gardens overgrown with weeds that looked like they were the only healthy living things in the area. A woman with a cigarette in one hand and a beer can in the other watched with narrow-eyed suspicion as Philippa and Moo stood at a bus stop, pretending to wait for a bus. Moo had said this would be good cover while they surveilled the terrace for some sign that number 74 was being watched by the fake fakirs.

"You don't think it will draw attention to us when we don't get on the bus," said Philippa.

Moo pointed up at an electric sign on the bus stop that indicated that the next bus was twenty minutes away. "I think we'll have decided our best course of action by then," she said. "Don't you?"

"There's no one hereabouts who looks like a fake fakir," observed Philippa.

"That's true," said Moo. "On the other hand, I don't think we're going to find them watching the house from the comfort of a bed of nails, do you?"

"I suppose you're right," said Philippa.

"Chances are they'll be a little more discreet than that," said Moo. "What I mean is that we mustn't expect them to look like fakirs. Chances are they'll probably look like any of the other men in this area. Blending in is the first secret of successful terrorism. We must also blend in ourselves. And it's fortunate we are what we are. I doubt they'll be expecting trouble from an old lady and an adolescent schoolgirl." Moo smiled kindly at Philippa. "Come on. The coast looks to be clear. Let's go and ring the doorbell."

"Suppose she's at work?"

"It's a Saturday," said Moo. "Nobody around here works on a Saturday."

Farther down the street, several men stood outside a betting shop, idly kicking cans and, sometimes, each other. They wore tracksuits and gold chains and tattoos, and most of them had cell phones attached to their studded or ringed ears.

Moo regarded them dimly. "Come to think of it," she added, "there aren't many around here who look like they work on any other day, either."

They halted outside number 74. It was in a better state of order than any of the other houses in the terrace. The door had been freshly painted, the mailbox polished, and the windows were clean. Behind them, thick net curtains prevented Moo from checking out the interior for any sign of trouble.

Moo pressed the little doorbell and an electronic facsimile of a famous song from *The Sound of Music* announced their presence at the front door.

They waited for almost a minute before the door was opened on the chain and a woman's long face appeared in the gap, accompanied by a strong smell of cheap perfume and air freshener, although in that part of the world it was quite possible they were one and the same. Seeing Philippa and behind her, Moo, the woman's narrow and suspicious green eyes seemed to become a little less suspicious and a little more green.

"Miss Shoebottom?" said Moo.

"Yes?" she said. "What do you want?"

"We're friends of the expected one," said Philippa.

Miss Shoebottom hardly batted one of her batlike eyelids. "Then you'd better come in." She closed the door, slipped off the chain, and opened it again to admit Philippa and then Moo.

"Can I offer you both some tea?" she said, and pressed a finger to her lips as if counseling their discretion.

"Yes, that would be very kind of you," said Moo.

Miss Shoebottom seemed quite nervous. She kept lifting her eyebrows at the ceiling of her little sitting room, and Philippa almost believed the woman had some sort of tic. What was more, she demonstrated absolutely no inclination to make tea, for which Philippa at least was grateful as she had no desire to drink any.

"Are you all right?" Moo asked Miss Shoebottom.

"Yes, I'm very well, thank you." Miss Shoebottom mouthed some other words that remained silent. Then she pointed upstairs. "Under the circumstances."

Moo nodded. "Yes, it is a nice day," she said. "We won't stay long, Miss Shoebottom. We heard you were expecting someone from the local church to come and visit. About your very kind offer to do the flowers in church on a Sunday."

For a moment Philippa wondered what on earth Moo was talking about.

"Of course, it would have to be real flowers that are used in the church. Not *fake* ones. Plastic or paper flowers. The reverend was quite adamant about his horror of fakes. He would have come to see you himself but he's burying someone today. And after all, I always say, a funeral is forever, not just for life."

Philippa looked at Moo and was about to conclude that the old lady had suffered some kind of stroke that was affecting her mind when she heard a creak on the floor upstairs and understood exactly what was happening. Moo and Miss Shoebottom were speaking in code. *Someone else was in the house.* Someone whom Miss Shoebottom was afraid of.

"Have you met the Reverend Swaraswati?" asked Moo.

"No," said Miss Shoebottom. "I don't think I have met him yet. The reverend. He's been away, hasn't he? For a long time?"

"Yes," said Moo. "A very long time. Much longer than he or anyone else had expected."

"You got that right, love," whispered Miss Shoebottom wearily.

"Well, we'd best be getting along," said Moo. "Perhaps we'll have that cup of tea another time."

"Yes, perhaps that would be best," allowed Miss Shoebottom. "Do send the Reverend Whatshisname my regards and say that I hope to meet him before very long."

Philippa reached for the door to the sitting room and found it swinging toward her.

Two long-haired, bearded men advanced into the room. They were accompanied by the same smell of Indian balm Philippa had encountered on the prison ship *Archer*. And but for their smart suits, they looked very similar, too, being dark and very thin as if they didn't eat much.

"Not leaving already, I hope," said one of the men. "We haven't yet been introduced."

"Please don't go," said the other.

And since each of the two men was holding a gun in his hand, Philippa felt obliged — for a moment at least — to delay her use of djinn power and their inevitable escape. Also, she hoped perhaps to discover something about whom these men were working for.

"I'm afraid we heard what you said," said the first mendicant fakir. "About the expected one. I'm afraid very little ever happens in this town. And certainly nothing has been expected here for a long, long time. Except perhaps our mutual friend, the fakir sent by the Tirthankar. We've been staying here with poor Miss Shoebottom for several weeks now in the hope that we might get to meet him, but so far without luck. We've even been accompanying her to her place of work at the town hall. So you can imagine how fed up with us she is."

Miss Shoebottom fetched a can of air freshener off the mantelpiece and started to spray the air around the mendicant fakirs.

"It's not you I mind so much, luvvy, as the smell of that horrible Indian balm you rub into your skin," she said.

The first mendicant fakir grinned apologetically. "See what I mean? But none of this matters now. Not now that you have turned up. We're rather hoping now that you can take us to our friend, the fakir. In fact, we're certain you can. Which really is a stroke of luck. We were rather beginning to think that the run of bad luck that we afflicted on Bumby had started to affect us, too."

"I'm afraid we haven't the foggiest idea what you're talking about, young man," Moo said sternly. "And I suggest you put that gun down before you get into trouble."

"It would be bad luck for Miss Shoebottom if you can't take us to the fakir," said the second mendicant fakir, brandishing his gun meaningfully. "On top of all the other bad luck that she and this disgusting little town have had to put up with."

"Yes, indeed," said his colleague.

"Perhaps we can help each other," said Philippa.

"I know how you can help me," said the first mendicant fakir. "But I fail to see how I can help you, beyond doing you the obvious favor of not shooting you and your friend."

"Perhaps if I could meet your employer," said Philippa, "I might explain that I know the location of all five fakirs of Faizabad. Not just the one here in Bumby. But the other four as well."

"How is that possible?" said the second mendicant fakir.

"It's possible," said Philippa. "You'll have to take my word for that."

The two mendicant fakirs looked at each other uncertainly.

"Not even the Tirthankar, if he were still alive, could know that," said the first mendicant fakir, and started to shake his head with disbelief. "No, it's not possible."

"Your employer, whoever he is," insisted Philippa, "will be very upset when he learns that you settled for just one fakir when you could have had all five. By the way, who is your employer? Perhaps I know him."

"The emir does not make deals with little girls," said the first mendicant fakir.

"Please yourself," said Philippa. "But you really should ask him first. Why don't you give him a call? Is this emir here in Bumby?" Philippa grinned. She was starting to enjoy herself. "I can find out, you know."

The second mendicant fakir laughed. "And how would you do that, please?"

"I could torture you."

Both the mendicant fakirs were laughing a lot now.

"However, the use of torture diminishes me as a person," said Philippa. "And I wouldn't care for that. Besides, if my uncle Nimrod's right, you guys are kind of used to a bit of pain already, so clearly that's not going to work. Unless of course —" Philippa sounded thoughtful now. "Unless it's a really inhuman kind of pain. Yes. I bet that might work."

"Does she always talk such rubbish?" one fakir asked Moo.

"It's not rubbish," said Moo. "She's a person of enormous supernatural power. Unless you put that gun down, I fear you're in for a very nasty shock, young man."

"So," continued Philippa, "here's what's going to happen. You're going to tell me who this emir is and where he is to be found. Or else you're going to regret it. And you can comfort yourself with the knowledge that you never really had any choice in the matter. So you'd best do as my friend says and put that gun down, or else."

"You mean this gun?" said the second mendicant fakir and pointed it at Moo's head. To her credit the old lady did not even flinch.

"FABULONGOSHOOMARVELISHLY —"

"She's talking rubbish again," said the first mendicant fakir.

"— WONDERPIPICAL!"

Almost immediately both of the mendicant fakirs screamed as each realized that he was no longer holding a gun but a living ferret, which is a local species of weasel. Now, ferrets do not like to be held by strangers, and each immediately bit the hand of the mendicant fakir holding it.

Another curiosity of ferrets and weasels is that once they bite, they are reluctant to let go and so it proved with these two ferrets.

"Ouch! Ouch! Ouch!" squealed the first mendicant fakir.

"Leggo, ouch!" said the other.

"Yarooo!"

Miss Shoebottom laughed and then covered her mouth. "No, I shouldn't laugh, should I? Not when someone is in pain. Sorry, luvvy."

"Ouch!"

"My dad used to keep ferrets and he used to say —" Miss Shoebottom was laughing again. "He used to say that he reckoned there's nothing sharper or more painful than to be bitten by than a ferret's tooth. Not even an ungrateful child." More laughter. "Oh, no, I'm sorry. It's not funny."

"I should think you deserve a good laugh at the expense of these two rogues," said Moo. "Don't you?"

"You've got that right, missus."

"Get them off!" yelled the second mendicant fakir.

"How did you do that then?" Miss Shoebottom asked Philippa. "Turn those guns into ferrets. Are you some kind of magician, love?"

"I'll explain in a moment," said Philippa. "After I've finished dealing with these two."

"Owwww!" said the first mendicant fakir. "I can't stand the pain any longer."

"Oh, jolly well done, Philippa," said Moo. "So that's what you meant by inhuman pain."

"And since I'm not the one who's actually inflicting it," said Philippa, "I guess I can look myself in the mirror when I go to sleep tonight."

"Please get it off me," begged the second mendicant fakir.

For their part, the ferrets were enjoying themselves, for in truth there is nothing a ferret likes more than to sink its teeth down to the bone of a human finger.

"As soon as you tell me some more about this emir," said Philippa.

"The emir is His Excellency Jirjis Ibn Rajmus," yelped the first mendicant fakir. "And he lives in Cairo."

"You mean the Cairo that's in Egypt?"

"No, the one in Georgia, U.S.A.," yelled the second mendicant fakir. "Where do you think I mean?"

Philippa thought the mendicant fakir was being sarcastic, but let it go. "All right. Why's he doing this?"

"He wants to know the great secrets of the universe, of course. Anyone who knows anything about these five fakirs knows what important information they possess. Really! You could have worked that out for yourself, surely."

"Er, yes, all right," said Philippa, who wasn't used to interrogating people. "Um." She looked at Moo. "What else should I ask them?"

Moo took over. "Tell me about this organization of mendicant fakirs."

"It's called the Chariot," said the first mendicant fakir.

"How do you get your orders? Who told you to come here, to Bumby?"

"We get our orders from the emir on the Internet. He tells us what to do and we obey."

"And how did you go about creating the bad luck in the world?" Moo's tone stiffened. "That is this emir's plan, isn't it? To create such a bad atmosphere in the world that the five fakirs who remain buried alive will be persuaded that they are needed and come forth to reveal their secrets?"

"Yes, ouch!"

"So how did you do it?"

"I don't know about the world," said the first mendicant fakir, grimacing with pain. "But I can tell you what we've been doing here in Bumby, if you like."

"Yes, I think you'd better," said Moo.

"Mostly we just went around and secretly sabotaged things so as to create an impression of enormous bad luck. I was working at a local Indian restaurant so it was very easy for us to add dangerously hot chilies to the curries."

"And I was working at the local chemical factory so it was easy to let a large quantity of pink dye escape into the local river."

"But we also came equipped with a Jinx, the phrase book with incorrect translations, and a supply of stink bugs."

Miss Shoebottom tutted loudly. "So that was you." She picked up a copy of the *Radio Times*, rolled it quickly, and struck each mendicant fakir on the head several times. "Blasted nuisance, the pair of you. You want locking up, really you do."

"I was behind the two accidents at the circus," said the other unhappily. "When the Magnificent Mikhail managed to saw a lady in half for real and Leonid the Lion Tamer got eaten by a tigress."

"Murderer," said Moo.

"And I created the computer virus, the Bumby Bacteria," said the other fakir.

"And it was me who salted the deep caves with gold nuggets so as to make everyone think there was a gold mine."

Miss Shoebottom hit him again with the *Radio Times*. "Blast you, man, if you knew the trouble you've both caused."

"They know," said Moo. "They know."

"I hope they send you both to prison for a very long time," said Miss Shoebottom.

"Most probably they'd enjoy that," said Moo. "We saw three of their colleagues on Her Majesty's prison ship *Archer* and they gave every impression of being in a holiday camp. Didn't they, Philippa?"

"Yes," admitted Philippa.

"You ask me, prison's too good for 'em," Moo said fiercely. "Plus the taxpayer has to pick up the tab for looking after them."

"So what should we do with them?" said Philippa. "We can't let them go. There's no telling what they might do. Create more havoc. Report back to this emir. Hurt Mr. Swaraswati."

"We should execute them," said Moo, taking the gun from her handbag. "Shoot them. I'll do it."

"Not in here, you won't," said Miss Shoebottom. "This is a new carpet."

"In the garden then. On the lawn. People will just think a car backfired. Twice."

"Aiee!" squealed the first mendicant fakir. "You can't mean that. Please."

"No," said Philippa. "She doesn't mean it."

"I do mean it," Moo said fiercely.

"What's your favorite animal?" Philippa asked Miss Shoebottom.

"Well, it's not ferrets, love." Miss Shoebottom laughed bitterly. "Can't stand them. They're just like emaciated rats, so they are. I can never understand why people put them down their trousers."

"They do?" Philippa was horrified.

"Poachers do it," explained Moo. "To hide them from gamekeepers when they go hunting rabbits."

Philippa looked at the ferret still attached to the ball of the first mendicant fakir's thumb and winced. "That looks kind of hazardous, to me."

She shook her head. Sometimes it was hard to believe that so many Americans could be descended from people in Great Britain. The people here were so totally weird.

"What's your favorite animal?" she said again.

Miss Shoebottom shrugged. "Budgies," she said. "I always liked budgies. I used to have one when I were a little girl. Cheeky, he was called. I loved that budgie."

"What color was he?"

"The budgie? Blue. Powder blue. Why?"

Philippa looked at the two mendicant fakirs. She'd never before turned people into animals. John had been obliged to turn Finlay McCreeby into a peregrine falcon once and had felt guilty about it for months, almost until the very moment when he'd found an opportunity to turn the falcon back into Finlay McCreeby. Of course, her mother had done it all the time, until she'd renounced her djinn power completely. For a long time her two uncles had lived with the Gaunts as the family pet dogs. And even the family cat, Monty, was a former contract killer called Montana Retch. And according to her father, it was thanks to Layla that New York's Central Park Zoo had a Cuban solenodon, a hairy-nosed wombat, and an American red wolf, because these were all that remained of the three men who had kidnapped him the previous year.

Philippa thought there was something terrible about turning a man into a hairy-nosed wombat. Maybe it was better just to send these men to prison like the others, after all.

"FABULONGOSHOOMARVELISHLYWONDERPIPICAL!"

As Philippa spoke her focus word, the two ferrets finally let go of their prey and disappeared under the sofa, while the two mendicant fakirs sank onto their knees holding their hands. But instead of being grateful, one of them looked at her with hate in his eyes.

"You demon," he said. "Now you're in for it." He stood up menacingly. "I'm going to clock you one, you devil. Just see if I don't."

Philippa felt something harden inside her. A little iron in her soul. In truth, this iron in the soul was something she had inherited from her mother, although she did not know it. Anger took hold of her, which is never a good way to use djinn power. For one thing, it creates a strong smell of sulfur and often makes a loud bang.

The fakir raised his fist to Philippa. "Demon," he said.

"FABULONGOSHOOMARVELISHLYWONDERPIPICAL!"

There was a loud bang and a cloud of smoke and a strong smell of sulfur. Miss Shoebottom screamed and then reached for the air freshener.

Two blue budgies were hopping on the carpet, with one of them still chirping the budgie word for "demon," which sounds a lot like "cheep." Philippa was just about to bend down and pick up the two budgies when the two ferrets beat her to it.

"Darn it," said Philippa, who'd quite forgotten about the two ferrets.

Miss Shoebottom screamed again, grabbed a broom, and then shooed the greedy ferrets out the door. Still holding the budgies, they ran away along Muckhole Terrace to enjoy their unexpected meals.

Miss Shoebottom dropped onto her sofa and closed her eyes. "What a morning!" she exclaimed.

"Sorry about that," said Philippa. "I sort of meant those birds to be pets for you."

"Don't apologize. A pet's the last thing I need right now,

luvvy. A holiday's what I really need. I have to get away from here, and soon."

"What about Mr. Swaraswati?" asked Moo.

"What about him?"

"After all these years of being buried alive, he's keen to meet you," said Philippa.

"Is he now?" Miss Shoebottom's mouth turned down. "Well, I'm not sure I want to meet him. Not anymore. Stuck here in this crummy little town all these years, like me dad and his dad before him, for generations, I tell you it's me that feels buried alive. Not him. So. Now that he's come back and he's not in any danger, I've decided. I'm going on vacation in Spain and then I'm going to live my life."

"But what shall we tell Mr. Swaraswati?"

"You can tell him what you like, love, but I've had enough," said Miss Shoebottom. "My family's been waiting here for centuries for that old man to turn up and I reckon I've done my bit by not leading those two characters to where he was staying. Of course, I knew where he was all the time. There's not much that happens in Bumby I don't know about, luvvy."

Miss Shoebottom sighed, kicked off her shoes, and rubbed her stockinged feet painfully.

Philippa looked at Moo and shrugged, hardly knowing what to do next.

"She makes a fair point, Philippa," said Moo.

"Look," said Miss Shoebottom. "Philippa, is it?"

Philippa nodded.

"You seem to know what you're doing," said Miss Shoebottom. "You look after him. All this Indian stuff is a complete mystery to me. I don't even like curry. Hundreds of years ago, when my family first moved here, it probably meant something, but not anymore. Now it means zip. And I certainly wouldn't know what to do with one of the great secrets of the universe. Not if I lived next door to Professor Stephen Hawking."

"You have no wish at all to meet him?" Moo sounded a little disappointed.

"Stephen Hawking?"

"No, Mr. Swaraswati."

Miss Shoebottom thought for a moment. "No." She shook her head. "It's been too much for me and my family, all these years. I just wish — I wish I was on holiday right now."

"Very well," said Philippa.

"You mean —?"

"I do mean. If that's really what you want. There ought to be some sort of reward for keeping faith with the fakir all these centuries."

"I'm glad you understand," said Miss Shoebottom.

"Spain, you say?"

"Majorca'd be nice."

Philippa nodded. "FABULONGOSHOOMARVELISH-LYWONDERPIPICAL!"

And Miss Shoebottom disappeared.

Philippa sat down on the sofa where Miss Shoebottom had been sitting and let out a sigh.

"What are you thinking?" asked Moo.

"I'm thinking we'll have to take Mr. Swaraswati with us," said Philippa. "And I'm also thinking I need a new focus word. That one is getting a little too easy to say."

"Why is that a problem?"

"I've realized something important. Something I never knew before. If your focus word is too easy to say, it's too easy to turn people into budgies. And that is a heck of a thing to do to anyone. When you turn a man into a budgie you take away all he had and all he's ever going to be." She smiled thinly. "As a man, that is. Not as a budgie."

CHAPTER 25

RUMBLE IN THE FOREST

Groanin had two things going for him as he ran away from the grizzly bear. One thing was that he'd been attacked by a large and fierce animal before — a white tiger — and, hardly wanting to repeat the experience, this helped to make him run much faster.

On that previous occasion, the tiger had torn off his arm and eaten it and for a long time Groanin had lived his life as a butler with one arm. But then John and Philippa and their friend Dybbuk had been obliged to create a new arm for him so that he might more easily wind them up and down a well in an old British fortress in India. And, of course, being djinn they had endowed him with not just any old new arm but an arm that was much, much stronger than his previous one.

That was the other thing he had going for him.

The new, stronger arm was handy when removing very tight lids from those little pots of marmalade you got in hotels and showing off to young ladies who were struggling with heavy suitcases; it meant he could carry two bags of coal up from the cellar instead of one; and in Italy once, he'd had to fight an angel named Sam who fancied himself as a bit of an all-in wrestler. But apart from that, Groanin had not had much use for a significantly stronger arm. At least he hadn't until now and, turning around to face the bear — for Groanin realized he could run no farther — Groanin punched it hard on the nose.

The blow would certainly have rendered a grown man unconscious, but grizzlies can weigh up to a thousand pounds, which makes them a lot harder to knock out in a fistfight. Groanin punched the bear again, which hardly encouraged the bear to feel any more kindly disposed toward him. The huge grizzly roared with pain and backed away, lashing out with its huge claws at Groanin. Fortunately, it missed. The bear was not, however, inclined to give up on a promising-looking meal — even one that packed a good right hand. Contrary to what most people believe about bears, they like meat, especially when late snow on the ground makes it harder to forage for the other things they like to eat.

The bear rose up on its thick hind legs, lifting its vulnerable and already bloody nose clear of Groanin's lightning right hook, and calculating that, in this way, the man wouldn't have the reach of arm to hurt it again. It was a shrewd calculation. The man would have to come in close to land a blow in the bear's belly, and risk getting mauled in the clinch.

Shuffling around in a circle, the two combatants faced each other off. The bear threw a couple of clumsy haymakers.

Groanin kept his right hand up high, ready to throw it if the bear dropped down on all fours again. The Englishman figured he had the speed of his arm on his side while the bear's raw power was its greatest strength. Now if he could only stay out of the clinch. There was little point in trying to take the fight to the bear. That would have been fatal. All he could do was shoot straight punches to the bear's nose whenever it dropped on all fours.

They did this for more than two hours.

"Come on, tough guy," said Groanin, taunting the bear. "Let's see what you've got."

The bear roared back in the butler's face — so loud it almost blew the fur hat off his head. And when the bear roared, Groanin had a perfect and unnerving sight of all of its teeth, which looked very large indeed. *A white tiger looked like a little kitten next to this beast*, he told himself.

"My God, your breath doesn't half stink, you stupid great fur rug," yelled Groanin, who was trying desperately to keep his spirits up in the face of the grizzly's obvious grizzliness.

The bear was tiring now, knocked off balance by Groanin's punches, which had taken a toll on the creature's nose. Every time the bear dropped its head, blood dripped into the snow and if the fight had been fought according to the rules of the Marquess of Queensberry, the referee — assuming there had been one on hand — would have stopped the contest and given the decision to Groanin. And feeling its appetite for the fight beginning to drain away, and sensing it was now or never, the bear dropped onto all fours again and rushed the butler, ignoring the hard right that flashed in from nowhere straight onto the point of its wet black nose.

Groanin let out a yell of terror as the bear knocked him flying with one sweep of its mighty paw. He flew through the cold air and landed ten yards away. Groanin turned on his belly and tried to crawl away, but the bear was on him in a second. He felt the heat of the animal's breath on his neck and heard the low rasp of its angry growl in his ear. Something sharp against his shoulder made him cry out with pain and he felt himself lifted high in the air. Like a dog worrying a toy, the bear shook him in its mouth for almost half a minute, dropped him on the snow, and then pounded him with the full weight of its front feet.

Feeling himself mortally wounded, Groanin turned to meet his fate, hoping to land one last good punch on the bear's nose, and was just in time to see something gray and furry fly through the air and attach itself to the bear's throat. For a moment his eyes, which were filled with blood from a cut on his head, struggled to separate the fur of the bear from whatever it was that had attacked it.

And it was only when the bear flung off the attacking creature and finally ran away that Groanin realized he had been saved from being eaten by a bear by a wolf. And the question that now occupied him was why. Why had a wolf saved his life?

The wolf picked itself up off the snow and limped toward him. Groanin found he could not move and laughed at the irony of his own situation.

"I suppose you're going to eat me now," he said as the gray timber wolf got nearer. "My — what — big teeth — you have." Groanin sighed and closed his eyes in resignation to his fate. "All the better to — eat you with, little Red Riding Hood."

But instead of eating him, the wolf bent down and started to lick his face. One of Groanin's eyes blinked open, met the blue one of the wolf's, and seemed to find a flicker of something he half recognized.

"Don't tell me," he whispered. "Don't tell me that's you, Rakshasas. That really would be a coincidence. And a great blessing, old friend. Feel tired now. Like I was reading *David Copperfield*. One of the classic English novels. Great book for bedtime. Good night, old friend."

Then he closed his eyes again and this time he did not open them.

Rakshasas, for it was he, sat down on his haunches. He licked his injured paw for a moment. Then he pointed his thin muzzle up at the breaking dawn and began to sing the lonely song of the wolf into the cold air.

CHAPTER 26

THE DREAM OF LIFE

John recognized the howl of his old friend and hurried across the snow to find him, certain from the plaintive tone of the wolf's howl that something was very wrong. Then, in the distance he saw a big grizzly bear running away and was gripped by a terrible feeling of déjà vu — as if somehow all of this had already happened to him before. This sensation was so strong that it made John nauseous and, for a moment, he stopped running and just stood there trying to rationalize it. Finally, he retched into the snow; and then, feeling a little better and telling himself that he was just worried about Groanin, he picked up his feet and carried on running along the huge tracks that had been left behind by Zagreus.

About a half mile farther up the trail, he found a trio of furry shapes that broke up as he got nearer. Rakshasas ran toward him and licked his hand and whined. Zagreus stood up and John saw that his large, low-set forehead was even lower on his huge, pointed head than before and his eyes were full of sadness.

Only the third shape remained motionless on the snow.

For a moment John did not recognize that it was Groanin. For a moment he thought it was Nimrod, for was that not Nimrod's red fox fur coat he saw crumpled on the ground? For several seconds he just stood there until Zagreus mumbled a sentence that included Groanin's name but which John, his ears singing with shock as if he had been struck by a bolt of electricity, could not otherwise understand.

"Groanin?"

John threw himself down on the ground and saw that the unconscious butler was gravely wounded. There was a large gash across his forehead, and as John unbuttoned his coat he saw that the fur had been cut through and was sticky underneath. Hardly hesitating now, he bent forward, placed his head on the butler's chest, and gradually made out the irregular sound of a failing heartbeat. Groanin was dying.

This realization drew John's hands to his face and feeling them wet, he saw that they were covered with blood and instinctively he wiped them on the snow. Something fell out of the butler's inside pocket and John picked it up and wondered why it seemed significant. It was Groanin's fountain pen.

And then he remembered what Mr. Burton had said. . . .

To be given a vision of the future is a rare thing. Upon seeing such a thing, however, it is difficult not to act on it. And yet you must also be aware that what you might see would only be a fragment and not the whole picture, therefore understanding might be similarly incomplete.

John screamed very loudly and sat down in the snow. All was clear to him now where it had not been clear before — that much was obvious. The death foretold was not that of Nimrod but that of poor Groanin. And the only reason Groanin had followed John to Yellowstone was because John had gone there to seek advice from Mr. Rakshasas on what to do about the foretelling of Nimrod's death that he thought he had seen in Mr. Burton's ink spot. It was exactly as Mr. Burton had said.

For some reason he could not explain, John looked up at the sky and for a fleeting second he saw in his mind's eye the whole sky as black and shiny as an ink spot and behind the ink, the image of an enormous eye. His own. And it was plain to John that he had had been right about one thing. It was all his fault.

"You stupid idiot," he said, punching the snow with both his fists. "You stupid, darned idiot."

"It wasn't his fault," said Zagreus. "Well, maybe. He was foolish to cook those sausages, sure."

"Not him!" John screamed. "Me! I'm the idiot. If I hadn't wanted to look into the future, none of this would have happened."

John threw himself into the snow and wished that he was dead and buried under several feet of the stuff.

Rakshasas barked loudly and then nipped John on the elbow as if urging some more practical course of action than merely feeling incredibly sorry for Groanin and by extension, himself.

"You're right," said John, wiping the tears from his face. "Maybe it's not too late. Zagreus, pick him up and carry him back to the tent. I can go for help. Get him to a hospital."

Rakshasas barked and took hold of John's sleeve.

"What is it? You want me to come with you?" John shook his head. "I need to get started right away. I figure if I walk west I can reach a town, or maybe get a signal on my cell phone."

Rakshasas barked again and, gripping John's sleeve, pulled him along the trail back to camp.

"All right, all right," said John. "I'll come with you. But there's not much I can do for him back at camp. I've got a small first aid kit but that's hardly going to be enough to fix him up. Not with these injuries. He needs a hospital."

Rakshasas barked and, lolling his tongue out of his mouth, panted loudly, as if he was hot.

"What the heck's the matter with you?" John asked.

Rakshasas did it again, only this time he splayed his legs out.

"You're pretending to be hot," said John.

Rakshasas barked once.

"Of course, the sweat lodge."

Rakshasas barked again.

"Maybe I can use djinn power to help him."

Rakshasas barked again.

Zagreus was already carrying the unconscious Groanin back to camp. His huge hairy legs and powerful arms made short work of the walk and Groanin's weight. For every one of his steps, John was obliged to take two or three, but he soon caught up with the Sasquatch. And racing ahead, he and Rakshasas ran all the way back to camp.

As soon as John saw the sweat lodge he started to throw off his clothes so that he might run straight inside and start warming up. To John's surprise, Rakshasas followed him in.

Sweat lodges were ceremonial saunas built by Native Americans for medicinal purposes. A hole was dug in the ground and a structure made with tree branches, and these were then covered with animal skins; stones heated in an exterior fire were then brought into the lodge, laid in the pit, and, when water was poured onto them, these produced steam and a considerable amount of heat.

John's sweat lodge was still hot from before, when he had needed extreme heat to bring about an out-of-body experience that could enable him to enter the wolf body of Mr. Rakshasas. And it was clear from the wolf's anxious demeanor that he wished this to happen again so that they might effectively communicate, for while Rakshasas the wolf was able to remember much of what he had once been, he was no longer in possession of the least part of djinn power and was quite unable to transubstantiate or to become pure spirit.

Indeed, when John in his mundane physical shape had first come upon Rakshasas, the wolf had hardly recognized him. The memory of his djinn life was locked away inside the wolf's unconscious mind like the contents of a hard disk on a very old computer.

As soon as he was able to, John lifted his spirit clear of his own parboiled body and stepped inside the wolf's, at which point the wolf, who found it too hot inside the sweat lodge, stepped outside.

Rakshasas watched as Zagreus lay Groanin on the snow, and licked his lips at the sight of so much fresh blood.

"Gosh, you really are a wolf, aren't you?" said John, a little shocked to discover that there was a part of Rakshasas that looked upon Groanin as a possible meal.

"I am that," said Rakshasas. "But it's apologizing for it, I'm not, John. Sure, any dog is always full of loyalty to a man until a cat comes by."

"Yes, of course, I'm sorry."

"It's a lot I've remembered since you were last inside my mind, John," said Rakshasas. "All of the adventures we had. Great times, eh? And there'll be more, I'm sure of it, now that you've found me again. Of course, I'll be a wolf from now on. Which is not so bad. To be honest, I'm relieved to be shot of the burden of all that djinn power. Such a responsibility. More than any decent spirit can cope with, I'm thinking."

"I'm not being rude," said John, "but I really don't have time for this. I need to get djinn power so that I can make a stretcher and some bandages so that I can get Mr. Groanin straight to a hospital."

Rakshasas lay down beside the unconscious English butler.

"There's no helping him now," said Rakshasas. "At least there's nothing medical science can do for him. Take it from me, John, poor Groanin is beyond the help of any doctor."

"What?" John's spirit was appalled. "What do you mean? You mean he is going to die? No. That can't happen. I won't allow it."

"'Peace, peace!'" said Rakshasas. "'He is not dead, he doth not sleep — he hath awakened from the dream of life — 'Tis we, who lost in stormy visions, keep with phantoms an unprofitable strife.'"

"What?" John sighed. "Make sense, will you? You were always hard to understand."

"Wisdom is a bit like that in the ears of them as have none of their own."

"Well then, what does it mean, what you said?"

"Just a little piece of poetry by Percy Shelley," said Rakshasas.

"Poetry! At a time like this? Are you mad?"

"There's wisdom in yon Percy Shelley. Take my word for it. A lot of wisdom. More than you might expect, given how young he was when he died. He was just thirty years old. It was him who wrote that poem you and Philippa were fond of. 'Ozymandias.' Well, I digress. Have you heard of purgatory, John?"

"Of course. But I don't know where or what it is."

"Purgatory is a spiritual condition or process in which

the souls of people who die are made ready for heaven. It's a kind of waiting room for souls to become pure enough to enter heaven. Well, the same is true of death. There's a kind of waiting room in between life and death where a soul can be held up, if you like. That's where Groanin is right now. For a while, at least."

"How long can it be held up?" John asked urgently.

"Oh, almost indefinitely. If the conditions are right. And it so happens, they are. They are here, I mean."

"What sort of conditions?" asked John.

"Extreme cold. Ice. Freezing."

"You're saying we should freeze Groanin until I can get medical help?"

"Yes. But perhaps I didn't make myself clear. Mr. Groanin is beyond the help of any doctor, John."

"How do you know? With respect, you're just a wolf."

"Instinct. Believe me, a wolf knows when something is close to death. No, something much more drastic than anything a doctor can do is now required if you're going to save Mr. Groanin. Isn't it always the way?"

"What must I do?"

"First of all, you'll have to bury him in snow and ice. To keep his body cold. Of course nothing in Yellowstone stays buried for long. And fortunate it is that your friend Zagreus is with us. If he's willing, he can stay here and keep an eye on Groanin's body while we're gone. To make sure that nothing tries to eat it. Even though he's a big fellow, it's fair to say he might have his work cut out for him. There's plenty a creature in the park that likes a free meal such as a dead human being. And there's a smell of blood that's in the air, right enough."

"Then what?" demanded John.

"We have a long and difficult journey ahead of us, John. A journey that is not without risks to us both. My life I count for little. But yours I value above a nice juicy steak, and that's saying something. Are you sure you want to do this?"

"It's my fault that Groanin's in this position," said John. "If I hadn't looked into the future —"

"The future is certain, right enough," said Rakshasas. "Sure, it's the past that's unpredictable."

"— he'd never have come here at all."

"He never did like foreign travel, that's the truth. When you meet an Englishman like Mr. Groanin, it's hard to believe the British ever had the largest empire the world has ever known. If it had been up to him, the likes of Sir Francis Drake, John Churchill, Lord Nelson, and Captain Cook would never have left their armchairs in Portsmouth dock. Well, well, we're all different colors on life's paint box and no mistake."

"Wouldn't it be easier to take him with us?"

"No, no, it wouldn't," said Rakshasas. "You see, there's a strong possibility that his spirit might already have left his body and be wandering around Yellowstone. If we took off with his body now, we might never bring him back."

"So, where do we have to go?" asked John.

"A long, long way. The other side of the world, and beyond all probability, more or less. It's lucky you have the carpet because we've hours of flying ahead of us. Sure, it'll be like old times. It's ages since I was on an old Marrakesh

Express. That's what we used to call a flying carpet when I was a lad."

"Where do we have to go?" John was beginning to sound exasperated.

"Didn't I say? Tibet. That's where we're going, John. To Tibet. That's the only place that can help him now."

CHAPTER 27

A MESSAGE FROM BEYOND THE GRAVE

Back at the King David Hotel, Nimrod lamented the passing of Mr. Rakshasas to his former butler, Mr. Burton. "If only Mr. Rakshasas were still with us," he said. "He would know exactly where to begin the search for a legendary place like Shangri-la."

"An earthly place of paradise has been an enduring myth in all human mythology, has it not?" said Mr. Burton.

"Yes. From the Bible story of the Garden of Eden, to Dilmun in the Epic of Gilgamesh, even Celtic literature has its Islands of the Blessed. Pretty much all great human civilizations have their traveler's tales about a legendary lost paradise."

"Then it is my opinion," said Mr. Burton, "that the best place to begin such a search would be with the tales themselves. In a bookshop or perhaps a library. It is the curse of our modern times that people live their lives paying such little reference to so much knowledge."

"By Jove, you're right," said Nimrod. "I could visit the library inside Rakshasas's lamp. There's a collection of esoteric books in there that rivals the Library of Congress. He must have some rare and antiquarian books about Shangri-la."

Nimrod retrieved Mr. Rakshasas's djinn lamp from his leather Louis Choppsouis luggage, set it on the coffee table, and, having become a thick cloud of transubstantiated smoke, made his way into the lamp's enormous and esoteric interior.

The lamp was almost completely given over to a huge library that was as untidy as a Cornish boatyard, with books strewn about everywhere, and which revealed no discernible organization. For anyone who had never visited the Rakshasas Library, it would have been hard to believe that it was cared for by a devoted librarian.

Liskeard Karswell du Crowleigh had curated the Rakshasas Library for more than fifty years. He was also the bottle imp.

There are the children of hell. There the creatures of Beelzebub. There are mocking imps and there are petty fiends. There are flibbertigibbets, which were once wont to hang about a place of execution, and there are imps that were once children. There are little demons and evil spirits and there are bottle imps that some djinn employ to guard the lamps and bottles in which they sometimes live. Bottle imps are sometimes regarded as venomous but, strictly speaking — and there's no better way to speak to a bottle imp — this was not true of Liskeard. Because of his unpleasant taste for rotting animal flesh, the bacteria in his mouth were extremely dangerous, and this was the main reason why Nimrod did not employ an imp in his own lamp — although not because he was afraid of being bitten; it was just that Liskeard Karswell du Crowleigh had terribly bad breath.

It was several minutes before Liskeard, who was a former sorcerer, appeared in the great reading room, however. He bowed gravely to Nimrod and hissed a polite greeting to the man he now regarded as his lord and master:

"Good day to you, ssssir," he hissed for, despite his neat gray suit and vaguely human ways, Liskeard Karswell du Crowleigh most resembled a monitor lizard. "I'm sorry I did not come more quickly, but I was in the lower library stacks and it takes all of ten minutes to climb the cast iron stairs up to the reading room."

"How are you, Liskeard?" asked Nimrod.

"Very well, sssir."

"Are you sure?" Nimrod smiled kindly. After Mr. Rakshasas had died, Nimrod had offered Liskeard three wishes as a reward for his long and faithful service, but these Liskeard had declined on the grounds that having any kind of wish would have implied a strong longing for a specific thing he did not already have and since his life was the library and nothing but the library, he could not conceive of an alternative to that. Besides, Nimrod was quite unable to change Liskeard's hideous appearance which, it is to be imagined, otherwise would certainly have been at the top of his wish list.

"You weren't always a bottle imp, though, were you?" said Nimrod.

"No, sssir," admitted Liskeard. "Once I was a poor excuse for a sorcerer. Many years ago, I made the mistake of trying to steal the synopados, the soul mirror of a wicked djinn. The mirror was armed with a very powerful binding that turned me into the hideous-looking imp you see before you now, sssir. As I'm sure you are aware, sssir, a binding made by another djinn is irreversible, and since I have no idea whose mirror it was I tried to steal, I fear I shall be like this forever. Which makes it better that I live in here, sssir. Where my abhorrent appearance is an affront to no one." He smiled a hideous smile. "Besides, I like reading."

"Er, yes, quite," said Nimrod. "Well, perhaps one day we'll find out who was responsible for turning you into an imp and then we can sort you out, what?"

"Yesssssir." Liskeard kept on smiling his malodorous smile. "It was Mr. Rakshasas who took pity on me and invited me to become his librarian, and here I have remained ever since."

"And you're doing a splendid job, I'm sure, old fellow," said Nimrod.

"Thank you, sssir. Were you looking for a particular book; ssssir? Do please bear in mind that in this particular library, you only have to wish for a book and it will bring itself to you. Which is why we don't bother organizing the books in any alphabetical or subject or author order."

"I was wishing like mad for everything on Shangri-la," said Nimrod. "But so far the only thing that's turned up is you, old chap."

"That is unusual, ssssir." Liskeard shrugged. "Shangri-la and other material regarding an earthly paradise is almost certainly held in this library, sssir. I know because I've read several books on that subject myself. Most recently, *Lost Horizon* by James Hilton. That was a very good book, sssir. Very good. I think the last time I read it was 1966." Liskeard paused for a moment. "Yes, most certainly the library has many books on Shangri-la." Liskeard paused. "Unless . . ."

"What?"

"Well, I was merely recalling the fact that not long before he died, Mr. Rakshasas burned all of the books in one of the lower sections of the library."

"I didn't know that."

"Although it wasn't my place to solicit or to receive explanations, nevertheless, Mr. Rakshasas told me that all of the books were burned in fulfillment of a promise he had made to the High Lama of the Meru Lamasery."

"Did you say the Meru Lamasery?"

"Yessssssir. A lamasery is a Tibetan monastery, for Buddhist monks who are called lamas, right? Is it something to do with Shangri-la? Does the name of Meru mean something to you?"

"Possibly, yes." Nimrod shook his head. "But I wish I

knew why. And I do wish he hadn't burned all those books about Shangri-la. Promise or not."

As soon as Nimrod had spoken these words — and it must be remembered that this was a wishing library — Liskeard bowed gravely and spoke again, although this time the voice was not his own but that of Mr. Rakshasas:

"Your wish, dear Nimrod, is my command. If you're listening to this, I must be dead and you must have a very good reason for wishing I hadn't burned all my books about Shangri-la, or you wouldn't be here now and wishing what you've wished. If you haven't and you don't want to go to Shangri-la then smack the bottle imp five times on the head and this message will self-destruct. Otherwise pay careful attention as I'll say this only once.

"Years ago, I think it was 1937, I visited Shangri-la. And yes, it does exist, although it's not called Shangri-la. Not exactly. In point of fact, the place is called Shamba-la. And no, you don't remember me ever talking about it because I made a solemn promise to the monks of the lamasery on Mount Meru that I would never speak about the place during my lifetime. I also promised them that before I died I would destroy all of my books and papers about Shamba-la in order that we might keep the place a secret. Sure, if people knew that such a place as Shamba-la existed, they'd be lining up to get in there and the paradise would be spoiled, right enough.

"However, I happen to know that the author, James Hilton, based his novel *Lost Horizon* on the notes of an Austrian-American called Joseph Rock. Now this fellow

Rock was a great explorer and knew Tibet very well in the 1920s. Almost certainly he visited Shamba-la, because when I was there I found some of his possessions. And they knew his name. Anyway, Rock died in 1962 and left all of his books and papers to the Jewish National and University Library."

"You mean the National Library here in Israel?" said Nimrod.

"*Are we* in Israel?" It was the voice of Liskeard interrupting, momentarily, the message left within him by Mr. Rakshasas.

"As it happens, we are," said Nimrod.

Liskeard was silent for a moment before Mr. Rakshasas continued speaking:

"It's Joseph Rock's papers you'll be needing, Nimrod, if you're ever going to find Mount Meru and Shamba-la. Because that's where you'll find it and you probably don't need me to tell you that Mount Meru is the same Mount Meru that exists at the center of the universe in Hindu mythology. Find that and you'll have found Shamba-la. I'm pretty sure that Rock's papers will tell you how.

"The last I heard, the head librarian at the Jewish Library was a djinn of the Jinn tribe by the name of Rabbi Joshua. He's an awkward customer, is Rabbi Joshua. A Kabbalist, which, among other things, means he believes that every number contains a secret meaning and, to get him to cooperate and lend you Joseph Rock's papers on Shamba-la, you may have to play a game of Djinnverso with him. And win. But beware, Rabbi Joshua is a bit of a gambler."

Nimrod groaned.

"You need the Rock papers, old friend, so you'll have to be polite to him," said the voice of Rakshasas. "Bite your tongue if you have to, but get those papers. There's no other way to get to Shamba-la. And by the way, there's something you'll need if they're going to let you into their earthly paradise. You're going to need to find a man or a woman who is genuinely content with his or her lot in life to keep you company on your expedition. Believe me, you won't get in without such a person. And you can take my word that he or she won't be easy to find because such people are rather thin on the ground these days."

"Too true," murmured Nimrod. "Especially these days."

"Good luck, Nimrod," said Rakshasas. "I wish I was coming with you. And keep a tight lip on where you're planning to go. Fences and ditches have ears when it's Shamba-la you're talking about. And if you get there and you come back, just remember that a man's eye should always be blind in the home of a friend. That's why I burned all those books. Good-bye. Good-bye, old friend."

CHAPTER 28

KABBAL BABBEL

Like many public buildings in Israel, the Jewish National & University Library in Jerusalem on Mount Scopus looked more like a military headquarters than a repository for all the nation's books. It was built of beige-colored stone and featured a little ornamental pool out front with three primitive-looking fountains that reminded Nimrod of drinking-water faucets in the lavatories at his old school.

Inside the dimly lit lobby of the building was a triptych, meaning "three," of modern stained-glass windows — one red, two blue — that also reminded Nimrod of being back at school: It looked like just the kind of thing that the art class might have painted on one of the larger walls.

"The red panel has exactly seventy-seven panels," Nimrod told Rabbi Joshua when he came to find him in the lobby. "I just counted them while I was waiting."

"I didn't know that," said Rabbi Joshua. "Gee, thanks a lot. Seventy-seven is one of my favorite numbers."

"Is it really?"

"It's the smallest possible integer requiring five syllables in English. Let's go and talk in my office."

Rabbi Joshua led the way. He was a tall, thin man with a long black beard and long locks of hair on the sides of his head. He wore a plain white shirt and black trousers, and on his head, a little skullcap.

"Hot out there," he said, changing the subject for just a second since, as it happened, he hadn't yet given up on the number seventy-seven. "Seventy-seven is one of the coolest numbers there is." His accent was American.

"Really?" said Nimrod.

"Oh, sure. It's the twenty-second discrete biprime as well as being a Gaussian prime since it's a multiple of two primes — seven and eleven. Which of course means it's a Blum integer. Not only that, but it's the sum of three squares: four squared plus five squared plus six squared. Believe me, I could go on all day about seventy-seven. Did you know that it's the sum of the first eight prime numbers?"

"Er, no," said Nimrod. He could see that it was going to be a difficult meeting. If there was one thing he disliked, it was a number freak.

"Like I said, it's a very cool number. In Islam. In Judaism. In Christianity. During the Second World War in Sweden, at the border with Norway? They used it as a shibboleth — a password — because it's not easy to say seventy-seven in Swedish and that way it was easy to work out if someone was Swedish, German, or Norwegian."

"And to keep them out," said Nimrod. "Yes, that sounds like Sweden, all right."

Rabbi Joshua's office was a shrine to numerology and the Kabbalah. There was a curious poster on his wall depicting a tree of life that looked more like an ancient family coat of arms, pictures of famous mathematicians, a coin-operated model of the Temple of Solomon, and an odd piano that Nimrod commented on: It had a normal-looking keyboard, but attached to the keyboard were a series of wooden cages in ascending order of size.

"That's an interesting piano," he said.

"It's a cat piano," said Rabbi Joshua. "The idea is you put cats of different sizes in the cages and when you hit one of the piano keys it pokes the cat and makes it scream. You put the kittens at the treble end of the keyboard and the fully grown ones at the bass end."

"What a horrible thing," said Nimrod, who was fond of cats.

Rabbi Joshua smiled. "I've never played it," he admitted. "Not yet, anyway. Hey, it's nice to see a fellow djinn. In here I'm kind of by myself, and I don't put myself in djinn society the way I should. How is Mr. Rakshasas?"

"Dead," said Nimrod.

"Gee, that's too bad. What happened to his books?"

"He left them to me."

"He had some rare ones, didn't he?" said Rabbi Joshua. "So, what can I do for you?"

"I'd like to borrow something from your archives department."

"That could be difficult. Some of that stuff is pretty valuable."

"Well, I'm not asking to borrow the Albert Einstein Archive," said Nimrod.

"Good, because I'd have to say no. Even to you, Nimrod. I could let you see it, though. Hey, did you know that Einstein's birthday on March 14, 1879, can be arranged as 3-14-1879 or 3.141879? Which means that his birthday is just 0.000287 percent away from being the number pi, which, as I'm sure you know, is 3.141592 and probably the most important number in geometry. I mean, no wonder Einstein's mind was in tune with the universe, right?"

Nimrod nodded. "No, it's the Joseph Rock Archive I want to borrow."

"Rock. Rock. Can't say I recall that name off the top of my head," admitted Rabbi Joshua.

"He was an explorer," said Nimrod. "An Austrian-American who traveled in Tibet a lot."

"Mind telling me why you want to look at it?"

"I promise you," said Nimrod, "it's got nothing to do with numbers."

"Everything's got something to do with numbers," insisted Rabbi Joshua. "That's what makes them so interesting."

"If you say so."

"Tell you what. I'll play you at Djinnverso. Best of five games. If you win, you can borrow this Joe Rock Archive."

"And if I lose?" asked Nimrod.

"You let me take a look at the Rakshasas Library. See what he's got in there. Maybe we could make you an offer for some of the good stuff."

"All right," said Nimrod. "It's a deal. Best of five."

"Five's an even cooler number than seventy-seven," said Rabbi Joshua, fetching his Djinnverso set from a drawer in his desk. "Five's a prime number, a Fibonacci number, a Catalan number, a pentagonal number, a Bell number, a centered square number; there are five elements including spirit, and five natural senses; five Sikh virtues, and five Sikh sins; in many ways five is my favorite number of all."

They started to play. Nimrod won the first game and Rabbi Joshua won the second. However, he was not content with the wager they had made and offered Nimrod what the djinn call a Pension Bet. This is when one djinn agrees to give another three wishes for his old age (or sometimes before), when full djinn power has begun to fade.

"You mean on top of the bet we already made?" asked Nimrod. "Concerning the Rock Archive."

"Sure," said Rabbi Joshua.

Nimrod didn't like Pension Bets because, on principle, he didn't like the idea of one djinn owing something to another. To make a Pension Bet was, as Rakshasas had once said, "Like one dog chaining itself to another, it stands to reason that two dogs will want to go two different ways." In spite of these reservations, Nimrod agreed to the bet, however, for he could see no other way of reaching Shamba-la than getting to borrow the Rock archives.

Nimrod won the next two games.

Which also meant he won the right to borrow the archives and the Pension Bet of having three wishes from the rabbi.

With anyone else but a djinn, Nimrod might have forgiven the debt, but djinn etiquette was very precise about such matters: To decline the three wishes won as a result of a Pension Bet would have counted as a grave insult and might have resulted in his being challenged to a djinn duel.[1]

"Double or quits," offered the rabbi.

"Six wishes from one djinn to another?" Nimrod shook his head. "Impossible. You know how it works. A fourth wish cancels out the first three."

"Not three wishes from me," explained Rabbi Joshua. "I own a lot of Pension Bets, from other djinn. Lilith de Ghulle, Jirjis Ibn Rajmus, Mr. Vodyannoy, to name but three."

"I bet you do."

Nimrod shook his head, which seemed to set something off in his memory because suddenly he recalled something that Zagreus had told him on the plane from London to Fez: that he believed his progression from one incarnation to another had been prevented by a Mr. Churches. To Nimrod, it seemed quite possible that the name Zagreus had heard had really been that of Mr. *Jirjis*, which sounds a bit like "churches."

[1] Djinn duels, also known as Cagliostro Duels, are always settled medicinally, which is to say that each djinn arrives at the duel with three apparently identical pills, two of which are harmless but one of which contains a diminuendo binding. Each djinn swallows the other djinn's pills in turn, until one of them starts to shrink and, as a result, is judged to have lost the duel. Nimrod had fought and won only one such duel in his lifetime — against Rajmus the Ifrit, who was the father of Jirjis.

"I don't think I'd like to have the son of Rajmus the Ifrit owe me a Pension Bet," said Nimrod. "I might not get the chance to call it in."

"Maybe you're right at that," admitted Rabbi Joshua. "He was kind of angry about it when he lost."

"How did you come to be playing a nasty piece of work like him, anyway?"

"Jirjis?" Rabbi Joshua shrugged. "It's a library. People want to borrow books and archives. Even wicked djinn from the deep south of the United States."

"What did an Ifrit want to borrow?"

"As a matter of fact, he wanted to borrow the Einstein Archive."

"Did you lend it to him?"

"No. Of course not." Rabbi Joshua shrugged again. "I won that bet. So, what do you say?"

"You mean double or quits?" Nimrod shook his head. "I should say not."

"All right, all right, you win, Nimrod," said Rabbi Joshua. "Let's go and see if we can find that Rock Archive for you."

Nimrod followed Rabbi Joshua downstairs into the library's basement and then beyond that into the deep rock of Mount Scopus, where, in A.D. 66, a Roman legion had camped in order to besiege the city of Jerusalem.

"Conditions down here are perfect for the storage of rare archives," explained Rabbi Joshua. "Air temperature is a constant sixty degrees Fahrenheit, with exactly fifty percent humidity. And of course, security is excellent. Quite apart from the usual electronic bits and bobs, I have installed one particular device I think you'll be interested in: a golem. You know? A man-thing, an artificial creature made from clay. To protect the archives."

"Was that altogether wise?" asked Nimrod.

"There's a great tradition of creating golems to protect us Jews," said the rabbi.

"Yes, but surely you remember what happened when the rabbi of Prague, Judah Loew ben Bezalel, made a golem in 1580? The thing ran amok and started killing not just people who were persecuting Jews but a lot of innocent people also."

Rabbi Joshua shook his head. "That's because he didn't make it properly. He was relying on an incorrect translation of how to make a golem contained in the Book of Creation. Mine is the correct word of power, which means the golem can only obey me."

"Nevertheless," argued Nimrod, "you would still have to write the word of power on a piece of parchment and hide it somewhere on the golem's body."

"Relax, Nimrod," said Rabbi Joshua. "Everything is under control. I know what I'm doing. I put the word of truth in its mouth. To deactivate it, you would merely have to say the Hebrew word for truth."

They reached a thick glass door that slid open when the rabbi tapped a series of numbers into a keypad on the wall.

"How often do you come down here?" asked Nimrod.

"In truth, hardly at all. That's the main reason I try to deter people from frivolously using the archive. We like to leave the atmosphere in the archive rooms undisturbed, to keep the temperature constant. We call these the Goldilocks rooms. Not too hot and not too cold. To protect the archives."

"And the golem lives in here?"

"It doesn't live," said the rabbi. "That's the whole point of a golem. It's not like a bottle imp. It's just a thing. A man with no soul."

"Wasn't Adam, in the Book of Genesis, a golem, too?" said Nimrod. "For the first twelve hours of his existence?"

"Yes, I suppose he was," admitted Rabbi Joshua. "But then the trouble only started after he was given a soul."

"True," said Nimrod. "But life — any kind of life, even life that's not much more than dirt — finds a way."

"Not this time." The rabbi operated another sliding door and led Nimrod down a long corridor that opened on to a series of archive rooms. But as soon as they had turned a corner in the corridor, it was plain that something had gone badly wrong. The glass door to the Einstein Archive had been shattered and papers were strewn all across the floor. Nimrod guessed this was the Einstein Archive because Albert Einstein's distinctive features were carved in bas-relief above what remained of the door.

Rabbi Joshua let out a wail of horror and rushed inside.

"Oh, my goodness!" he said. "We've had a break-in. The Einstein papers. They're everywhere. Just look at all this mess."

Nimrod picked a sheet of paper off the floor and glanced over a sample of Einstein's very small, black handwriting, which was in German, of course. Nimrod thought it looked like a fairy's handwriting, and he'd only seen one hand that was smaller and neater: his own.

"Can you tell if anything has been stolen?" he asked.

"No. It'll take ages to find that out. Who would do such a thing?"

"I can think of one person," said Nimrod.

"Who?"

"Jirjis Ibn Rajmus."

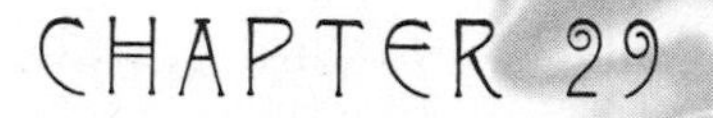

CHAPTER 29

MR. SWARASWATI'S FEAR OF FLYING

In a quiet field behind the black ruins of St. Archibald's Cathedral on the top of Bumby's forbidding North Cliff, Philippa rolled out her sapphire-blue flying carpet under an enormous gray cloud and prepared for takeoff, which is to say she sat down and gathered her thoughts prior to uttering her new focus word.

She had given a great deal of thought to devising a new focus word and had come up with an even longer word than her previous word, which was: FABULONGOSHOOMARVELISHLYWONDERPIPICAL. Philippa had chosen a new word that was easy for her to remember and articulate but which, at the same time, was extremely time consuming to say. The simple fact of the matter was that lately she was more than a little in awe of her own djinn power and had concluded it might be better to have a focus word that was so very long she might still be able to change her mind about using djinn power before she finished saying it; in which case she might leave the rest of the word unspoken. In this way, she hoped she might avoid the same mistakes her mother, Layla, had made that had resulted in her complete renunciation of her own djinn power. Otherwise, it was only too easy to turn two men into budgies. Or cats and dogs. Which was not a power Philippa much enjoyed.

Mr. Swaraswati sat beside Philippa on the carpet and, pulling his big toes toward him like the reins of a horse, nervously awaited its ascent. Having spent so much of his life buried six feet underground, the idea of flying several thousand feet above it left him feeling anxious and apprehensive and a little light-headed.

"And you're sure it's possible to breathe at such an altitude?" he asked Philippa. He looked pale and nauseous and his hands were trembling.

"It's possible to breathe at up to twenty thousand feet," said Philippa. "After that the oxygen gets pretty thin and you have to wear a mask."

"Is that so the gods will not recognize you and throw you back down to the ground for your impudence in coming among them?" he asked.

"Er, no," said Philippa. "It's a mask to help you breathe more easily."

Mr. Swaraswati took a deep breath and wondered if it might be best for him just to hold his breath until the flight was over. "I see. What speed will we travel at?"

"Oh, I dunno," said Philippa. "Two or three hundred miles an hour?"

"Is it possible?" Mr. Swaraswati was incredulous. "If a man traveled at such a speed, surely he would die a horrible, horrible death. His head would fall off and his flesh would be torn from his bones. His eyes would be squeezed out of his skull and his lungs would be sucked out of his chest."

"No, no," Philippa said airily. "Men have traveled in space at speeds of up to eighteen thousand miles per hour."

"Truly?"

"Truly." Philippa smiled. "Ask Moo. She flew to Yorkshire with me. From Morocco."

"Yes, it's quite true," said Moo. "And I'm still here to tell the tale. There's absolutely nothing to worry about, Mr. Swaraswati, I can assure you."

Mr. Swaraswati nodded gravely.

"I see," he said thoughtfully. "That is most reassuring. And if we fall off the flying carpet, then we will not die, either, yes?"

"Er, no," said Philippa. "That's not quite correct. A fall from the sort of height we'll be flying at would, most probably, be fatal. Nothing much has changed there, I'm afraid."

"Then I'm afraid, too," said Mr. Swaraswati.

"But it's quite a big carpet," said Philippa. "And these carpets tend to fly very hard and flat. So if you keep away from the edge and don't wander around, I think you'll be perfectly safe."

"Perfectly safe," said Moo, who was impatient to get back to London, especially now that it had started to rain.

When at last Mr. Swaraswati was reassured that he might fly on the carpet and live, Philippa set about taking off.

"DIDDLEEYEJOEFROMMEJICOFELLOFFHIS-HORSEATARODEOHANDSUPSTICKEMUP-DROPTHEMGUNSANDPICKEMUPDIDDLEEYEJOE-FROMMEJICO!"

As soon as Philippa had finished speaking her new focus word, which took all of eight seconds, the flying carpet began to rise up in the air. It remained as hard as a wooden floor, but while they remained untouched by the wind, there was little Philippa could do to avoid the rain except issue Moo and Mr. Swaraswati djinn-made umbrellas and try to steer the carpet above the clouds. But having entered a large rain cloud, she discovered that it was thousands of feet in height and width, and it wasn't very long before the carpet and its three passengers were being buffeted by some very turbulent weather.

"Sorry about this," Philippa told Mr. Swaraswati and Moo. "It's just a bit of air turbulence. I'll try and get us above this cloud as soon as I can and find us some smoother air."

"I say," said Moo as the carpet hit an air pocket that felt like an earthquake. "Quite a roller coaster this trip, eh? Whoops. That one felt like I was in a barrel going over Niagara."

Moo's description of the flight was extremely accurate. For a moment, the carpet fell several hundred feet, before another air pocket brought them up short with a loud bang as if they had hit a huge pothole in a road.

"Oh, God," said Mr. Swaraswati and, wiping the rain from his face and wringing out his beard, he began to pray, and pray quickly for the amber prayer beads he held in his gnarled hand were passing between his finger and thumb so fast that he might almost have been counting the individual air pockets that buffeted the flying carpet. "I think," he said, not unreasonably, "I have a tremendous fear of flying."

Philippa concentrated on taking the carpet even higher, but the gray cloud, a cumulonimbus, heavy with rain like a giant dirty sponge filled with water, seemed to be interminable.

Worse was to follow, however, as a sheet of lightning flashed in front of them and lit up the sky like a phalanx of photographers. And a few seconds later, a rumble of thunder turned into a virtual artillery barrage.

"This isn't good," murmured Philippa.

"I will never complain about British Airways again," Moo shouted above the tumultuous noise.

Mr. Swaraswati threw away his prayer beads and covered his ears with the palms of his hands. "Oh, calamity!" he cried. "Calamity!"

"You're not helping," Philippa told her passengers. "Gee, no wonder pilots lock the door to the cockpit."

"Can't you get us out of here?" Moo shouted again to make herself heard above the terrible storm.

"I'm trying for Pete's sake," said Philippa, mentally redoubling her efforts to lift them clear of the tempest that now threatened to destroy them.

"Use your djinn power to quiet the storm," suggested Moo.

Philippa frowned. *Who does she think I am?* she wondered crossly. *Moses?*

"Or to make us feel more comfortable."

"Not while I'm flying this thing, I can't," Philippa said through gritted teeth. "I don't dare take my mind off handling the carpet in order to do any of that. I might lose control."

That's what comes of having a focus word that takes eight seconds to finish saying, she told herself, and resolved to go back to something shorter as soon as they were out of the storm.

Another sheet of lightning illuminated the sky around them, only this time it seemed closer than before, flashing on and off like a huge neon light that was about to conk out.

"I thought you said it was perfectly safe," yelled Mr. Swaraswati. By now, he was completely prostrate on the carpet, eyes closed, face pressed down as if he hoped he was underground again.

"It is," said Philippa. "Just try to relax."

For a moment Philippa lost sight of Mr. Swaraswati and Moo as the carpet entered a particularly thick and dark part of the thundercloud. And she was reaching out to take hold of the old fakir's hand when a third sheet of lightning split the darkening sky in front of her.

It wasn't just the sky that was split, only Philippa hardly knew this yet.

She snatched her hand away as if she had been electrocuted. Her whole arm felt numb. And when she inspected her fingers she found they were black as if they had been burned. Being a djinn this was hardly a great problem and the realization that she had been struck by lightning quickly gave way to a fear that something had happened to Moo and to Mr. Swaraswati, who were still lost in the thick cloud that now enveloped them.

"Moo?" said Philippa. "Mr. Swaraswati? Are you all right?"

Hearing no reply, Philippa leaned to one side and stretched out her arm to reassure herself that they were still there. And not finding anyone, she leaned a little farther and then a little farther still until she almost fell off the carpet, or what was left of it.

Philippa let out a horrified scream, for it was quickly apparent to her that the flying carpet had been cut in two by the sheet of lightning and that Moo and Mr. Swaraswati were gone. She herself was so close to the new edge of the bifurcated carpet that there was even a scorch mark on the trousers she was wearing.

She shouted their names again, only this time more loudly; she did this several times until, to her huge relief, in the distance she heard them call back.

"We're all right," shouted Moo. "We're still in the air, but we seem to be going around in circles. That last bolt of lightning must have cut the carpet in half. Where are you?"

"On the other half," called Philippa. "Keep shouting, and I'll come and look for you."

"I've never been a very shouty sort of person," said Moo. "But I'll do my best. Perhaps, if I was to recite a poem, that might help."

"I don't see how reciting poetry could help the situation," said Mr. Swaraswati. "A prayer might be better."

"I mean that Philippa can hear me reciting it," shouted Moo. "There's one I know by Kipling that has five verses, so that should give her plenty of time to get a fix on us. I often used to recite it to the girls at my school in India. Many years ago."

"Good idea," shouted Philippa, and wheeled the carpet around in the direction of Moo's voice even as the storm died away.

"There's nothing like a bit of Kipling," Moo told Mr. Swaraswati, "to keep your spirits up." Moo started to recite the poem.

Philippa steered the flying carpet back and forth, up and down through the huge gray cloud, but she continued to fail to see her two companions, and having the strong impression that, if anything, Moo's voice was getting even farther away, Philippa shouted out again.

"I can't hear you," she said. "What's the matter? Moo? Answer me. Have you stopped? You said there were five verses of that poem. I've only heard three."

There was no reply.

On she flew, around and around until at last she started to fear that she might end up getting as lost as Moo and Mr. Swaraswati.

"It's no good," she said after almost an hour's search had passed without result. "I can't see you and I can't hear you. I'm hoping that maybe the strip of carpet you're on will carry you on to London and my uncle Nimrod's house, like it was supposed to do. That's where I'm going, too. And if you're not there then Uncle Nimrod will probably know what to do, so don't panic. Don't panic. We'll think of a way to find you. I promise."

CHAPTER 30

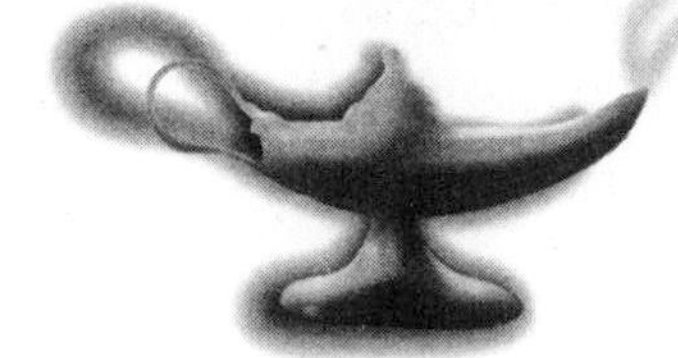

UNCLE NIMROD'S FLYING CARPET

Nimrod, flying back to London with Mr. Burton, tried to read the Joseph Rock papers that Rabbi Joshua had lent to him from the Jewish National Library. But his mind was elsewhere. Mostly his mind was back at the library in Jerusalem and the scene in the Einstein Archive where several hundred papers, including the great scientist's personal diary, were now missing, to say nothing of one golem.

"Remind me," said Nimrod. "The Lahore earthquake was when exactly?"

"April 1905," said Burton.

"A month before Einstein published his first great work on special relativity."

"Exactly. But why do you ask?"

"I was trying to think of a good reason why Jirjis Ibn Rajmus would want to steal Einstein's diary for the year of

1905. When he was working for the Swiss Patent Office in Bern. And I think I just thought of a good reason. Because the diary must explain something about the Faizabad fakir whose live burial was disturbed by the Lahore earthquake. There must be something in that diary about the man who quite possibly revealed to Einstein one of the great mysteries of the universe."

"Yes, I see what you mean," said Mr. Burton, stroking his long beard. "Who is this Jirjis Ibn Rajmus, anyway?"

"Jirjis is the son of Rajmus, who is himself the cousin of Iblis the Ifrit," said Nimrod. "Jirjis lives in the state of Georgia, in the southern United States of America."

"A djinn?"

"Yes, and a particularly nasty one, too," said Nimrod. "Jirjis killed his wife, you know — chopped her into pieces with an ax. And her, he loved. Imagine what he might do to someone he didn't like."

"It doesn't bear thinking of," agreed Mr. Burton. "But perhaps she provoked him in some way. The course of true love ne'er runs smooth, and all that sort of thing."

"The man who had tried to rescue her from a hole in the ground Jirjis turned into an ape."

"Better than killing him, I'd say," said Mr. Burton. "Still, I take your point. This Jirjis sounds like a thoroughly bad fellow."

"Oh, he is."

"Have you ever met him?"

"No, but I know his father, Rajmus," said Nimrod. "I fought a djinn duel against him once."

"Which I suppose you won," said Mr. Burton. "Since you're still here."

"Yes."

"So this Jirjis is not likely to feel particularly well-disposed to you or any member of your family," said Mr. Burton. "Or any of your friends."

"No, indeed," said Nimrod. "If ever we met, I think I can safely say it would be him or me."

"And you think he might be connected with the change in the world's luck?"

"It would certainly explain a great deal about what's going on," said Nimrod. "Possession of one or more as yet unrevealed secrets of the universe would be just the kind of power a djinn like him would crave. I imagine he wanted the Einstein papers for some clue that might be there as to how he might find one of the five remaining fakirs."

"But if he's a powerful djinn," said Mr. Burton.

"He is," said Nimrod. "Very powerful."

"Then what could he want with human knowledge?"

"Knowledge is knowledge," said Nimrod. "Whether it's human or djinn. And physics is physics. If there's another secret of the universe that's as important and momentous as *e* equals *mc* squared, then Jirjis would certainly want to have that knowledge. To build a weapon perhaps. To make himself more powerful. Who knows what's in a mind as warped as that?"

"I had forgotten how much wickedness is in the world," said Mr. Burton.

Arriving back in the garden of his house in Kensington and Bayswater, Nimrod eyed the flying carpet that was already lying on his lawn with concern because it was smaller than he remembered and scorched along one edge. And full of worry that something might have happened to Philippa, or to John — he was as yet uncertain to whom the flying carpet belonged — he hurried through the back door of his house.

Philippa was sitting in the kitchen nursing a cup of coffee, and seeing her uncle again she stood up and faced him nervously.

"It's not my fault," she said. "It's not my fault because there was this terrible storm, right? And the flying carpet got struck by a sheet of lightning. And the carpet got split into two and we got separated in a thick cloud and I flew around and looked for them for ages. And Moo recited a poem for me so that I might have some idea where they were. But it was no good because I couldn't see a thing inside the cloud and for all I know, she and Mr. Swaraswati are still up there, because they're not here like I hoped they would be. And I really didn't know what to do so I came back here, but they weren't and now you are, thank goodness, because we have to go back and look for them right away even though I'm tired and I just want to go to bed and sleep for, like, a thousand years."

Philippa sat down and looked miserable.

"Mr. Swaraswati?" asked Nimrod.

"Mr. Swaraswati is the fakir," said Philippa. "The real fakir. One of the fakirs who got told one of the secrets of the universe by the Tirthankar of Faizabad. And not one of those fake mendicant fakirs. I had to deal with them. Two of them.

They were really unpleasant. I had to turn them into budgies. Only they got eaten by a couple of ferrets. Which kind of upset me." Philippa swallowed with difficulty. "A lot, because I guess that means they're dead. Which makes it my fault. And I'm really not very happy about that. I mean, I'm beginning to see my mother's POV on this one, Uncle Nimrod."

Tears welled up in Philippa's eyes and, taking off her glasses, she blinked several times and tried to hold on to herself.

Nimrod handed her a handkerchief and she wiped her eyes and blew her nose loudly.

"And you left him alone on a cloud, with one of the last great secrets of the universe?" said Mr. Burton.

"And Moo," said Philippa. "He's not alone. Moo's with him." She offered Nimrod back his handkerchief.

"Oh, well, I suppose that makes it all right," said Mr. Burton.

"Keep it." Nimrod tutted loudly. "Budgies, eh?"

"Yes."

"Pity," said Nimrod. "It would have been useful to have questioned them."

"Oh, I did," said Philippa. "They told me they were working for some sheikh who lives in Cairo. A man called —"

"Jirjis Ibn Rajmus," said Nimrod.

"Yes. How did you know?"

Nimrod shook his head. "Never mind that. We've got to find that fakir before someone else does." Nimrod pointed at the garden. "Come on," he said. "There's no time to lose. A flying carpet without a guiding mind could end up just about anywhere, depending on the wind. Fortunately for us, when properly directed to do so, one rug will follow the other. I shall simply direct my own carpet to pursue what remains of your own carpet, much as I would instruct a bloodhound to go after a scent."

"I might have done that myself," explained Philippa. "But I didn't know how."

"Didn't you see me do it with Groanin?" asked Nimrod. "Back in the Atlas Mountains?"

"No."

"By the way, have you heard anything from Groanin? Or John?"

"No."

"Oh, well, I'm sure they're all right. I armed Groanin with a discrimens, just in case of an emergency. Not to mention enough stores to equip an expedition to the South Pole." Nimrod frowned. "Now where was I?"

"Telling me how to sic one carpet on another."

"Oh, yes. Well, it's quite simple," said Nimrod, and in the garden he showed Philippa how it was done.

"You take a very sharp knife or a razor," he explained. "And with it you lightly shave the surface of the carpet until you have collected a small amount of material on the blade's edge." Nimrod produced a disposable razor from his coat pocket and scraped it across the carpet until there were a few millimeters of blue fibers visible on the blade. "Now, the carpet is made of silk, of course, so you have to make a mark of respect to the carpet by crushing the larva of a *Bombyx mori* in your hand. That's a domesticated silk moth to an American like you, Philippa."

Muttering his focus word, which was QWERTYUIOP, Nimrod opened his palm to reveal a white lepidopteran larva, about one inch long, with a little horn on its back.

"Like this," he added. "Fascinating little creatures, really. Each one can make a cocoon that's made of a raw silk thread of up to three thousand feet long. Think of it: Just ten of these little blighters and you could have a thread that's the height of Mount Everest." He sighed. "Shame to kill it really, but that's the thing about a lot of old djinn bindings. It is rather cruel. But then so is meat, I suppose."

Philippa pulled a face at the sight of the worm in Nimrod's hand.

"Then you blow the fluff from the blade into the air above the carpet and strike it hard, three times with the palm of the hand in which you just crushed the silkworm larva, and shout '*suivi*,' as if you were playing baccarat or chemin de fer. I kid you not."

"I'm surprised I didn't work it out myself," said Philippa.

Nimrod shrugged. "I know it all sounds terribly arcane and old-fashioned, but this is one of the reasons we djinn abandoned flying carpets in the first place and took up riding whirlwinds. That and bad weather, of course. Flying carpets aren't so good in storms, as you've already discovered."

"And how."

When Mr. Burton and Philippa had seated themselves on the flying carpet, Nimrod blew the silk fibers into the air, crushed the silkworm larva in his hand, and banged hard three times on the surface of the carpet. Nothing happened.

"Ah," said Nimrod. "I was forgetting something." And taking hold of Philippa's thumb, he stabbed it quickly with a pin. "The scent."

"Ow," she protested loudly.

Nimrod held her thumb so that a large red pearl of blood dripped onto his carpet.

"Didn't you have some of my blood already?" she said, wincing as her uncle squeezed her thumb like the rubber end of an eyedropper.

"Fresh is best, I think," said Nimrod. "Besides, I already used that blood to set Groanin on his way from Morocco."

Once again, he slapped the carpet three times with the flat of his caterpillar-sticky hand and shouted "*suivi*," and, once again, nothing happened.

"Perhaps it already thinks it's found what it was supposed to be looking for," said Philippa, pointing to her flying carpet that lay a few yards away on the lawn of Nimrod's back garden.

"Yes, of course," said Nimrod. "Stupid of me." And uttering his focus word once again he flicked a small ball of fire at the remnant of Philippa's carpet, which disappeared in a cloud of smoke. "Sorry about that. But we'll get you another when we have to take Mr. Burton back home to Morocco."

As soon as Philippa's carpet was no more, the carpet rose in the air, and soon they were flying south.

"Er, are you sure about this direction?" Philippa asked her uncle. "Yorkshire's north of here, isn't it? Not southeast."

"A *suivi* binding is quite infallible," insisted Nimrod. "This must be the direction where the other half of your carpet is headed or has ended up."

"I hope they're all right," said Philippa.

And on they flew, across the English Channel and into mainland Europe.

"This is all to the good," insisted Nimrod. "We'd have to fly in this direction, anyway. Because as soon as we have rescued Moo and Mr. Swaraswati, we are headed for Tibet."

"Tibet?" said Philippa. "What's in Tibet?"

"When I was inside the omphalos at the Church of the Holy Sepulchre in Jerusalem," explained Nimrod, "the oracle revealed to me that if I wished to bring about the impossible — suddenly to make a great many people feel that the world is a better, happier place than it was before and that they themselves can actively share in the world's new good fortune — then I should find Shangri-la."

"Shangri-la?" said Philippa. "You mean there really is a lost paradise in the Tibetan Himalayas where time and history have no meaning?"

"Apparently so," said Nimrod. "Except that it's not really called Shangri-la but Shamba-la. This archive, the Joseph Rock Archive I brought with me from the Jewish National Library, explains exactly how to get there. Wherever we seem to be going now appears to be vaguely southeast, which is on the way to Tibet, as the crow flies."

As if to confirm this, a crow flew alongside them for a while, and even perched on the edge of the carpet for a short rest before Mr. Burton, who held that crows were birds of ill-omen and therefore unlucky, shooed it away.

Finally, after almost ninety minutes, the flying carpet dipped toward what Nimrod declared to be Germany's Main River, which is not the main river in Germany — that's the Rhine — but a tributary of the Rhine called the Main.

"We seem to be heading for Frankfurt," said Nimrod.

The carpet dipped again and seemed to aim itself at the city's tallest buildings in Frankfurt's banking district, and then at one building in particular — a rather ugly-looking skyscraper with a signal mast and a yellow logo that enabled Nimrod to identify it as the Commerzbank Tower. Like many other European banks, the Commerzbank had gone bankrupt several months ago, and there was an enormous sign on the uppermost window that read ZUM VERKAUF, which in German means "for sale." Next to the signal tower was a flat roof on which, some eight hundred feet above the city of Frankfurt itself, was a small blue carpet and two people waving at them.

"It's Moo and Mr. Swaraswati," said Philippa.

The carpet circled over the rooftop for a moment and then descended slowly.

"Thank goodness," said Moo. "I thought we were going to be stuck up here for ages. We've been waving to those blasted window cleaners on that building opposite for almost an hour. They were waving back, too. They must have thought we were just being friendly."

"Not waving but drowning, eh?" said Nimrod as his carpet settled on the rooftop. "Well, it looks like they've got something else to think about now. Us. We'd best get going soon, before a television crew turns up. It's not every day people see a flying carpet."

"It's been a very trying time," said Moo. "After we lost you, Philippa, we thought we were done for. Especially when we crossed the North Sea. Where on earth are we, anyway?"

"Germany," said Philippa. "Frankfurt. The Commerzbank Tower, I think."

"These carpets are designed to land somewhere safe, eventually," said Nimrod. "When they lack direction and control. And you can't get anywhere safer than a bank."

"That only used to be true," said Moo. "Either way, I'm very happy to see you all. Very happy."

"That reminds me," said Nimrod, and having explained to Moo and Mr. Swaraswati that they were all now going to Tibet, he added, "I'm reliably informed that to gain admittance to Shamba-la we are going to need a really happy man in our company."

"This is Germany," said Moo. "Finding a really happy man here isn't going to be easy. At least not until the beer festival in October."

"Mr. Burton?" said Nimrod. "Would you say that you're really happy?"

"My life has not been of sufficient benefit to others for me to say that I am truly happy," he said. "What happiness I have known has been like a beautiful butterfly that settled upon my shoulder when I wasn't looking."

"I'll take that as a no, then. Moo?"

"I don't know why we're on this earth," said Moo. "But I'm darned sure it's not in order to be happy." She shrugged. "But whatever it is, I should think that being the head of the British KGB and happiness are an impossible combination."

"Mr. Swaraswati?"

"Since it seems I must ride on another of these terrible flying carpets, I could hardly describe myself as being truly happy, no," he said.

"We could always fly back to England," said Moo. "My local milkman is always whistling a happy tune. Drives me mad with it. Of course he doesn't look very happy. We English never do. Our teeth aren't good enough for us to smile a lot." Moo punched Nimrod gently on the shoulder. "What about you, Nimrod? You're wise enough to seem quite happy."

"Too kind, dear lady, too kind," said Nimrod. "It's true that wisdom is the greater part of happiness. And I feel very happy. But strictly speaking, I'm not a man at all. And nor is Philippa. Which is to say, she's a djinn, not a human being, and we have a bit of an advantage when it comes to being happy."

Philippa nodded. "There is no greater happiness than making other people happy, I think. Although as I've discovered, granting someone their dearest wish isn't always that easy."

"Well said, Philippa," said Nimrod.

"Which reminds me, Uncle Nimrod," said Philippa. "Yes, of course. Why didn't I think of him right away? A really happy man. I think I know exactly where to find one. And it so happens that it's on the way to Tibet. As the crow flies."

CHAPTER 31

THE HUNGER CRY

Zagreus, the bigfoot, watched the flying carpet carrying John and Rakshasas the wolf until it was just a dot on the western horizon and then let out a big, smelly yak-sized sigh. Already he felt the parting from John acutely, for he was of the opinion that he owed the boy djinn everything: But for John he'd still have been stuck in Bumby, a Jinx with no idea of who or what he was supposed to be.

At the same time, Zagreus was feeling comfortable in his shaggy skin for the first time ever, as far as he was able to tell, and had quite forgotten who and what he had once been before being a Jinx; and even that would soon fade from his memory.

The bigfoot sat down heavily next to the burial mound of snow that contained Groanin's body and occupied himself for several minutes throwing snowballs at a lodgepole pine. He was good at throwing snowballs. There is no creature better at throwing snowballs than a bigfoot — not even a small boy with a policeman in his sights. But after a while he got bored throwing snowballs and, feeling hungry, he went over to the tree he'd been aiming at and, ripping off several branches, ate several pounds of crunchy, scented pine needles. Then he burped and sat down again.

There was nothing else for him to do now except await their return. Until then, he knew what he had to do. Indeed, he was thoroughly alive to the very real danger that existed inside the park. Somewhere in the immediate vicinity was a hungry wolf pack and at least one grizzly bear. If what John had said was correct, they would both have caught the scent of Groanin's blood on the snow and even now would very likely be trying to track down its source. Simply put, the bigfoot's job was to see that neither the bears nor the wolves were able to dig up the butler's body and eat it.

Zagreus burped again and brought something up. Still getting used to being a bigfoot, he was a little surprised to discover a large portion of his own meal arriving back in his mouth from his stomach to be chewed a second time. It was only now that he realized he was a ruminant, and that his body was unable to produce the enzymes required to break down the cellulose in plant matter, and that he was going to have to chew the cud that was what the bolus of semi-degraded food he'd just regurgitated was properly called.

That might have disgusted him as a human being, but it didn't disgust him as a bigfoot. Chewing the cud felt as natural to Zagreus as it would have felt to a well-adjusted cow. Chewing the cud was something to do at least. And he was chewing that cud for quite a while before the pine needles were all chewed enough to swallow a second time. Chewing was hard work.

Silence settled on the thick and brilliant Yellowstone snow — so bright that Zagreus felt obliged to close his eyes against the glare and, for a while, he dozed quite unaware of the fact that Groanin was sitting next to him and had been for some time.

"Wake up, you great daft lummox," said Groanin, and punched Zagreus on his enormous hairy shoulder, but the bigfoot did not respond to the butler's fist.

Groanin, who had overheard John telling Zagreus that the butler was in a place between life and death, knew it was absolutely crucial that his body remained cold and uneaten by any wild animals if ever he was to be revived, but he already despaired that the sleepy bigfoot would prove unequal to the task of guarding him that now lay ahead.

"You're supposed to be guarding my body," he said. "I say, you're supposed to be guarding my dead body. Not snoring away like a flipping lumberjack's saw."

Groanin shook his head irritably.

"By heck, I pity the female bigfoot — assuming there is such a thing — that has to live with that flipping sound," he muttered. "I've heard some snoring in my time. My old dad could have snored for England. But that. That's superheavyweight champion-of-the-world snoring, is that. Bigfoot, my elbow. Bignose, more like. Big lungs. You big daft lummox."

In the far distance, a wolf howled a quavering note that was full of melancholy and hunger.

"Did you hear that?" Groanin felt a spasm of fear pass through him like a cold wind and then another one as suddenly he realized that he wasn't much more than a breath of cold wind himself. For the first time he had an insight into what it was like to be a djinn, albeit a djinn in a transubstantiated or spiritual out-of-body state. "That was a wolf, wasn't it?"

But Zagreus remained loudly asleep.

Another wolf howled a reply to the first as if they were coördinating a search for the butler's body.

"Wake up, you outsized chimpanzee," said Groanin. "Before them wolves start to chow down on my corpse. Come on, you hairy baboon. Wakey-wakey."

Zagreus opened one large brown eye. He had not heard Groanin's voice, but he had heard the wolf. His hearing was as sharp as any predator's.

He stood up — by now he was almost nine feet tall — and walked around in a circle for a while. Groanin didn't know it but the bigfoot was leaving his strong scent on the snow like an invisible stockade in the hope that the pack of wolves would smell it and treat it with caution. He was correct in this respect; wolves were afraid of a bigfoot, almost as afraid as they were of a man with a rifle.

"Here, shouldn't you build a fire?" said Groanin. "To help keep them wolves off?" Then he shook his head. "On second thought, ignore that suggestion. A fire might start to melt that heap of snow that is keeping my body cold. I'm nothing but a bag of frozen peas, I am."

When he'd finished marking out his territory, Zagreus sat down again, and this time he sat down on top of the burial mound.

"If you don't mind, that's my head you just parked your enormous backside on top of," complained Groanin.

Zagreus stayed put even when the first wolf turned up and lay down like a contented dog at a safe distance from the burial mound. A big silver-gray wolf, he licked his jaws and glanced around as another wolf came and lay beside him, and then another. None of them seemed fierce so much as patient — very patient, as if they realized it was only a question of waiting there long enough before Zagreus fell asleep or got bored and abandoned his lonely outpost.

Zagreus grinned a bigfoot grin and made a snowball — the cruel kind, with a piece of ice at its core — and hurled it at the first wolf, striking it full on the muzzle.

The wolf yelped with pain as the piece of ice connected with its nose, and retired to a safer distance. So did the others.

"Good shot," said Groanin.

Zagreus hurled another snowball and then another, both of which fell just short of the wolves in their new position.

"Looks like they've found your range," Groanin said redundantly.

Zagreus beat his leathery chest and roared, but the wolves stayed put at this display of bluff.

"I can't bear to look," said Groanin, beside himself with

worry. "I think you've got your work cut out and no mistake, Zagreus, old mate."

The butler got up and walked away, almost certain that it would not be very long before the wolf pack was tucking in to a full English breakfast. He didn't look back. The sight of his snowy burial mound with a great hairy man-ape sitting on it surrounded by wolves was too depressing to contemplate.

"If I come out of this alive," he told himself, "I am never ever going to buttle for that man Nimrod again."

It was a conversation that lasted for several miles.

"This is what comes of going abroad and mixing with foreigners," said Groanin as he walked effortlessly through the snow and into trees. "None of this would have happened if I'd stayed on in Kensington like I wanted. There are no grizzly bears in London. Not even at London Zoo, which is the way I like it. Nasty animals with teeth and claws. What was God thinking of making such a beast? I didn't want to come to this horrible place. Or any of the other horrible places I've been with that blasted man Nimrod. But would he listen? Would he, heck. All His Lordship cares about is that he has his tea made by a proper English butler. As if that made any difference. Well, I'm through with all that. From now on he can make his own tea. And cocoa. And coffee."

Groanin wiped his nose and realized that he was wiping it not because it was wet but because he could actually smell fresh coffee. Real coffee. Had he imagined it? Quickening his invisible footsteps, he crested a hill and saw the bright little yellow diamond of a campfire in the distance. And having little idea of what else to do with himself until he was either properly dead or safely rescued, Groanin thought that this was probably as good a place to await John's return from Tibet as any. There was something cheerful and welcoming about a campfire that called to him in the unmistakable accents of civilization: a hearth, the sound and conversation of another human being, the smells of cooking food and hot coffee.

Nearing the fire, he saw that he had arrived back at his own campsite, the one the bear had chased him away from earlier.

And with nothing better to do, Groanin crawled back inside his tent and started to read *David Copperfield*.

CHAPTER 32

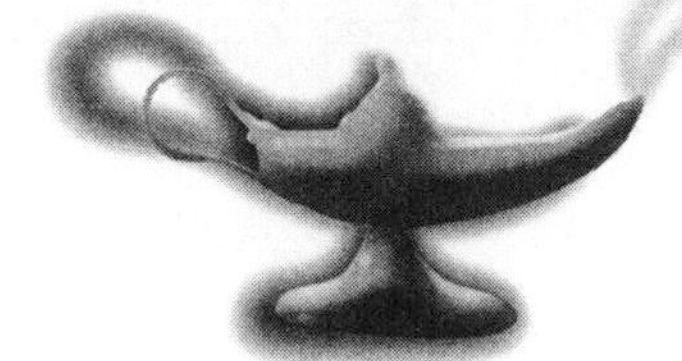

GOOD HEALTH AND A BAD MEMORY

As usual, Silvio Prezzolini started his day in the tourist shop at Pompeii by carefully dusting all of the merchandise, of course paying special attention to the Roman cameos. As he worked he tried to ignore the scientists from Princeton University who sat in a trailer outside, observing him from a safe distance in an effort to determine if the effects of random or so-called unlucky events could be measured scientifically. So far the scientists hadn't measured anything very much, except that it got very hot in Pompeii and that they were putting on weight as a result of all the pasta and pizza they were eating. And certainly nothing unlucky had happened to Silvio in a while.

As he worked, Silvio sang a little tune called "Guaglione," which always reminded him of good food and wine, and pretty girls, and riding around Rome on a Vespa, and sunshine, and a day on the beach; and as usual it wasn't long before he quite forgot all the terrible things that had happened to him since the age of two when he had fallen from a third-floor window and, uninjured, been run over by a Neapolitan pizza delivery van.

When he'd finished singing "Guaglione," he sang "Ciao, Ciao, Bambina" — and sang it very well, too — which put him in an even better mood as it made him think of smiling Italian children, and friendly dogs, and delicious ice cream, and blue skies, and certainly nothing at all of being sucked out of an Alitalia aircraft when the door fell off, or being struck by lightning on a football pitch, or his forty-two car accidents. He was even able to grin when he saw a little girl carrying a toy panda without any memory of his time at the Rome zoo when he'd been severely assaulted by an escaped panda named Felix.

When Silvio had finished dusting his merchandise, he opened the shutters on the shop, took a deep, euphoric breath of life, and told himself he was the luckiest man in the world to have such a wonderful job. Which was enough to make the small, balding man with a limp (from the time he was hit by a piece of debris from a failing Russian satellite) start singing "La Pansè." Everyone who lived and worked in Pompeii liked hearing that song a lot as Silvio sang it just like Renato Carosone.

As well as his many accidents, Silvio had almost forgotten the little American girl with reddish hair and glasses, and he took a few moments to remember that she was a genie and had offered to grant him three wishes because *Il Foglio*, an Italian newspaper, had described him as the unluckiest man in the world.

This time the girl was accompanied by a tall man wearing a red suit. The man had a big nose and a wide mouth and a full head of curly dark hair. He looked clever, like a scientist: not a mad scientist exactly, but perhaps an eccentric one, if the color of the suit was anything to go by. Or maybe a Renaissance prince. Someone distinguished and extraordinary, anyway. Instinctively, Silvio guessed that the man must be a genie, too, if only because he was with the girl and because there was something in his large eyes that was more than just intelligence. It was power. Not a frightening sort of power, but something else. A kind of imperturbable strength, perhaps. An inner glow, like a holy man or even an angel.

"Hello," said Philippa.

Silvio smiled uncertainly. "Hello," he said.

"This is my uncle Nimrod."

"How do you do, sir?"

"We were very much enjoying your singing, Signor Prezzolini," said the tall man. "Weren't we, Philippa? Let me have people around me who sing, I say. People like you, Signor Prezzolini, are the real artists of this world — the painters who put some color into our dull hearts. But for you, all would be quite monochrome, sir. An imperfect daguerreotype of some long-forgotten place."

Silvio looked modest and wondered what a daguerreotype might be.

So did Philippa.

"I don't know about that, boss," said Silvio. "You are English, yes?"

"Yes. Had we but a little more sunshine in our little island, we might look and sound as happy as you, signor." Nimrod sighed and looked around him with a smile. "Like a strawberry or a tomato, the greatest part of happiness is cultivated in sunshine, is it not?"

"Yes, perhaps you are right," allowed Silvio. "Are you a genie, like your niece?"

"Yes," said Nimrod. "Although we ourselves tend to use the word *djinn*. These days we tend to consider the word *genie* outdated or offensive, much as Native Americans prefer to be called that instead of Red Indians." Nimrod smiled kindly. "Not that I would be offended, of course. It takes something really quite repulsively offensive to offend me."

"If you don't mind me saying so, boss," said Silvio, "you don't look much like a djinn, either."

"You mean about thirty feet tall?" said Nimrod. "With silk trousers, bare chest, little waistcoat, turban, and with a big curly mustache?"

"Yes."

"Take my word for it. We're a little more modern nowadays. It's easier to get around if you dress for Wall Street instead of *The Thief of Baghdad*."

"I hope you were not insulted, boss," Silvio said carefully, "that I didn't want three wishes. It's just that I thought there might be more deserving cases for your help than me."

"Light my lamp, I was not insulted at all," said Nimrod.

"Intrigued, perhaps. Fascinated, certainly. It's rare one hears of someone as selfless as you. I wanted to meet you myself. Given all that has happened to you during the course of your life, you could have been forgiven a little self-pity."

Silvio shook his head. "Boss, the way I see it is this: I'm still here. It's true, some dreadful things have happened to me, but I've survived them all. You'd have to be pretty lucky for that to happen. In fact, you'd have to be the luckiest man in the world. This is the way I look at myself. More like the luckiest man in the world." He smiled wryly. "Maybe it helps that I've got a bad memory, I don't know. But most of the time, unless I try to remember them — and why would I do that? — I manage to forget all the really bad things that have happened to me."

Philippa looked at her uncle. "Didn't I tell you?"

"Remarkable," said Nimrod, and nodded at Philippa. "Yes, it's just as you said, my dear. This is a really happy man."

Silvio grinned. "That's right, boss," he said. "I'm a very lucky fellow."

"And you're happy the way you are?" said Nimrod.

Silvio nodded. "Very happy."

"This world has need of men like you, Silvio," said Nimrod. "Especially now."

The Italian looked sheepish. "It's kind of you to say so, boss, but . . ."

"I mean it. This world has need of a man like you. And that's why we're here. To enlist your help. Seriously."

"You? Need my help?" Silvio shook his head. "You're kidding me, boss. You're a djinn. With the three wishes and the magic lamp and everything. You make people's wishes, they come true. Just like in the *Arabian Nights*, yes? So how can a guy like me help a djinn like you? I'm just an ordinary Joe."

"You might think that's true," said Nimrod. "But it isn't. Not these days. Happiness might look like something small and of no account to you, but that's because you've got it. Ask a man who isn't happy and he'll tell you just how important it is. You see, happiness is a kind of magic. The kind of magic that even I can't make." Nimrod shook his head. "You're important, Signor Prezzolini. More important than you know. We have need of your magic, signor. We're on a mission to save the world from a run of bad luck and unhappiness that even now threatens a world that has no idea what it wants and is destroying itself to get it. Will you help us?"

Silvio thought for a moment. "It's true, things have been pretty bad in Italy, of late," he said. "What with the banks, and unemployment, and the economy, of course. Not to mention corruption. There's a lot of corruption."

"Will you come with us, now? Right now."

"Yes, of course," said Silvio. "If you really think I can be of assistance."

"I do, I do."

"All my life I've wanted to do something that matters," said Silvio. "For my life to mean something." He looked at Philippa and smiled kindly. "That's something better than three wishes, my dear."

"Well said," said Nimrod. "Stout fellow."

"Where are we going?" asked Silvio, starting to lock up the shop that he had only just opened.

"Tibet."

"Tibet?"

"The roof of the world," said Nimrod.

CHAPTER 33

UP ON THE ROOF

Until John learned to understand all the wolf's different barks and whines — John even had to put up with a few nips on the hand and the leg when Rakshasas thought he was being particularly obtuse — communication between the two was difficult. Of course, understanding what Rakshasas was saying was easy when John was able to enter the wolf's body as a spirit, but the boy djinn could hardly do that while he was flying the carpet. This made navigation difficult as only Rakshasas knew how to get to Shamba-la in Tibet.

So John chalked a drawing of a compass on the carpet and, from time to time, he would show Rakshasas the army compass he held in his hand or tell him the bearing, whereupon the wolf would bark an affirmative, whine a negative, or place his paw on the chalk circle according to the direction his nose told him that they should fly in.

And in this way they flew from Colorado to Lhasa in Tibet, west to east, crossing the Pacific Ocean and then mainland China — a distance of seven thousand five hundred miles.

John had never been to Tibet before and, but for the wolf's lack of speech, Rakshasas would certainly have told his young friend something of the beautiful country in which they were soon to arrive. He would have told him that Tibet is the highest region on Earth, with an average elevation of sixteen thousand feet, and that it had been an independent country until the People's Republic of China had invaded it in 1950. He would also have told him that ever since then the Communist Chinese had cruelly tyrannized the Tibetan people and that the true leader of Tibet, a holy man of great wisdom and presence called the fourteenth Dalai Lama, Tenzin Gyatso, was forced to live in exile.

Almost certainly, Rakshasas would also have told John that Tibet had a large population of wolves, which were black and the most prominent predator in the country, accounting for 60 percent of all livestock losses. Black Tibetan wolves — known locally as *chanko nagpo* — were considered bolder and more aggressive than their paler European cousins, which was why they probably killed more people than all of Tibet's tigers, leopards, and bears put together.

This would have been quite a lot of information for John to have been told about wolves, but then it must also be remembered that Mr. Rakshasas was now a wolf and that there is no subject a wolf finds more interesting than other wolves, except perhaps its next meal — even a wolf like Rakshasas who had formerly been a djinn.

Anyway, John didn't know any of these interesting facts about Tibet or wolves, but he guessed they had almost reached their destination when they came in sight of a snow-covered mountain range shrouded in clouds, which was so high, so ethereal, so inaccessible it looked like a holiday home for the gods. The air tasted unusually pure and John thought it was as if the hyper-real blue sky had been scrubbed clean by some celestial housekeeper. He had never seen anything quite so beautiful. But it was cold — very cold — and John felt glad of the thick fur coat he was wearing and hugged Rakshasas close to him for extra warmth.

Hundreds of feet below them was a vast and — apart from a very long river that turned out to be a railway line — featureless green valley.

The wolf whined and wrestled itself away from under John's arm, and took up a position on the flying carpet like an English pointer, which is a breed of dog developed as a bird dog. With his tail held straight out behind him, one paw raised, and his muzzle aimed directly ahead as if indicating the probable direction of a quail or a pheasant, Rakshasas barked a couple of times and looked ahead, his back almost as straight as the railway line below, until he was certain that John understood where the wolf was directing him to fly the carpet.

"You want me to follow the railway line?" said John. "Is that it?"

Rakshasas barked.

"All the way to those high mountains?"

Rakshasas barked again, licked John's hand in approval, and sat down next to him.

"I guess they're the Himalayas."

The sky was so bright that John was obliged to put on a pair of UV-protected sunglasses.

"When were you last here, in Tibet?" John asked the wolf.

Rakshasas stretched out his paw and scratched the carpet once; then he scratched it nine times; then he scratched it another three times, before scratching it again another four times.

"One-nine-three-four." John frowned. "You mean 1934?"

Rakshasas barked and licked John's hand again.

"I forgot you were so old," said John. "I mean, before you died and got yourself reincarnated."

Rakshasas pointed his muzzle at the sky and howled.

"You sound like you've missed this place," said John.

Rakshasas barked.

"It is very beautiful," admitted John.

Nearing the foothills of the Himalayan mountains, Rakshasas jumped up onto his hind legs and jerked his nose at the sky.

"We go up now?"

The wolf barked again and lay down.

They flew onward and upward until John's frozen ears started to pop and his billowing breath began to grow short. At the top of a sheer rock face several thousand feet high, he found a dust-bowl plateau surrounded by a ring of small peaks that was home to two enormous freshwater lakes. John might have counted twenty-one of these peaks, but he was too busy being amazed at the size of the mountain at their center. This was shaped like a pyramid but so very much larger: The Great Pyramid of Cheops would have occupied only the snow-covered peak of this huge mountain, and even though he was a djinn, John suddenly felt extremely small.

"What is this place?" he whispered in awe of the gemlike mountain to which Rakshasas had brought him. "It's not Everest. But it looks every bit as high and, if anything, those four walls look even more difficult to climb." He shivered involuntarily.

Rakshasas pressed his muzzle at the back of John's neck and pushed him down.

"You want me to go down?" said John. "To land?"

Rakshasas barked.

John nodded. "You're right. Already I can feel that cold mountain air beginning to get into the marrow of my bones. If I don't warm up right now, I won't have any djinn power left for the journey ahead. From now on the only heat I'm going to get I'll have to make myself."

Rakshasas barked again.

John landed the carpet smoothly and stood up. The plateau was empty, with no human presence or habitation. Another planet couldn't have felt less deserted. Even the air — sparkling with crystals of moisture, as if someone had tried to saw through a diamond, or sprinkled fairy dust over everything — seemed utterly unearthly. John couldn't explain it, but he felt like it had just snowed on Christmas morning.

"This place is really magical," he said.

While Rakshasas found a dead rabbit and ate it, John put on some extra winter clothing: two pairs of woolen long johns, a woolen T-shirt, a zip-up merino jersey, a woolen shirt, a pair of down-filled overtrousers, a goose-down vest, a pair of Baffin Island boots, a balaclava, huge furry mittens on a string, and a fur hat. With his fur coat on, John looked like a short, fat bear, but he found he walked more like a penguin. Quickly, he made a fire and toasted himself beside it. And when John felt djinn power strong in him again, he slipped out of his body and into that of Rakshasas.

"What is this place?" he asked the wolf, vicariously enjoying the taste of rank rabbit meat.

"This is Kailash, the holy mountain," explained Rakshasas. "It's the earthly manifestation of the celestial Mount Meru that Hindus believe to be the spiritual center of the universe and the home of the supreme god, Lord Shiva. Kailash means 'crystal' in Sanskrit, which is perhaps because the mountain looks like an uncut diamond."

"It's weird," said John. "You'd think that with a mountain that size some of the world's mountaineers would be here to climb it. And that there'd be some sort of base camp here. Like at Mount Everest. But there isn't. There's nothing."

"Sure, Mount Kailash is forbidden to climbers and explorers," said Rakshasas. "And there have been no climbing attempts. But you are right to compare it to Mount

Everest. And here I must tell you its first great secret, which you must promise never to reveal to anyone."

"Of course," said John. "I can keep a secret."

"Kailash is actually much higher than Everest," said Rakshasas.

"What? You're kidding."

"It hides its true height. Sure, Everest is a mere pimple at twenty-nine thousand feet. Kailash is more like forty. Now that's what I call a mountain."

"How does a mountain do that? Hide itself?"

"This is no ordinary mountain, John. There is much that is hidden here and must remain so. Forbidden or not, the place would still be full of climbers if the news ever got out that this was actually the highest mountain in the world."

"Yes, I can imagine it would," agreed John.

"Even pilgrimages are banned by the Chinese, who are afraid of Mount Kailash," explained Rakshasas. "They may be Communists, but they are very superstitious. According to all the religious traditions that revere this mountain, to set foot on it is a great blasphemy. And anyone who dares to do so will die in the process."

"That's a comforting thought," said John.

"Fortunately, we're not actually going to set foot on it," said Rakshasas.

"What? Then why are we here?"

"There is only one way into Shamba-la that I know of," said Rakshasas. "And it is not to be found by climbing. I doubt that any climber could ever get there. You've heard of the expression 'blue sky thinking'?"

"Yes, of course," said John. "I think it means the kind of thinking that's not in touch with reality."

"This is where that expression originates from," said Rakshasas. "When you look at the north face of Kailash, especially close up, it is so large and the rock so hard and shiny that it seems to reflect the very sky. Indeed, there are some who say it looks like the sky itself."

"Don't say what I think you're going to say," said John.

"You must fly the carpet straight into the north face of the mountain at a low spot where the snow looks like cloud and the rock most looks like the sky," said Rakshasas. "At least that's what I did before."

John groaned. "That's what I was afraid you were going to say."

"And if you are sufficiently courageous, you will discover that the rock is not rock at all, but sky."

"And if I am not?"

"Sure, then you will fly into solid rock and we'll both be killed."

"How will I know where to aim for?"

"You must aim at what you consider to be the bluest part of the north face," said Rakshasas. "Although this changes according to the time of day and the weather. This part of the north face is called Milarepa's Window. But in truth, your aim is not so important as your state of mind, John. To some extent this is an exercise in mind over matter."

"Blue sky thinking."

"Precisely."

"So why do I need to fly at speed? Couldn't I just ascend slowly until I found this window?"

"From time to time there is a very strong current of air that emanates from this part of the rock face," explained Rakshasas. "Like the blowhole of a whale. If you were not moving at speed, you would be blown off the carpet."

"It all sounds very hazardous," said John. "Isn't there some kind of mountain route?"

"There is, but I simply don't know where that is," said Rakshasas. "Or if I did, I've forgotten. It was 1934 when I was last here, after all. Believe me, there's a lot that gets forgotten in seventy-odd years. Besides, the land route is every bit as dangerous. Perhaps more so."

"What am I doing here?" said John. "I should be in school."

"Quite apart from the difficulty of the route," continued Rakshasas, "and the obvious blasphemy that a good djinn should always seek to avoid, there are many wild animals."

"When this is all over and I'm not dead, I'm just going to stay home and do my homework and watch TV. Really."

"Anyway, the land route would take many weeks and poor Mr. Groanin does not have many days, let alone many weeks."

"Point taken," said John. "In which case, we'd better get moving. The sun will be setting soon and we can't afford to wait another day to identify this Milarepa's Window you spoke of."

"One more thing," said Rakshasas. "If and when we see the Lamasery — that's a monastery for the lamas who live up there — let me do the talking. It's hoping they'll remember me, so I am."

"How are you going to do that?" asked John. "You're a wolf."

"There's more than one way to talk to one of these lama fellows," said Rakshasas. "You'll see."

"I sure hope so," said John.

He slipped out of the wolf's body and back into his own, whereupon he spent several minutes retching onto the ground, so strong was the taste of rank rabbit meat in his mouth. (This is an occupational hazard for all djinn following an animal transformation.)

When he was recovered, John sat down on the carpet again and, with Rakshasas sitting beside him, he took off, flying as fast as he could and aiming squarely for a center spot on the north face of Kailash where the rock seemed bluest. But try as he might, John could hardly imagine that suddenly the rock was just going to transform itself into air. He'd seen a lot of strange and wonderful things since discovering that he was a djinn, but solid rock that had the power to change its shape and mass wasn't one of them.

Increasing speed, they rapidly neared the huge rock face. Thousands of feet below them lay the immense plateau. Thousands of feet above them rose the forbidding north face of Kailash. And the nearer they got, the less John thought that any climber alive could ever have scaled it. Kailash made an ascent of the north wall of the Eiger or the south face of Annapurna look like a stroll in the park.

The sacred mountain now filled his whole field of vision. Ahead of him, everywhere he looked there was just the blue mountain and more blue mountain. And for the first time John began to understand how Mount Kailash could have been mistaken for the sky. The snow hugged the rock surface like thin cirrus clouds reflecting the blue sky against the silver granite rock face.

When there were just a few hundred feet to go, Rakshasas sat up and barked loudly and John had the idea that the wolf was encouraging him to go even faster, although that seemed like suicide.

If John got it wrong now, they would smash into the mountain and be dashed to pieces.

"Blue sky thinking!" he yelled, and willed himself to think that the rock would turn to air.

Rakshasas barked an excited bark and ran back and forth on the flying carpet as if he'd caught the scent of a rabbit.

John tried to empty his mind of everything except flying the carpet and the outcome he was praying for.

Suddenly, in his mind's eye, he seemed to see an image of himself, cross-legged on the carpet, like some ascetic monk engaged in meditation. And for no reason he could think of he raised one hand in salutation to the mountain even as he thought they must crash into it.

But instead of hitting a wall of solid rock, John now perceived how an optical illusion operated here, and that the apparently solid north face concealed a fissure about as wide as the length of a bus. Near its opening, the walls of the fissure were veined with abundant deposits of silver reflecting rock and sky like an enormous series of mirrors, more than enough to have persuaded any observer from the ground that the north face was one unbroken mass.

"Milarepa's Window! We found it!"

At the same time it was plain to see why Rakshasas had urged John to focus all of his concentration on their flight into the north face of the mountain: The narrow fissure was cut into the rock at an acute angle and almost as soon as John navigated the carpet successfully through the opening, he had to swerve suddenly to the right. At the very same moment a strong gust of wind blew out of the fissure and if John had not been flying at speed, the carpet would have been flicked back out again like an old shuttlecock. As it was, the gust carried them several dozen feet up in the air so that a sharp outcrop of rock narrowly missed John's head by inches.

John uttered a cry of fright at this narrow escape and then a cheer, and Rakshasas howled triumphantly as the flying carpet sailed on through the fissure, like a silken thread through the eye of a needle. Out of the sunshine, the temperature dropped suddenly and John was glad of all the warm clothing he was wearing. But the djinn power that burned within him was still strong.

"We did it," he yelled, his voice bouncing back and forth between the steep walls of the fissure like a ball in a racket court.

Rakshasas nipped John on the hand as if to remind him to pay attention to where they were going. And it was as well he did, for the fissure was full of sharp turns and twists and unexpected gusts of wind, and to John it seemed that their rapid passage through the rock was like the aerial equivalent of white-water rafting.

After ten minutes of flying, they emerged not of the other side of the mountain but on the edge of an enormous, extinct volcano crater.

"We made it," said John, hugging Rakshasas close to him. "We're through."

He was just about to punch the air and emit an exhilarated whoop when something hit them hard from below, and a second later they heard what sounded very like a gunshot.

The carpet spun like a flying saucer, collided with the wall of the fissure they had just vacated, and then fell backward. John struggled to regain control while Rakshasas scrambled to stay aboard, and failed. The boy djinn turned, reached for the collar of fur around the wolf's neck, missed, and then cried out as Rakshasas fell twenty or thirty feet down to the snow-covered ground. When he turned back, he had a brief view of a semi-ruined lamasery high on the side of the mountain he had collided with, and several people looking down at him and pointing as if he was an object of curiosity. A second later, the carpet still carrying John hit the ground a few yards from where Rakshasas was already lying. The snow cushioned the worst of the impact, which was still enough to loosen every filling in John's mouth and, for a few minutes, he lost consciousness.

He felt something sharp in his arm and when he opened his eyes he saw that he was surrounded by several pairs of polished black riding boots; a very tall man helped him to sit up, while another knelt in front of him and looked inquisitively into John's eyes. The second man was wearing a curious little silver skull-and-crossbones badge on his hat and for a minute John wondered groggily if he was a pirate.

John looked around for Rakshasas and didn't see him. Then he blinked and rubbed his eyes and shook his head, convinced that he must be hallucinating: There were several men in a circle around him now, and they were talking in German, which, fortunately, was a language John already understood. They were all wearing a symbol he recognized only from his schoolbooks.

"How many fingers?" The man with the skull-and-crossbones badge was holding up three fingers.

"Three," John heard himself mumble.

The men seemed most concerned about his welfare and were already reproaching another man carrying a rifle for having shot down John's flying carpet. But what concerned John was the idea — surely he was hallucinating, he told himself — that all of these men were wearing the distinctive black uniforms and Nazi armbands of Hitler's SS.

CHAPTER 34

THE MAN IN BLACK

The lamasery was situated high on a ridge inside the Kailash crater and reminded John of a goat trapped on an inaccessible mountain ledge. On the outside at least, the lamasery was typically Buddhist in its appearance: Made of white stone, there were five main halls separated by courtyards with high walls, small windows, and pagoda-like roofs. But on the inside, things were very different from a traditional Tibetan temple; the place was full of swastika banners and flags, and instead of images and statues of the Buddha, there were images and statues of Adolf Hitler — a man who would surely appear in everyone's top ten of History's Most Horrible Men.

The Germans carried a still groggy John through the main gate and into a kind of hospital dispensary. The Tibetan wind blew under the door and through a gap in the window, like a sigh from some unseen spirit. There were glass cabinets filled with medicines, a couple of beds, and, on the wall — between a couple of medical charts — yet another picture of Hitler. It was a most unsettling place. A man in a white coat sat down in front of John and examined him for broken bones before taking his temperature.

"Goodness," he said, "you're burning up."

"No, I'm fine," insisted John. "This is my normal temperature."

"Nonsense," said the man and, before John could prevent him, his warm fur hat and coat had been removed. Immediately, he felt his core temperature drop. "That's better."

"Could I have my coat back?" said John. "I'm feeling kind of cold now."

"This thermometer says different," said the man in the white coat. "Look. Ninety-eight point six."

John, who thought it best not to mention that his normal body temperature was several degrees higher than that, nodded his agreement. At the same time he tried to gather his remaining body heat so that, in the event of the Nazi turning nasty, John might turn him into some kind of animal, but instead he found himself quite unable to focus his djinn power. Every time he tried to gather all of his concentration in one mental place, his mind seemed to wander off somewhere else.

He remembered feeling something sharp in his arm outside on the snow.

"Did you give me something?" he asked suspiciously.

"When you were unconscious," said the man in the white coat, "I gave you a shot to help you recover."

John nodded. That explained it.

"Um, where's my dog?" he said. John hesitated to use the word *wolf*; it hardly sounded normal. People were a bit funny about pet wolves.

"One of our men who has veterinary experience is taking care of him," said the man in the white coat.

"Is he all right?"

"Yes, he'll be fine, I think. He has a concussion. Much like yourself, probably."

"I'd like to see him, please," said John.

"Just as soon as you answer a few questions," said the man in the white coat. "Look, who are you and what are you doing here?"

John shook his head. "That's rich," he said.

"What do you mean?"

"I have one or two questions myself," said John. "Such as, what the heck do you think you're doing taking potshots at people like that? You could have killed me."

"I'm very sorry about that, but one of my men mistook you for a game bird," said the man in the white coat. "We don't get a lot of meat up here at the Mopu Lamasery. That's what this place is called. I'm afraid he shot you for our pot before he realized his mistake. To be quite frank with you, we were all rather surprised to see a boy and a dog on a flying carpet. Even here, in the Kailash crater, where things can hardly be described as normal."

John nodded. "That's fair enough," he said. "All right. My name is John Gaunt. And I'm from the United States of America."

"An American? How is it that you speak perfect German?"

John answered carefully. "My mother is German," he lied. "We were brought up speaking German."

The man in the white coat shrugged. "Interesting," he said. "But perhaps not as interesting as how it is that you come to be on a flying carpet in the first place."

"I'm still trying to work it out myself." John, hardly wanting to admit that he was a djinn, felt obliged to keep on lying to the German. "I'm here on vacation with my father," said John smoothly. "He's a diplomat. Yesterday, while he was in an important meeting somewhere, I went to the marketplace in Lhasa, to buy a present to take back home to my mother. Anyway, I met this strange little man. His name was Daliah Lavi and he claimed he was a sort of holy man. He promised to sell me a very special carpet — a magic carpet — if I gave him all my money. At first I didn't believe him. Then he showed me how the carpet could levitate itself and I was so impressed that I bought it.

"I took the carpet back to the hotel room and laid it out on the floor. My father wasn't very pleased when he saw it, especially when it didn't levitate at all. He thought I'd been ripped off and threw the carpet out the window. Then he went to another diplomatic meeting. And I went to have lunch with someone. But when I came back the carpet was back in our room, which was when I figured that the holy man, Daliah Lavi, had perhaps been telling the truth after all. That it really was magic. So the dog and I sat on it, and the next thing, we were flying through the air. Which sounds fine, except that the carpet wouldn't stop. Not for hours. Leastways not until your friend winged it with his gun."

The man in the white coat smiled patiently. "An interesting story," he said quietly. "One might almost say, a fairy story. Indeed, I am reminded a little of the story of Jack and the Beanstalk. In fact, it's one of my favorites. But you're hardly as stupid as Jack, I think."

John shrugged. "It's the truth."

"Is it?" The man removed his white coat. Underneath, he was wearing a smart black SS uniform with lots of medals, including a little Iron Cross on a black-and-white ribbon. "Permit me to introduce myself."

The man brought the heels of his boots together with a loud click. He was tall with thin blond hair and a sunburnt, bony face that might have been called handsome. In front of one of his cornflower-blue eyes was a monocle, and there was a dueling scar on his cheek that was the shape of a check mark in a schoolboy's exercise book, which gave the impression that a teacher had looked at his face and marked it "correct."

"I am Obersturmbannführer Dr. Heinrich Hynkell of the Waffen-SS and I have been wearing this uniform for long enough to know when someone is lying."

"Can you think of a better explanation?" said John.

"No, I can't." Hynkell nodded thoughtfully. "Frankly, your story is a most reasonable explanation for how you come to be flying a carpet in the company of a wolf. Yes, a wolf. I know a wolf when I see one, John. I also know that carpets cannot fly except in fairy stories. And yet the fact remains that all of us saw you arrive here on a flying carpet. Hence, this is a situation in which the most reasonable explanation is perhaps the least likely to be true. Especially when one considers our proximity to Shamba-la and the very many magical things that happen there. In such a case as this one, where the impossible, however improbable, cannot be eliminated, then everything else, no matter how reasonable, must be discounted."

John shook his head and then yawned as he tried to hang on to the German's impeccable logic.

"Look," said John. "A kid flying a carpet is hardly usual, I'll grant you. But I'm telling you the truth."

"My men are examining the carpet now in the hope of finding out its secrets," said Hynkell. "It would save a lot of time if you told us how you came to be flying on it. This might also save your pet wolf a great deal of pain, John. In addition to being a veterinarian, the man looking after him is a skilled torturer."

"Please don't harm him," said John. "I know this looks strange. But you've got to admit, I don't exactly have the monopoly on what's strange around here. It's none of my business what you wear in this place, but you guys aren't exactly dressed for the Sunday school picnic, are you? After all, you're all dressed as Nazis."

"That's because we are Nazis," Hynkell said stiffly. "And what of it? Adolf Hitler was elected by the democratic will of the German people in January 1933. And while I prefer the name National Socialist to Nazi, there's nothing inherently wrong with being a Nazi."

"A lot of people might disagree with that," said John. "What with the Second World War and everything."

"The Great War of 1914 to 1918, I have heard of," said Hynkell. "But not this second war you speak of."

"Sure you have," said John. "Everyone's heard of the Second World War. 1939 to 1945?"

"I'm beginning to think your concussion is more severe than I had supposed," said Hynkell. "This is still 1938, John. And there will be no war. The British don't want a war any more than we do."

John paused for a moment and tried once again to gather his thoughts. There seemed little point in arguing with Hynkell. Clearly, the German believed it was 1938 and John felt he would only have angered him with a contradiction about something as basic as the year in which they were living. Instead, he thought to come at an explanation from a different angle.

"Do you mind me asking why you're here?" he inquired of Hynkell.

"I'll ask the questions," said Hynkell.

"Very well."

"Let me tell you what I think."

"That's not a question," said John.

"When I was a child, there was only one kind of being who could ride on a magic carpet. A genie."

"I read those stories, too," said John.

"I think we both know that they weren't just stories."

"You can't mean what I think you mean," said John. "Listen to yourself. Please. You're German. Surely that means something. You're too sensible to believe in all that Aladdin stuff. Look, the carpet's yours, Dr. Hynkell. Take it, with my blessing. After what happened to me, I never want to see the thing again."

"Well, that's very generous of you," said Hynkell. "But I think I should feel like a bit of an idiot if I gave up an object made of solid gold for something made of silver plate. What kind of fool would I be if I held on to a magic carpet and let a real-life genie slip through my fingers? Yes. In spite of what you say, I really do think you're a genie, John."

"A genie?" John grinned. "You mean like out of a magic lamp? The whole *Arabian Nights* deal?"

Hynkell nodded.

"Come on. Do I look like a genie? I'm not even an Arab."

"A great German named Friedrich Nietzsche once said that appearances can be deceptive."

John sighed. He was getting nowhere fast. The German was about the first mundane he had ever met who seemed to believe in genies without ever having met one.

"I feel tired," he said. "What was in that shot you gave me?"

"Just a mild stimulant," said Hynkell. "It's more likely the effects of the concussion that are making you feel tired."

John shook his head and yawned. "Look, if I really was a genie, do you think I'd sit here and let you push me around?" He yawned again. "You ask me, it's you who's talking like he's had a bump on the head, doctor. Next thing, you'll be asking me for three wishes."

"Oh, don't worry, I'll get to that." Hynkell shook his head. "All in good time. But, you know something? When I was a boy, three wishes never seemed quite enough."

"I guess you're a typical Nazi, all right," said John.

Hynkell smiled and then slapped John hard across the face — hard enough to knock the boy djinn off his chair.

John picked himself up and, rubbing his cheek, sat down again. "I'm trying to figure out," he said through clenched teeth, "why you think I would give a Nazi jerk like you three wishes. Supposing I could do something like that."

"To stop me from torturing your pet wolf, of course," said Hynkell.

"And what's to stop me from turning you into a rabbit?"

"I'm still trying to work that out. But something's stopping you. I suspect it's the proximity of Shamba-la that's preventing you from using your genie powers. The place exerts a strange effect over everything." Hynkell nodded. "Yes, of course, that must be it. Shamba-la affects you like it affects everything else."

John shrugged, but he was wondering if Hynkell might just be right. By now his mind had cleared and the room felt warm enough for him to have focused some djinn power. But somehow the use of his power still eluded him. "Maybe. Where is it, anyway? Shamba-la?"

"A couple of miles away. Across the other side of the crater."

"Why not ask them for three wishes? Or the local equivalent."

Dr. Hynkell emitted a hollow laugh.

"Don't think we haven't tried," he said. "But they wouldn't ever let us in. Not without a truly happy man in our number. And, well" — Hynkell shrugged — "who can say that he's truly happy these days? Especially since we're here in Tibet. Things are improving under Hitler, it's true. But there's none of us who's here who wouldn't prefer to be back home in Germany."

"So why did you come?"

"Because last year —"

"That would be 1937, right?" said John, humoring the Nazi.

"Of course, 1937." Hynkell nodded irritably. "We were ordered to find Shamba-la by SS Reichsführer Himmler," he said. "What's more, he told us we couldn't return home without some evidence that we'd found it. Not ever."

"Surely if you explained how things were here," said John. "He'd understand."

"You don't know Reichsführer Himmler," said Hynkell. "He's not a very understanding person."

"So what is it that he expects you to find up here?"

John was careful to use the present tense, as if Himmler was still alive. In fact, he had committed suicide in 1945. But he hardly thought Dr. Hynkell was going to believe that.

"In particular, we were told to obtain documents about Tibetan paranormal powers; to find evidence of a common ideological heritage between Adolf Hitler and the Lord Buddha; and to discover the secret of eternal life."

"Is that all?" said John.

Fortunately, the Nazi didn't get John's sarcasm. If he had, he might have hit him again.

Instead, Hynkell said, "That's all. What more could there be?" But then he pulled a face. "Except you, of course. Because they won't let us in to Shamba-la, we've gotten nowhere with our mission, so far. But you might prove to be the next best thing in Himmler's eyes. Yes. Why not? With a real genie in the bag, we might finally be able to go home. Always supposing that we could get you back to Germany safely. Away from this place and its peculiar influence, you might be rather harder to handle than you are now."

"Hasn't it occurred to you," said John, "that Himmler might regard me and my flying carpet with no more enthusiasm than my own father did back in Lhasa? Especially when we fail to take off in Berlin."

"I told you I didn't believe that story."

"And you think Himmler will believe yours?"

"Why not? It was him who sent us on this stupid expedition."

"Good point," agreed John.

By now John had formed the conclusion that Hynkell and his men really did believe that it was 1938, and as a result of this observation he had begun to form a theory of what might have happened to the Nazi expedition during its close proximity to Shamba-la. Back in Yellowstone National Park,

Rakshasas had told him that the place exerted a curious effect on time and arrested the aging process in people — not to mention the effect that Shamba-la was supposed to have on those like Groanin who were mortally wounded. It now seemed to John that perhaps it wasn't just Shamba-la that arrested the aging process but the whole of the Kailash crater. He supposed these SS men were all of them at least a hundred years old, and yet none of them looked a day over forty.

Hynkell nodded. "Yes, I think I have a solution."

"Have what?"

"The solution to the problem of how to handle you outside of the Kailash crater. How to get you back to Berlin."

"Do tell," said John.

"From what I read in the *Arabian Nights*, it always seemed to me that genies were creatures of their word," said Hynkell. "Even evil genies. Once they swore to do something, they generally always did it."

"And?"

"I want you to swear," said Hynkell, "by all that you hold dear that you will not use your genie powers against us. That you will accompany us back to Germany. If you do that I'll release your pet wolf unharmed. Agreed?"

Now John was of the opinion that giving his word to a Nazi didn't really count, especially when the word was given under duress, and agreed with alacrity, thinking that he might recover his djinn power as soon as he could sit in front of a fire and warm up again.

"Agreed," he said.

But the Nazi wasn't about to let the boy off with swearing an oath quite so lightly.

"I want to hear you swear it on the life of your mother and your father," he said. "Say, 'I wish that they might die a terrible death if I ever break this oath.'"

John hesitated. This was different. This was *wishing*, and John knew better than to wish things lightly, especially when it involved the lives of others. He thought of Groanin's mortally injured body back in Yellowstone and then he thought of his mother and his father. He loved them all but, forced to choose, he realized he owed his parents life itself and discovered that he would always choose them.

"Swear that you will accompany us to Berlin and grant Reichsführer Himmler and Adolf Hitler three wishes," said Hynkell. "Swear it or I will order my men to roast your pet wolf alive. And I'll make you watch. Believe me, my men won't hesitate. It's been ages since they ate fresh meat."

John nodded his agreement; without his djinn power he had little choice. "I swear it," he said sullenly, and consoled himself of what he was going to do to these Nazi thugs when finally he reached Berlin.

"Say, 'I wish that my mother and father will die a terrible death if I break this oath.'"

"I wish that my mother and father will die a terrible death if I break this oath," he said.

The Nazi smiled. "Excellent. I'll tell my men to prepare to leave for home immediately. You've no idea how eager they are to return to their wives and families. I think it's fair to say that you've made their day."

"Delighted," growled John, already plotting his revenge.

Once Hynkell and his men discovered that Hitler and Himmler were long dead, John decided he could consider himself free from his oath and turn them all into a colony of ants. A colony he would take great pleasure in stamping on while wearing one of their jackboots. Forever.

CHAPTER 35

A BIGGER SPLASH

Flying east-southeast at a speed of almost three hundred miles per hour, Nimrod steered a perfect course through clear Eurasian skies, crossing several countries and seas that Philippa had only ever read about in the newspapers or in her geography textbooks: Serbia, Romania, Moldova, Ukraine, and the Black Sea. Somewhere over the Russian steppes, every vestige of cloud vanished and, as the sun increased its fiery intensity, Philippa basked lazily in the heat and warmed her djinn blood like some idle government official in a play by Anton Chekhov. A lingering concern for her brother, John, and Mr. Groanin stopped Philippa from feeling entirely at ease, however; she couldn't help but think it strange that they hadn't heard from them. She'd even tried sharing her concern with Nimrod, who told her that there were bigger fish to fry.

"We have to fix the world's luck and quickly, Philippa," he had said, "or else there will be a disaster, and I do mean disaster. Chaos, anyway. When we're on our way back from Shamba-la with some sort of solution to the world's woes, we'll talk about it again. Until then, try to relax. I need your mind rested and keen, my dear, for what may lie ahead."

So Philippa lay back on the silken azure and stared up at the sun and marveled at her own being. After a while, she closed her eyes and then dozed quietly.

Even Mr. Swaraswati, who was less than enthusiastic about flying carpets, managed to relax a little, performing a series of yoga-meditation poses that left Moo speechless with admiration that a human being could twist and contort himself in such a fashion.

Mr. Burton smoked a water pipe through a rubber tube and lay on a bed of nails that he assured everyone was very comfortable but, oddly enough, no one else seemed inclined to try for themselves.

Silvio Prezzolini read an Italian newspaper, smoked cigarettes incessantly, combed his hair, drank small cups of coffee, and occasionally sang one of his favorite songs such as "Arrivederci Roma" or "Lo Vivo per Lei." Moo, who was a big fan of Dean Martin and Frank Sinatra, particularly enjoyed Silvio's singing and told the Italian that she thought his voice was every bit as good as theirs. Silvio thanked her and felt very flattered by this comparison, as well he might have done.

Meanwhile, the sapphire-blue carpet behaved faultlessly, sliding straight and level through the air like an enormous fish slice, its silk thread shining brightly so that seen from the window of a passenger jet it would have resembled a beautiful swimming pool on the French Côte d'Azur, or perhaps Palm Springs.

Things were going well; perhaps too well, for it cannot be denied that the djinn gave up flying carpets and took to flying whirlwinds of their own manufacture for several good reasons, only one of which was how these outmoded modes of supernatural transport performed in adverse weather conditions. They were about to discover another reason why flying carpets are not all that might be imagined by someone with, well . . . a lack of imagination.

It was over Kazakhstan that it happened. One minute they were enjoying perfect flying conditions and the next a large bird landed heavily in the center of the carpet and broke its neck.

"What the heck?" exclaimed Philippa.

"Bird strike," said Nimrod. "Happens to planes, too. No cause for alarm because we don't have any windshield to break or jet engines to fail."

But when another bird hit the carpet and then another, Mr. Swaraswati turned pale. "Rama," he said, which means "God." "Rama."

"It's raining birds," said Moo. And when several more birds killed themselves dive-bombing the carpet, she felt obliged to put up an umbrella.

"I think they're pelicans," observed Mr. Burton.

"What's wrong with the birds?" exclaimed Mr. Swaraswati.

"Eees just like Alfred Hitchcock," said Silvio. "They crazy."

"Why are they attacking us?" said Moo.

The flying carpet shimmered in the sunshine as it gently undulated upon a current of air and suddenly Philippa guessed what was happening.

"They're not attacking us," she said as another bird crashed onto surface of the carpet like a small fighter plane, and expired in a mushroom cloud of blood and feathers. "I think they're mistaking the blue carpet for the surface of the ocean. Seen from above, it moves like the sea. They're not attacking us. They're diving for fish."

"Light my lamp, but you're right," said Nimrod. "Well, I've never seen that before. What an extraordinary . . ."

But this was the last thing he said as a split second later a diving bird struck him hard on the head and knocked him unconscious. The bird itself uttered a squawk of surprise and disappointment that the carpet was not made of water, staggered a few feet away from Nimrod's body, and fell over the edge.

"Oh, Lord," said Moo. "That's torn it."

Moo leaned across Nimrod, wiped some blood from his head with her handkerchief, and started to gently slap the djinn's face; then she found some smelling salts in her handbag and waved them under Nimrod's nostrils, all to no effect. The djinn remained quite insensible.

The flying carpet banked steeply like a damaged bomber and began a slow descent.

"We're doomed," moaned Mr. Swaraswati. "Doomed, I tell you. I should never have agreed to come on this thing. Not after what happened before."

Not hesitating, Philippa took control of the flying carpet and tried to steer it carefully toward the ground. It seemed much heavier than she had expected, almost as if it was carrying a lot more weight than she had supposed. As soon as she had brought the carpet to a standstill on an arid plain in a valley surrounded by rugged peaks, she jumped up and went over to see how seriously her uncle had been injured.

"How is he?" she asked Moo.

"He's still breathing, thank goodness," said Moo.

Mr. Burton picked up one of the lifeless birds. "*Pelicanus crispus*," he said. "The Dalmatian pelican. The largest of the pelicans. On average, it's the world's heaviest flying bird. Which means —" He hesitated. "Which means it's jolly bad luck it landed on someone. Oddly enough they're a symbol of self-sacrifice in medieval bestiaries."

"These birds were certainly conforming to their image." Philippa continued to look anxious.

"I'm sure he'll come around in a minute or two, my dear," said Moo, trying to reassure her.

But when after fifteen minutes, Nimrod remained unconscious, Moo shook her head and said, "I think he needs a doctor. Perhaps even an X-ray. He might have a fractured skull. That bird must have hit him a lot harder than we supposed."

"I daren't use djinn power to help him," said Philippa. "Not without knowing precisely what's wrong with him."

"No, indeed," agreed Moo. "I expect you've got to know what you're wishing for when you wish it. Otherwise, you could end up doing more harm than good."

"We've got company," observed Silvio.

Philippa turned and looked where Silvio was now pointing and saw three figures who were squatting in the grass about forty feet from them; there was a man wearing a striped padded jacket, a small boy with a green padded jacket, and a woman with a large quilt bundled on her back and a very large turban on her head as if she had just washed her hair. Behind them were several odd-looking camels and a couple of tentlike dwellings.

Philippa waved at them, trying to appear friendly. "Hello," she said. "Can you help us please? We need a doctor for our friend. He's injured."

The trio stayed put and gave no indication that they had understood what Philippa was saying.

"What language do they speak here?" she asked Moo.

"I'm not even sure where *here* is," admitted Moo, and then shouted something in Russian because they had been flying over Russia, and Russian was a language that she knew well, being a KGB British spymaster.

The man stood up, snatched off his skullcap, and, bowing several times, came forward to greet them, speaking all the time in a language Philippa had never heard before. His face was weatherworn and vaguely Asian.

"That's Kazakh he's speaking," said Moo. "I think we're in West Kazakhstan, and luckily, I speak a bit of Kazakh as well as Russian. It seems we're only a few miles from a town called Atyrau, where there's a doctor. This chap says he's willing to take us to the town on his camels but only because he's afraid that we're Cossack devils. For that reason alone —

I mean, in case anyone else mistakes us for Cossack devils — it might be an idea to leave the carpet here while we go into Atyrau. I should say it's too heavy to carry, wouldn't you?"

"Mr. Swaraswati could stay here and look after it," said Philippa. "Couldn't you, Mr. Swaraswati?"

"It would be a pleasure not to go anywhere except where I am now," said the old fakir. "Especially if this involves my being very firmly on the ground."

"I'll take that as a yes," said Philippa.

"I'll stay here with him," volunteered Silvio. "To keep him company."

"Me, too," said Mr. Burton. "No sense in us all going to town."

"Thank you," said Mr. Swaraswati.

The Kazakh, whose name was Mr. Bayuleev, wasn't tall but he was very strong; he picked Nimrod up by himself, carried him to one of his Bactrian camels, and laid him across a saddle that sat between the beast's two humps. Then, leaving his wife and child in a little leather igloo, Mr. Bayuleev traveled into Atyrau with Philippa and Moo, which was a distance of about two miles along a road that improved the nearer they got to the town.

Situated on the edge of the Caspian Sea at the delta of the Ural River, Atyrau is a largish fishing town with a nice new mosque and several high-rise buildings. The air is clear and the river is clean. Kazakhstan is a country that's rapidly improving itself and becoming more affluent than when it was part of the old Soviet empire. Which is why everyone seemed friendly and kind, especially the doctor at the local hospital, Dr. Bazayev, who had studied medicine in London.

By the time Dr. Bazayev had X-rayed Nimrod's head and bandaged it (the doctor pronounced himself very impressed at the size of the Englishman's skull and brain), the djinn had partly recovered and was sitting up on the edge of his hospital bed and asking what had happened to him.

The doctor left Nimrod with Philippa and Moo and went to attend to some other patients.

"I remember a bird landing on the carpet and not much else," admitted Nimrod.

"You got hit by one of them," said Philippa. "Mr. Burton said it was a pelican."

"Ah, yes," he said. "They were dive-bombing us because they mistook the blue carpet for a lake with fish in it."

"That's right," said Philippa. "How are you feeling now?"

"My head feels like a hot-air balloon," said Nimrod. "But I'll be all right."

Philippa looked relieved. "I was worried about you, Uncle Nimrod."

"We both were," admitted Moo. "We may have the Joseph Rock papers at our disposal, but neither of us really knows the way to Shamba-la. Let alone Tibet."

"Yes." Nimrod nodded. "There's still a long way to go. About two thousand four hundred miles, to be exact. Tibet's not called the roof of the world for nothing. You need a long ladder to get up there."

"Mr. Swaraswati *will be* delighted," said Moo. "To be flying again."

Nimrod glanced around the room where he had been receiving treatment. "By the way," he said. "Where *is* Mr. Swaraswati?"

"I left him where we landed," explained Philippa. "With the flying carpet."

"And where is that?" asked Nimrod.

"Well, we're in Kazakhstan," said Philippa. "And this is a town called Atyrau. So I guess you could say that we left them a couple of miles outside Atyrau. In a kind of valley. It's all right. He's with Mr. Burton and Mr. Prezzolini."

"And who's with them?" Nimrod sighed.

"Er, no one," said Philippa.

"That was stupid, stupid, stupid. Haven't I made it clear that Mr. Swaraswati is much too valuable to leave anywhere? The importance of what that man knows cannot be exaggerated."

"Don't be an idiot, Nimrod," said Moo. "Philippa was only trying to help you. We thought you might be seriously injured. I might have known it would take more than a bird crashing onto your big head to knock some sense into it."

"You're right, of course," said Nimrod. "Philippa, I'm sorry. It was churlish of me to complain. All the same, we'd better be getting back. It'll be dark soon and we wouldn't want to lose them, would we?"

Mr. Bayuleev took them back to the spot where they had landed and where Mr. Swaraswati and Mr. Burton and Mr. Prezzolini were waiting for them; but they were no longer seated on the blue carpet. They were standing up and waving their arms and looking thoroughly alarmed.

"The carpet has been stolen," said Mr. Burton. "Just fifteen minutes ago. By local bandits. In my opinion they were Tatars."

"There wasn't much we could do to prevent them," said Mr. Swaraswati.

"No, of course not," said Nimrod. "Can't be helped. These things happen."

"You're taking this very calmly," observed Moo. "How are we going to travel to Tibet without that carpet?"

Nimrod frowned. "Am I? I certainly don't mean to take it calmly."

"They were armed with guns," said Mr. Prezzolini. "They threatened to shoot us unless we gave them the carpet."

"As a matter of fact, I'm not calm at all." Nimrod shook his head. "Whatever gave you that idea? Because if there's one thing I really hate, it's a thief," he said. "I get really angry about theft. If I wasn't so tired I'd go after them myself and —" He shook his head. "I don't know what I'd do. I'd probably do something terrible, if you really want to know. Something really awful. I'd give them what for, that's what I'd do. That's what thieves deserve. *Proper punishment*. Real punishment instead of the smack on the wrist that the law gives thieves these days."

"To be fair, I think the punishment for thieves in Kazakhstan is a bit harder than it is in England," said Moo.

"Well, it's probably still too good for them," grumbled Nimrod. "Whatever it is." Nimrod snorted. "Thieves? I'd skin them alive."

"What are we going to do?" asked Philippa.

"Go after them, of course," said Nimrod. "Go after them and get the carpet back. What do you think we're going to do? The *Times* crossword?"

"You can see their tracks," said Mr. Burton, pointing at the ground. "They should be easy to follow. They can't have gone far in fifteen minutes."

Nimrod let out a sigh. "Philippa, you'll have to do it. Go after them. I can't. I'd probably overreact. You do it."

"Me?"

"That's right. You. Look, if you knew how I was feeling, you wouldn't argue."

"But what shall I do when I catch up with them?" she asked.

"Do?" Nimrod laughed. "Do? Light my lamp, child, you're a djinn. What do you think you should do with someone who's stolen your flying carpet? Cook them a cake or scare the skin off their feet? You scare them, of course. That's what you do. And if that doesn't work, then you do whatever seems horribly and poetically appropriate in the circumstances."

"Such as?"

Nimrod shook his head, which was a mistake as it was still aching terribly. "Ow," he said, wincing with discomfort. "My head. Talk about Jack and Jill. I don't know, Philippa. Why ask me? You've been doing this sort of thing for a while now. You've read the *Arabian Nights*. You know what we djinns are capable of. Sometimes we just have to be cruel, I think. Especially to thieves. So do what your mother does. Boil them in oil. Drown them. Tie them to a railway line.

Make them swallow rats. Set some wild animals on them. Better still, turn them into animals that other animals can eat, I suppose. *They're thieves*. Just get that flying carpet back."

Philippa gave her uncle a look. Usually, he wasn't as intolerant as this and she wondered if the blow on his head had affected him in some way. She pulled a face and started to follow the trail of the Tatar bandits.

CHAPTER 36

GETTING THE HUMP

Mr. Bayuleev had lent Philippa one of his Bactrian camels so that she could go after the bandits in comfort. Unlike Dromedary camels, Bactrians have two humps, and as she climbed up onto the beast and settled herself between two enormous hairy pepper pots, she wondered which had come first in the evolutionary process: one hump or two.

The camel walked quickly along the trail left by the Tatar bandits. They were on foot and their boot prints were clearly visible even from the height of the camel's back, so they weren't difficult to follow and Philippa was able to spend some of the time thinking about what she was going to do when she caught up with the bandits, which she soon did. But before she had arrived at a satisfactory answer to the problem of how she was going to deal with them, almost inevitably it seemed to her, they refused to return Nimrod's carpet.

There were three of them and they were easy to identify carrying Nimrod's carpet on their broad shoulders like a long, saggy tree log. They wore sleeveless sheepskin jackets and all of them looked like the actor Charles Bronson, with narrow eyes, drooping mustaches, and salient cheekbones. They also wore pistols thrust under their belts.

Seeing Philippa, they stopped for a moment and waited for her to say something.

"*Aye?*" said one, which is Tatar for "yes."

"Excuse me." Philippa smiled. "That's my uncle's carpet," she said, "and he wants it back."

The Tatar leader smiled a big friendly smile. "*Zinhar öçen,*" he said. "Say please."

"*Zinhar öçen.*" Philippa shrugged. "Please."

The bandits thought that was very funny. Then one of them waved at her. "*Saw buliğiz,*" he said. "Bye-bye."

"No," said Philippa, jumping down from the camel. "I can't let you do that. Look, you can't go around stealing things. It's not right. If you don't put that carpet down, I'm going to have to stop you. I'm asking you nicely, all right?"

"*Yuq,*" said the leader and, since he shook his head as he said this, Philippa guessed, correctly, that "*yuq*" is the Tatar word for "no."

"Yuck, indeed," she said. "I really hate this. Why won't people listen?" She stamped her foot and raised her voice. "You're not listening to me."

Blocking their way now, she said to the leader, "Look, I know you speak a bit of English."

"I speak English," said the leader.

"Good, because I want you to know that I'm not fooling around here."

"I not fooling around, also," said the bandit leader. "I warn you to go away. Or maybe I take your camel as well as your uncle's carpet."

"That would be an even bigger mistake than the one you made already," said Philippa. "Please don't make me use force. You've no idea what I'm capable of. Don't make the mistake of underestimating me. Some other people did and now they're budgies. Or at least they would be if some ferrets hadn't eaten them. I don't like using force. But if you give me no choice, then I will."

"Force? What kind of force?" He grinned. "Maybe you gonna hit me with your glasses, huh? Or slap my face?"

"I can do much worse than that," said Philippa. "But the thing is I don't want to, you see?"

The bandit leader sighed and it was clear he still didn't believe Philippa could stop him, which was, she decided, hardly surprising since grown men have a bad habit of ignoring children, especially girls, and not taking them seriously. So she decided to make the carpet much heavier by the simple device of causing a length of solid cast iron weighing several hundred pounds to appear inside the rolled-up carpet. Which was the same moment she remembered that she'd forgotten to change the focus word back to something more easily usable.

"DIDDLEEYEJOEFROMMEJICOFELLOFFHIS-HORSEATARODEOHANDSUPSTICKEMUP-DROPTHEMGUNSANDPICKEMUPDIDDLEEYEJOE-FROMMEJICO!"

Immediately, the three bandits staggered and then collapsed under the heavy weight; then the carpet rolled off their shoulders and onto the ground.

"I told you," she said. "Now if you'll just leave it there and walk away, nobody will get hurt. Or turned into an animal."

The bandit leader stood up holding his shoulder painfully and said something that even in Tatar sounded unpleasant to Philippa's ears. Then he reached for his pistol.

There was no time for her to think about anything except getting all of the focus word out of her mouth before the bandit could get his gun out of his belt; but even as he was thumbing back the hammer, Philippa still hadn't finished uttering it. And he was actually pointing the pistol at her when the very last syllables crossed her lips.

There was a loud bang and a strong smell of sulfur, as is often the result following an angry or urgent demonstration of djinn power. The bandit leader disappeared, and another Bactrian camel was now standing in his place.

This prompted the second bandit to reach for his pistol, only he did it a little more quickly than his friend, which meant that he was able to get off a single shot that Philippa ducked, before she finally managed to utter all of her focus word again, and he, too, was turned into a burping, saliva-drooling Bactrian camel.

It wasn't that she liked Bactrian camels so much as the fact that, what with all these guns being pointed at her, there was little time to think of anything else but guns and camels. And she might just as easily have turned the bandit into an old service revolver of the kind that the bandit had been holding, except that she disliked camels just a little less than she disliked guns.

"At this rate, I'm going to end up with my own camel train," said Philippa.

The third bandit was sufficiently alarmed by what had happened to his friends that he was not inclined to stay and offer Philippa any further resistance. He was quite convinced that Philippa was some kind of alien, or at the very least a Cossack devil of the kind his grandparents had told him about. He yelled with fright and quickly reached for his gun to throw it away.

The trouble was that Philippa was unable to read his mind and assumed that he, too, was intending to shoot her, and before the pistol could hit the ground, there was a third Bactrian camel standing beside the other two.

Philippa let out a weary sigh and felt sick. It wasn't the fear of almost being shot that made her feel nauseous so much as the idea of turning a man into an animal. Having experienced being an animal herself, she knew this wasn't so bad. All the same what she had done felt pretty drastic and, for a moment or two, she looked hard for a silver lining inside the cloud of what she had done.

"They may be camels but at least they're still alive," she told herself. "Unlike those two budgies back in Bumby. Although it wasn't really my fault that they got eaten by those two ferrets. How was I to know that ferrets eat budgies?"

She found a length of rope on the back of Mr. Bayuleev's camel and used it to tie the other three to the saddle.

"And I suppose I can always make a gift of these other camels to Mr. Bayuleev in return for him helping us. He looks pretty poor. I guess three camels would be very valuable to him."

Then, using djinn power again, she made the length of cast iron inside the flying carpet disappear before lifting it up in the air and laying it across one of the bandit camels.

"And I suppose that those three wicked bandits can't rob anyone else now. Or worse. I mean, it is possible that they might have shot me. Equally they could shoot someone else. So I guess that has to be a good thing, too."

She mounted Mr. Bayuleev's camel and started back to where she had left the others.

"All the same, I can't helping thinking that it still doesn't feel right to do that to someone," she said. "It feels cruel and unusual. Like something prohibited in the Constitution. And that has to be bad."

This feeling lasted as long as it took Philippa to arrive back at the collection of leather tents Mr. Bayuleev called home, because when she presented him with three extra camels he was so grateful he started to kiss her hand and to cry. And she began to feel that maybe something good had come out of what had happened after all.

Nimrod, however, was less impressed.

"I hope you terrified them properly first," he said. "Before you turned them into camels."

"Of course I did," said Philippa, hoping to change the subject.

Nimrod looked disbelieving.

"They don't look like they've been terrified very much."

"Well, I did."

"Go on then, what did you do?"

"I'd rather not say, if you don't mind."

"That's because you didn't do it, did you?" argued Nimrod. "Which makes me wonder why you turned them into camels."

"What's wrong with camels?"

"Nothing," said Nimrod. "That's my point, really. I mean, given that these were three desperate thieves with guns, and given that you couldn't bring yourself to terrify them a bit first, couldn't you have turned them into something a bit more horrible than camels?"

"Such as?"

"I don't know. Tortoises. Fish. Better still, gerbils. That way something would be bound to eat them before very long. Especially around here. Snow leopard. Eagle. Lynx. A gerbil's a nice snack when you're a lynx or an eagle. And serve them right, too. In my opinion, all thieves should squeak a bit for their crimes. Especially when they go around pointing guns at people. That's only justice. Don't you agree, Moo?"

"I've never liked gerbils," said Moo. "Or anything that squeaks. But I happen to believe in the rule of law. There can be no real justice without a trial."

"Well said, lady," said Silvio.

"If I hadn't seen your X-ray," said Philippa, "I'd swear there was something very wrong with you, Uncle Nimrod."

"I agree," said Mr. Burton. "You're behaving in a most peculiar way."

"I feel fine," insisted Nimrod.

"Anyway, I thought three camels would make a nice gift for Mr. Bayuleev."

"That's fair enough, I suppose."

Nimrod chuckled as Mr. Bayuleev proceeded to kiss Philippa's hand once again.

"Bless him, look. He thinks you're an angel. A real one, probably. Tell you what. I've had a great idea. Three camels, right? Why don't you hang a bit of tinsel on them and maybe he'll think it's Christmas?"

Nimrod laughed out loud at his own rather tasteless joke, which left Philippa staring up at the sky and hoping that before very long another large bird might fall and hit her uncle on the head. Either that or she was going to have to get used to liking Nimrod a lot less than before.

"Come on," said Nimrod. "Let's roll out that carpet and get out of here before he starts worshipping you and this gets really embarrassing."

Philippa shot her uncle a withering look. "Yes, well, I certainly know what that feels like," she said.

CHAPTER 37

AUF WIEDERSEHEN

It was midnight, for they were to leave before it was light, and the moon made everything in the Kailash crater a strange and unearthly shade of blue.

At the Mopu Lamasery, the Nazis made their preparations to return home to Germany from Tibet with a cheerfulness that John found easier to understand than to share. They rolled up their flags, packed away their pictures and statues, and sang jolly German songs about how they loved to go wandering in the mountains (especially when they were in countries that belonged to other people), a man called Horst Wessel, and how someone's rotten bones were trembling. Several of them grinned happily at John and clapped him on the shoulder. A few even thanked him for "agreeing" to accompany them to Berlin.

"You've no idea what this means to us," said one. "To go home. To see our families again after all this time. Seventy weeks in Tibet. It felt more like seventy years, I can tell you."

John didn't have the heart to tell the Nazi that something had happened to time while he and his comrades had been staying in the Kailash crater; that seventy weeks had been at least seventy years, and that very likely all of their families were dead — either from old age or as a result of the Second World War, which none of them seemed to know about. So he kept his mouth shut and bided his time.

Meanwhile, Hynkell kept his word and released Rakshasas, who sprang upon John in a frenzy of affection, licking his face and playfully biting his hand. John took hold of the thick collar of fur around the wolf's neck and spoke quietly into his ear, explaining what had happened.

"They know that I'm a djinn," he said. "Well, of course they suspected something of the kind when they saw us arrive here on a flying carpet. Seventy odd years ago, Himmler sent them here to find out the secret of eternal life and a load of stuff about Tibetan paranormal powers, but the monks at Shamba-la have always refused to let them in the door. I guess they must have showed up after you were last here, huh? Otherwise you'd have mentioned it, right?"

Rakshasas barked once.

"Anyway, they think I'm the next best thing to Tibetan paranormal powers. So they're planning to take me back to Berlin instead of some monk from Shamba-la. And yes, I've agreed to go with them."

Gradually, the wolf settled down until he was just standing there looking at him, with an expression of disappointment and reproach in his blue eyes — as if to say, "You made a deal with some Nazis?"

"What could I do?" John said to Rakshasas. "Since I've been in the Kailash crater, I've had no djinn power. None at all. It's completely deserted me. I couldn't have resisted them even if I had wanted to. And I had to give my word to go back to Berlin with them or they'd have tortured you. Roasted you alive, they said, and made me watch."

Rakshasas stared at him some more and then shook his head, and John didn't need to put his spirit inside the wolf to know what he was thinking.

"That might not seem important to you," said John. "But I certainly couldn't have endured it."

Then Rakshasas put his nose into the air and emitted a long howl, which of course made John think of Groanin and what was happening in Yellowstone Park.

"Yes, I know. I'm thinking about poor Groanin, too. But he's a shrewd one, the Nazi commander. He made me make a wish, see? They made me wish that something would happen to Mom and Dad if I broke my word to them. And I know better than to wish things lightly, especially when it involves the lives of others. You know how that stuff works. So I *had* to choose."

John punched his hand as he tried to explain himself to the wolf.

"I had to choose Groanin or my own mother and father. So I had to choose my parents. That's what anyone would do, isn't it?"

Rakshasas stepped forward and licked away the tear that was rolling down John's face. Then he nipped him on the hand again as if to say, "Pull yourself together."

John pulled himself together and watched helplessly as the flying carpet was rolled up and tied on top of a climbing pack, and although he had his doubts that the carpet would fly at all within the confines of the crater, he still felt compelled to mention it to Hynkell. Even to tease him with it a little.

"I don't get it," he said. "Don't you want me to fly some of you out of here? It'd be a lot easier than walking, I'd have thought. And certainly a lot quicker."

Hynkell, who was tying a rope around his middle for the descent, shook his head. "I can't ask some of my men to wait behind," he said. "Either we all go back together or not at all. Besides, I'm not quite ready to put myself completely in your control, John."

"I already gave you my word," said John.

"It'll be a different story in Berlin, but up here it's best that I don't put too much temptation in your way. So I think we will climb down, yes?"

John shrugged. "It's your call," he said. "But it looked like a very difficult climb when I flew in here. I'd have said it couldn't have been done on foot. It's a sheer wall at the foot of that fissure. You must all be excellent mountaineers. I certainly hope so since I'm putting myself in your control."

"We're the best in Germany," said Hynkell. "Which is to say, the best in the world. That's why we were sent here in the first place."

"I don't mind telling you," said John. "I'm not much of a climber. And nor is Rakshasas."

Hynkell smiled thinly. "Then we shall teach you." The Nazi approached John and tied a rope around his middle.

"Is that in case I escape?"

"No, it is in case you fall."

When all the Nazis were assembled and ready to leave the crater, Hynkell made a speech about the journey that lay ahead of them and passed around a bottle of schnapps. After that, they sang the German national anthem. And just before dawn, they set off.

For about an hour they walked along a knife-edge traverse until they came to the entrance to the fissure and Hynkell led the way in, but not a man followed him without halting breathlessly for a moment, and glancing back at the crater where they had lived for such an unfeasible length of time. Yet there were no expressions of regret at leaving behind their secret Himalayan sanctuary. For all of the Germans, this was not a departure but an escape and, in spite of his dislike of their leader, Hynkell, John couldn't help but feel a strong sense of concern and foreboding for what lay ahead of them. How soon would they discover the truth about what had happened to them? When they reached Lhasa and saw the first television? And how would they react to the discovery that even the youngest of them was at least ninety years old? Would they take it out on John and Rakshasas?

The passage through the fissure was anything but easy going. The floor was nonexistent and most of the time they had to traverse the passage in an acute angle between the two walls. Sometimes the gap between the two walls was very narrow, which meant that the larger climbing packs had to be removed and in some cases abandoned because they were too bulky to be squeezed through. Only Rakshasas, being the smallest of all the travelers, moved through the fissure without any real difficulty.

After several hours in the fissure, they stopped for food and some of the kinder, friendlier Germans fetched Mr. Rakshasas some food, and John learned that not all of the men were fanatics like Hynkell. Some were just ordinary men who had found themselves drafted into the German army and, because they were skilled mountaineers, detailed to join the SS and, in particular, Hynkell's expedition to Tibet.

"Don't worry," one of them told John. "We'll look after you and your furry friend here. Back in Germany, I have a dog that looks a lot like him. My brother has been looking after him while I've been away." The German smiled. "He'll go crazy when he sees me again."

"After all this time, do you think he'll recognize you?" John asked carefully.

"Of course," said the German. "He's my dog. Not my brother's. German shepherds are one-man dogs. For life. Once they're yours, they're yours forever."

"I'm sure you're right," said John.

"My name is Fritz," said the man, holding out his hand.

John nodded and took it. "John," he said. "Pleased to meet you. I think."

"Have you been to Berlin before?" asked Fritz.

"Yes, once," said John. "I went to the Pergamon Museum. It was very interesting. The Blue Gates of Babylon."

"Your German is very good," said Fritz.

"Thanks." John thought it best not to mention that the only reason he spoke fluent German was because he'd wished it with djinn power. That was the only reason he'd done a lot of things. And he wondered how much Fritz knew about who and what he was. Kind or not, John certainly didn't want to get into a conversation with the German that ended with being asked for three wishes.

"How is it," asked Fritz, "that you are able to fly a magic carpet?"

John shrugged. "Practice," he said.

Fritz smiled at John's joke but there was no time for him to reply as one of Hynkell's staff sergeants blew a whistle, which was the sign for everyone to get moving again.

The second stage of the journey through the fissure in Mount Kailash was even harder than the first, and while John found the going difficult he did not find it as difficult as most of the Germans, who seemed surprisingly unfit. By the time they reached the other side of the mountain, the Germans were all puffing like steam trains and many of them were exhausted. And it was with a sense of relief that John heard Hynkell give the order that they would make camp in the fissure that night and begin the descent of the rock face first thing in the morning.

As soon as the order was given, Fritz collapsed against the rock wall and might have lain down except that there was no room to lie down, and almost everyone except John spent the next few hours asleep on their feet like a collection of statues. Even the man carrying John's flying carpet was asleep, and John might actually have stolen it back but for the fact that he had given his word to Hynkell.

To take his mind off such considerations, John went to the edge of the fissure, stared down the rock face, and shuddered at the very thought of trying to climb down the mountain. The descent looked impossible and the real wonder was how these men had ever made the ascent. If he'd felt sufficient heat in his bones, he might even have contemplated helping out the Germans with better rope and some more up-to-date climbing equipment like a few dozen belay and rappel devices, quickdraws, carabiners, and climbing boots. But it was a bitterly cold night, and John felt as helpless as a kitten stuck up a tree.

"Thinking of escape?" said a voice.

John looked around and saw Hynkell was immediately behind him. He looked very tired. There were deep lines in his face, and John wondered if he or any of his men would be up to the physically demanding feat that lay ahead of them.

"No," said the boy djinn. "I told you I gave my word. Maybe you Nazis are in the habit of breaking a promise, but I'm not."

Hynkell nodded. "Good," he said. Then, producing a Luger pistol, he added, "Just remember. I'll be bringing up the rear tomorrow. So if you do break your word, I shan't hesitate to use this. On you, or your furry friend."

John looked over the edge once more. "Anyway, right

now I'm more worried about breaking my neck than breaking my word. If you ask me, none of your men are up to this climb. They're already exhausted. What are they going to be like when they're on that wall?"

"Don't worry about my men," said Hynkell. "They'll be all right. They made it all the way up here. They'll certainly make it back again."

"I hope so," said John. "For my sake."

As soon as it was light, the best of Hynkell's climbers moved out onto a narrow ledge, roped in threes, and began to traverse along the sheer face of Mount Kailash; this first climber was roped to a second man who followed, and a third, and so on until it was John's turn. Tied onto his back was Rakshasas, for John trusted no one else to carry his old friend. If they fell they would fall together. But before John stepped out onto the ledge, Fritz tapped him on the arm and handed him a pocketknife.

"Just in case," he murmured.

For a moment John wondered what he meant and realizing this, Fritz explained:

"Just in case you need to cut the rope," he said.

"Cut the rope?" John looked horrified at the very idea. "Why would I want to do that?"

"You might have to, lad." said Fritz. "To save yourself. And there would be no shame in that. My own son would be about your age. I hope that another man, in similar circumstances — if such a thing were possible — would do the same for him."

"Thanks," said John. "But I'm sure I'll be fine."

"Naturally." Fritz grinned. "It's just a precaution, that's all."

Ignoring the sharp wind that whipped his face with reproach for having dared to set foot on the holy mountain — John had hardly forgotten what Rakshasas had said about the blasphemy of climbing Mount Kailash — he edged his way onto the traverse and began to inch his way along the wall. And, one by one, Fritz and the others followed until they were all on the wall, like a daisy chain.

For about half an hour, the movement of the climbers along the traverse was steady, but gradually it slowed and eventually came to a halt. At first, John thought it might have something to do with the wind, which was quickly building up to a gale, and he braced himself for an order from the front to go back to the fissure. He felt that would only have been sensible; perhaps they might attempt a descent later, when the wind had dropped. But when no such order came, John became impatient.

"What's happening?" he asked the man in front to whom he was roped, whose name was Kurt.

Kurt turned to tell John that he didn't know, and John hardly recognized him. At first, the boy supposed that it was the cold that had turned the man's hair white; but he realized the cold could hardly have affected his voice, which was now weak and halting, or his back, which was now bent. There could be no doubt about it, thought John: Kurt was aging in front of his very eyes.

"There's something wrong with Kurt," he said, turning

to speak to Fritz, and was even more shocked to see that Fritz, too, was aging rapidly. Instead of the tall and blond and handsome man that John had seen leaving the Kailash crater, Fritz was now an infirm and very elderly man.

Farther up the ledge, there was a shout and then a cry, and John looked around just in time to see three of the men leading the way along the traverse slip and fall to their deaths. Except that they looked dead already. Outside of a grave in a horror movie, John had never seen anyone look quite so old.

Rakshasas uttered a whine of fear, and even through his thick fur coat, John could feel the wolf trembling.

"Outside of the crater," John yelled, "their true age is catching up with them."

Rakshasas barked once to agree.

One by one, the men ahead of John fell from the traverse. And he realized that it would be only a matter of seconds before Kurt and Fritz, the two frail old men to whom he was still roped, fell, too.

Feebly, Fritz indicated that John should hammer in a piton and tie himself on. John hardly needed telling a second time. He put in a piton and was shocked to find it badly rusted and crumbling in his fingers as if it, too, was old — as old as the SS troop Himmler had sent to Shamba-la. This discovery — that it wasn't just the Nazis who were rapidly deteriorating but their equipment as well — shocked John almost as much the faces of his two immediate climbing companions. He had no idea if the piton or even the rope would hold his weight if he fell.

He looked back at Fritz and nodded and saw him lay his head wearily against the rock as if he was too tired to go on. By now Fritz's hair was completely white and his hands were shaking noticeably. He looked at least a hundred years old.

"Now cut the rope," shouted Fritz. "Cut the rope and save yourself. Before Kurt and I take you down with us."

John took out the pocketknife and held the blade over the rope still attaching him to Kurt and Fritz. He hesitated to cut the rope, knowing that without it these two frail old men were certain to die.

"I can't do it," he shouted.

Farther along the ledge, three more aged Nazis fell, very quietly, to their long overdue deaths.

"You have to," said Fritz. He pointed a doddery hand behind John. "Look."

John looked at Kurt and saw that he was already dead. He knew he was dead because the man was aging so rapidly his head was little more than a skull. The next second, Kurt's skeleton collapsed in a pile of dust and bones that slipped over the edge of the traverse simultaneously removing the need for John to cut that section of the rope.

"Cut the rope, John," shouted Fritz even as, feeling faint, he swayed on the ledge.

Rakshasas barked urgently and then nipped John on the ear.

John cut the rope and then closed his eyes as Fritz slipped, sat down heavily on the ledge, and then tipped forward into thin air like a man falling asleep for the rest of eternity.

He heard a few more feeble screams farther down the traverse and when he opened his eyes again he found that he was the only one left on the rock face. The SS men were gone, including the flying carpet that might have saved John's life. And all that was left of them was one skull and a couple of thigh bones silvered with cold that occupied the center of the traverse like an SS man's cap badge.

Rakshasas whined meaningfully.

"No way am I dropping you down there after them," said John.

The wolf barked once.

"I don't care how heavy you are. We'll either make it together or we won't make it at all."

Half frozen with fear, John tried to gather his courage. It wasn't easy. He didn't look down. He didn't dare. The sight of so many men falling thousands of feet to their deaths would, he was sure, remain with him for the rest of his life. And begged too many questions he didn't even want to think of. There was no point in staying where he was. There was no one to come and rescue him. He took a deep breath and prepared to move.

"Look on the bright side, Rakshasas," he said, his face pressed close to the wall. "At least now I don't have to go to Berlin."

He slipped the rope out of the rusted piton and, reasoning that their best chance was back in the Kailash crater, he started to inch his way back along the traverse. But the wind seemed to have other plans and buffeted John like an invisible cat playing with a mouse. Desperate to keep up his spirits and hoping that somehow he might wish it true, John began to sing. He didn't always sing the right words, but the sentiment was utterly true and heartfelt. John had never before wished anything with such sincerity:

"Oh, I wish I was in the land of cotton,
Old times there are not forgotten,
Look away! Look away!
Look away! DixieLand.
Oh, I wish I was in Dixie,
Hooray! Hooray!
In DixieLand, I'll take my stand
To live and die in Dixie.
Away, away,
I wish I was in Dixie."

John's hands stayed flat against the wall, for there was nothing to hold on to. There was just a toehold on life and nothing else. Rakshasas closed his eyes against the wind and stayed silent, hardly daring to distract the boy djinn from the important business that was happening beneath his feet.

Ten minutes passed, and then fifteen. John thought it could not be long until he was in the safety of the fissure again. He didn't dare lift his head away from the wall to check on his progress. But when, after almost half an hour on his toes, he risked a look, he was shocked to find that the fissure was nowhere to be seen.

"That can't be right," he said and, looking back along the

way he had come, he was horrified to discover that somehow he had come along a second and lower traverse and that the bottom of the fissure was now ten or fifteen feet immediately above his head.

John swore loudly for almost a minute and then reached up, looking around for any toeholds and handholds.

Breathlessly, he outlined the options for himself and Rakshasas:

"As I see it, we have two choices," he said loudly in the teeth of the wind. "We can go back along the traverse, straight into the wind, and pick up the right trail again. It's about fifty or sixty feet. Times two because we'll have to come back this way again, but on the right ledge this time. I figure that way's maybe twenty or thirty minutes."

He sighed and glanced above his head again. "Or we can try to climb this bit of wall above our heads. I think I can do it because there are several hand- and toeholds. I think we can make it up there in less than half the time it would take to make the traverse along the ledge."

He closed his eyes, wishing that he could sleep and wishing that he might see his family again. So much wishing, it seemed ironic that he was a djinn with the power to grant wishes and yet couldn't even grant his own least wish, which was simply to stay alive.

"We'll climb. Because I don't have the energy to walk back along this traverse."

Rakshasas whined quietly and glanced over his shoulder. It was not a prospect that inspired him with much confidence.

"Thanks for that," said John. "It's nice to know you believe in me."

Rakshasas barked once to disagree.

John nodded. "Right," he said, reaching for one of the handholds he'd found above his head. "Let's get on with it."

He fixed the back of his heel on a small step, pulled himself up, and found himself halfway up to the ledge already. With hand and foot stretching out to his right, he found another handhold and a crack that was just wide enough for him to squeeze the toe of his boot into, enabling him to move up again; this time his hands were on the wider ledge in front of the fissure and safety.

Rakshasas barked his encouragement as John pulled himself up until he was looking over the edge.

"We made it," he grunted, scrabbling up the wall. "We made it."

For the first time in ages, John felt a smile spreading on his face. He reached for another handhold inside the fissure and then winced as something else caught his hand and squeezed it tight.

It was another hand.

Except that it was hardly a hand at all but the thin, bleached bones underneath a human hand — all twenty-seven of them — which was still attached to something that was more corpse than body; something unutterably old and loathsome and decayed and yet still half recognizable as Obersturmbannführer Dr. Heinrich Hynkell of the Waffen-SS. A skull beneath skin as yellow as parchment grinned horribly and then leered in John's face, and instinctively the boy drew back and pulled his own hand away from the foul creature's grip. And John heard himself cry out, not from fear of Dr. Hynkell, for it was certain that this had been the despicable Nazi's last living act, but from the realization that he was about to fall off the ledge.

Rakshasas yelped loudly and shifted on John's back, trying to carry the boy a few vital inches forward to safety. But it was to no avail.

With his other hand, John grabbed at the one solid object that still remained in reach, and found himself holding Hynkell's skull, which immediately snapped off the Nazi's bony, thin neck. And like Hamlet holding Yorick in an empty theatre, John found himself parting company with the mountain.

With his legs now cycling an invisible bicycle and his arms swimming frantically in a dry sea, John somersaulted backward into thin air like a doomed bungee jumper and began the inexorably long fall to earth and the death he had struggled so very hard to avoid.

And he could not help thinking of the question he had tried not to think of earlier, which was this: Does a person falling thousands of feet to his death remain fully conscious right up until the moment that he hits the ground?

It seemed that John was about to find out.

CHAPTER 38

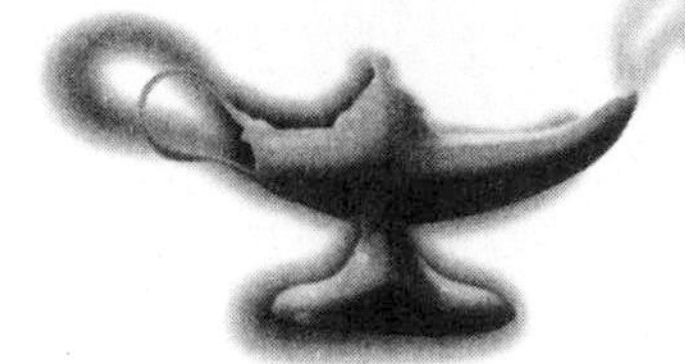

FINAL THEORY

Nimrod regarded Mr. Swaraswati with something like concern.

The fakir's eyes were closed and he didn't appear to have taken a full breath for quite a while. He sat cross-legged in the same position he had been sitting in since leaving Kazakhstan several hours before. Nothing about him appeared to be moving: Not even his hair and beard in the wind and for all Nimrod knew, there was nothing moving inside the man either — not his heart nor his lungs nor the blood in his veins. The djinn couldn't help but worry that perhaps the old fakir had expired without telling anyone his secret, which seemed a terrible waste in Nimrod's new, slightly addled way of thinking.

"So come on then, Mr. Swaraswati," said Nimrod. "What is it? Are you going to tell us? Or should we try and guess?"

They were flying over that part of China that only the Chinese government calls China, but which the rest of the world calls Tibet. Beneath them were high mountains, capped with snow and wrapped in clouds.

Mr. Swaraswati inhaled a deep breath through his nostrils and, after several seconds, his eyes flickered open.

"What is what?" he asked.

Nimrod grinned. "The secret of the universe that the Tirthankar entrusted to you all those years ago," he said. "About the meaning of everything. Which one did you get?"

"Really, Uncle Nimrod," protested Philippa. "I think it's very unfair of you to ask Mr. Swaraswati that question."

"He's got to tell someone, hasn't he?" insisted Nimrod. "I mean, look at the poor old thing. He's not exactly in the best of shape, now is he? I've seen healthier-looking people in an anatomy class. And I don't mean the ones standing up wearing the white coats. If he doesn't tell someone soon, well, who knows?"

No one said anything, least of all Mr. Swaraswati.

Then Philippa said, "I think you have a delayed concussion, Uncle Nimrod. You don't know what you're saying."

"Rubbish," said Nimrod. "I mean, what's the point of being buried alive for a thousand years with one of the secrets of the universe locked away inside your mind if you snuff it before you can tell anyone." Nimrod shrugged. "That's a mystery to me, I don't mind telling you." He chuckled at his own tasteless joke, and added, "I bet even Mr. Swaraswati would feel like a bit of a chump if he checks out of life's motel before he can tell anyone what he's remembered. Always supposing he can remember it, of course. I'm not actually convinced of that. To be honest with you, he doesn't look like he can remember if he has milk in his coffee." He nodded at Mr. Swaraswati and, raising his voice as if the old man were deaf, he smiled a patronizing sort of smile. "All right?"

"I say," protested Moo. "Speaking as an old person myself, I think you're being a bit insensitive, Nimrod."

"Don't get me wrong, I'm not having a go at old people," said Nimrod. "I've nothing against them at all."

"I'm glad to hear it," said Mr. Burton, who was no spring chicken.

"I expect to be old myself, one day," said Nimrod. "*Horribly* old. But there's old and there's old, right? There's old like you, Moo, and there's an archaeological discovery. Mr. Swaraswati's off the normal scale of what's old. He's like a living fossil. Aren't you, Mr. Swaraswati?" Nimrod nodded at him again. "And I'm just saying that if he's going to tell anyone, it ought to be one of us." Nimrod shrugged. "After all, who else is there? It's not like he's got a lot of mates, has he? If he's going to entrust the Tirthankar's secret to someone, it ought to be one of us, that's all I'm saying. In case something happens to the poor old thing. Just think about it. We wouldn't be having this conversation if that pelican had landed on him instead of me."

"Exactly," said Philippa bitterly. She hardly recognized her uncle since the accident. She still hoped his personality change wasn't permanent. It wasn't that he was a nastier person since the accident, just a less caring and less courteous one.

"What I mean is that it might easily have killed him," added Nimrod by way of explanation.

"Well," said Philippa, "if you ask me, the only way Mr. Swaraswati can be absolutely sure that he can trust us is if we don't ever ask him to reveal the Tirthankar's secret."

"You're wrong," said Mr. Swaraswati.

"What?" Philippa frowned.

"Nimrod is right," said Mr. Swaraswati. "Mr. Burton was asking me about this very thing earlier on, when you were both in Atyrau."

"Was he, by Jove?" said Nimrod.

"And I've been thinking about what he said," said Mr. Swaraswati. "You know, ever since I stepped upon this flying carpet I have had the constant thought that I might easily be killed. That is why I have been so anxious. The idea that I might fall off this thing before I have had the chance to impart the Tirthankar's great secret has been most worrying to me. And, as Nimrod says, if I can't trust you, whom can I trust?"

Nimrod smiled triumphantly at his niece. "There you go," he said. "Was I right, or what?"

"So I will tell you."

"Heads up, everyone," said Nimrod. "This could be important."

"Centuries ago," said Mr. Swaraswati, "I made a tryst with destiny. In truth, I had little appreciation of quite what I was committed to and that I would have to wait buried in the dark and loamy earth of Yorkshire for as long as I was. But now the time comes when the pledge must be redeemed.

Not wholly or in full measure but very substantially, for the Tirthankar cannot be here himself and share the true extent of his enlightenment. And it is certain that I have no real understanding of that which I have so long remembered. He told me that before I revealed this, one of the great secrets of the universe, I should say this: That a moment comes but rarely in history when we step out from the old to the new, when an age ends and a new age begins, when that which was hidden or long suppressed is now revealed, and how it is fitting that at this solemn moment we should all take the pledge of dedication to put this knowledge to the service of humanity and the still larger cause of the world we live in."

Nimrod shrugged. "Sure," he said glibly. "Why not? Everyone? We can do that, yeah? Swear that none of us will try to profit from this secret? For the sake of humanity? On a count of three, everyone says 'we so swear,' right? One, two, three . . ."

"We so swear," said everyone.

There followed a moment's silence while Mr. Swaraswati looked nervously over the edge of the flying carpet.

Nimrod nodded at Mr. Swaraswati. "In your own time," he said. "When you're ready."

"Does anyone have a pencil?" asked Mr. Swaraswati.

"Here," said Nimrod. "You can borrow my pen. But I want it back. That's gold, that is."

Mr. Swaraswati took the pen. "And something to write on?"

Moo opened her handbag. "You may use my British secret service notebook," she said.

Mr. Swaraswati thanked her and scrawled something on a sheet of paper. He looked at it for a second, nodded, and then handed it to Nimrod, saying, "Where *e* equals 'experience.'"

Nimrod read it, tore out the page, read it, and nodded. "Yes," he said, almost to himself. "That would make sense. If the signum function is the derivative of the absolute value function . . . hmm. The resultant power of *e* is zero, which is similar to the ordinary power of *e*. The numbers cancel each other out and all we are left with is *e*. My goodness. That's right. So it does."

So keen was his concentration that for a moment the flying carpet dipped a little, which was enough to persuade Nimrod to fold away the piece of paper Mr. Swaraswati had given him, and put it in his pocket.

"Well?" said Mr. Burton. "Come on. Aren't you going to read it out to the rest of us?"

Nimrod shook his head. "You wouldn't understand it," he said.

"Really," said Moo. "I'll have you know I went to Cambridge University."

"Course you did," said Nimrod. "And that's why you're a spy. But this is complicated stuff about the nature of the universe. As complicated as *e* equals *mc* squared. Perhaps even a bit more complicated than that. And to be honest, I'm not sure I understand it myself. Yet."

"All the same," said Moo. "I think Philippa and I would like to hear it. After all, it was us who found and rescued Mr. Swaraswati."

"Hear, hear," said Mr. Burton.

Nimrod shrugged and handed Moo the page torn from her own notebook. "Please yourself. But it's theoretical physics, and unless you know about that stuff, you're wasting your time trying to understand it."

Moo read what was written on the page aloud. "It says: *d [e]* equals *sgn (e) de*," she said.

"It's very clever," said Nimrod. "Elegant. Simple. I'd never have thought of that myself. Well, who would?"

Moo glanced at Mr. Swaraswati. "What does it mean?"

Mr. Swaraswati shrugged. "I am merely the medium," he said. "I have no understanding of the message."

"Haven't you heard?" Nimrod chuckled. "The medium *is* the message."

"All these years," said Moo. "You must have some understanding of what it means."

"Perhaps a little," said Mr. Swaraswati.

"This I've got to hear," said Nimrod. "Come on then, Professor."

"Please, Uncle," said Philippa.

"You see, *e* equals experience," said Mr. Swaraswati. "And *d* equals a derivative function. In other words, what you can get from *e*. What the equation means is that unless we explain *how* it is that we experience things, we cannot begin to explain the nature of the experiences themselves. In other words, all perception is affected by being. And only when you explain being can you truly explain perception."

"Clear enough now?" Nimrod laughed again.

Mr. Burton stood up holding his head in both hands as if suddenly he had understood something. He shook his head as the implications of what Mr. Swaraswati had just said made a profound impact on his thoughts. "That's it?" he said. "That's it?"

"Oh, oh, I think he's got it," observed Nimrod. "Now watch his skull explode as he realizes the true implications of what this means."

"Please, Uncle," said Philippa. "Do try to be serious for a moment. What *does* it mean?"

"What does it mean?" Nimrod looked evasive. "Are you sure you want me to tell you? Sometimes it's better not knowing these things. Like old Mr. Dishwasher here said. You can't put the genie back in the bottle, so to speak." He shrugged. "When of course you can. We're the living proof of that statement. But you get the general idea."

"I want to know what you know," said Philippa.

Nimrod looked Philippa straight in the eye.

"That's not so easy," said Nimrod. "And in a way that's what is at the bottom of the equation." He pulled a face and tried to look thoughtful. "You might say that it's the ultimate truth. You see, however we describe the universe we live in, the fact remains that all the experiments we carry out and theories we elaborate in order to do that are based on our own ability to experience things or not experience things. In other words, we can only start to understand the physics of the universe that we live in when we have first clarified how it is that we have any experience of a universe at all. And because we can't ever do that it means that the ultimate truth is —"

Nimrod stopped speaking for a moment; he was no longer looking Philippa in the eye, but over Philippa's shoulder. Something had distracted him.

"What?" she asked impatiently. "What's the ultimate truth?"

"It's John," said Nimrod.

"John?" said Philippa. "What's he got to do with this?"

"Everything," said Nimrod, pointing ahead of them. "Look."

In the distance, Philippa saw a figure wearing a fur coat falling down the side of an enormous mountain. The figure was upside down and moving at considerable speed and seemed almost resigned to the prospect of landing, fatally, on his head. The apparent calm of the falling figure was unusual enough. But what was particularly strange was that the figure appeared to have a wolf tied onto his back. And it was only now that Philippa realized that the plaintive, siren-like sound she had ringing in her ears for several seconds was the wolf howling. Philippa wore glasses. But there was nothing wrong with her sight when she was wearing them. And straightaway she saw and felt that Nimrod was right: It *was* John and in just a few seconds he would be dead, unless someone did something. In the same second she realized this, Philippa let out a scream of horror as being John's twin kicked in and she felt herself at one with her brother, plummeting through the air, with everything around her a speeding blur of the world upside down. So powerful was this telepathic sensation that her stomach turned over and she almost vomited. The scream emanating from her lungs grew louder and turned into a cry for help.

Nimrod might have suffered a personality change, but there was nothing wrong with his sense of urgency, nor his ability to deal with this crisis. Even before he had finished pointing John out to Philippa, he had changed the flying carpet's course to intercept his nephew's fall.

"Sit down," he yelled at Mr. Burton, who was still taking on board the full implications of what Mr. Swaraswati had been carrying in his head for a thousand years.

The carpet banked steeply in the air like an attack aircraft, and Mr. Burton sat down and rolled perilously close to the edge before Silvio Prezzolini grabbed his hand and kept him on board; no less rigid — with fear — than the surface he was sitting on, Mr. Swaraswati lay down on his stomach and closed his eyes.

"As anyone who has ever used a flying carpet to field . . . a falling cat . . . or a falling baby . . . will tell you," Nimrod shouted through gritted teeth, "the trick is . . . to keep your eyes on them all the time. . . . to line yourself up with their flight . . . and to *catch* them . . . rather than . . . let them just . . . fall on top of you. . . ."

Even as he spoke, Nimrod was accelerating down to the ground alongside John, trying to match his velocity.

Mr. Burton, Silvio, and Moo all began to scream as the certainty began to take hold of them that they would surely hit the ground at the same time as John. Philippa was already screaming, of course. Mr. Swaraswati had his eyes closed and was muttering a last prayer to Rama. Only Nimrod and John appeared to be completely calm. Nimrod even appeared to be enjoying himself.

"You'll kill us all, you fool," yelled Mr. Burton as, at the last possible second, Nimrod steered the carpet underneath his nephew and, slackening the surface tension a little to soften the boy's landing, caught him as neatly as if he had been wearing a baseball mitt.

Rakshasas barked once and began to lick John's ear, which, for entirely telepathic reasons, Philippa could have sworn belonged to her; the sensation was so strong, she even grimaced a little and wiped her own ear with her sleeve.

The carpet continued its precipitate descent for several terrifying seconds before Nimrod brought the dive fully under control and they leveled off, clearing the ground at the foot of Mount Kailash by a matter of a few feet.

"You should see your little faces," said Nimrod as the carpet slowed and then dropped onto the ground as lightly as a sheet of notepaper. He guffawed loudly. "You all look like you're about to have a heart attack." He laughed again. "Apart from Mr. Swaraswati, who looks like he's already had one. And John, of course. Crumbs. What happened to you? You look like my granddad."

"What?" John snatched off his glove, half expecting to see the exposed phalanges, carpals, and metacarpals of a skeletal hand. But his hand looked normal enough.

Philippa jumped up and hugged her brother with relief.

Everyone else was just hugging themselves and waiting for their heartbeats to return to normal. But John was rather more concerned with the possibility that he, too, was aging rapidly, like Hynkell's SS troop.

"What do you mean?" he asked Nimrod anxiously. "Like your granddad? Am I old?"

"Your hair," said Nimrod. "It's white."

"It's true, bro," said Philippa. "It's white as snow."

"What?" John touched his hair. "How?"

"I dunno." Nimrod tutted, muttered his focus word, and gave John a hand mirror. "But it is."

John grabbed the mirror and stared at himself, half expecting to see the face of Methuselah, who was a very old man in the Bible. He was enormously relieved to see his face did not look old. He felt as if he was still a young man. But it was certainly true his hair was white. He shivered to see himself, for he was still brimful of terror. "Could being really afraid have done that? Or something else?"

"You mean the kind of fear that you have when you're falling through the air at one hundred and twenty miles per hour?" asked Nimrod. "That's terminal velocity, in case you didn't know."

John nodded. "It's true what they say," he whispered. "You're aware of everything. Just like on a bungee jump. And it's horrible."

"Yeah," said Nimrod matter-of-factly. "That'll do it, all right. Fall like that, no problem. Interesting fact: History records that the hair of some condemned prisoners, like Thomas More and Marie Antoinette, turned white overnight before their executions." He laughed his cruel laugh. "Not that it mattered all that much to them the next day, after they both got their hair cut."

"I thought I was a goner for sure," said John.

"You *were* a goner," said Nimrod. "By rights you should be strawberry jam. Oh, yes. We should be scooping you off the ground with a spoon and onto a scone with some cream and some tea. Talking of tea, I could do with a nice cup of tea. Where is that butler of mine? Where's Groanin?"

Moo stood up angrily, "Oh, for goodness' sake," she said. "Do you have to be so selfish? Ever since that pelican landed on your head you've been insufferable."

"I like that," said Nimrod. "Here's me, trying to solve the world's problems. And all you can do, Moo, is moan about my personality. I don't have to be here, you know. I could be somewhere with my feet up. It's you who got me into this mess, you silly old bat."

"I beg your pardon?" said Moo.

"I said you're a silly old bat. Something old and creepy and a bit leathery, anyway."

"What did you say?"

"Have you thought about a hearing aid?" said Nimrod. "Blimey, it's no wonder the British spy service is so up the creek if you're one of the ones who's in charge. Call yourself a spy? You should be selling cakes at the local church fete, dear." Nimrod bent down and smiled at the wolf. "And I suppose this rabid-looking mutt must be Rakshasas."

"I've never been so insulted in all my life," said Moo, and swung at Nimrod with her handbag. It was a large handbag, full of stuff, including a laptop and a gun, which made it all the heavier.

"What's that?" Nimrod straightened just as Moo's heavy handbag came his way and struck him on the head with an audible *clunk* that sounded like a large wrench being dropped on a garage floor.

"Oh, I say," said Moo. "That sounded a bit too solid."

Nimrod spun around on his heel, reeled to one side, and then walked unsteadily, like someone drunk, for several paces before sitting down heavily. He held his head for a moment and groaned quietly for several seconds.

"Ow, ow, ow," he said.

Moo glanced inside her handbag and, finding the gun, looked at Philippa anxiously. "I forgot I had my computer in there. I certainly didn't mean to hit him that hard." She followed Nimrod, full of apologies. "I'm so, so sorry, Nimrod. Are you all right?"

Nimrod shook his head and blinked through the pain. "Light my lamp, but I feel most peculiar," he said. "Like I've got a brain-freeze headache."

"Perhaps you need to see another doctor," said Moo.

Nimrod remained silent for a moment or two.

"Moo's right," said Philippa. "You should have an X-ray."

"No," said Nimrod. "That won't be necessary. It's going now." He let out a deep breath and flexed his neck. "The fact is, I feel as if I've not been myself for a while. And now, I think I am again. In fact, I'm certain of it. You know, I really don't know what came over me."

Philippa ran to her uncle and hugged him. "You had a

bang on the head. In Kazakhstan. And for a while, you were insufferable."

"Yes. I was, wasn't I?" Nimrod stood up slowly and looked very embarrassed. "Light my lamp, I seem to remember saying some terrible, monstrous things to you all. I hope you can find it in your hearts to forgive me."

"Of course," said everyone.

"Especially you, Moo," said Nimrod. "Did I really call you an old bat?"

"Please don't mention it," said Moo.

"And you, too, Mr. Swaraswati."

"Your apology is wholly and in full measure acceptable," said Mr. Swaraswati.

"Thank you," said Nimrod. He looked at John. "John. I'm so very glad you're all right. Tell me everything, dear boy. For a start: Why are you here? And where is that butler of mine?"

John explained everything that had happened to him since leaving Morocco, after which Nimrod and Philippa asked him many questions. But after a while, Mr. Burton observed that John looked tired and suggested that the rest of their questions ought to wait until John was feeling a little stronger.

"Thanks," said John. "I do feel kind of tired after all that climbing. Not to mention all that falling."

"But if I might be permitted ask a question," said Mr. Burton. "Of you, Nimrod."

"Of course," said Nimrod.

"Before you rescued John on the flying carpet," said Mr. Burton, "you were about to tell Philippa something important. About what Mr. Swaraswati has told us."

"Was I? Yes, I was, wasn't I?"

"What was it? That you were about to say? About the ultimate truth of the universe." He shrugged. "I'm curious."

"Curious?"

"I've spent my whole life seeking this kind of enlightenment and I don't feel I can wait another second to find out what it is that has been revealed here."

Nimrod shrugged. "It's a mathematical proof," he said.

"Yes, yes, but of what?"

"God, of course," said Nimrod. "It's the mathematical proof of God."

CHAPTER 39

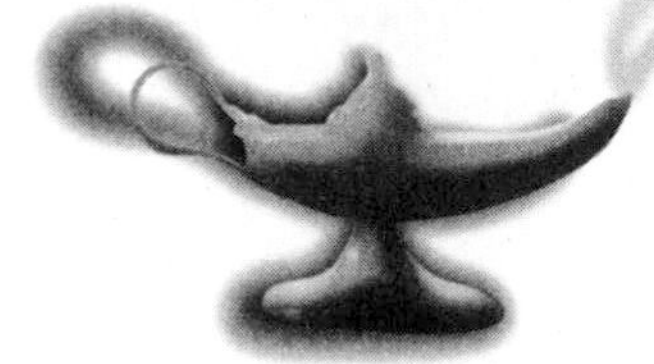

ENGLISH AFTERNOON TEA

"Is that all?" said Mr. Burton.

"Is that *all*?" Silvio frowned at him. "About the mathematical proof of God? Is that *all*?"

"I meant no offense." Mr. Burton looked apologetic. He fiddled with the beads around his scrawny neck and shuffled his dirty feet. "I was being ironic for the purpose of rhetorical effect. And irony can be hard to detect when English is not your first language. I expect that's why Americans can't understand it."

"Hey," said Philippa, who thought she understood it very well.

Nimrod chuckled. "Oh, very good. Very good."

"It was a sort of joke," Mr. Burton told Silvio. "After all, what could be more important than a mathematical proof of God?"

Somewhat placated — for he was a good Roman Catholic — Silvio nodded. "If this is true, it's no laughing matter for people," he said.

"It's true," said Mr. Swaraswati. "When he told me this great thing, the Tirthankar said that this was the most important truth of all."

"More important than *e* equals *mc* squared?" said Mr. Burton. "I find that very hard to believe."

"That is what he said," insisted Mr. Swaraswati.

Meanwhile Philippa untied Rakshasas from John's back and hugged the animal closely. It licked her face more like a dog than a wolf, but seeing it untied, Silvio backed away from the creature nervously.

"What's the matter?" Philippa asked him.

"This is a wolf, is it not?" said Silvio.

"Yes," said John.

"I used to work at the Rome Zoo. Before I got attacked by a panda and left this employment, I see many wolves." He pointed at Rakshasas. "Every night they howl. Isn't it dangerous? Wolves eat people, don't they?"

"This fellow is quite all right, I can assure you," said John. "He won't harm you, Silvio. This wolf contains the reincarnated spirit of a very dear old friend of ours. Isn't that right, Nimrod?"

"Absolutely right, dear boy." Nimrod knelt down and took the wolf's paw in his hand. "It's a pleasure to see you again, Mr. Rakshasas. I can't tell you much we've missed you."

Rakshasas barked once.

"Here, let me quickly introduce you to everyone," said Nimrod. "This is Silvio Prezzolini, who is the truly happy man we will need to gain admittance to

Shamba-la, as you instructed. Yes, I got your message, from Liskeard. And I already have the Joseph Rock Archive."

Rakshasas barked again and looked sideways at Moo.

"What lovely blue eyes he has," said Moo.

"This is my dear friend Moo," said Nimrod. "She is chief of the British KGB. This is Mr. Swaraswati, one of the fakirs of Faizabad."

"Delighted," said Moo.

"Pleased to meet you, Mr. Rakshasas," said Mr. Swaraswati.

"And this, of course, is Mr. Burton, your former butler, whom you already know."

Rakshasas greeted Moo and Mr. Swaraswati and Silvio Prezzolini with an alert expression and a wagging tail. But as soon as Nimrod had introduced Mr. Burton, the wolf backed away growling, with ears folded back and teeth bared, which was a thoroughly alarming sight.

"Hey, what's the matter?" said John, taking hold of the collar of fur around the wolf's neck, just in case he was thinking of attacking anyone after all.

Mr. Burton looked sheepish. "It's true, I've changed quite a bit since he last saw me. Living at the top of a rope in the Atlas Mountains will do that to a chap." He patted his stomach with the flat of his hand. "I'm somewhat thinner. And of course I didn't have the beard or the long hair. Plus, I do need a bath."

"We all need a bath," muttered Moo.

Rakshasas kept on growling fiercely.

"All the same," said Mr. Burton. "It is rather disappointing. I felt sure that he'd recognize me."

"He looks a bit different himself," observed Philippa. "And when you have the eyes of a wolf, you see things as a wolf does. Not as a djinn or a man. Who can tell what he's thinking?"

"I can," said John. "At least I can when I enter him as spirit."

Philippa tutted loudly. "Well, anyone can do that."

"What's the matter?" Nimrod asked the wolf. "Don't you know your former butler?"

"He didn't recognize me right away, either," said John. "I had to enter him as spirit before we were able to bond properly."

"Yes, that must be it," said Nimrod.

"Perhaps if he can get my scent it will jog something in his memory," said Mr. Burton. Bravely, Mr. Burton held a hand toward the wolf for him to smell. But Rakshasas just barked viciously and backed farther away.

"Nope," said John. "He's not having it."

"Well, it has been a very long time." Mr. Burton looked a little hurt. "It's obviously going to take a while for him to remember me," he said.

"Don't worry," said John, who had formed the closest attachment to Rakshasas and now felt he knew him better than anyone. "After what we've just been through, I think maybe he's a little nervous. And maybe a little worried about Groanin."

"You're right," said Nimrod. "As soon as we've had a cup

of tea we should get going again. It'll be getting dark soon. The sooner we can reach Shamba-la, the sooner we can get back to Yellowstone and rescue that big-hearted butler of mine. Light my lamp, but I don't know what I'd do if ever he decided to retire and go and become a holy man in Morocco. Really I don't." He shook his head and smiled at Mr. Burton. "How long were you in the service of Mr. Rakshasas, anyway?"

"Twenty years," said Mr. Burton.

Nimrod nodded. "Ten years Groanin's been with me," he said. "Just ten years and he's become quite indispensible. Not to mention my best friend since Mr. Rakshasas here moved on to his next incarnation. I hate to think how much I'd miss that man after twenty years of service. Especially his tea. No one makes tea like Groanin." Nimrod wagged a finger at Mr. Burton. "You know, I bet you can make an excellent cup of tea. All that time buttling for Mr. Rakshasas. He may have dressed as an Indian, and sounded like an Irishman, but Mr. Rakshasas was as English as I am. And he did like his Darjeeling tea, didn't he?"

"Yes," said Mr. Burton. "That he did."

"I, for one," said Moo, "would love a cup of tea."

"Me, too," admitted John. "Something hot, anyway. I'm cold."

Philippa confessed that even she was cold enough to drink tea.

"Of course," said Nimrod. "Why didn't I think of it earlier? I wonder if perhaps you would be kind enough to make us some tea, Mr. Burton. As only a great butler can."

"Of course," said Mr. Burton. "I'd be delighted."

"You make the tea and I'll make some scones."

Nimrod dug out the tea things from the luggage and gave them to Mr. Burton, who set to work collecting snow in the kettle and then lighting a fire to boil some water. And while Mr. Burton prepared the tea, Nimrod, whose personality seemed quite recovered from his bump on the head, had John explain to him precisely how to fly a carpet through the fissure in the north wall of Mount Kailash and into the secret crater.

"You must fly the carpet straight into the north face of the mountain at a low spot where the snow looks like clouds and the rock most looks like the sky," he said. "You must aim at what you consider to be the bluest part of the north face. Although this changes according to the time of day and the weather. This part of the north face is called Milarepa's Window. But in truth, your aim is not so important as your state of mind, Uncle. To some extent this is an exercise in mind over matter."

"Blue sky thinking."

"Precisely."

"So why do I need to fly at speed? Couldn't I just ascend slowly until I found this window?"

"From time to time there is a very strong current of air that emanates from this part of the rock face," explained John. "Like the blowhole of a whale. If we are not moving at speed, we could be blown off the carpet."

"Perhaps you should fly the carpet," said Nimrod.

"I'm much too tired," John said. And in truth, with his head of white hair, he looked tired, too.

Nimrod nodded. "Before we get back I'm going to have to fix that," he said. "Your hair."

"With djinn power?" asked John.

"No, with some hair dye."

"Ladies and gentlemen, tea is served," said Mr. Burton. Smiling broadly, he laid a large silver tray in the center of the carpet and started to hand around cups and saucers. "You know, when I was up that rope on Jebel Toubkal, in the Atlas Mountains, I often used to think of English afternoon tea. With cucumber sandwiches, buttered tea cakes, fairy cakes, and hot scones. Many's the time I thought of hot scones with cream and jam — apricot jam mostly."

"Excellent," purred Nimrod. "Excellent. Thank you, Mr. Burton."

"It almost makes me want to have my old tailcoat back," said Mr. Burton. "And my stiff collar. So that I might serve tea properly. And look like a proper English butler."

"Well, there's nothing wrong with the way you make tea," said Nimrod happily.

"Except for one thing," said Moo.

Nimrod raised his hand. "Please, Moo. I'm enjoying my tea. Don't say another word."

"Why?" she said indomitably. "I'll say what I like. I don't know what kind of English butler he was, but he can't have been a very good one."

"Please, Moo, not now," said Nimrod. "You'll spoil everything."

"Why?" asked Philippa.

"Because he didn't serve the tea with milk," said Moo. "The fool served it with lemon. That's the sort of thing you might expect from an American. And easily excused. But it's quite unforgivable in an English butler."

Mr. Burton stared at her with hard incredulity.

"You stupid, crabby, stuck-up English snob," he said, and then kicked the cup and saucer from the old lady's gloved hands.

"Was it something I said?" said Moo.

It would have been hard to say exactly what happened next, except that Nimrod threw away his own teacup and leaped to his feet. There was a huge flash and a loud explosion, as if a grenade had gone off, and a strong smell of sulfur, as if someone had just struck a couple of thousand matches.

Even John, with his quick eyes, could not have said what happened to Mr. Burton except that where the quietly spoken English fakir had been standing not one second before, there was now a roaring, beastlike man, seven or eight feet tall, who was smooth and uniformly red in his nakedness and almost entirely without human features, as if he had just sprung half formed from a giant clay modeler's wheel.

Grimacing horribly, the creature stamped its clay foot violently and the whole ground seemed to shake. Then it swung a right hook at Nimrod, narrowly missed the tip of his long, thin nose, and struck a rock that shattered into a thousand pieces. Dust and small fragments of rock and bits of clay rained down on everyone's heads like a shower of hailstones.

Still roaring like a tiger, the thing took another step forward and swung again. There was no time for Nimrod to duck or dive, and such was the clay creature's raw destructive power that the hammer blow seemed certain to remove the djinn's head at the shoulders.

Philippa screamed, which was why no one heard the word that came out of her uncle's mouth. And all that John could've said with certainty was that the word was too short to have been his focus word. But whatever it was, it worked and even as the huge fist made the beginning of contact with Nimrod's cheek, the creature wielding it stopped dead, as if someone had flicked a switch and paused an old horror movie.

Nimrod stepped away and, trembling just a little — for he was acutely conscious of how close he had come to death — let out a breath and touched his cheek, very much aware that a split second later might have seen the clay creature's ham-sized fist follow through with its killer punch.

"Light my lamp, but that was close," he said.

"What the heck is it?" said John, inspecting the clay creature more closely.

"And what in the name of Sam Hill just happened?" added Philippa.

"It's all over now. Nothing to worry about. We're all quite safe." Nimrod let out a nervous laugh. "This is a golem," he said. "An animated being created entirely from inanimate matter such as earth or clay. Rather like the first man, who was Adam, of course, except that Adam had a soul. Anyway, this particular golem was made by my old friend Rabbi Joshua Loew ben Gazzara for the purpose of protecting the Einstein Archive in Jerusalem. Except that it didn't. A few weeks ago, the golem and a part of that archive were stolen from the Jewish National Library by Jirjis Ibn Rajmus, who, as Philippa knows, is an evil djinn of the Ifrit tribe. At the time, I wondered why anyone, let alone a djinn, would want to steal the Einstein Archive and a golem. Well, now I know."

Nimrod took out a handkerchief, mopped his brow for a moment, and then lit a cigar.

"You see, Jirjis needed an adsuesco, which is what we djinn call a spare shape or a familiar creature, and rather useful to have around as a means of escape when you are using someone else's body. As Jirjis was. Goodness only knows where his own body is. Probably somewhere back in Morocco. Jirjis had stolen the body of Mr. Burton and was doubtless awaiting my own arrival on Jebel Toubkal in the Atlas Mountains, to seek Mr. Burton's advice."

"You mean Jirjis has been hiding inside Mr. Burton all along?" exclaimed Philippa. "But why?"

"Jirjis had already been to a great deal of effort creating an atmosphere of bad luck in the world so that he might provoke one or more of the fakirs of Faizabad to reveal themselves. So that he might gain control of one of the great secrets of the universe as revealed by the Tirthankar of Faizabad. I think he must have gotten the idea from the Einstein Archive, which, according to Rabbi Joshua, includes a rather cryptic entry in Einstein's diary about being visited by 'the Man from Lahore' while Einstein was still working rather anonymously at the Swiss Patent Office in Bern. The diary item suggested that a great secret was revealed to Einstein and that another similar great secret lay buried in Bumby, Yorkshire. That's why Jirjis sent his mendicant fakirs to Bumby. So that they might find Mr. Swaraswati's *dasa* — the servant of the buried fakir — and that she might lead them to him when he revealed himself.

"But his plans started to fall apart when his men found the *dasa* but failed to find Mr. Swaraswati. And when he realized that I was on the case, he decided to enlist my unwitting help. To have me and by extension you, Philippa, bring the fakir to him."

"But how did he know?" asked Moo. "How did he know you were on the case?"

"That day you came to my house in London," said Nimrod. "You were followed, were you not?"

"Yes, I was." Moo nodded. "I remember now. At the time I thought he was just a mugger."

"Most probably he was employed by Jirjis," said Nimrod. "I dare say, he had you followed in your capacity as the head of the King's Gambling Board of the Secret Intelligence Service. After all, luck, whatever its color — good or bad — is your departmental pigeon, isn't it? He wanted to see what you would do. How you would react to the crisis. And when you involved me, he immediately thought to take advantage of that."

"But when Moo and I arrived back in London with Mr.

Swaraswati," said Philippa, "why didn't he just kidnap him? Why accompany us on this journey?"

"Because you lost Mr. Swaraswati, Philippa," said Nimrod. "When your carpet got split in two by lightning. We didn't find him again until we got to Frankfurt. Remember?"

"Oh, yes," said Philippa. "I'd forgotten that."

"I hadn't," said Moo.

"Nor me," said Mr. Swaraswati.

"Of course, by then Mr. Burton had gained my trust," explained Nimrod. "And Jirjis must have reasoned it would not be long before Mr. Burton had gained Mr. Swaraswati's trust, too." Nimrod patted Rakshasas affectionately. "But he never gained your trust, did he? You knew as soon as you saw him."

Rakshasas barked once.

"Of course, by then it was too late," continued Nimrod. "In my stupidity, I had already persuaded Mr. Swaraswati to reveal his secret."

"You did have a bump on the head," said Philippa.

"The revelation of the secret was another thing that made me start to suspect him," said Nimrod. "A man like Mr. Burton, who has spent the last twenty years of his life seeking spiritual enlightenment, would have greeted the mathematical proof of God with perhaps a little more obvious enthusiasm. But Jirjis needs no such proof, of course, and therefore he was more than a little disappointed to discover that the great secret of Mr. Swaraswati was not some earth-shattering physics formula like *e* equals *mc* squared, but something else, something that's of no practical or financial use to him whatsoever."

"If you suspected him," said Philippa, "what on earth was all that nonsense about tea?"

Nimrod smiled. "I wouldn't expect an American to understand, Philippa."

"I think I understand," said John. "It was a test. To make absolutely sure of your facts. You knew that the real Mr. Burton would only have served afternoon tea with cold milk, and never with lemon."

"Precisely. Not only that, Mr. Rakshasas couldn't abide Darjeeling tea. He always much preferred Ceylon tea."

"Only Moo was about to blow it and you couldn't shut her up," added John.

Nimrod nodded. "I'm afraid so."

"Sorry, I'm sure," said Moo. "But how was I to know?"

"Dear lady," said Nimrod. "It's not your fault. For the life of me I couldn't remember the word of power that Rabbi Joshua used when he made his golem. But for that blow on the head I suffered, I might have remembered it much sooner."

"What was it, anyway?" asked Philippa. "The word, I mean?"

"One moment," said Nimrod. "Before I say it aloud, there's something I have to do."

He went over to the golem, stood on a rock, and put his fingers into the creature's mouth, from whence he removed a small piece of calfskin parchment.

"This is the word, here," he said. "It's written in Rabbi Joshua's blood and if it was uttered while it was still a part of the golem, the creature would come back to life. If life it can be called. You see, the word that activates the creature, *emet*, which means "truth" in the Hebrew language, also contains the word for death, *met*, when the first letter in *emet* is subtracted. Uttering the word *met* stops the golem in its tracks, thank goodness. And that's what I was trying to remember. Anyway, as soon as Jirjis realized I was onto him, he abandoned Mr. Burton's body and took the shape of the golem in order to defend himself against me. But he didn't ever gamble on me knowing Rabbi Joshua's word of power."

"But where was it?" asked Philippa. "The golem?"

"Right here, with us," said Nimrod.

"Are you saying that the golem has been with us all this time?" said Philippa.

"Yes," said Nimrod. "Ever since Morocco he's been sitting invisibly on this carpet."

"Well, that explains a lot," said Philippa. "When I was flying the carpet, I had the sense that there were more people on it than I knew about."

"Then you're to be complimented," said Nimrod. "Your senses are keener than mine, I'm afraid."

"The Einstein Archives," said Moo, brandishing some papers she had found. "The papers that were stolen. It would appear that they were in Mr. Burton's bundle all along."

"Rabbi Joshua will be relieved," said Nimrod.

"Where is Mr. Burton now?" asked John. "The *real* Mr. Burton."

"That's a good question," said Nimrod. "Really, he ought to be around here somewhere. I do hope he's all right. When a djinn leaves someone else's body that quickly it can be rather dangerous."

"I'll go and look for him," offered Silvio.

Rakshasas barked and ran off to help search for his former butler.

"Me, too," said Mr. Swaraswati.

"And Jirjis?" asked Philippa. "Where is he?"

Nimrod indicated the golem. "Stuck in here," he said. "Because this object was made with djinn power, it doesn't behave like any normal animal, vegetable, or mineral. The only way he could escape from this clay figure now is if I were to put the parchment back in the creature's mouth and speak the word of power again. Which I'm afraid I can't risk doing.

"Of course, this discovery changes everything. Now that we have found the culprit responsible for adversely affecting the amount of luck in the world, the Homeostasis — the balance of luck that exists in the world as measured by the tuchemeter — will, to some extent, fix itself. However, now that we are here, in such close proximity to Shamba-la, it would seem prudent to go ahead and consult with the monks at the lamasery as to how a quick-fix event of almost mythical good luck might still be achieved. Just to make up for all the bad luck that happened before. They will know what to do, I'm sure. Just as they will surely know how to help poor Groanin."

There was a bark and a shout and Nimrod said, "Sounds like they've found something."

They walked over to where Silvio and Rakshasas were staring at something lying on the ground. It was Mr. Burton. And he was quite dead. The shock of Jirjis leaving his body so quickly had killed him. Rakshasas sat down beside the dead fakir and, pointing his nose at the sky, began a plaintive howl. Philippa knelt down and put her arms around the wolf.

"That's a pity," said Moo. "Poor Mr. Burton."

"We'd best take him with us," said John. "It may be the monks at Shamba-la can offer him some kind of burial."

Nimrod nodded.

"What kind of monks are these, anyway?" asked Moo.

"To be honest I don't know," confessed Nimrod. "But I've heard stories, of course."

They walked back to the flying carpet.

"What are we going to do with him?" Philippa pointed at the golem.

"We're certainly not taking *him* with us," said Nimrod. "Not after all the trouble he's caused."

Philippa shook her head. "We're just going to leave him here?"

"There's not much we *can* do," said Nimrod. "Except perhaps alter the golem's image so that it becomes something rather more in keeping with the landscape and culture of Tibet."

Nimrod puffed an enormous smoke ring from his cigar into the air, which he sucked back into his mouth and then blew out again while at the same time he uttered his focus word. For a moment the cigar smoke hovered above the golem like a halo and then slowly descended like a curtain of gauze, momentarily obscuring the shape of the now inanimate clay being. When the smoke cleared, the golem's shape had changed, and instead of a fierce and brutal-looking human shape, there existed a rather more benign statue of the Lord Buddha. The statue was made of weathered stone and looked as if it had been there for a century or so.

"That's better, I think," said Nimrod.

Philippa winced. She realized that she was never going to get used to the idea of turning people into animals or, for that matter, imprisoning wicked djinn inside stone statues. "Says you," she said.

"Says me," said Nimrod.

"Don't you get it?" yelled John. "He killed Mr. Burton."

"That's no reason," insisted Philippa.

"It's not always easy deciding issues like this, Philippa," said Nimrod. "And believe me, I take no pleasure in doing this. But if nobility obliges, then being a djinn must do so still more."

"If you ask me, he had it coming," said John. "If it hadn't been for those stupid ink spots, I'd never have gone to Yellowstone and Groanin would never have come after me. And poor Groanin would be with us now, instead of buried under a mound of snow and ice." He shook his head. "Why did he do that, anyway?"

"I told you, I once fought a djinn duel with his father, Rajmus," said Nimrod. "It was a duel that ended in Rajmus being shrunk to the size of an atom. In effect, he was destroyed. That was most regrettable. Anyway, I imagine Jirjis saw an opportunity to be revenged on me through John, without revealing who he was, and could not resist it. He hoped to hurt me and perhaps even to destroy you. At the very least, I imagine he thought it might be easier dealing with two djinn instead of three. And, doubtless he intended some further revenge upon me and mine as soon as the Tirthankar's secret was known to him."

CHAPTER 40

THE DICKENS OF A FRIGHT

Inside his tent, wrapped up tightly in his orange sleeping bag, Groanin tossed aside *David Copperfield* and sighed irritably. Despite the usually reliable help of Dickens's greatest novel, the English butler was finding it impossible to drop off to sleep. And he wondered if his sleeplessness had anything to do with being neither completely dead nor properly alive. Which, upon sober reflection, seemed to Groanin like an accurate description of almost every one of the characters in *David Copperfield*.

"I wonder if people were ever like that," he said out loud. "So boring and lifeless that they might as well be dead."

He shivered and, still inside the sleeping bag, wriggled out of the tent like a large, fat orange caterpillar to warm his hands next to the embers of the fire. But there was no warmth in them. Not even when he threw a few twigs on to build up the flames. And he thought it odd how he couldn't warm himself, like there was no heat in the fire.

"Well, perhaps that's another thing about the state I'm in," he said. "Perhaps it's hard to stay warm when you're neither one thing nor the other. Hardly surprising, I suppose, when my earthly body is buried under several feet of snow and ice."

Somewhere in the darkness an owl hooted and a coyote yelped and then a cloud moved away from the moon, flooding the scene with a ghostly silver-white light. The wind whispered something in the treetops, which shifted like some kind of huge animal, and Groanin realized that he was talking to himself just to stop himself from being afraid of the dark.

"Not that there is much to be afraid of when you are already halfway to becoming a ghost," he told himself. "It's not like that blasted grizzly bear can maul me again." He looked reproachfully at the book that was lying in the doorway of the tent, where he had thrown it.

"But if I do end up being dead and there is a place called heaven and I manage to get in through the gates, I shall go and find Mr. Charles Dickens," said Groanin. "And if he's there, too, I shall make a point of telling him exactly what I think of his silly boring book."

"You may tell me now if you like," said a voice.

Groanin let out a yell and jumped out of his sleeping bag.

Groanin looked and saw a small man about sixty years old sitting next to the fire. The man was wearing a frock coat with a velvet collar, and a beard that was as big as a fire brush.

"What the Dickens do you mean, sneaking up on someone and frightening them like that?" Groanin demanded crossly.

"I'm only here because you said you wanted to tell me what you thought of my book," said the man. "And since you are what you are and I am what I am, I decided to come and save you the effort of trying to find me."

Groanin gulped loudly. "You mean you're Charles Dickens?" he said.

"That's correct," said the man. "So what have you got against *David Copperfield*? Some people think it's my finest book."

"But you're dead," said Groanin.

"That's right," said Dickens. "I died on June ninth, 1870. What of it? And do stop opening and closing your mouth like a fish."

"It's just that I never met a ghost before," said Groanin. "Not a real one."

"You know, you remind me of Ebenezer Scrooge in another book I wrote called *A Christmas Carol*," said Dickens. "But I don't suppose you like that one, either."

"Er, no, I didn't," admitted Groanin. "I thought it was too sentimental by half."

"You know, since you are the sternest critic of my work I've met in a long time," admitted Dickens, "and since you have nothing better to do with your time, it occurred to me that I might read you a new book I've been working on for the last hundred years. It's called *Philip Ironfilings*. I'd appreciate your comments on it."

But Groanin was already running away; he kept on running and did not look back.

"I do not like this place," he complained as he ran across the snow. He ran and talked without getting out of breath, which was easy since you have to be breathing to be out of breath. "I do not like being visited by the ghost of the writer I most dislike in the world. I wish John and Rakshasas would come back and get me out of here because I wish I was back at the house in London. Do you hear that, Nimrod, you daft idiot?"

He stopped for a minute to shout at the moon like a real lunatic.

"Do you hear? I wish I was back at the Carlyle hotel in New York and tucking into an enormous lunch like the one we had just a while ago. That's what I wish more than anything else in the world. But there's a fat chance of me getting that wish granted, is there? What's the point of being the butler to a powerful djinn if I can't even have that wish come true?"

Groanin looked back at his campfire and started running again. He kept on running until, just after dawn, he came in sight of the place where he had left Zagreus guarding his body.

Two things struck him right away.

One was that Zagreus was now very hard pressed by the pack of hungry wolves surrounding him. Every time he managed to drive one wolf away with a well-aimed snowball, another wolf would creep forward to take its place. They lay in a neat circle around the bigfoot, whining, howling, and licking their chops hungrily. It seemed obvious that Zagreus could not keep up his defense of Groanin's body for much longer.

But the other thing that struck the butler was that the snow and ice covering his body and preserving it from decay was melting. The air temperature was warmer. The early morning sun was shining brightly and Yellowstone's late spring snow was starting to thaw. Suddenly, the national park was getting warmer, much warmer. And things were looking extremely serious for Groanin.

"That's all I need," grumbled Groanin. "Nature's deep freezer to break down on me now."

If John and Rakshasas didn't come back soon, it would be too late. And whatever disembodied afterlife limbo state Groanin was now in would become something horribly permanent.

CHAPTER 41

SHAMBA-LA

It seemed utterly impossible that human beings could ever have built anything so high and inaccessible on the gray and perpendicular mountainside of the Kailash crater as Shamba-la. There was no visible way up to the monastery and no obvious way down. A condor would have thought twice about alighting on such a place in case it lost its nerve about taking off again. Even the thick snow that covered the crater seemed unable to stick to the narrow outcrop of rock where the monastery was situated. Shamba-la was both exquisitely beautiful and wholly improbable at the same time — a collection of immense, fortlike white walls, several stories high, with many golden windows, and all topped with pinkish curling rooftops, like so many rock anemones and mountain primulas picked by the hand of some intrepid climber. If someone had placed a luxury hotel midway up the north face of the Eiger or on top of Annapurna, it could not have looked more compelling to the eye.

Descending through thin clouds onto the uppermost roof — for there was nowhere else for them to land — Moo almost wondered if the sun and altitude were affecting her, so splendid did she find the sight of the ancient Tibetan monastery.

No less moved by the majesty of the lamasery, Silvio Prezzolini felt as if, in a strange way, he was almost coming back to a place he had visited once before, albeit in a long-forgotten dream, and had longed to visit again. The Vatican in Rome he had seen many times, but this was more impressive. The Vatican looked dull and solidly temporal by comparison with this ethereal palace.

Mr. Swaraswati, convinced that he was about to encounter a kind of heaven, closed his eyes and began to pray one of his strange mumbling prayers.

Rakshasas wagged his tail and excitedly sniffed the air, which smelled of mint and sugar. It was more than seventy years since he had set eyes on the lamasery and he wondered if any of the monks would recognize him. He only vaguely recalled the interior of Shamba-la. He remembered fountains and warm, spacious rooms and silent feet crossing marble floors. But most of all, he remembered a *girl*.

The twins, John and Philippa, who were too young to have a real appreciation of magnificent buildings and architecture, were silenced by the beauty of Shamba-la. Even Nimrod, who was used to having an eagle's view from a flying carpet, thought the place impressive.

"I felt my djinn power just desert me," said Philippa.

"Mine hasn't worked since I came to this crater," said John.

"I sense we won't have need of djinn power," said Nimrod. "Not in this place."

Drums and a huge bass trumpet announced their arrival; it sounded like the foghorn on a celestial ferryboat and was quite the loudest thing any of them had heard since their arrival in Tibet — louder even than the explosion that had heralded the arrival of the golem.

Nimrod pointed at a man standing on one of the high terraces, who appeared to be blowing into a long wind instrument that might have doubled as a pipe on an oil well.

"A sacred Tibetan long horn," shouted Nimrod. "I've heard them before, but never one as loud as this."

"What does it mean?" shouted John.

"Mean?" said Nimrod. "The noise is meant to drive away devils and evil spirits, of course. So if we're not driven away, then I suppose we're not devils and evil spirits."

Nimrod brought the carpet to a halt and everyone stood as a small man wearing the claret-colored toga of a Tibetan monk came toward them. He put his hands together, raised them to his forehead, and bowed gravely. He did not say a word, but to everyone's surprise, they all clearly heard him ask if they had come in peace.

Nimrod answered in similar fashion. *We come in peace*, he said silently.

Philippa glanced at her uncle. "Telepathy?"

Nimrod nodded. "One of many secrets known to the monks at Shamba-la."

"Er, we bring a happy man with us," Nimrod said uncertainly. "Mr. Prezzolini."

The monk said nothing.

"We can prove it if you like," said Nimrod.

That will not be necessary, said the silent monk. *Since you have also brought someone else.*

Rakshasas trotted forward and the monk, seeming to recognize the wolf — or at least the reincarnated spirit that the wolf carried — bowed several times and, grinning a broad, gap-toothed grin, stroked the animal's head fondly.

"It would appear that these two have met before," said Nimrod.

Oh, yes, the monk said silently. *We know each other very well. Rakshasas was in human shape the last time he was here; but he is no less welcome in his new incarnation. As are you, friends of Rakshasas. You are all welcome to Shamba-la.*

Only Nimrod was able to control his thoughts sufficiently to communicate with the monk telepathically. *Thank you,* he said. *We also have a friend with us who has died. I hope you won't mind us bringing him here. We meant no disrespect, but we didn't want to leave him behind. We thought you might give him a decent burial.*

The monk said silently, *He is welcome. And we shall see what we shall see. It may be that he is not as dead as you thought. Few things ever are. The original nature of things is neither born, nor extinguished. Leave him here for now and I shall ask some of my brothers to come and fetch him.* He bowed again. *Please come this way.*

The monk led the way through a heavy oak door that seemed to open by itself and, immediately, they were in a very long marble corridor with one wall that was made of dozens of enormous golden prayer wheels that the monk turned as he passed. Beyond an enormous library that was full of silent scholars, they walked through a kind of dojo, where dozens of monks sat chanting a sonorous deep mantra that sounded sinister to the ears of the twins but which Nimrod assured them was merely the recitation of a kind of poem called the heart sutra, which was all about wisdom.

"What do the words mean?" whispered Philippa.

This chant is the only sound that we make out loud, explained the silent monk. *For the wisdom of enlightenment is the true knowledge that all the five senses are empty.*

Which prompted Nimrod to air his own thoughts on the matter: *It's true that we could all listen a bit more and speak a bit less. That's the trouble with the world, I think. There's simply not enough listening. Most of the words that are spoken today are full of emptiness. Emptiness is something the world has plenty of right now.*

The monk nodded his agreement.

"Yes, but what does that mean?" asked John.

You don't have to understand the words, explained the silent monk. *The words say what is beyond words for this, John, is the sound of the universe breathing.*

"You know my name?" said John. "You read my mind?"

Of course.

"Can you read everyone's mind?" asked Philippa.

Yes.

"I don't think I care to have my mind read," observed Moo. "There are some things an Englishwoman regards as inviolable and private."

The monk took the visitors into a great hall, where he bowed and told them that the High Lama knew they were there and that he would speak to them soon, and then he left them on comfortable armchairs beside a refectory-style table with a big vase of yellow flowers and some tea and home-made Tibetan cakes.

The hall was about the size of a good-sized cathedral. The high walls were covered with ancient paintings, many of which depicted scenes of a Tibet that, thanks to the Chinese army, probably no longer existed outside the walls of Shamba-la. A golden statue of Buddha sat in an alcove at one side of the hall. He had curly blue hair and lipstick and although he was thirty or forty feet tall, he appeared to be wearing a real robe made of yellow silk.

"Wow," said John. "I bet that Buddha is made of solid gold."

"It is," said Nimrod. "But up here gold is just another metal and has no real value."

Philippa shook her head to clear it of the geometric pattern on the floor. "How long has this place been here?" asked Philippa.

"Joseph Rock's papers speak of a monastery on this site since the year A.D. 996," said Nimrod. "Few westerners have ever seen this place and lived to tell the tale."

"Are we in any danger?" Moo asked him, although she did not sound as if she would have believed him if he had answered that they were.

"No, not at all," said Nimrod. "Not from the people who live here. I meant that most of the travelers who got this far chose to stay. And from what John has told us about those Nazis, it seems clear that if you stay here for long enough, time itself begins to have no real meaning. Which makes it impossible to leave, I suppose."

"Leave?" Mr. Swaraswati shook his head silently. "I don't think so."

"Does anyone else find it peculiar?" said John. "That we're so high up in the Himalayas and there's no fire and yet this place is plush and warm. It feels kind of like an expensive hotel."

"It's better than the El Moania hotel in Fez, anyway," said Philippa.

John laughed. "I'd forgotten about that place."

"I wish I could," said Philippa.

"It's odd," said Silvio, "but ever since I got here I feel relaxed and invigorated all at once. Like I've been on holiday for a very long time."

"I've been thinking the same thing," confessed Moo. "If you put a *Times* crossword in front of me now, I swear I could do it in five minutes." She glanced at her watch.

"All my life," continued Silvio, "people have told me I was bad luck. But here I think that maybe it's impossible to believe in bad luck. I always tried to think of myself as a lucky guy. But here, I really believe it. I think maybe that to come here, to Shamba-la, this is the luckiest thing that has ever happened to me."

"Speaking for myself" — Mr. Swaraswati wobbled his head — "I feel as if this is journey's end." He shrugged. "But only in a good way. This is a good place, not a bad place. The last time I felt like this was when I was in the enlightened presence of the Tirthankar himself, in Faizabad. I can feel a tremendous energy here."

"I hope so," said John. "That's what we came for." He smiled a knowing smile.

"What?" asked Philippa.

"I was wondering how long it would take to read all those books in the library and thinking I might like to try it."

"It's the altitude," said Philippa. "He's not getting enough oxygen. I can't think why he would say such a thing otherwise. I can't remember the last book he read, and I dare say neither can he."

"I think that's why I said it," said John. "There's something about this place that makes absolutely anything seem possible."

"It's an odd thing," admitted Philippa, "but for some strange reason I seem to agree with you."

"Then anything *is* possible," said Nimrod.

Philippa took off her glasses. "That's another odd thing. My glasses don't seem to work." She frowned and rubbed her eyes. "No, that's not it at all. The fact is, I can see much better without them."

"This tea tastes better than any tea I've ever drunk in my entire life," said Moo.

"I was about to say the same thing myself," said Nimrod. "These Tibetan cakes are delicious. I must see if they'll give me the recipe."

"And —" Moo squeezed her wrists and shook her head. "No. I'm a foolish old woman, I must be imagining things."

"No," said Philippa. "Say what it is."

"My joints have stopped aching. Just like that." She smiled happily. "For years I've had pain but suddenly, the pain left me." She snapped her fingers. "Just like that. And look at that: I can snap my fingers. It's years since I was able to do that." She sighed wistfully. "Suddenly, all the dirt and bustle and noise and bad manners of London seem a long way off."

"That's for sure," said John.

Silvio wiped a tear from his eye. "Not since I was a kid have I felt like this," he said. "I feel like I have been here before. I keep looking around for my mama."

Moo looked at her watch again and shook her wrist vigorously. "That's odd. My watch has stopped."

"Mine, too," said Silvio. "But who needs a watch when you're somewhere like this? That's what I say."

Somewhere a door opened and, hearing footsteps, they all turned around to see that the monk had returned. Silently, he said that the High Lama would see them in the garden.

"A garden?" said Moo. "Up here?"

"There's no doubt about it," said Nimrod. "This is Shangri-la, all right."

The monk bowed and led them through a long stone tunnel into a walled garden that beggared belief: There were broad green lawns and well-stocked flower beds that filled the air with their scent.

"Remarkable," said Moo. "It's just like the Chelsea Flower Show."

"But without the crowds," added Nimrod.

Beside one of the flower beds was a young woman. She was in her early twenties and very beautiful. She wore a long, yellow, embroidered dress that was slashed to the thigh and her shiny black hair was bound in an elaborate knot in which a veritable garden of yellow flowers had been tied. But it was her smile that everyone noticed most. It never stopped. Which is not to say that ever it looked forced. It seemed that she was just one of life's natural smilers and the kind of person who made smiling infectious.

As soon as he saw her, Silvio Prezzolini broke out in an equally wide smile that the woman acknowledged with a polite bow. But her attention was mostly reserved for Rakshasas, whom she hugged on her knees as fondly as if he had been her own pet dog.

For his part, Rakshasas was no less pleased to see the young woman in yellow. He licked her face and barked and howled several times, which echoed in the walled garden until it sounded as if there was a whole pack of wolves on the lawns.

"I think we're witnessing a reunion," observed Nimrod. "These two seem to know each other of old."

"How did she recognize him?" asked John. "I mean, Rakshasas has only recently become reincarnated as a wolf. The last time he was here, in 1934, he was in human shape."

But he is still the same as he was back then. The woman's voice was as silent as the monk's but no less audible for all that. Her voice was sweet and gentle and full of the rushing of water and the sunshine sound of her radiant smile. *We say he is gone, gone, gone over, gone fully over, awakened, and then reached the other shore.*

Rakshasas licked the young woman's face again and lay down loyally at her feet.

You have brought us a great gift, she said silently. *You have brought an old friend back to us. I am grateful and hope that you can all stay a while and enjoy the hospitality of the monastery. But I seem to sense that three of you are already in a hurry to leave.*

"We have a friend who is injured, perhaps dead," explained John.

But this is not the man you left outside, the woman said silently. *Mr. Burton. This is Mr. Groanin of whom you speak, yes? The one in Yellowstone National Park.*

"Yes," said John. "We were hoping you could help us to help him. Can you?"

The young woman kept on smiling broadly but did not answer John's question. Philippa had the strong sensation that the woman was some kind of mystic; at the same time she formed the impression that Shamba-la was a place where such mysticism was common.

Perhaps the High Lama, when he comes, will offer a solution, Nimrod said in silence.

That is up to the High Lama, she said in her peculiar quiet way.

When will he be here? Nimrod asked her.

The young woman hugged Rakshasas again.

"Do you know him well?" asked Moo.

When the young woman spoke, she spoke aloud: "Oh, yes. I know him very well. My name is Yang Jin and I have been the wife of the High Lama for as long as I can remember."

The travelers bowed politely.

"I'm very pleased to meet you, Yang Jin." Nimrod spoke out loud, too. "I think you know everyone's name by now since you also know the secrets of our hearts. Will your husband, the High Lama be joining us?"

Yang Jin's smile widened, although such a thing seemed hardly possible, and there was amusement in her narrowing brown eyes. She put her hand up to her mouth for a moment and then buried her face in the thick fur around the wolf's neck. A thin gold necklace around her slender neck shimmered in the sunlight and the silk of her sarong rustled like the sound of sand under a soft brush.

Nimrod smiled patiently and repeated the question, after which Rakshasas barked once. Yang Jin looked at him and nodded.

"Very well," she told Rakshasas. "If you wish it."

Yang Jin stood up, bowed again, and lifted a hand in the direction of the wolf.

"This *is* the High Lama," she said. "Rakshasas is the great Abbot and High Lama of Shamba-la. For many years he stayed with us here. Then he went away. And now he has come back to us. He has told me the secrets of his heart, which is how I can tell you that he is back home forever, I think. This is the reason for the great horn. And for the chanting of the heart sutra. Our prayers have been answered. Lord Rakshasas is with us again."

IN THE PRESENCE OF THE HIGH LAMA

John felt his jaw drop to the ground. Philippa gasped out loud. Even Nimrod was surprised by the extraordinary revelation that Rakshasas had been, and possibly still was, the High Lama of Shamba-la.

"Whoa," said Philippa. "That is so unbelievable."

"Light my lamp," said Nimrod. "I can hardly believe it myself."

Only John seemed inclined not to believe what he had heard. He looked suspiciously at Yang Jin and said, "Is this some kind of trick so that you can keep Rakshasas for yourself?"

Rakshasas stood up and stared quizzically at John with his bright blue eyes.

Sure, don't be breaking your shins on a stool that's not in your way, John, said a silent but instantly recognizable Irish voice that sounded like it came from the air.

"Mr. Rakshasas," said Philippa. "Is that really you?"

If it's me jaws you want to see moving, then you'll have to take the consequences. The wolf ran forward and nipped her on the hand.

"Ow," said Philippa.

Of course it is me, you young eedjit.

"Nimrod, look," said Moo, and pointed across the garden, where Mr. Burton was walking toward them and looking as well as anyone could ever remember seeing him.

"Extraordinary," said Silvio. *"Fantastico."*

"Truly, this is a place where the extraordinary is commonplace," said Mr. Swaraswati.

"Mr. Burton," said Nimrod. "I'm delighted to see you. I thought you were dead. Indeed, I was quite sure of it." He smiled. "I think I need to shake your hand to quite believe it, though."

The two men clasped hands.

"I'm at a loss to explain it myself," confessed Mr. Burton. "I don't remember anything much, except that there was someone else in my head beside me. A djinn called Jirjis. I tried to warn you once, but he stopped me. The next thing I knew, I was lying outside alone on that carpet, drinking a glass of water from the glacier here at Shamba-la."

What the glacier water at Shamba-la won't cure, said the voice of Rakshasas, *there is no cure for.*

"Why didn't you mention something before?" John asked the wolf. "Like when we were back in Yellowstone?"

Sure, if I spoke to you as a wolf, John, you'd need to be a wolf to understand what I said. Besides, it's only now, since I got back to Shamba-la, that I've managed to find the still small voice of spirit again.

"Is it true?" asked Nimrod. "That Yang Jin is your wife?"

Who would say that she was married to a wolf if it was not true? said Rakshasas.

"Good point," admitted Nimrod.

"And that you're the High Lama?" added Philippa.

Sure, Yang Jin is just being polite, said Rakshasas. *But it's true that the last time I was here I was also the High Lama.*

"But why ever did you leave?" asked John.

"Yeah," added Philippa. "This place is really great. It's like — Shangri-la."

What's in the marrow is hard to take out of the bone, admitted Rakshasas. *I left Shamba-la because it was my duty to come back and help with the djinn education of your mother, Layla, and your uncle Nimrod. Just as your uncle Nimrod has helped to educate you as true children of the lamp. But after all these years, it's good to be back. And I shall always be grateful to you, John, for making that happen.*

"Since you mention the need to serve the world," said Nimrod, "I wonder if I might mention our mission to you. We wish to restore people's faith in things. If you like, we wish to turn the clock back to how things were before Jirjis Ibn Rajmus started to make people believe that the world was an inherently unlucky place. Or to put it another way, we need to draw from your reservoir of hope."

Rakshasas sighed. *Ah, Nimrod. And after all that I've told you about the hazards of wishing anything,* he said silently.

"Nevertheless I do ask it," said Nimrod. "Can you help us, old friend?"

"And Groanin," said John. "We mustn't forget him."

Not me, said Rakshasas. *Shamba-la. If it can be done at all, it can only be done here. But this is not an easy thing you ask. Sure, great mansions have slippery floors, and no mistake. And to go in is not without its risks. A wish is a dish that's a lot like a fish . . .*

"I know." Nimrod smiled. "Once it's been eaten it's harder to throw back."

For that reason you must always remember this, said Rakshasas. *You are what you wish. With this particular wish most of all. To have this wish come true you must give up a little of who and what you are. Your past and your future. For they are one and the same. Not only that, but you will never knowingly realize that which was lost.*

"Willingly," said Nimrod.

John and Philippa looked at each other and nodded.

"For sure," said John.

You say more than you can comprehend, children, said the voice of Rakshasas. *But I doubt not the truth and sincerity of what is in your hearts. This thing will be done. But it would be well that it were done quickly. For I sense that time is short for Mr. Groanin. The three of you will leave. But it is clear to me that the others — Moo, Mr. Burton, Mr. Swaraswati, Mr. Prezzolini — are all united in an earnest desire to stay here in Shamba-la. For they have glimpsed the eternal. That is an easier wish to make come true. Even for me. I only have to ask Yang Jin.*

"It's true," admitted Moo. "I'd like to stay. At my age you don't often feel like you've been given a second chance."

Nimrod glanced at Messrs. Burton, Swaraswati, and Prezzolini, who all nodded back.

"Well," he said, "I can't say that I blame you." He turned his attention back to the wolf. "And you, dear friend? Will you stay, too?"

It was hard for me to leave the first time, announced Rakshasas. *It would be impossible for me to leave again.*

Nimrod nodded. "What must we do?" he asked.

Even while we were speaking here, said Rakshasas, *I have given the order to make the preparations for your departure.*

The wolf turned to lead the way back toward the great hall. *And now you must say all your good-byes,* he said. *To me, and to the wonderful friends you brought with you.*

Their good-byes took a while as sometimes they do when people are reluctant to be parted and more especially when people and, for that matter, wolves who used to be people, think they might never see one another again; as Rakshasas said he thought was more or less certain in this case.

Hands were shaken. Kisses were exchanged. Promises to remember forever were given. Moo kept a stiff upper lip. Mr. Burton and Mr. Swaraswati made more reverential salutations, especially to Nimrod, to whom they obviously felt great respect was due. Silvio Prezzolini tried not to smile through his tears but could not help himself.

"I'll miss you, Silvio," said Philippa, wiping a tear from her own eye.

No need to worry about Mr. Prezzolini, said Yang Jin. *This is a place of hope. There is no worry here. He will never have a bad night's sleep again. None of them will.*

"Somehow I suspected as much," said Philippa. "And I'm glad."

Nimrod was inclined to say his good-byes quickly. John

and Philippa, being children, were given to take a lot longer saying them, much to the disgust of Rakshasas, for he was a wolf after all and wolves are ruthless by nature.

Sure, if these two went to a wedding they'd be inclined to stay for the christening, observed Rakshasas. *Will you hurry up?*

"You can't rush these things," insisted Philippa. "Sometimes the best things are said last of all. Otherwise where is the good in good-bye?"

We'll make a wise Irishwoman of you yet, Philippa, said Rakshasas.

"Besides," said John, hugging the wolf to him, "the last time we parted forever we didn't get to say good-bye at all."

This time it is forever, insisted Rakshasas. *You'll forget this place. And you'll forget about us. It's in the way of things.*

"Never," said the twins.

The twins thought Rakshasas was exaggerating, of course, but Nimrod knew or strongly suspected that he was not.

The wolf licked the tears from their faces. *Sure, I'm only doing this because I need the salt*, he joked.

And then: *May you have warm words on a cool evening, a full moon on a dark night, and a smooth road all the way to your door.*

The good-byes were over. It was time to be on their way.

CHAPTER 43

THE MANDALA

Back inside the lamasery, Rakshasas and Yang Jin led the three djinn through the great hall to the temple, which, to everyone's surprise, was even bigger than the great hall. Everything in the temple was red, except a marble floor that was the color of the sky, and which was decorated with an enormous and elaborate concentric diagram that Philippa found exercised an almost hypnotic effect on her when she looked at it for more than a couple of minutes.

"This building reminds me of a djinn bottle," said Philippa, blinking her mind clear of the effect of the circle. "It seems bigger on the inside than on the outside."

Yes, said Rakshasas. *It is.*

Yang Jin invited them to sit within the inner circle.

"What is this thing, anyway?" asked John. "A magic circle?"

Nothing so crude, Rakshasas said impatiently. *Will you listen to the child? Tell him, Nimrod.*

"It's a mandala," explained Nimrod. "Which is a Sanskrit word for 'circle.' Only it's far more than a circle with a decorative center. It's a kind of cosmic diagram that reminds us of our relation to what is infinite, to the world that extends beyond."

Oh, I think you'll find it does a lot, lot more than that, said the voice of Rakshasas.

"Whatever it is, it's very pretty," observed Philippa. "Although it makes your eyes go kind of weird when you start to look at it closely."

"I noticed that," said John. "I thought it was just me."

"I've never seen a mandala as complex as this," confessed Nimrod. "It's quite extraordinary. There are so many intricate shapes and colors. It makes the ceiling of the Sistine Chapel look like a caveman's daub."

"This is the holiest place in Shamba-la," said Yang Jin. "Perhaps in all Tibet. Here you are reminded of the divinity that lies within all of us."

"Some more than others," said John.

Philippa glared at him.

John shrugged. "I was thinking of Jirjis," he said. "And that golem. There was nothing divine about them."

"Be quiet, John," said Nimrod.

"Yes, sir," said John obediently, for he could see that his remarks were inappropriate in a holy place.

This mandala took about three hundred years to create, said Rakshasas. *That is because it's more than just an actual design; it represents the universe itself. This mandala is an actual moment in time. And, as such, it can be used as a vehicle to explore the nature of existence, of the universe, and of time itself.*

"I was afraid you'd say something like that," said Nimrod.

"Whoa," said John. "Did you say vehicle? You mean like a car or something?"

"I think he means something a lot more complicated than just a car, John," said Nimrod. "Rakshasas? Is this really the only way?"

I'm afraid so, said Rakshasas.

"You don't mean — ?" Philippa took a deep breath.

"I *do* mean," said Nimrod. "This is a journey that's going to make a ride on a flying carpet look very ordinary." Nimrod frowned. "That reminds me. Rakshasas? What about our luggage? What about the carpet?"

You won't need it, explained Rakshasas. *Not where you're going.*

"Oh, Lord," said Nimrod. "I don't think I'm going to like this. Always supposing I can remember it."

"What?" said John. "What's happening?"

"I think we are about to experience a major case of déjà vu," said Nimrod.

The next second, the floor turned. Or at least one of the outer circles turned.

"Where *are* we going?" he asked.

Around in circles, said Rakshasas. *Sure, did not you know that there is no circle that is not made from within a single point that is located in the center? And it's this point that receives all the light and illuminates the body, and all is enlightened.*

With one of the outer circles turning one way, one of the inner circles began to turn in the opposite direction. Soon, both were turning at speed and started to produce a ring effect in which all the light was being bent into a circle spinning around them.

The temple, Yang Jin, and Rakshasas were now invisible to the three occupants of the mandala.

"That's the Einstein ring," said Nimrod. "The gravitational lensing effect as predicted by Albert Einstein."

Of course if you take away all the light, said the invisible voice of Rakshasas, *if all of the light is absorbed, if nothing is reflected, then what you end up with is a gravitational or space-time singularity.*

The floor turned faster and faster.

Good-bye, Nimrod, said the voice. *Good-bye, children.*

"I think he means a black hole," yelled Philippa as the floor turned faster and faster.

"Hole? What hole?" John looked up at the ceiling.

"Not up there, John," said Philippa. "Look."

Now there was just the light of the circle and, beneath them, what looked like an enormously deep and dark well.

"It's a wormhole through space-time," said Philippa. "The kind of singularity that would allow someone to travel from one part of the universe to another. Or one part of time to another part of time. Isn't that right, Uncle?"

"It's just a theory," said Nimrod. "But the idea does seem to be sound."

The three djinn started to sink into the now invisible temple floor.

"You mean we're going back in time?" said John.

"It would appear that way, John," Nimrod said calmly. "We're going back to a time before any of this ever happened."

"But won't time just repeat itself?" asked Philippa.

"No," said Nimrod. "Not with Mr. Swaraswati, Moo, Mr. Burton, and Mr. Prezzolini remaining behind here in Shamba-la. That changes everything. Mr. Swaraswati was the reason that Jirjis began his nasty little scheme to change the world's luck in the first place. With him gone from Bumby, there's no point in doing anything. With Moo gone, there's no one to ask me to investigate an alteration in the world's luck on behalf of the British KGB. With Mr. Burton gone, there can be no human body for Jirjis to use to trick us. There can be no prophecy given to John in an ink spot that takes him to Yellowstone. There can be no reason for Mr. Groanin to follow John to Yellowstone and get himself mauled by a bear. We're going back to a universe in which everything that has happened to us in the last few weeks and months never happened at all."

"That must be what Mr. Rakshasas meant when he said that you are what you wish," said John. "With this particular wish most of all. That's what he meant when he said that to have Uncle Nimrod's wish come true — to turn the clock back to how things were before Jirjis Ibn Rajmus started to make people believe that the world was an inherently unlucky place — we must give up a little of who and what we are, our past and our future."

"For they are one and the same," said Philippa. "And that we will never knowingly realize that which was lost. That's why he said we'd forget about him and Shamba-la. Because none of it ever happened." She looked anxiously at the black hole that now seemed to envelope her. "Will it hurt?"

"I don't think so," said Nimrod. "But I don't actually know. All I really know for sure is that . . ."

. . . Mandala, temple, Chelsea Flower Show, yellow dress, Yang Jin, prayer wheel, Shamba-la, Kailash crater, golem, falling, Fritz, Hynkell, SS, Nazi, Bactrian camels, Mr. Bayuleev, bandits, pelicans, Zagreus, omphalos, Jerusalem, Dickens, Groanin and the bear, Yellowstone, Commerzbank, Frankfurt, the wolf pack, lightning, cloud, Mr. Swaraswati, ink spots, Falernian wine, Jebel Toubkal, riddles, Mr. Burton, the flying carpet emporium, Asaf Ibn Barkhiya, the El Moania hotel, Fez, HMS Archer, *the mendicant fakirs, Moo, Silvio Prezzolini, Pompeii, Sheryl Shoebottom, Bumby . . .*

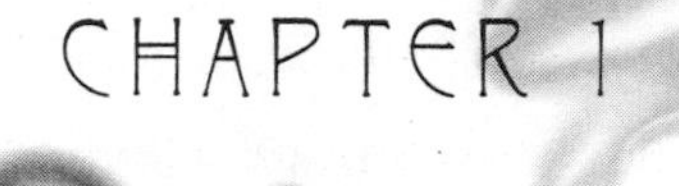

CHAPTER 1

REVISITED

The twins John and Philippa left their house on East 77th Street in New York, and walked around the corner to the Carlyle hotel where their uncle Nimrod, who was staying there with his butler, Groanin, had invited them both to come and have lunch.

Following her complete and irrevocable renunciation of her djinn powers, Nimrod's sister, Layla, who was also the twins' mother, had made it adequately clear to her brother that she and her husband no longer cared to have any djinn matters even mentioned in their presence. Although Nimrod strongly disapproved of any djinn denying his or her true nature, his impeccable British manners required that he respect his sister's decision — enough to have written a short note to her informing her exactly why he had invited her two children to lunch.

Since no objection to their lunch had been forthcoming, Nimrod had gone ahead and booked a table in the hotel's swanky restaurant where he and Groanin now met the twins.

After a very large feast of Cornish lobster bisque, peekytoe Maine crab, pan-seared Hudson Valley foie gras (which Philippa did not eat), Atlantic black bass, roasted Amish chicken, and desserts from the trolley, Nimrod finally arrived at the subject he wished to discuss with his nephew and niece.

"Since you have both recently turned fourteen," he said, "the time has come when you must observe a tradition in the Marid tribe that we call *taranushi*."

"Why is it called *taranushi*?" asked John.

"Well," said Nimrod, "as you may know, Taranushi was the name of the first great djinn. Before the time of the six tribes, he was charged with controlling the rest, but he was opposed by another wicked djinn named Azazal, and defeated. This Marid tribal tradition is meant to commemorate his overthrow by wicked djinn."

"Why was he opposed?" asked Philippa.

"For the simple reason that he tried to improve the lot of mundanes —" Nimrod glanced at Groanin, who was loosening a button on the waist of his trousers to accommodate his enormously full stomach. "Sorry, Groanin, I was speaking about human beings. I meant no offense."

"None taken, sir."

"Yes," continued Nimrod. "Well, as I was saying, Taranushi tried to improve the lot of human beings by occasionally giving some of them three wishes. In fact, it was he who initiated the custom of giving three wishes."

"So what's the tradition?" asked John.

"The tradition is that each of you will go somewhere of your own choosing and find someone you consider to be deserving of three wishes. But it has to be someone truly deserving because upon your return, you have to justify it to a panel of adjudicators that includes me, Mr. Vodyannoy —"

"*After* I get back from my holiday," said Groanin. "I say, after I get back from my holiday. And not before. It's been ages since I had a proper holiday."

Nimrod continued with the names of the panel of *taranushi* adjudicators. "There's Jenny Sachertorte, and Uma Ayer the Eremite. Also, it ought to be a secret where you two go, just in case anyone tries to put themselves in the way of being granted three wishes. So, even I shouldn't know where that is. Although that's not so important, given it's me. But either way, you're very much on your own for this one."

"Anywhere we want?" said John.

"Anywhere you want," confirmed Nimrod.

"Maybe I should go on holiday with you, Groanin," said John. "There must be something I can do for that funny little town in Yorkshire where you take your vacation. Bumby, isn't it?"

"Oh, no," said Groanin. "You're not coming there and that's final. Bumby is just fine the way it is without you messing the place up with three wishes 'n'all."

"There must be something I could do for it," teased John.

"Nothing," said Groanin. "Nothing at all. Things are just dandy in Bumby the way they are."

"Please yourself." John shrugged. "Either way, it doesn't sound so difficult."

"Doesn't it?" Groanin laughed. "It's also traditional," he said, "in case you'd forgotten, for a young novice djinn like you to make a complete pig's ear out of granting three wishes. And to have little or no idea of how a wish will turn out. That's why I don't want you within a hundred miles of Bumby, young man. Especially not when I'm on me holiday."

"All right, all right." John laughed. "I promise not to go."

"Ever," insisted Groanin.

"Yes, okay," said John. "I was just kidding, all right?"

"Maybe," said Groanin. "But just remember what old Mr. Rakshasas used to say? 'A wish is a dish that's a lot like a fish: Once it's been eaten it's harder to throw back.'"

"I remember," said John. "I'm not about to forget anything he said, okay?" He frowned. "I just wish I knew what had happened to him for sure."

There was a moment's silence while everyone spared a thought for Mr. Rakshasas who, it seemed, had been fatally absorbed by a Chinese terra-cotta warrior in the New York Metropolitan Museum of Art.

"Groanin makes a good point," said Nimrod, returning to the subject in hand. "Because it's not just that the recipient has to be judged deserving of three wishes. You also have to justify what they do with their three wishes. And, as I think you know, that can be a very different kettle of fish. People are unpredictable. And greedy."

Groanin managed to stifle a burp. "You can say that again," he said and, waving the waiter over, he ordered himself a second dessert.

"Even the most honest, upstanding sort of person can turn rapacious when three wishes are involved," added Nimrod.

"Aye, it's not everyone that wishes for world peace," said Groanin. "I say, it's not everyone that wishes for world peace these days. Even if that was something within your power."

"Which, sadly, it isn't," said Nimrod.

"How are we going to discover if someone is really deserving of three wishes?" said John.

"Research," said Nimrod. "Read books. Read the newspapers. Find out what's happening in the world."

John groaned. "I might have known that there'd be some reading involved."

"It saves time finding out things for yourself," said Nimrod.

"It does that," agreed Groanin.

"Maybe I'll go to Canada," said John. "I bet there are lots of people in Canada who could do with three wishes." He grinned. "Stands to reason, doesn't it?"

"Don't tell me," insisted Nimrod. "Even your parents aren't supposed to know. It's a secret, remember?"

"He doesn't know how to keep a secret," said Philippa.

"I like that," said John. "You're the biggest gossip I know."

Noticing that Groanin had a newspaper in his pocket, John asked to borrow it and, absently, Groanin agreed. It was an English newspaper called the *Yorkshire Post* and, hardly to John's surprise, there was nothing of any interest in it.

Privately, Philippa thought she might go to India. For one thing, in India they believed in the djinn, and experience had already taught her that it was a lot easier granting someone three wishes when they believed such a thing was even possible. Another thing was that there were lots of deserving people in India. Just about everywhere you went you could see them. Yes, India seemed like a good idea. She would go there. Besides, India was hot, and being hot meant she would have maximum power. That seemed important, too.

And she thought John could do worse than go to Africa for some of the same reasons. She thought she might suggest this to him when they were back home.

"Suppose you and these other adjudicators decide that the three wishes were not justified," said Philippa. "What happens then?"

"I'm glad you mentioned that," said Nimrod. "There's a penalty to be paid."

"You mean like a punishment?" said John.

Philippa grinned.

"What?" asked John.

"Nothing."

"What?"

"It's just that I had this incredible déjà vu moment," said Philippa. "I remembered you asking that question over lunch in here once before."

"Well, that's easy to shoot down," said John. "We've never had lunch in here before."

"I'm not surprised," said Groanin. "At these flipping prices. I say, I'm not surprised at these flipping prices." He leaned back in his chair and, raising his voice, added for the benefit of the waiter, "Sixty-five dollars for a Dover sole? They're trying it on for size, if you ask me. There's not a fish in the sea that's worth sixty-five dollars on a dinner plate."

"Groanin, please," said Nimrod. "Behave yourself or I'll send you back up to your room."

"Yes, sir." He chuckled. "Hey, listen. What do you call a meal you've eaten before? Déjà stew."

Philippa groaned.

"Every day is like déjà vu with you, sis," said John. "The things you say, the clothes you wear, the things you do."

"Thanks."

"Of course, strictly speaking," said Nimrod, "it shouldn't be called déjà vu at all. Properly, it should be called *déjà vécu* — the sense of having lived before."

"I just knew you were going to say that," said John. "Weird." He started to laugh.

"No, really," insisted Philippa. "Whatever you want to call the feeling I had, it was very strong."

"You've eaten too much lunch," said John.

"Not as much as you."

"With all this talk about déjà vu, I'm reminded of a poem called 'Sudden Light,'" said Nimrod. "By Dante Gabriel Rossetti."

"I think I've never heard of him before," said John. "You know? Like *déjà who?*"

"Do shut up," said Groanin. "There's a good lad."

Nimrod said:

I HAVE been here before,
But when or how I cannot tell:
I know the grass beyond the door,
The sweet keen smell,
The sighing sound, the lights around the shore.

You have been mine before —
How long ago I may not know:
But just when at that swallow's soar
Your neck turned so,
Some veil did fall, — I knew it all of yore.

Has this been thus before?
And shall not thus time's eddying flight
Still with our lives our love restore
In death's despite,
And day and night yield one delight once more?

John shrugged. "I really don't know what that tells us."

"That Philippa is hardly the first person to have felt this way," said Nimrod. "As a matter of fact, I had quite a déjà vu moment myself when I saw the two of you coming in here today."

Philippa's eyes narrowed as she tried to hang on to the thought and the feeling that had prompted her own déjà vu. Then she sighed. "It was there and now it's gone."

"I know," said John. "Maybe you've been reincarnated."

"If that's true, it must be some kind of a punishment," said Philippa.

"How's that?" asked John.

"Because I'm closely related to *you*."

"Whooaa," said John. "I just had the déjà vu thing myself."

"Stop it," said Philippa.

"No, honestly," insisted John. "I swear I really did. Oh, man, that was creepy. I just looked at that big vase of yellow flowers and it was like I'd seen it someplace before."

"You know something, John?" Philippa smiled. "I guess maybe it's true after all. You do get everything I get, only it takes just a little longer."

ABOUT THE AUTHOR

P. B. Kerr was born in Edinburgh, Scotland, where he developed a lifelong love of reading. Although the Children of the Lamp books are P. B. Kerr's first for children, he's well known as the thriller writer Philip Kerr, author of the Berlin Noir series, including, most recently, *If the Dead Rise Not*; *A Philosophical Investigation*; *The Grid*; *The Shot*; and many other acclaimed novels. Mr. Kerr lives in London with his family. Visit P. B. Kerr at his website, www.pbkerr.com.